"You got a name?" he said curtly.

After a brief hesitation: "Neville."

"That's it? Neville."

Neville nodded.

"All right, Neville, now why don't yuh just state your business?" Rawlins said in a more friendly manner.

Neville breathed out a sigh. "I do have a matter to talk over with you, Sheriff. But—I'd suggest you handcuff me 'fore I say anything more."

Rawlins regarded Neville with a deliberate look and folded his arms across the width of his barrel-like chest.

"Now why would you be askin' me to do that?" he said.

Neville hesitated, then focused his eyes solidly on Rawlins and spoke outright the words he'd come to say. "'Cause I'm the man that killed your mayor."

Praise for the novels of Stone Wallace

"This unusual Western mines some fairly fresh ground . . . The plot is engaging in a *Butch Cassidy and the Sundance Kid* kind of way."   —*Booklist*

"Stone Wallace will become an institution to Western fans after they read this novel . . . It's a page-turner that you won't want to put down!"

—Tommy Garrett, editor-in-chief of the *Canyon News*

Berkley titles by Stone Wallace

BLACK RANSOM
MY GALLOWS HANG HIGH

My Gallows Hang High

STONE WALLACE

BERKLEY BOOKS, NEW YORK

THE BERKLEY PUBLISHING GROUP
Published by the Penguin Group
Penguin Group (USA) LLC
375 Hudson Street, New York, New York 10014

USA • Canada • UK • Ireland • Australia • New Zealand • India • South Africa • China

penguin.com

A Penguin Random House Company

MY GALLOWS HANG HIGH

A Berkley Book / published by arrangement with the author

For information, address: The Berkley Publishing Group,
a division of Penguin Group (USA) LLC,
375 Hudson Street, New York, New York 10014.

ISBN: 978-0-425-26535-2

PUBLISHING HISTORY
Berkley mass-market edition / February 2015

PRINTED IN THE UNITED STATES OF AMERICA

10 9 8 7 6 5 4 3 2 1

Cover art by Robert Hunt.
Cover design by Diana Kolsky.
Interior text design by Laura K. Corless.

*To my great friend and fellow writer
Lisa Kopochinski,
with all of my very best wishes
for continued happy trails*

We laugh, we cry, we are born, we die
Who will riddle me the *how* and the *why*?

—ALFRED, LORD TENNYSON

PROLOGUE

He called himself Neville. Whether that was his family name or the name given him at birth, seldom was he asked and never did he offer.

Where he came from, no one knew. Where he was headed, no one could say. He was looked upon as a loner, a man who neither sought nor welcomed companionship, and a man whose mysterious presence would elicit conversation among the citizens in those dusty dirtwater towns through which he would pass. Saloon patrons would eye him curiously, watching in silence, as he entered the premises, unwashed, unshaven, the denim fabric of his shirt and trousers faded from long exposure to the sun, walking with purposeful wide strides, spurs jangling against the sound of his brisk footfalls, and stepped up to the bar, where he adhered to the routine he observed in each town he stopped in, ordering a schooner of beer with which to wash away the taste of trail dirt, followed by a straight shot of whiskey that he'd toss back in a swift, single swallow, before leaving as silently as he had come and riding off to whatever his eventual destination.

Who was that stranger? the men would then ask among

themselves. Cowboys passed through trail towns all the time, and outwardly in dress and appearance there appeared to be little to make him stand out from others, but there *was* something distinctly different about this lean-faced, tawny-haired man whose brow was furrowed in a perpetual look of concern: an indefinable yet somehow penetrating quality that he carried with him as surely as the six-shooter that rested in his holster—an unsettling presence that captured attention and prompted suspicion.

The man called Neville never failed to notice the stares that followed him, and yet he never acknowledged them. Even with his back turned as he stood at the bar, leg bent with boot resting on the foot rail, he could feel those piercing glares. He minded his own business and expected the same consideration. Most people were obliging, but on occasion someone just a little too curious or whiskeyed up would sidle up beside him at the bar, usually with a friendly offer to buy him a drink, though Neville was wise to the true intent. Neville always declined the offer, with thanks. One glass of beer, one shot of whiskey as a chaser; his order never varied. Only rarely was the refusal of this gesture met with offense, but to avoid the possibility of trouble it seemed all Neville had to do was slowly turn his head and fix his eyes on who-ever might attempt to challenge him, and inevitably the man would back down and try to hold on to his dignity as he returned to his table. Neville's deep-set eyes, of a deep brown color that appeared almost black, embedded in dark, expressionless features, were desolate. Some might assume they were the eyes of a man who had seen too much. Others could say they reflected the soul of a man resigned to death. And that made him a potentially dangerous adversary.

He discouraged any attempt at conversation from bar-keeps prone to talk, keeping cordial by responding to a question with either a "yep" or a "no," but refusing to elaborate. Soon the bartender would get the idea and return to other duties. Saloon girls did not approach the stranger to ask him to buy them a drink. They could sense his aloof, brooding temperament and kept away.

None of his stays in any saloon exceeded ten minutes, but within that short time he stimulated the imagination of the customers. Once Neville strode out the batwings and rode off slowly on his horse, whispered conversation would rise in an excited tempo as drinks were swiftly consumed, prompting more orders from the bar, and theories were tossed about: He was thought to be a gunslinger, an outlaw, maybe even an army deserter or a man on a mission of revenge. While no one could know for sure, all agreed that the stranger harbored a dark, perhaps even a tragic past.

There was a tragedy in Neville's life, though it existed not in his past . . . but in his future.

Neville knew he wouldn't come upon another town for many a mile. It promised to be a long ride through the sun-baked prairie landscape where grasses were yellow and fields parched, thirsty. The trail was hot and dry and the air still, and he was unable to catch even the whisper of a cooling breeze. He kept the brim of his Stetson tilted low against the glare of the sun. He rode the horse he'd named Daniel at a steady, even pace, so as not to deplete the animal's strength under the exhausting heat. The horse was old and tired and they had come a long ways together, and still had a fair distance to travel. Neville kept the fingers of one hand draped over the pommel and held his canteen at the ready with his left hand. He drank frequently but not liberally, consuming just enough to sustain him until he reached another creek or stream. As the hot midday sun bore down upon him like a blinding white fireball he had to fight the growing urge to take more aggressive swallows from the canteen, only strong self-discipline preventing him from what he knew was an unwise temptation. He had to keep mindful of the importance of conserving his water until he came to another source—or rode into another town where his thirst would be satiated by a somewhat more potent beverage.

Luck seemed to be with him. As the sun reached its peak

and with Neville's willpower beginning to diminish, he noticed a familiar reflection . . . and what he prayed was not a mirage . . . shimmering under the sunlight in a gully not too far in the distance.

He kept himself steady on the saddle, tracing his upper lip with the tip of his tongue, squinting under the brim of his hat to see if his eyes were merely playing tricks and that the image would fade.

Satisfied that he was not hallucinating, he prepared to urge Daniel forward, but the pinto had also already noticed the little creek and didn't need guidance; in anticipation of the cool refreshment he picked up his pace toward the free-flowing waters.

Neville gave a slight tug on the reins to slow the animal, then proceeded.

It took a couple of minutes to navigate the slight but rocky descent, but once they were on level ground Neville released his hold on the reins and let the horse tread on alone across the dried mud bank toward the creek. The animal was smart, displaying an intelligence that intrigued Neville. He kept back and watched as Daniel tentatively dipped his muzzle into the water to taste it, testing it as if to give his approval. Neville waited . . . until the horse raised back his head in a strong, abrupt movement, then thrust his muzzle back into the creek to quench his mighty thirst, snorting into the water. Neville watched until Daniel began drawing from the creek, then strode across to the water's edge, dropping to his belly, and after allowing himself a taste of the water, he slapped off his Stetson and plunged his head whole into the slow-running current, giving his head a vigorous swishing beneath the surface to clean the dust and sweat from his face. When he finally lifted his head and wiped the moisture from his eyes he noticed that his horse was still contentedly enjoying his own refreshment, lapping up water at a leisurely pace.

"That's right, fella," Neville muttered as he pulled himself up from his belly and rested on his haunches. "Drink easy."

Neville knew he had to heed his own advice or risk suffering a bellyache, so he merely cupped his hands and scooped up a couple of small handfuls of water, which he slowly sipped.

The water was cool and clean and Neville swept his canteen through the gentle flow, filling it near to capacity. He rinsed out the canteen, then refilled it, taking a final taste before tightening the cap.

He stood up, brushed back his wet hair, and put his hat back over his head against the beating sun, then placed his hands against his hips and took a slow, absorbing look around his surroundings. He inhaled, then exhaled a long breath and savored the feeling of freedom that suddenly washed over him. As brief as it was, he would keep this memory. He felt good in this little oasis and wished it were possible for him to stop longer to rest. Camp out for the night before heading onward. He sighed again. As much as he dreaded what awaited him in Commercial City he knew he couldn't allow himself the luxury of a prolonged stopover anyplace. Circumstances—and a bargain he intended to honor—demanded that he keep riding.

His horse had drunk his fill and was standing back from the creek, cropping a small growth of grass. Neville waited until the pinto lifted his large head, and then he walked over and rubbed his hand affectionately along his muzzle. Daniel responded with a nicker and slight rock of his head.

"Okay, fella, time for us to get movin'," Neville said.

Taking the animal by the reins and tensing the slack, Neville carefully maneuvered them both up the rocky slope back onto the trail.

He mounted the horse and paused just long enough to tip his Stetson back up over his forehead and wipe away the pellets of sweat that had again started to dot his brow. His lips stretched in a slight, self-conscious smile. He wasn't fooling himself that the perspiration that glistened on his skin was due solely to the heat.

No, he was considering that the next stop on his journey could likely be his last.

And as night rapidly approached, a black canvas over-taking the burnt-orange hue of the prairie sunset, Neville sat with his horse atop a small rise where he noticed the distant dotting of lights, looking to flicker like the flames of tiny candles reflecting against a vast charcoal tapestry. Next to him, at the side of the road, was a wooden sign driven into the dirt whose neatly printed wording confirmed to Neville that his long, slow ride had indeed come to an end:

COMMERCIAL CITY
2 MILES

Now that he had come this far, his destination in sight, he fought back a growing apprehension and, finally, sum-moning all of his courage, he rode forward with a singular purpose.

Prepared to complete those last couple of miles to enter a town he had never visited.

Arriving for an appointment with a lawman he had never met.

To confess to the murder of a man he had never known.

Some weeks before . . .

Commercial City was a community grown prosperous due to the steady influx of hardworking and enterprising families moving west into the lush green landscape of Gila Valley, a territory rich with fertile grasslands and bordered on the eastern perimeter by Pomosa Spring, which provided plenty of fresh, clean drinking water. Farther west, the valley was watered by the Salisaw River. Families lived in sturdy clap-board houses spread out across the landscape, their proper-ties neat and well maintained and colorfully decorated with flowerbeds and gardens tended to by the housewives.

The town's primary road, named Archer Street, was built on a slight elevation with wood-framed stores, shops, and other business enterprises standing side by side in a mostly unbroken row, mainly populating the north edge of the road, though there was continued construction activity on the opposite side of Archer Street as further development of the town was encouraged. Currently there was much excitement among the citizens as work had begun on a major undertaking: the building of a theater intended to showcase top entertainment acts from across the country.

Not many years previously the town had existed as a raw boom camp: settlers living in canvas tents and lean-tos, families huddled together for shared warmth against the bitterly cold nights, enduring spare meals cooked over outdoor fires. It was a tough existence, made worse by inevitable illness and death, most particularly among the very young, the elderly, and the physically feeble who had endured much hardship during the long journey west. There were also those who did not survive the journey due to misadventure. One of these casualties was Emmanuel Archer, who lost his life while attempting to rescue a girl who had wandered too close to a river's edge and fallen into the rushing currents during their trek. Sadly, his valiant act was in vain as the girl also perished, but because of his heroism it was decided that the town's main road would be named in Emmanuel Archer's memory.

Yet gradually the town developed as buildings and houses were constructed in a determined community effort. These were God-fearing folk, and the first two structures erected were a church for worship and a schoolhouse for learning. Their credo, engraved on a gold plaque soon to be affixed to the outside wall next to the main entrance of the Municipal Building, proudly proclaimed: *Strong of body. Clear of mind. Pure of spirit*. Throughout their labors they echoed the battle cry of "*Faugh a Ballagh!*" (Clear the Way!), and since many of the men were veterans of the War between the States, what they expressed was not a shallow optimism.

A town government had been established; a mayor was appointed by unanimous decision, supported by a council composed of merchants and businessmen. The town sheriff had also been elected by a majority vote, prompted by an enthusiastic endorsement from the mayor. Both men had been leaders in the establishing of the community. The mayor, Thaddeus Ford, possessed qualifications that made him well suited for overseeing the affairs of the town as it strove to live up to its name of Commercial City and gain a secure economic foundation.

The sheriff, Tim Rawlins, was a big, bearlike man whose mere presence inspired confidence in the people of Commercial City. He had worked as a police constable in Philadelphia, establishing a fine arrest record, before accepting the invitation to head west to partake in a new adventure.

With two highly competent individuals handling municipal affairs and law enforcement, Commercial City expanded and, indeed, thrived. Its reputation as a clean, safe community encouraged others to make their home there, and most were received with welcome.

Of course, the growth of the town also attracted more unsavory types who saw the potential for other opportunities. These small groups or individuals who tried to insinuate corrupt methods into the business community were quickly discouraged in their ambitions by swift action from the sheriff's office.

A town like Commercial City offered another incentive for shady entrepreneurs. Its prosperity and expanding population made it a prime location to scout out with the purpose of establishing gambling parlors and other questionable venues of recreation. It wasn't long before intriguing wire correspondence led to a meeting between Mayor Ford and agents from San Francisco who claimed to represent an interest eager to discuss a serious business proposal that they assured the mayor would prove beneficial to the town.

Thaddeus Ford was a clever and careful man who through his past exploits and leadership had come to understand human nature, and he became suspicious when he received a final telegram sent during their journey suggesting that they meet in the saloon and discuss the proposition over a few drinks. Thaddeus immediately formed the impression that the true intention of the message was to learn if the town *had* a saloon. In any case, for the moment he pushed that aside as an unnecessary consideration; he believed it proper and professional that a meeting regarding town matters should be held in his office in the Municipal Building, which held significance not only for its status, but also because it was the only stone-constructed building in Commercial City, situated at the end of Archer Street, bordering the western limits of the town, beyond which lay the farming communities.

When the three associates finally arrived in town by Concord stagecoach, Thaddeus, accompanied by Sheriff Rawlins, was standing at the depot to provide his visitors with an official greeting. After Thaddeus welcomed the gentlemen to Commercial City, he suggested his preference of discussing business in his office—he *suggested* but did not insist, curious to gauge a reaction from these business agents; upon meeting each personally, he could not quite quell his sense of distrust of them. The associates, however, agreed to the mayor's request, and a time for their meeting was arranged for later.

That afternoon Thaddeus was affable while maintaining a professional deportment. He poured his visitors a glass of premium imported brandy, while he himself abstained. He opened a decorated box on his desk and offered cigars, which only one of the men accepted. Thaddeus himself did not smoke.

The three men were immaculately groomed and conservatively attired in white shirts with starched collars and suit coats, their brocade vests complemented by either an ascot or cravat. Two had bowler hats, which they rested upon their laps while they sipped at their drinks. When they'd entered the office, the fragrance of bay rum accompanied them, which Thaddeus, who did not favor perfumes or colognes, found rather cloying.

They presented themselves as successful businessmen and exuded an air of confidence bordering on arrogance. When they shook hands with Thaddeus, their grips were dry and strong. The mayor noted this, as well as the maintaining of eye contact when one of them was speaking.

Thaddeus admitted that they introduced themselves most
admirably, but that only heightened his intention to stay on
his guard. These were clearly skillful men.

The man who called himself George Stadler appeared
to be the spokesperson among the group. He also looked to
be the oldest of the three, approximately the same age as
Thaddeus, but thin- rather than thick-framed, and whereas
the mayor's hair was dark if thinning, Stadler's own head
of hair was full and wavy and silver. He had a mustache and
neatly trimmed goatee that gave him the appearance of an
academic. The precision of his speech offered another indi-
cation as to his education and intelligence. He was sitting
at his ease, perfectly relaxed, comfortable in this environment, with his legs crossed in one of the plush armchairs
opposite the big second-floor arc window that overlooked
the east side of town where the muted sounds of construction
on the theater could be heard and through which filtered the
midafternoon sun, bathing the brown and rust tones of the
office in a warm yellowish glow.

Stadler puffed on the cigar he'd been given, pulling it
from his lips and nodding in approval of its fine taste while
carrying on with small talk. He seemed initially hesitant if
not downright evasive about getting to the point of the meeting, first stressing through carefully modulated tones the
various economic considerations to a growing community
like Commercial City; Thaddeus quickly realized that
Stadler was employing his comments and arguments to cleverly segue into the thrust of the conversation.

Stadler soon confirmed the mayor's suspicion when he
spoke of the financial benefits towns out west were enjoying
by permitting the operation of gambling parlors. Thaddeus
felt his gut tightening but purposely did not change expression. His first urge was to bring the meeting to an immediate
end; instead he held himself in reserve and decided to hear
out the whole proposal.

"It's simple economics, Mayor Ford, that as these parlors
profit, so shall the towns where they are employed," Stadler
said. "The additional revenue generated, which should be

considerable, would go a long way toward aiding in the expansion of Commercial City."

"That's an eventuality, of course," Thaddeus countered, his features impassive. "A more immediate question would be where do you propose to secure the funds to finance the building of these . . . establishments?"

Stadler spoke confidently. "The funding will be handled on our end. And just to put your mind at rest, we don't plan to populate Commercial City with gambling, Mayor Ford. Just one parlor—at first, to test the waters, as it were."

"And if this enterprise should prove successful?" Thaddeus asked.

Stadler gave a practiced response. "As I said, best if we proceed one step at a time."

Thaddeus got up from his chair to add more brandy to Stadler's glass, which Stadler accepted. The other two men declined refills.

"I take it then that you have investors," Thaddeus inferred.

"We have the support of backers, yes," Stadler said.

"Mmm," Thaddeus said in a dubious tone.

"These are serious men, Mayor Ford," Stadler elaborated, his face drawn in a frown. "They've built a solid financial structure that has made a number of people quite wealthy."

Thaddeus didn't seem impressed.

"But of course I'm speaking of those who have seen the profitability of allowing for expansion," Stadler added slyly.

"So if I understand correctly, we provide no cash outlay and merely reap the benefits," Thaddeus said carefully, with a smile that was difficult to decipher.

Stadler returned the smile and shifted slightly but a little too noticeably in his chair. "Well, *share in the profits* may be a more polite way to express it."

Thaddeus nodded perfunctorily.

Stadler detected the mayor's skepticism, and he decided on another approach.

"Something you may want to keep in mind is that the construction and operation of such an enterprise would provide employment for your town . . . and later, I'm sure we could offer other incentives to assist in the continued financial welfare of Commercial City."

Thaddeus lifted an eyebrow. He wasn't sure what Stadler meant by "other incentives," but frankly he didn't like the sound of it. He cleared his throat, and with both hands clasped behind his back he turned toward the arc window and gazed out onto Archer Street. It was another quiet day in town, people pleasantly going about their usual business, no particular excitement outside the ongoing work on the theater. It was the vision he had seen for the town—one that he had realized through sweat and hardship, pain and sacrifice, and by earning the people's trust. One he intended to both foster and maintain.

Thaddeus spoke with his back toward the three men, his voice firm yet reasonable.

"Gentlemen," he said, addressing them as a group, "the people of this community aren't of the type to either patronize or be employed in a gambling establishment, dealing cards or spinning a roulette wheel. I know personally almost every one of our citizens. They're simple, basic folk. Those who don't operate businesses are satisfied farming the land outside town. Commercial City is still a new town—yes, still developing, which I'm sure you know, based on your coming here with your . . . *opportunity*. These people traveled far and worked hard and a long way to help build this town, and today they are content in their endeavors."

Stadler started to speak, but Thaddeus turned to face the group and raised a hand to silence him.

"Whether or not you can appreciate it, we look upon ourselves as a Christian community," he said. "In fact, our faith is what brought us to where we are today . . . and where we hope to be tomorrow."

Another of the partners, Harwood Finch, spoke up. Of the three agents, he looked to be the most rough-hewn. Not so much in appearance, but attitude. His tone was mildly brusque.

"Yet your town has a saloon," he noted. "A right fancy one, too, I hear. Drinking alcohol isn't prohibited. Isn't that a mite hypocritical . . . if, as you say, you promote Christian values?"

Thaddeus smiled indulgently. "No one *promotes* Christian values, Mr. Finch. The people make their own choices. As for the saloon, we're not what you might call fanatics. People drop in for a glass of cold beer on a hot day or come in to relax with a drink of whiskey, and I can see no harm in that. No one abuses the privilege. I enjoy the occasional drink myself. Gambling, on the other hand, presents a different sort of problem."

Finch frowned. "How so?"

Thaddeus spoke forthrightly. "People here work hard for their livelihood. I admit some of our local merchants are still having a difficult time, and I don't need to tell you gentlemen that those working the farms are dependent each season on good harvests. Most everyone in town has a family to support, so that can be a challenge. What I'm saying is that in such circumstances the chance to maybe earn some easy money can be a strong temptation. Entice them with gambling and it's like spinning the cylinder of a six-shooter loaded with five bullets. One time against the odds you may get lucky. In any case, it's intoxicating and the next thing you know families go hungry, desperation sets in, and our streets become unsafe. Decent people turn bad because they've fallen into a trap and can't see any way out except to turn to crime." He paused to capture his breath and to reach into his breast pocket for his handkerchief, with which to wipe beads of sweat from his brow. He spoke with more fervor than he had intended. He was satisfied that he had presented a telling argument . . . but didn't doubt his words had fallen upon deaf ears.

"You're presenting an extreme situation, Mayor Ford," Stadler said, "and one that I can say we have yet to encounter through any of our establishments. We have no desire to see any of the towns we visit turned into Dodge City."

Thaddeus drew a deep breath and went on. "There's another consideration. A gambling parlor would almost certainly attract people of, shall we say, questionable character.

I assure you, Mr. Stadler, those are types we do not wish to encourage into our city."

"Our intention . . . our plan, as it were, is to open a respectable establishment, Mr. Ford," the third man, Cyrus Connelly, finally said, speaking thinly and with a slight tremor in his voice. He was a pear-shaped individual, balding and round-faced, bespectacled with watery eyes, and appeared to be of a nervous disposition. Thaddeus determined that had he been dealing with Connelly alone, he could have ended this conversation much sooner—which would have been to his preference.

"It is not our desire to cater to riffraff," Connelly concluded.

"No? But how do you judge who's the, as you say, riffraff?" Thaddeus argued. "I know of gunfighters who present themselves as affluent gentlemen, yet they'd shoot you dead just for looking at them the wrong way. The irrefutable fact is, intentions aside, you cannot guarantee the character of each customer who walks into your establishment."

Connelly presented no rebuttal. He turned his head aside, coughed obviously, and settled back even deeper into his chair.

It was Harwood Finch who answered, offering a noncommittal shrug. "There are no guarantees either in business *or* in life."

"Very true, Mr. Finch," Thaddeus acknowledged solemnly. "But we also don't light the fuse hoping the dynamite won't explode."

The room fell into silence. The atmosphere was not exactly tense, but a slight tangible uneasiness was present. Thaddeus absorbed it, and he hastened to bring the meeting to a close.

"Gentlemen, I have other business to attend to this afternoon. I apologize for having disappointed you, especially given the distance you had to travel. But as I stated, your proposition is simply not something I feel would be an asset to Commercial City. In fact, if I may speak frankly, I see it as a detriment to the positive growth of our town."

The three agents exchanged furtive glances among

themselves before George Stadler rose and stubbed his cigar in the tableside ashtray. He looked a little disappointed but managed a thin smile as he extended his hand. His own expression grave, Thaddeus accepted the handshake, once again noticing the dry firmness of the grip.

Stadler, though, was not quite ready to surrender. With his hand still clasping the mayor's, maintaining that physical connection as if not wanting to sever the bond, he said, "I assume this decision is solely yours, that it would be of no advantage to arrange another meeting . . . with your town council?"

"On this matter and in the interest of not wasting any more of your time or encouraging further discussion, yes, I'm making the final decision," Thaddeus said, the tone of his voice official. "I feel I can say with assuredness, knowing the council members as I do, that they would side with me, unanimously."

As the men prepared to leave the office, Thaddeus returned to the chair behind his desk, though not immediately seating himself. Instead he stood there for a moment, head held upright, the fists of both hands pressed against the walnut surface. He looked to be considering. Finally he spoke his final say, beginning by addressing the partners individually, fixing his eyes on each.

"Mr. Stadler, Mr. Connelly, Mr. Finch, I debated saying this because the intention wasn't defined, but something mentioned earlier . . . not that it had any bearing on my decision . . . but what *you*, Mr. Stadler, said about the success of a gambling establishment providing our town with 'other incentives.'"

Stadler responded with a cautious nod.

Thaddeus shook his head. "It now seems clear to me that you and whoever your backers are had planned your own agenda for Commercial City, and that gambling would just be the start."

Stadler's face remained impassive. But then his lips peeled back in a sly smile that for the first time seemed to reveal his true personality and intent.

He said, "The West is open, Mayor Ford. What we're offering is simply the first step toward progress."

The agents had hoped for a better outcome, and once the documents were signed they were prepared to start back for San Francisco the next day to deliver them. But Mayor Ford's obstinance now forced a delay in their schedule. While they never admitted it, these men, despite their authoritative bearing, were merely messengers for the West Coast syndicate they represented, a group that originated out of the Barbary Coast and hoped to expand its interests into the opening of the frontier. George Stadler and his two associates were sent out to seek new settlements within these territories. Most importantly, they were expected to obtain results, and up until Commercial City their discussions and persuasions had yielded success with other towns they'd visited throughout the Southwest. On occasion, tactics had to be employed that were not entirely honorable, such as inserting a subtle threat into the conversation—but a measure necessary only when there was an obvious hesitation and a little prodding would prove beneficial to sway the decision in their favor. Otherwise it was always intended for these matters to be handled in a polite, businesslike manner.

Through their dealings with various officials they had gained valuable knowledge as how best to handle each negotiation—and George Stadler, in particular, developed a keen insight into individual personalities: where one's strengths and weaknesses could be discerned and effectively manipulated. What he most often discovered was that, intentions aside, the mercenary nature of most politicians prevailed.

Much to his dissatisfaction, for he was anxious to secure the Commercial City deal swiftly, that seemed not to be the case with Thaddeus Ford. Greed did not motivate him. He presented himself as a thoroughly honest and moral man— though whether that truly was his character or a mere facade was difficult to determine. However, it was a part of his

personality that Thaddeus Ford had so assiduously culti-
vated, he could not be swayed from what he believed was
right. Stadler also discerned from his talk with the mayor
that not even a blatant threat would prove effective against
his tenacious stand. With options at a premium, Stadler
understood that Ford would have to be dealt with another
way. A necessary if not preferred method of persuasion.

Stadler and his partners were given the authority to recommend any course of action necessary to guarantee a successful resolution. Mayor Ford obviously had a great deal
of influence over the community. With him removed from
office, it likely would be easier to convince a man of less
authority to agree to their way of thinking.

With the right incentives.

Book 1

ONE

Times had been tough for the family, and as each day passed with no relief in sight, desperation continued to set in—a desperation that bore into the man's soul like some unrelenting virulent disease. He felt he had done all he could. With blistered, bloody hands he'd cleared the land, planted the crops, and then—with what little he'd been able to put aside as collateral—he'd applied for credit, only to be told outright that his meager assets, including a pair of near-crippled draft horses and a favored though aged pinto he'd named Daniel that he used as a saddle horse, were not sufficient for him to borrow against and there was little sympathy for his plight. As if in a pathetic attempt to soften his disappointment, bankers reminded him that he was not the only farmer going through hard times in this part of the country. The soil was poor to start with, but when the drought hit that summer the earth was cracked and had the consistency of solid clay, which even weeds could barely inhabit.

It wasn't his fault—the elements had conspired against him—but he still blamed himself. *Farmer*, he thought miserably. What right did he have to call himself that? What did he really know about successfully working the land, yielding a saleable crop? As he thought about it with bitterness, what did he really care? He should have learned from experience. Why didn't he heed the memories of laboring in dismal fields alongside his pa?

It was a question he really did not have to ask. The answer was simple. He chose this life. No . . . that wasn't right. He *pursued* it after that terrible day those many years ago. He returned to it both out of necessity and because it brought him back to his roots, where at least there was a familiarity, as painful as that memory often was. And it was where he hoped to live his life in relative peace, in anonymity, free of the worry of those who might remember he owed them a debt.

Free . . . of everything, except his conscience.

But there was more. He had to provide for his wife and children and knew of no other way to care for them. Hardly any schooling. No training with which to work a trade. He didn't possess any other damn skill.

Still . . . for just a moment his face could lighten. His family was the only bright spot in his life. The one thing he could always count on was the love of his wife and the affection of his two young daughters: Rose, age seven, and Penelope, just turned five. It gave him comfort until stark realization that at times struck like a mule kick to the gut returned to remind him that he could barely support the family he had been blessed with. The house in which they lived was a cabin that could more accurately be called a shack, a spit-and-tar structure framed with poor-quality lumber that hadn't been cured and was weathered, warped, and split. A dwelling that perhaps offered shelter from the rain and occasional late-season snowfalls but provided little protection against the accompanying biting cold that penetrated walls weakened by storms and heavy winds and forced the family to huddle together, sharing their body warmth under woolen blankets.

While he knew he had put out his best effort, he felt he had failed as a man. He would often sit up on those cold nights, unable to sleep, haunted as he was by troubled thoughts. He'd try to warm himself with a hot cup of coffee— a damn luxury, seated at the kitchen table watching his little ones shiver against the night chill—and he'd curse himself for ever bringing children into such an environment. Certainly it was never how he planned it, but circumstances or, as he more often began to regard it, judgment and condemnation—a perverse providence—had thrust this miserable existence not only upon him, but also on his family.

He was resentful. It wasn't fair. It wasn't fair that his wife and children should be made to suffer for the wrong he had committed.

That one youthful decision had changed his life forever. It existed in his past, but despite periods of respite now growing ever more infrequent as the days of desperation became ever bleaker, he never forgot or truly forgave himself, and he suffered with the knowledge of what he had done, the memory of the people he had betrayed. Despite other influences he could not deny, he could never stamp out the truth that ultimately he alone was the one responsible for a desperate act that had made him a criminal—one who might still carry a bounty eager to be collected by parties on both sides of the law.

Often during these troubling days when he worked tirelessly yet fruitlessly on tending his fields, he reflected on how it all began . . .

He was a boy of fourteen. A farmer's son who worked long days with his widower pa, busting sod from sunup to sundown to scratch out a living harvesting poor crops that only wholesalers with the most generous of hearts would purchase—at a humiliating discount. But every penny helped, and as his pa would remind him when he was of a Christian mind, if they didn't show gratitude for what they had, they couldn't expect more. There was a coldness in the old man, as Pa suffered from the same frustrations and disappointments that his son was now experiencing. His pa was prone to vent his discouragements in violent outbursts, directed at him. Occasional beatings that were delivered for

the slightest provocation, deserved or not. But one day he'd
simply had enough and gotten up before dawn, packed a few
necessities into a canvas sack that he tossed over his shoulder, and walked away from Pa and his home. He remembered stopping by his mother's grave, which was on a
peaceful hillside not far from the farm. Pa had wanted her
laid to rest in a special place where each morning the sunrise
would meet the grave—and she was, but the burial plot was
not on the meager stretch of grassland that he owned. It
stretched just beyond the border of his property and intruded
upon the land owned by a neighbor.

The neighbor, a man without wife and children named
Caulfield, was of somewhat better means than the boy's pa,
and sympathetic to Pa's grief. He had not objected upon
discovering that earth had been opened on the land to which
he held claim without permission and a coffin lowered deep
within the soil. Caulfield held the right to issue a complaint
with the land title office, which would have resulted in a
penalty: financial restitution and/or jail time. But Caulfield
made no such charge against his neighbor. A thoughtful,
considerate gesture, but not looked upon as such by the boy.
To him, it was a blatant act of charity, which his adolescent
mind resented. He regarded it as another humiliation for Pa,
who was so overcome with grief that he remained ignorant
that he had trespassed onto another man's property.

It also grieved Pa that he could not pay for a minister to
officiate at the burial. Preacher Roberts did, however, come
by the house shortly afterward to speak with Pa. His words
were intended to offer comfort, but to the boy they sounded
hollow. While he could not conceive of the eternity Preacher
Roberts spoke of, the boy struggled to find comfort in the
concept of eternal peace, for his mother had suffered long
with her illness, her body wasting away until what was
finally placed into the cheap coffin resembled little more
than a flesh-stretched skeleton.

It was on that damp September predawn while the boy
stood before his mother's grave, his small, thin form framed
in the blossoming of an eager sunrise soon to reach over the

grassy mound beneath where his mother lay, his head bowed and hands folded in reverence, that old Mr. Caulfield happened to come by.

Caulfield thought it odd to see the boy standing by the gravesite at such an early hour. While he was a neighbor, Caulfield had never had much dealing with either the boy or his pa. Barely a word had been exchanged between them in the dozen or so years they'd sided property.

Caulfield was by nature an early riser and he'd already prepared his buckboard for the two-hour ride into town, where he'd hit the wholesale market early to sell his own vegetable crop—a yield only slightly better than his neighbor's but only because Caulfield put more effort into trying to keep his land fertile. His neighbor's attempts to maintain a quality yield, not impressive to start with, declined as the man fell deeper into a state of depression, and his son felt the growing urge to break away from a stifling and dirt-poor existence and therefore did not see the need to assist in trying to improve the family livelihood.

The boy had some schooling, but the fundamentals of education—facts and knowledge that would hold no importance in the world that *he* knew and soon would fully enter—provided little incentive for achieving a better life. To that end, he wasn't unhappy the day his pa, embraced in another of his miserable moods, took to drink and, under an influence that propelled him to a dark place, once more released his rage on his son. The boy withstood the undeserved punishment, almost welcoming each blow of the beating, gritting his teeth and clenching his jaw in defiance as his pa, beyond comprehension, perhaps not even understanding the reason behind his cruel actions, continued his drunken assault.

He recalled how after his pa came to his senses, he gazed at his son with the saddest, most regretful expression the boy could ever remember seeing. The old man's eyes glistened with tears as his face fell to resemble a countenance much older than his pa's forty-three years.

His pa looked stricken, regarding the boy's bloody face

with a look of incredulity, a combination of horror and revulsion. His mouth twitched as he struggled to utter what might have been an apology, but it was as if such words were foreign to his tongue.

The boy did not want to hear his pa say he was sorry. An apology might have penetrated the protective shell the boy had built around himself—a shield of armor he barely was aware he'd constructed in anticipation of the time when his pa would finally release all of his despair, regret, and guilt on the boy he had come to regard not as his son, but as his wife's child.

Yet a more gentle memory existed, one placidly within his brain. He recalled the nights when his pa would bring out his fiddle and express his emotions through music. The boy would stretch out at his pa's feet and be swept away in glorious melodies that represented both the prairie life and origins that extended through two generations and were a part of his family's old-country heritage. Those were the best times, but these memories were infrequent and faded fast in the harsher realities to which the boy had been exposed during those years following his mother's death—those times when he had come close to knowing a family.

Because there were also the occasions when his pa's music would reflect his heartbreak, his sadness at how life had been so unfair, taking from him the only person he claimed to have loved, the one woman he could ever love. The woman who had brought him a son but who fate had decreed would leave him to raise the boy alone. The boy recalled the heaviness that descended upon the little house when Pa, usually after consuming a jug of corn whiskey, would either stretch his violin strings to the breaking point through fierce renditions of songs that terrified the boy, or succumb to his sorrow and bow the strings while tears clouded his eyes.

The violin music, the recollected melancholy strains, faded from the boy's brain as tears dried while he said his final good-bye to his mother. He knew that after this day he would never return. He was surprised at how fast the sorrow passed. It was almost as if his mother were speaking to him, her voice distant and whispered, comforting, encouraging him in his decision to set out on his new life.

The boy nodded in silent acknowledgment . . . and then he felt a hand rest upon his shoulder.

The boy started. As he spun around, the hand lifted from his shoulder in a pacifying gesture.

"Whoa, hold on there, son," Mr. Caulfield said. "Didn't mean to startle you."

The boy exhaled a rattled breath before he relaxed. Caulfield's brown and lined-as-leather ancient face creased even more as he offered a kindly smile.

"Just kinda early to be seein' yuh out here," he explained.

The boy gave a wary nod as his eyes shifted back to his mother's grave.

"Visitin' . . . or sayin' good-bye?" Caulfield inquired with a slight twitch of his head.

The boy responded to the old man's question by assuming a defensive posture, as if to convey that the reason for his being there was none of the old man's business.

Caulfield understood and smiled gently. "Ain't nosin', son, just maybe figgerin'."

"What—would you be figgerin'?" the boy said tersely.

Caulfield lifted his head and looked off toward the distant valley as it responded to the breaking of dawn, announced by marmalade-tinted skies brimming bright over the eastern horizon.

"Looks to be a beautiful day," he said broadly, as if intentionally ignoring the boy's question.

The boy spoke again, with emphasis. "I said what would you be figgerin', Mr. Caulfield?"

The old man regarded the boy with a look of gentle astonishment.

"Feisty one, ain't yuh?" he chuckled.

The boy's tone became subdued. "Just wanta know what you was meanin' by what yuh said."

"That you'd be movin' on," Caulfield replied.

The boy narrowed his eyes as he scrunched up his face. He didn't speak, though he was puzzled and somewhat perturbed that his neighbor had figured out what he was planning. He'd wanted to be gone long before anyone would notice.

"You won't be sayin' nothin'?" the boy asked cautiously.

Caulfield didn't answer outright. Instead he furrowed his brow. "Gonna be hard on your pa, though, havin' yuh go."

The boy shook his head and looked away. "Pa will get along."

"Know things ain't been easy for you folks," Caulfield said in a sympathetic tone. "Had my own share of rough times. Hell, still do. But they're a lot tougher when you gotta go through 'em alone."

"Pa's been alone ever since my ma died," the boy retorted.

The old man rubbed his fingers along the back of his thinning scalp. "Can't rightly see that."

The boy shifted his weight from one foot to the other in an impatient gesture. Caulfield waited for him to explain his odd comment, but the words didn't come.

Finally Caulfield spoke. "I can't be tellin' yuh what to do. There are times when a man's gotta follow through with what he sees best for himself."

Upon being referred to as a "man," the boy turned to Caulfield and managed a faint but appreciative smile. To his own pa he'd never been anything more than "boy," and the word had taken on a contrary connotation. His mood softened. He turned to look at his mother's grave.

"Never placed no marker here," he said wistfully.

Caulfield merely shrugged. "Reckon . . . reckon maybe your pa didn't want to be reminded too much."

The boy shrugged and murmured, "S'pose."

Mr. Caulfield indulged himself to a deep breath of the dew-moistened morning air. "Yep, fine day ahead."

The boy's voice was muted when he next said, "I never thanked you for lettin' my ma rest here."

Caulfield nodded and resisted the urge to place his hand affectionately on the boy's shoulder.

"Don't know if Pa ever thanked you, either," Neville added sensitively. "So I'm thankin' yuh . . . for the both of us."

"That's fine, son," Caulfield said, touched by the sincerity of the gesture.

Caulfield's tanned and weathered face took on an expression that suggested he was in a debate with himself, considering. After a few moments his eyes veered off into the distance and his features took on a pensive look. His lips puckered and finally he gave a firm nod. Then he reached inside the breast pocket of his shirt and pulled out a small piece of colored cloth that he opened with great care. He looked contemplatively at whatever he had revealed; to the boy it appeared to be some sort of shiny object. But it wasn't showing clear enough for the boy to make out precisely what it was.

The old man regarded the object for several moments, again as if considering. Finally he popped a breath and fixed his eyes firmly on the boy. The hand in which he held the object was swaying.

He said, "What I got here is somethin' my own pa handed me when I decided to go out on my own. Was probably just 'bout your age."

The boy tried to see exactly what it was that the old man was referring to, but Caulfield deliberately kept the fingers of the hand closed in a loose fist that concealed the item.

Then, with slow ceremony, Caulfield lowered his hand toward the boy and relaxed his fingers. Resting in the palm of his hand was a ten-dollar gold eagle. The boy thought the coin was pretty but didn't recognize its significance, as he had never seen a gold piece before. But once the old man explained what it was, the boy was so impressed that he almost choked on his breath.

Caulfield cleared his throat to quell the emotion he could feel rising in himself.

"This piece is the most valuable thing I own," he said. "Ain't easy for me to part with it . . . but got no kin to leave it to and can't see no point in havin' it buried with me, when my time comes."

The boy looked up at the old man, wide-eyed. "Are—are you sayin' . . . are you tellin' me you want *me* to have it?"

"Let's say I'm entrustin' it to yuh, yeah," Caulfield said. "Served me well all these years. Or maybe it just gave me a contentment when times got hard. Well, reckon I'm just about as content as I'll ever be. But . . . well, maybe since you're startin' out on your own . . . maybe . . ."

The old man's voice faded. He didn't—or couldn't—finish what he was saying. But it hardly mattered, as the boy was so overwhelmed with being presented with the coin that he wasn't listening much to Caulfield anyhow. He'd rarely received any kind of gift and never one this valuable.

Caulfield said sternly, "Give me your word, son, that you always keep this piece with yuh. Never decide you're gonna go 'bout spendin' it. Myself, sure, I was tempted many times: on food, lodgings, even at times on a thirst I needed quenched. But I'd rather go hungry, sleep out on a cold night, and save myself from a miserable 'morning after' than part with it. Y'hear what I'm sayin'?"

The boy gave a perfunctory rock of his head. The old man sighed and pondered whether he had made the right decision in handing over a treasured heirloom to a kid he really hardly knew. Perhaps he was too hasty in his generosity. The gold piece held much more than monetary value to Caulfield, and he questioned whether the boy would look upon it the same way. The coin was still in his hand; he could still pull it away and drop it back into his shirt pocket and come across in the boy's eyes as some crazy old eccentric. The temptation was there, but Caulfield was an honorable man who could not go back on his gesture.

Still, he said, "I need to hear yuh tell me, boy."

The boy half lifted his eyes so that they just met Caulfield's gaze.

"I—give yuh my word," he said.

Caulfield handed the boy the gold piece and could only hope that his words had made some impact.

He watched as the boy admired and studied the coin, flipping it over from side to side. Then the boy glanced up at Caulfield. While perhaps he was too overcome to voice his thanks, to the old man his appreciation was reflected by the genuine look in his eyes. The boy held on to the coin as he walked away, turning back a couple of times to acknowledge Caulfield, who never moved from his spot until the boy became just a speck in his sight.

The boy walked away from his pa, the farm, and a past he wanted forgotten.

"Good luck to yuh, son," Caulfield said when the boy could no longer hear him.

The boy began his travels that morning with no destination in mind; perhaps, he wondered, setting the pattern for his life—just drifting aimlessly. He quickly discovered that while he enjoyed the freedom of being away from the volatile moods of his pa and the labors of the farm, he was also forced to discover the true meaning of being hungry. More than once the words of his pa came back to haunt him: "'Less you been hungry poor, you don't know the meanin' of poor."

Throughout the days preceding his leaving home, he had prepared by stashing away bits of food both from uneaten meals and by stealing into the meager offerings provided from what Pa called "the food chest," which was kept under lock and key under his pa's direct supervision, but his pa was not so careful about keeping the key out of his son's sight when drunk, so its whereabouts were eventually no longer a secret. The boy would wait until his pa was sleeping before taking small items from the food chest that he then hid in a sack in the shed. Some meat, but mostly eggs, which he would have to consume raw. Still, even with this supply, out of necessity, he had to eat sparingly. He ate enough to survive and maintain most of his strength, but his belly was never satisfied and the frequent rumblings in his stomach kept him aware of that.

Mostly he traveled by foot, but occasionally he could sneak a ride by leaping in the back of a passing wagon or buckboard, though he usually never went very far before he was discovered and chased off. He slept outdoors unless late

at night he might come across a barn or some other suitable
enclosure where he could catch a few hours of shut-eye in
comparative comfort—though his sleep was never entirely
restful as he had to waken and be off before sunrise lest he
be discovered by a farmer armed with a load of buckshot
and hostile to trespassing travelers.

All the while he held on to the ten-dollar gold eagle the
old man had entrusted to him. He naturally experienced
moments when he struggled with the decision to part with
the coin to ease his plight but, strangely perhaps, he recalled
Mr. Caulfield's words, and he would feel a sense of pride at
honoring his request and not releasing the coin from his
possession. In fact, during many of his solitary pondering
moments along his long journey he entertained the thought
of someday returning to Mr. Caulfield and surprising him
by returning the coin.

Yet as his trek wore on, each day proved to be a more
difficult temptation. Often he'd come to a town and spot a
restaurant as he passed like a vagabond through the streets,
sniffing the cuisine and watching with envy as the diners
consumed real food off plates and with silverware, and he'd
find himself fingering the ten-dollar gold piece, imagining
what a good meal would taste like while his stomach rum-
bled its own urging. Maybe his mind was beginning to play
tricks on him, but it almost became like his belly was a
separate part of him—more of a nagging companion, like
a hungry dog.

Finally the day came when his food supply was exhausted
and attempts at living off the land provided little sustenance,
other than feeding off berries when he could find them. The
boy's strength was rapidly fading and he barely staggered
just to the outskirts of the town called Brewer's Gulch before
he collapsed in a semiconscious heap on the dirt road. His
final awareness came with the tinny saloon music he heard
emanating from down the street. His final thought before
totally losing consciousness was of the gold piece tucked
away in his trousers pocket—the strange satisfaction that
through his travels and travails, he'd held on to it.

When he awoke he found himself in a dim room lying on a comfortable bed. He had a real mattress under him, not rough material sewn together and lined with chicken feathers, and a warm quilt over top of him. His head lay on a pillow that had a plump softness he never before had enjoyed. He felt as if he were resting on a cloud.

But—where was he? How long had he been here?

After a while the door to the room opened and a female form entered. Although the room was too dark for the boy to clearly make out her features, she looked to be middle-aged, about the age the boy's ma would have been, but dressed in fancy finery he could not recall ever seeing on a woman, especially in the county whence he came. His ma had always dressed poorly in clothing stitched together from wheat cloth. This lady was obviously a person of refinement, wearing a fashionable white blouse and bluebell calico skirt that made her look softer and prettier than his ma ever could.

And in that instant he was hit with a wave of guilt and wished he hadn't had that thought.

Without speaking a word, the lady walked over to the side of the bed and lighted the wick on the bedside table lamp. That corner of the room illuminated with a whitish glow that instantly brightened the atmosphere, and the boy took his first good look at the face of this lady. She had pleasant features highlighted by bright blue eyes and natural ruby lips with flaming red hair piled loosely atop her head. In contrast to these striking colorings, her complexion was strangely pale, though perhaps it was more a reflection from the light of the table lamp.

She seated herself on the edge of the bed and smiled warmly as she stroked the boy's forehead and began brushing back his hair. Still she didn't talk.

The boy regarded her curiously and was uncomfortable at this display of affection. He was confused, weak, and disoriented, and couldn't understand the reason for her kindness.

Finally he found the strength to ask, "Who are you?"

"A friend," she replied simply.

"H-how long have I been here?"

The lady continued brushing his hair back over his forehead. "I think for now you should rest. We can talk later."

That was not what the boy wanted to hear. Maybe this was nothing but a dream brought on by hunger and exhaustion. If so, he needed to know. Summoning his strength, he lifted himself on an elbow and leaned his upper body forward.

"No," he said determinedly. "No, I have to know now. Please—tell me what happened."

The smile subtly faded from her lips and her eyes gradually lowered. The boy felt he had enough of his wits about him to judge by her reaction that whatever she could tell him would not be good.

Still she hesitated, and once more the boy pleaded for an explanation.

"You were found out on the street," she finally told him. "At first you were thought to be dead. But once they saw that you weren't . . . the sheriff wanted to put you in jail, but I said I'd look after you until you were well."

The boy widened his eyes and said with alarm, "Jail? Why—"

Once more the lady seemed reluctant to go on, but she acceded to the begging look in the boy's eyes.

"When they checked you over they found a ten-dollar gold piece on you. The sheriff figured that no one in your condition could have gotten that money fairly."

"I came a long ways with that gold piece," the boy explained tautly.

"Collapsed in the mud on the street, dirty, your clothes filthy, looking like you hadn't had a decent meal in weeks . . . yet walking around with ten dollars in your pocket. Just didn't add up to the sheriff."

The boy swallowed and tempered his attitude. "Reckon it does look kinda funny. But there's a reason I never spent that money. A sorta promise I made to myself . . . and to the fella who gave it to me."

"I suppose you'll have to tell that to the sheriff," the lady suggested.

"Do yuh think he'd listen?" the boy asked anxiously. "Would he believe me?"

"Sheriff Bridges is a fair man. If you're telling the truth, he would, I'm sure."

"Sheriff—Bridges?" the boy echoed.

The lady spoke comfortingly. "Dan Bridges. You won't have to be afraid of him."

The boy began to feel a little more at ease. He wasn't guilty of any wrongdoing, and if necessary he could have someone get in touch with old man Caulfield to have him verify his story.

He looked across at the lady and met her eyes. "Wanta thank you . . . for takin' me in. Don't know how it woulda been, me wakin' up and finding myself in a jail cell. Much nicer here."

"Maybe I'm just used to taking in strays," the lady joked timidly.

"Reckon I should tell you my name. Seems kinda proper since I'm . . . well, sleepin' in your bed."

The lady smiled broadly. "Not *my* bed. A bed in my house."

"Sorry," the boy said with a flush of embarrassment. "Didn't mean for it to come out the way it did."

The lady brushed aside his apology.

"Name's Neville," he said.

"Neville," she repeated. Then she asked, "Is that your first name or last?"

"Just Neville," he said.

"Seems a bit—*odd*," she remarked.

"Odd?"

"Having just the one name."

Neville merely lifted a shoulder. "It's what I always been called. Never rightly gave it no thought."

"Well, Mr. Neville, that aside, you can call me Sadie."

Neville looked slightly perplexed. While he wasn't raised with much of an emphasis on manners, he was taught to respect his elders, and he was reminded that this woman looked close in years to what would have been his mother's age.

He spoke politely. "Ain't sure if that's right, ma'am, callin' you by your given name."

"Well, you'd better, young man," she playfully chided him. "'Cause I don't take to being called *ma'am*."

Neville twitched his neck. "Well . . . I reckon. If you insist, that is."

"I insist." The inflection in her voice left no room for argument.

"Yes, ma'am—uh, Sadie."

Sadie rose from the bed. "Now I made some supper. Some soup and biscuits. I'll bring you a tray."

"'Preciate it," Neville said. "One thing I sure am is hungry."

"Well, you won't be eating too much—or too fast," Sadie said firmly. "For now, just enough to start getting your strength back."

"So I'll be ready to talk to your sheriff?" Neville said with a downcast expression.

"Well, we won't be worrying about that 'til the time comes," Sadie said soothingly.

Having eaten the tasty meal that Sadie prepared for him and also having slept well, Neville felt much better when he woke the following morning. The comfort of a soft bed was a new and pleasant experience. He felt as if he'd slept for hours, but when he opened his eyes the room was still dark, indicating that it was not yet sunrise. He wasn't surprised; it was a pattern bred into him from nearly as far back as he could remember, rising before dawn to start his chores with Pa on the farm. So within minutes of waking he was itching to start his day and knew he couldn't lie in bed waiting for Sadie to come to waken him, possibly with a breakfast tray that, with the appetite he'd woken with, he could appreciate.

And . . . the more he thought about it, perhaps he shouldn't wait. With the household apparently asleep, he could easily take advantage of the opportunity to get out and away and save himself the trouble of speaking with the sheriff. Suppose the sheriff didn't want to check his story with old man Caulfield? He'd heard about how ornery some of these small-town lawmen could be, looking for any excuse to stir up a little diversion both for their own and the town's benefit.

For a brief instant, Neville decided to do just that—throw on his clothes and get himself away. But the idea faded once he remembered the gold piece. It had been taken from him and he wouldn't get it back unless he convinced the sheriff of the truth of his story—that it hadn't been stolen—for the lawman surely was holding the coin. With a sigh of resignation Neville decided just to wait it out and hope for the best, trusting Sadie's word that the sheriff would prove fair. He needed that gold piece; he'd discovered the hard way that he wouldn't get far without food and, to that end, the coin had taken on a practical rather than sentimental significance.

Still, with his own natural restlessness and with all that was churning around inside his head, he knew he'd couldn't just lie around the room waiting for the sun to come up. Instead he made up his mind to get out of bed and tiptoe about the house and maybe even see if he could find himself something to eat. The nibbles he'd had the previous night had hardly satisfied him. He was awfully hungry.

His shirt had been taken off when he was put into bed, but he was still wearing his trousers, for which his modesty was grateful. He found the sweaty, soiled shirt draped over the back of a chair next to the bed. He pushed the quilt aside and got to his feet. He was careful not to move too fast since he wasn't sure if he might still be weak and didn't want to chance getting dizzy and falling flat on his face. His boots were at the side of the bed, but he thought it prudent to roam about the house in his socks, to keep his footsteps muffled. He debated putting on his shirt, since it smelled bad, but thought it proper in case he should meet Sadie. It was one thing to lie in bed shirtless; to be caught padding throughout the house bare-chested was another matter. He put on the shirt, though leaving it unbuttoned to air out its unpleasant odor, and then he gently opened the door to his room and crept out into the hallway, which was alive with shifting shadows in the predawn gloom. Neville looked about. There was the opening to what appeared to be the parlor and another room with its door closed just down the corridor and off to his left. Neville paused and listened to snoring sounds coming from within that room. Most likely Sadie. But maybe not. Naturally he had no way of knowing if anyone else lived in the house.

He moved slowly until he reached a left turn in the hallway. Almost at once he got a whiff of coffee brewing, a welcoming aroma at this hour of the day. He also noticed a closed door at the end of the corridor, with a sliver of light slanting out onto the floor. Apparently someone else was awake, but whether it was Sadie he could not know, for there was still that someone snoring in the other room. What that did indicate was that Sadie did not live here alone. He held himself motionless while he debated going into what he assumed was the kitchen, not wanting to risk startling whoever might be there—if by chance it wasn't Sadie behind the door. Then he rationalized that if it was someone else, Sadie surely must have told that person about his being in the house so his appearance should not really come as a surprise, once he introduced himself. Convincing himself of that being the case, Neville started to walk toward the door, at the same time buttoning his shirt to look at least halfway presentable to whomever it was he would greet.

Still . . . he hesitated. He stood outside the door, his right hand raised with his fingers splayed against the wood frame, as he contemplated first knocking—then finally deciding just to throw caution to the wind and step inside.

That decision might have been a mistake, for as soon as Neville entered the room his eyes fell upon a sight he'd hardly expected to see.

Off to the side of the room by a woodstove atop where the coffee was brewing stood a tall, solidly built, stern-looking man with thick, curly black hair and a bushy, drooping mustache, wearing gray-and-black-striped trousers, a stiff-collared white shirt, and a vest—on which was pinned a silver star.

Neville unglued his gaze from the man and his eyes began to nervously dart about the room, focusing on a wide wall map of the territory, a gun rack fitted with rifles standing upright and, most telling, a room protected by a solid wood door next to the woodstove where, with the door now ajar, he could just barely make out a row of barred enclosures.

A jail, by God! He was looking into the sheriff's office—with the sheriff himself now eyeing him fixedly.

For seconds that seemed much longer to Neville, the only sounds in the office were the steady, rhythmic ticking of the wall clock and the simmer of the coffee heating up in the pot.

"So you're the young fella we brung in last night," the sheriff finally said with a neutral inflection as he lifted the pot from the stove and poured coffee into a tin cup. He paused before adding, "The one my wife has taken a likin' to."

Neville swallowed, still too stunned to speak. He couldn't comprehend how he could walk from the warm comfort of his bed into a cold jail with a clearly rough-edged sheriff standing there to greet him and offering a comment that likely was intended to make him uncomfortable. He suppressed his instinct of pure panic but wasn't sure what to do next. Should he just turn and walk calmly back to his room—or maybe surrender to the urge that was tugging at him and make an impulsive dash from the office out onto the street?

The sheriff wasn't making it any easier for him; his dark, squinty eyes were locked tight on Neville, nearly petrifying the boy with their steely penetration.

"Get your butt in here and help yourself to a cup," the sheriff finally said in a brusque tone, gesturing to the coffeepot.

Neville was hesitant to step into the office. Yet he knew that under the circumstances, he'd be making a big mistake to reject the invitation. The last thing he needed to do in front of the intimidating presence of the sheriff was to act in any way that might cast further suspicion on him.

Forcing down a heavy swallow that he hoped the sheriff didn't notice, Neville walked forward into the office, his steps slow and deliberate. The sheriff easily detected his discomfort and was amused. Still, the stern expression with which he regarded Neville didn't disappear, nor did his piercing eye contact. The sheriff was a careful man, used to dealing with desperados both young and old, and wasn't quite ready to put the boy entirely at his ease.

Neville decided he didn't want coffee—well, he did but was not willing to walk next to the sheriff to get it. The sheriff showed no sign of stepping aside to make it easier for him. Neville stood on the opposite side of the office from where the sheriff was standing.

"Take a chair," the sheriff told him. He spoke sternly, like a schoolmaster commanding a pupil.

Neville stepped over to the sheriff's desk and seated himself on the chair nearest it. The sheriff didn't budge from his place by the stove, taking noisy slurps from his coffee while he continued to study the boy.

Neville tried to make himself look relaxed but found it difficult with the sheriff seeming to stare right through him, either directly or, more unnerving, peering narrowly at him over the rim of his tin coffee cup. Neville was sitting with his back arched forward, his hands clasped together with the fingers of his left hand massaging the knuckles of his right. He was guilty of nothing but reckoned that to the sheriff his awkward body posture might have given the impression that he was responsible for half the crimes in the territory.

Finally, the sheriff took pity on the lad. His eyes seemed to lose their harshness as a slight smile crept across his lips, the curvature just visible under the woolly thickness of his mustache.

"Ain't gonna bite yuh, son," he exhaled. He ambled over toward his desk.

Neville's body pressed back into the chair in an involuntary response.

The sheriff shoved aside some papers and seated himself on the edge of his desk, resting his body just a couple of feet from where Neville was sitting. Despite the softening of the sheriff's expression and his friendly words, Neville still felt nervous and restless.

"Yeah, my wife's kinda takin' a liking to you," the sheriff repeated matter-of-factly.

For the first time Neville looked directly at the big man, reflexively, with a bewildered expression painted across his face.

The sheriff smiled. "Told me you two got introduced last night—Neville."

The boy's mouth started to move, but no words escaped his lips.

"Heh, heh, boy, you gotta learn to breathe easy," the sheriff chortled. "You're too tensed up."

Neville swallowed again. Finally he got the words out—perhaps with more emphasis than he'd intended.

"Can't ease up!" he exclaimed. "You—you're accusin' me of things that I ain't done!"

"Accusin'?" the sheriff echoed, bemused.

"Yeah, accusin'."

The sheriff looked offended and raised his hand in a sort of pacifying gesture. "I ain't accusin' you of nothin', son. Not if you ain't got nothin' to hide. Less'n if you're referrin' to you and my missus. In which case, I'd be askin' where'd yuh conjure up such an idea?"

"I . . . I dunno," Neville said awkwardly. "Reckon from all what you're sayin'."

The sheriff gave his wide shoulders a shrug. "Ain't sayin' nothin'."

"Then—you're just tryin' to get a rise outta me."

"That what you think I'm doin'—Neville?"

Neville reddened in the face. "Second time you said my name that way."

"What way?"

Neville was both heated and agitated, and he began waving his arms in frustration. "Sayin' it with that . . . with that

pausin'. Like you're tryin' to get me to admit to somethin'
I ain't done."

The sheriff calmly shook his head. "You're too suspicious, boy." He finished up the last of his coffee and placed
the cup off to the far side of his desk. Then he wore a smile.
"But least I got yuh to talkin'."

After several seconds, Neville came to understand the
sheriff's strategy, and he puffed out a short breath. The flush
dissipated from his face, though a look of wariness still
clouded his features. The sheriff had employed a clever tac-
tic, one intended to break down all unnecessary defenses,
coaxing the boy to speak truthfully, without resistance.

Neville bit his lip. "I—know what you done."

"Good," the sheriff said, slapping his knees with the
palms of his hands for emphasis. "Now we can stop blowin'
wind up the horse's butt and have ourselves an intelligent
talk."

Neville was quiet.

"Agreed?" the sheriff said in his deep, resonant voice.

Neville lifted a tentative shoulder. "S'pose."

"But 'fore we get to talkin', how 'bout you gettin' yourself
that cup of coffee," the sheriff suggested.

Neville was still unsure of his situation. When he'd set
out on his travels he'd never imagined finding himself where
he was now. First being tended to by a kind lady, then being
made to feel as if he'd committed some criminal offense by
a tough lawman. Now . . . well, he didn't know what to
expect.

But he got up and walked over to the stove, his gait only
slightly less tentative than before. He poured himself coffee.
He took a sip and grimaced. He'd tasted better.

He returned to his chair and then braced himself for his
talk with the sheriff.

Their conversation was surprisingly revealing—even a
mite startling. Neville was taken aback to find out that the
woman who had cared for him the night before, Sadie, was
the sheriff's wife. He was curious as to why she'd never
mentioned it when she'd spoken of the sheriff. He also found

it interesting to learn that the couple housed themselves in accommodations attached to the sheriff's office. Still, it all made sense to Neville after he absorbed it.

It required some gentle prodding from the sheriff, but Neville finally agreed to give his story. He found himself strangely reluctant to share it, yet he understood it was the only way to convince the sheriff that he was guilty of no wrongdoing and to explain how he came into possession of the ten-dollar gold eagle. The sheriff, who introduced himself as Dan Bridges—and insisted upon being called Sheriff Dan, forgoing formalities as had his wife—listened sympathetically as Neville told of leaving his home and his father, accepting the gold piece from old man Caulfield, his long travels where he remained unsure of where he might end up, and finally, not having eaten for days, collapsing face-down in the road just outside Brewer's Gulch.

It took Neville two cups of black coffee to relate his adventures, and by the time he was finished, the new day's sun was blazing a white light through the wide front glass of the office.

"Coulda picked a better town to end up in," Sheriff Dan remarked. "I'da tried to hold out 'til I got to Albuquerque," he added as a joke.

Neville wasn't much up for levity. He nodded vacantly without comment.

Sheriff Dan could see that the talk had taken a lot out of the boy, and so he allowed him some time to sit in quiet while he started rooting through the paperwork spread out on his desk.

A few moments later Neville was apologetic. "I probably talked too much."

"Glad you did, son," Sheriff Dan said, considerate of the boy's mood and speaking earnestly.

Neville scrunched up his features as he considered. "Don't think I ever talked so much—to no one."

"Not to your pa?" Sheriff Dan queried.

Neville lowered and then shook his head. "We never talked hardly at all—'specially after my ma died. Reckon the closest we came to sharin' was when he'd pick up the fiddle and start playin'. That's 'bout the most I remember 'bout havin' good times with him." He sighed pensively. "Not that even them was always the best times."

"Well, yuh feel better for jawin' with me?" Sheriff Dan asked expansively.

The boy hesitated, and then, as if suddenly enlightened, he said, "Yeah. Yeah, I do."

Sheriff Dan said, "So what do you do now?"

"Huh?"

"Your plans," the sheriff clarified. "Where you're headed. What you'll do once yuh get there."

Neville tried to come up with an answer, but he couldn't. He could not give an answer since he'd never worked out a definite course to follow. That was one decision he hadn't completely thought out. As far as he could determine, his future saw him just drifting. Maybe at some point stumbling upon an opportunity.

In the meantime, he had something else he felt he should say.

"Sheriff . . . Dan," the boy said meekly. "Kinda . . . lied 'bout somethin'. Both to you and Sadie—your missus."

Sheriff Dan gave a slight lift of his head to encourage the boy to continue.

"Don't know why I do it," the boy said uncomfortably. "Reckon I just prefer it if'n people don't know too much 'bout me. But . . . but I do have 'nother name."

"Makes no never mind whether you tell me or not," Sheriff Dan said straightly. He was sincere in his neutrality. Whether the boy who called himself Neville was ready to offer more than he already had would solely be his own decision. Sheriff Dan respected that. Because he'd already determined that whatever else there might be about him, there was honesty in the lad.

Perhaps it was Sheriff Dan's acceptance of the boy making his own decision—or possibly his apparent indifference, made evident by his getting up to fetch another cup of coffee,

that prompted Neville to start to rise from his chair and
blurt out:

"Tom! My name is Tom Neville!"

Sheriff Dan turned to him. He recognized that his telling
the sheriff this was of mighty importance to the lad. But he
also understood that for himself to acknowledge with more
than a nodding approval or appreciation for his honesty
could possibly be detrimental. The boy might be testing
him, hoping for a reaction that could set him off. From
professional . . . and personal experience, and now getting
some insight into Neville's personality, Sheriff Dan detected
that this boy was possessed of a short fuse. It was too early
in the day for the sheriff to risk detonating it.

So Sheriff Dan merely nodded. "That's fine."

The discouraged expression that appeared on Neville's
features seemed to indicate that he was waiting—perhaps
hoping for more of a response. It was clear that Sheriff Dan's
simple unquestioning acceptance was not what he'd wanted
to hear.

Sheriff Dan noticed the look on his face and said, "Somethin' wrong, boy?"

Neville felt his blood start to quicken. He had only the
vaguest idea why he was consumed with this sudden hostility, an emotion building beyond his comprehension, a
potential rage that both frightened and, in an odd way,
thrilled him. Sheriff Dan saw what was brewing; he had
hoped against it, but was prepared.

"Hang on, boy," he said reasonably. "No need to get all
fired up with snake spit."

"Why can't yuh just say my name?" Neville blasted, his
words thick as they passed through gritted teeth. "I have a
name! I told yuh—it's Tom. It ain't *boy* or *son*. It's Tom!
Why can't yuh just call me by who I am?"

To the sheriff it was as if Neville were giving vent to what
might have been years of pent-up anger and resentment.

"My pa could never say my name, neither!" he said, his
voice trembling with barely controlled fury. "Always just

boy! *Boy*, y'hear me? *Boy*, there's chores to be done. *Boy*, you're just plain lazy. He never even called me *son*."

"I ain't your pa, Tom," Sheriff Dan said sternly.

Neville wasn't listening. Instead his eyes shot daggers at the lawman, who readied himself for what he saw coming— an impulsive move.

Neville thrust himself from his chair, his temper nearing a fever pitch, and Sheriff Dan immediately responded. He dropped his coffee cup to the floor and stepped away from the stove, assuming a defensive stance that he hoped would halt Neville's aggression. Neville held himself back only for a moment, then advanced, a foolhardy move pitting his weak physique against Sheriff Dan's solid, muscular build. The sheriff halted Neville as the boy lunged at him. Sheriff Dan grabbed him tightly by the shoulders, holding firm against Neville's fierce struggles until after minutes, Neville's frantic efforts and muttered curses finally weakened and his body collapsed, deflated, wholly into the sheriff's arms.

Sheriff Dan pulled Neville upward, distressed that the boy now felt almost like a sack of rags in his two-fisted grip. The sheriff held him momentarily at a distance, trying to make eye contact though unable since Neville would not raise his face from the floor. Then with a strange sadness reflected in his eyes, he instinctively drew Neville close to his chest and comforted him as the boy broke down, his body convulsed with sobs.

Sheriff Dan permitted himself this physical intimacy with the boy because he understood. He empathized because he, too, had a son. Rather, he'd *had* a son. A boy close to Neville's age, a son whom he had not been able to reach, but from whom he had learned much through mistakes for which he blamed himself, coupled with a guilt that had intensified in the nearly three years since his only child, Jim, had been killed. A stupid, needless death for which he believed he was at least indirectly responsible.

Neville couldn't know, but as he was being held in Sheriff Dan's arms, the sheriff's wife, Sadie, had entered the room. She stifled a startled breath and, as she recovered, responded to her husband's uncharacteristic gesture with a tentative smile. Breakfast was ready, but it could wait. What she had hoped for when she'd insisted the boy be put into a warm bed rather than a jail cell had been realized—but even more dramatically than she could have anticipated. Her husband was not a demonstrative man; he'd forgone affection and compassion for their own son in lieu of the discipline he believed was essential for a boy raised in the still untamed wilds of the West, the toughening of spirit and backbone. But such influence had ultimately failed, drastically, as Jim, a sensitive youth feeling abandoned by the love he sought, showed signs of going wayward. Then one night, through an accident or by an error in judgment . . .

Sadie hastily pushed that memory from her mind.

Yet now as a witness to this unfamiliar tableau, as tears began misting her eyes, Sadie also felt a strange concern. She'd never seen her husband display such swift affection. Not to her, not to their son. Perhaps he was merely responding to the needs of the boy, who even she had sensed was lost and seeking something of value in his life.

Sadie could accept that. She, too, had grown fond of Neville in the short time she had gotten to know him.

But maybe . . . it was something more. Sadie understood, because she also shared some of the guilt that her husband had suffered with over the past years. Guilt that he tried to restrain under his gruff professional exterior but the pain of which seeped through whenever he spotted a father and son together, or when looking at a boy who would have been the same age as Jim.

A boy . . . like Neville.

What troubled Sadie, what she now could not keep herself from considering, was whether the blame with which her husband had burdened himself might have motivated him to accept into their home another troubled boy.

She didn't know if either of them could survive another heartbreak.

TWO

Yet in a most natural way, Neville shortly became part of their family. He seemed to fill a void in their lives, especially with Sheriff Dan. While Sadie initially had reservations about her husband growing close to the boy, she noticed a change in Dan that was both welcome and admirable. He had always been a stern, serious man, but following the death of their son he also fell victim to bouts of melancholy, which at times made it difficult for Sadie. He often became sullen and withdrawn and would lock himself in his office for hours, just sitting at his desk alone with his thoughts, and when she tried to talk with him, he would either answer in as few words as possible—or simply pretend not to hear her.

Even more troubling was that he'd taken to drinking more than he usually did. He never really became drunk or belligerent, but it upset Sadie to see him substitute his usual glass of beer for whiskey and then come into bed hours after she had retired, his breath smelling of liquor. There were times during this period when Sadie seriously considered leaving Dan.

For in truth, she'd never cared for living in Brewer's Gulch. It was a dusty, dirty town that offered no diversions outside the saloons, and for Sadie, used to the excitement of the city, it seemed as far removed from civilization as one could get. But she loved her husband, and her son, Jim, and also held on to the hope that eventually Dan, too, would tire of the town and decide to pack up his family and move onward, and maybe even seek another line of work.

Dan enjoyed being a lawman and made no guarantees that he would ever give up his badge . . . but he had promised Sadie he would think seriously about moving the family out of Brewer's Gulch. As their son grew older Sheriff Dan saw that the town was not an ideal place for an adolescent boy who was starting to feel and exhibit his own restlessness. Brewer's Gulch offered few opportunities; it seemed to exist mainly as a trail town, a welcome stopover for drovers, ready to drink and whoop it up after a long cattle drive. This was where Sheriff Dan earned most of his pay, trying to keep the peace when the cowboys rode into town. They were out for a good time, wanted nothing more than to spend their wages on whiskey and women and let off some steam, but inevitably things would get out of hand and Sheriff Dan together with his scattergun and a few reliable citizens would be summoned to one or more of the Brewer's Gulch saloons to restore order. And those were the times Sadie dreaded most. She knew how rowdy these trail dusters could get when liquored up; the whole of the town could hear their hollers and laughter and occasional gunfire from a drunken drover who "neglected" to turn in his six-shooter at the sheriff's office, and her heart would palpitate as she never knew if her husband would walk back through the door or be carried in.

As it turned out, it wasn't her husband, a most capable man, she had to be worried about. Their son, Jim, had begun getting into mischief, and outside of administering scoldings, Sheriff Dan seemed unable to curb his wild leanings. He had never built a strong relationship with the boy. The truth was that Sheriff Dan was more dedicated to his duty than to his family. Although this troubled her, Sadie had the maturity and patience to tolerate while not wholly accepting her husband's attitude, but Jim just grew resentful. Whereas he wanted acceptance and affection from his father, Sheriff Dan imposed discipline (to the point where he ordered his son not to refer to him as Dad or Pa, but as Sheriff Dan), and, as the situation between them grew more tense, with truancy now added to Jim's troubles, the sheriff had his boy pulled out of school and put to work cleaning out Hank Jenkins's livery stable. It was a lesson the sheriff believed was in the boy's best interest. Working long hours at a menial job would surely demonstrate to Jim the importance of an education.

Yet each day that Jim came home stinking of manure, clothes stained from his labor, all his folks could see was a bitterness festering inside him. It appeared the only lesson he was learning was indignation. Sadie pleaded with her husband to move the family away from Brewer's Gulch before something terrible happened.

Sheriff Dan stalled, stubborn in his certainty that hard work and a sense of responsibility would set the boy right . . . until finally his wife's fears were proven true.

One Saturday night when Jim was working late, there was a fire at the stable. However it started, Jim was not able to escape the flames, and his badly burned body was later found amid the charred wreckage.

Sheriff Dan never knew for sure what happened, though he had his suspicions. Troubling suspicions. He kept those to himself, not even sharing them with his wife. As far as he was concerned, she did not need to know. Better that she and the town believe as they did that it was an unfortunate accident. Sheriff Dan could not quite convince himself that it was. He couldn't surrender the thought that his son had started the fire deliberately, perhaps intending it to look like an accident, getting himself trapped inside. What would prompt him to do such a thing would remain a mystery . . . though Sheriff Dan could never forget that it was he who had made his boy take the job at the livery stable, and that

Jim had clearly resented him for it. Whatever the true cause of the fire that killed his son, Sheriff Dan could not ignore that he had to accept some of the blame. Only later could he come to understand that he wasn't so much a dad as a disciplinarian.

What he could not know was that his wife also challenged the official conclusion. Sadie had observed the changing attitude in her son; as she reasoned, how could a mother not notice? Although she, too, would never express it, she possessed her own doubts that the fire was an accident. She couldn't bring herself to say outright that gentle Jim had intentionally caused the blaze, which killed not only him but three stabled horses and totally destroyed Mr. Jenkins's livelihood, but deep in her soul she knew that was probably what happened.

That was only one of the crosses that she bore. For a long time afterward she struggled with herself not to affix blame to her husband for their son's death. A part of her would always hold Dan responsible, but as she witnessed the change that came over him, the deep inner torment he lived with each day, the lengthy silences, the drinking, she quietly found it in herself to forgive him without Sheriff Dan ever truly realizing that she had accused him. She couldn't add to the burden he was already carrying.

She forgave, but she never would forget . . .

In the weeks that followed Neville's acceptance into his home, Sheriff Dan became almost like a real father to the boy. He spent more time with Neville than he ever had with his own son, not grudgingly but willingly, and there were moments when this realization haunted him with a terrible guilt. Those were the times when the sheriff would go off on his own to try to cleanse his conscience. Neville was never told the reason for these brief departures, but Sadie understood.

In the beginning Neville was wary; even when his ma was alive he'd never really known the true comfort of a

family. But the sheriff and his missus treated him with a
genuine kindness that soon eased many of Neville's doubts.

It still seemed strange to him how all this had come
about. At night he'd lie in his big, comfortable bed feeling
safe and protected and in his own pensive moments regret
how he couldn't have felt this way with his pa. But as time
passed, the figure of his father clouded into an indistinct
memory. As far as Neville was concerned, through circumstances he never could have imagined when he set out from
his home that morning not so very long ago, he had found
his family.

Sheriff Dan and Sadie discussed with Neville his going
back to school. This embarrassed Neville, as he was a boy
of almost fifteen and had hardly seen the inside of a class-
room. His pa had seen no value in education. One didn't
need to know how to read books to plow fields or plant crops,
was how he looked at it. The way Neville saw it, he'd have
to start right back at the beginning. He'd feel foolish sitting
in a room filled with kids half his age.

Neither Sheriff Dan nor Sadie pushed the issue. After
all, while they had taken him in, Neville was not their child,
and they held no parental privilege. But Sadie did offer a
compromise. She would set aside one hour each night after
the supper dishes were done to teach Neville the basics of
reading and arithmetic. Those were important to know. Neville thought too much of Sadie to disappoint her, and he
agreed to sit with her.

Sheriff Dan still believed in the importance of a strong
work ethic, and he got Neville a job working at the Grain
and Feed. Sam Grafton was the fellow who owned the store
and he proved a good man to work for, kind and fair to the
boy, and Neville found that his hours at the Grain and Feed
passed pleasantly.

He'd been at the store for about two months when one
afternoon toward the end of the week the bell above the door
jingled, likely announcing a customer who needed servicing.
Neville was alone in the shop, stocking shelves. He climbed
down off the step stool, wiped his dusty hands against his

apron, and turned to see Sheriff Dan standing just inside the threshold, both arms raised, a sapling fishing pole in each hand.

"Ain't much goin' on around town, Tom, kinda slow," the sheriff said with a grin. "Thought maybe we might get in some fishin' at the crick."

Neville's face dissolved into an expression of disappointment. "I—I'd like to, Sheriff Dan. But Mr. Grafton had to leave town to pick up some supplies from Cranston and he left me in charge. Said he won't be back 'til just 'round suppertime."

"I'll square it later with Grafton," the sheriff said. "Think it a good idea if we talk some."

It was the afternoon when Neville was finally told the story of the couple's heartbreak. He knew there had been a son, a boy named Jim who had died, but each time Sheriff Dan or Sadie spoke of him, and those moments were few indeed, Neville could see their pain, so conversation promptly ceased and the boy remained a mystery to him.

He finally learned about Jim and the tragedy while he and Sheriff Dan sat next to the water's edge on a small rise, a grass-bedded clearing bordered by thick underbrush. They sat protected from the midday heat by the wide, shady overhang of a willow tree, their makeshift lines cast into the calm waters.

Sheriff Dan noticed how Neville became quiet after he'd been told the story. He debated telling the boy more. He wasn't a man open to revealing intimate feelings, but after some consideration he decided to take this opportunity to speak frankly with Neville.

"Never told yuh this, but in some ways you remind me of Jim," he said solemnly. "Yet no matter how much I might try to talk myself into thinkin' maybe it could be, I know you can't never step into my son's shoes. Maybe . . . maybe that's what I was thinkin' at one time, after takin' a likin' to yuh. But, no, it ain't what neither me nor my missus needs,

Tom. I know that now. Maybe you just come 'round at the
right time. Yuh told us how it's been for you, and Sadie and
me . . . we just felt we could help. But reckon each of us gotta
get on with our own life, no matter what hurt we might be
dealin' with."

"You sayin' that you'd like me to move on?" Neville
asked with a hint of despair.

"No, ain't sayin' that," Sheriff Dan assured him.

"Then you want I should stay?" There was a hopeful note
in Neville's voice. To the sheriff, at that moment, he came
across like a child fearful of abandonment.

Sheriff Dan raised the Stetson over the back of his head
and scratched with emphasis an imaginary itch on his neck,
his persistent effort creating a red blotch on his skin.

"Tom, I'm sayin' that you gotta do what *you* think is
right," he said, speaking plain and straightforward. "Reckon
I pretty well explained to you what yuh needed to hear."

Now it was Neville's turn to speak, and he considered
his words carefully.

"You and Sadie have been awful good to me," he said,
holding check on his emotions. "What yuh told me . . . 'bout
your son . . . well, reckon I can understand. Guess the way
I look at you, Sheriff Dan, is . . . you bein' the man I wish
my pa was. But I can't never see me ever bein' the boy your
son was. And I don't mean no offense, but I wouldn't want
to be. You and Sadie have those memories and you gotta
keep 'em."

Neville turned his head to the side and looked away. He
felt a little embarrassed saying what he had. As with the
sheriff, he'd had few opportunities to express his personal
thoughts. He wasn't even sure if he was making any sense.
But to Sheriff Dan his words and the sincerity behind them
held a lot of meaning. They were true and heartfelt. The
sheriff appreciated hearing them.

Sheriff Dan spoke quietly, a faint emotion coming
through in his own words. "Tom, one thing I learned, the
hard way, is that every boy needs a man in his life. Someone
who can teach him, someone the boy can look up to. Well,

course wasn't that way with me and Jim. Thought I was doin' the right thing but I was mistaken, 'cause turns out I really didn't know him. Couldn't . . . maybe *wouldn't* take heed of his needs. I'd kinda like to make up for those missed opportunities, Tom. Don't mean I gotta be takin' the place of your pa to do that." He took a long pause. "And that don't mean you gotta go thinkin' you're replacing Jim."

Neville responded with a slow nod.

The two sat sharing a prolonged quiet. The air was still, and not a stirring disturbed their solitude. Neville became lost in his thoughts. He looked ahead, beyond the waters of the creek to the lush green rolling landscape on the opposite side, spread out before him like an emerald carpet rich in color, and farther off in the distance the cresting of the Boda Valley Hills. He wondered what lay beyond. Perhaps had circumstances been different, had he not surrendered to an empty belly, he might have made that discovery. Maybe he still would.

He wanted to own a piece of that land, to settle upon, perhaps raise a family. Something that he could nurture and cultivate on his own, owing to no man.

But as he pondered a possible future, a sad memory of his pa intruded upon these pleasant thoughts, blunt words he remembered when Pa was ready, as he was on many occasions, just to accept failure for his labors:

"Boy, the only land a man truly owns is the six feet he's buried in."

Sage words or an expression of bitter discouragement? Neville fortunately didn't have long to contemplate, as he heard the voice of Sheriff Dan speaking to him.

"You listenin' to me, Tom?"

"Huh?"

"Or are you out there somewheres?" Sheriff Dan asked with a half smile, offering a vague hand gesture into the distance.

Neville shifted his attention back to the moment. He concealed his embarrassment and nodded briskly.

"Can't rightly blame yuh for driftin' off," Sheriff Dan

said with a chuckle. "That's why I like to come out here when I can. Gives a man a chance to think."

"I like it here," Neville agreed. He pulled in a deep, appreciative breath. "It's clean. Even the air tastes pure. From where I come it's dry land, not good for farmin' or much else." Then his tone held an edge of bitterness. "Don't know why my pa ever decided to settle there."

Sheriff Dan acknowledged with a nod but otherwise thought it best not to pursue the comment. He understood that Neville held a lot of resentment when it came to his pa.

"Tell you what we'll do, Tom," he said instead. "Before the weather gets cold let's plan a campout. Just you and me. We'll build us a fire and catch us some good eatin' fish. Y'ever taste trout cooked over an open fire?"

Neville shook his head with a hint of sadness, the gesture indicating to Sheriff Dan that the boy had never even gone fishing before today.

The sheriff again resisted commenting. To lighten the mood he said expansively, "Well, we pull some in and fry it in butter and you're in for a treat."

Neville looked out at the still waters of the creek, nary a ripple to disturb the surface, then frowned and glanced askance at the sheriff.

"We been sittin' here for close to an hour and neither of us got a bite," he remarked.

"True 'nuff, Tom," Sheriff Dan conceded, hefting a sigh. "Don't think it's no reflection on us, though. I'd venture the fish in this crick are gettin' pretty smart." He then tossed Neville a wink. "Well, in that case we might be smart ourselves to get the missus to pack us a lunch for our outing."

THREE

W̶hat transpired that afternoon proved a turning point in the relationship between Neville and Sheriff Dan. The honesty they both expressed while lazily awaiting a tug on their sapling fishing poles seemed to produce a bond between the two. The respect for each other's needs was both recognized and acknowledged—and appreciated by both.

This also was of another value. Although it would not occur until two years later, Neville had been made to realize that he had to go back home and make peace with his pa. He was holding on to too much bitterness, and while Sheriff Dan and Sadie provided him with a stable and calming influence, there remained those moments when Neville would suddenly and unexpectedly lash out. The fear and resentment he still held toward his pa would erupt at the slightest provocation, a word or an insult that stimulated a reminder of the past—or would startle him awake in the grip of a nightmare. It was Sheriff Dan who recognized what needed to be done to finally purge Neville of all the negative feelings he still harbored, and it was he, supported by Sadie, who encouraged Neville to go see his pa.

After some doubt and soul searching, Neville finally
agreed to make the trip. While he still hadn't mapped out a
definite future for himself, he thought that after the passage
of these years and seeing that he was neither dead nor des-
titute, and now able to present himself proudly in a crisp
new suit, purchased equally by the sheriff and himself from
a portion of his store wages, it might also be the time to
return that ten-dollar gold eagle to Mr. Caulfield. In truth,
it provided Neville with a better justification for his returning home than a dubious visit with his pa. And although he
really hadn't thought about it, perhaps that coin had brought
Neville good fortune, as the old man had said it did for him.
Not through value, but simply by possession.

"Don't know how things are gonna turn out for you, Tom,
just know if'n you decide, you're welcome to come back
here," Sheriff Dan said to Neville the morning of his departure.

The comment sort of surprised Neville. He hadn't
planned on saying good-bye forever; he'd hoped his adopted
family wasn't expecting that, either. While he wouldn't voice
it, he didn't believe there was the remotest chance he'd consider staying back on the farm with his pa.

"I 'preciate that," he said, meeting Sheriff Dan's extended
hand with a strong grip.

Sheriff Dan grimaced playfully.

"Couldn'ta grabbed me that hard a few years ago," he
joked, impressed by the firmness of the boy's handshake.

"No, reckon not," Neville replied, tightening his lips
against an emotion beginning to well in him. "Lotta things
I couldn't have done back then."

He turned to glance at Sadie, who he sadly noticed
looked so much more aged than when he'd first met her and
she had shown him such kindness. Now her head was bun-
dled in a shawl, only partially concealing the thinning gray
strands that had replaced the flaming red hair of only a few
years earlier, her pallid skin now sallow and prematurely
withered, each shift of her features further defining the lines
around her mouth and deep-borne wrinkles that creased her

forehead. Her once-bright eyes had become cloudy. Neville knew she hadn't been well, and that fact had caused him to reconsider making this trip. But Sadie had insisted that he go. For the first time since that night when he was brought into the house and she had come into the room to see him, Sadie had again entered his bedroom on an evening not a week ago to speak with him. She could not hide or deny her sickness but, as was her nature, maintained a selfless, valiant demeanor, setting her personal concerns aside for the benefit of someone else. She would not permit him to not carry through with visiting his father on account of worry for her.

Neville also learned something about Sadie that night. At one time she had worked as a saloon girl in Wichita. That was where Sheriff Dan met her, during a particularly raucous night when he was serving as temporary sheriff and he and his small group of hastily appointed deputies had to prevent a near-riot with the cowhands of a cattleman named Frenchie Hosteler, who were responding to a challenge from a rival cattle rancher as to who would be awarded the contract to supply needed beef to a cavalry outpost presently stationed in the Southwest near the Tacoma Mountains in preparation of the threat of an Apache skirmish. Friendly if alcohol-enhanced betting grew out of proportion and before long fists were flying, then guns drawn. Sheriff Dan managed to gain control over the potentially powderkeg situation, with the most severe injury suffered by one of his own deputies who received a broken jaw for his stepping in to try to diplomatically settle a whiskey-heated disagreement.

Once a semblance of order was restored, Sheriff Dan surveyed the situation and noticed how one particular girl had seated herself at a far table and was looking at him admiringly. Dan wasn't much for saloons, but he had seen this gal once or twice, but not until this night did he *really* take notice of her. As Sadie told the story to Neville, one thing led to another and soon she was giving up her "hostessing" duties to move away from the city to settle in a succession of prairie towns as the bride of a lawman. A future, she admitted, she could never have imagined for herself.

Neville was remembering the story when Sadie stepped over to him. He took her delicately by the shoulders, then tilted his head and breathed out a sigh.

"You keep well 'til I get back," he said, looking directly into her eyes.

Sadie started to say something, but words seemed to fail her. She met Neville's gaze and gave a brisk nod before her eyes lowered, either sadly or thoughtfully. The scrawny lad who had been brought into their house only scant years before had developed into a man. His voice had deepened, his body had grown and filled out, and both his face and his attitude had taken on a handsome maturity. While she would not express it through her words, Sadie couldn't help thinking that she and her husband had raised their "son" well.

Neville kissed her tenderly on the cheek. Sadie responded by taking his hand in both of hers. It troubled Neville to feel almost no strength in her grip and the very slight tremor in her fingers.

The stage was pulling up to the depot. While not generally given to profound observations, he commented on the irony of his change in fortune.

"Two years ago I stumbled into Brewer's Gulch, landing facedown on my belly, and now today I'm leavin' in comfort in fancy duds on a stagecoach." His eyes revolved around the dirty buildings and dusty main street of the town before he paused. "Place kinda grows on you."

Sheriff Dan and Sadie looked at one another and exchanged a smile.

Neville sighed. "Thing is, I ain't even sure I'll find my pa alive."

Sheriff Dan and his wife exchanged another glance, suggesting that they, too, had considered that possibility.

"Still better that you know, Tom," the sheriff said. "However you choose to move on with your life, don't figger you'll go very far without knowin' for sure. That'll always be holdin' yuh back. And if you don't find exactly what you're lookin' for, least you can say yuh tried."

Neville gave a slow nod.

Sadie finally spoke up, her voice weak, her words faint. "Just know that whatever you come upon . . . and whatever you decide, we love you, Tom."

Neville tried not to react with surprise. This was the first time Sadie had ever spoken those endearing words. He wanted so much to reciprocate her sentiment, to voice it not only to Sadie but also to Sheriff Dan. He did love them, he was sure they both knew it, yet throughout those years they shared together, from the day when he had been accepted into their home, he'd never been able to say "I love you." They were words that carried too much emotion and were just too difficult for him to speak.

Just before he boarded the stage, he leaned forward and again kissed Sadie on the cheek—but this time suddenly consumed with the painful thought that this might be the last time he would see her. He quickly became aware that this despondency was reflected in his expression, his features downcast. He hastened to force a smile. His eyes went toward Sheriff Dan. The sheriff had caught the look Neville had tried to shield. He offered a solemn nod to let Neville know that he need not feel ashamed; that he, too, understood the concern.

And there was more. In his own stolid way, in the manner that he and Neville understood because of the many times together that did not require conversation, just the quiet sharing of each other's company, along with thoughts that both had come to recognize and respect in one another, the sheriff was expressing to Neville that he had been a good son.

Neville stepped up and took his seat inside the coach, wedging his way through the tight compartment with the valise he insisted on keeping with him. There were three other passengers with whom he would be sharing at least part of the ride: two heavyset, middle-aged women who looked like spinster sisters and a handsomely dressed man probably in his mid- to late sixties who presented himself as either a prosperous businessman or a successful retiree. Neville had offered a polite smile and nod to the others as he'd entered, but only one of the sisters returned the greeting, and that with only a very slight stretching of her lips, maintaining, it would seem, a proper decorum. It was going to be a quiet ride, Neville figured, but that was fine with him. He had a lot to think about on his journey.

A journey that, once it was under way and he was riding away from the waving hands of Sheriff Dan and Sadie, he debated the wisdom of agreeing to undertake.

The roads were hard and most often dusty, trail powder frequently billowing into the compartment, the narrow wheels of the stage occasionally responding harshly to deep ruts in the road, jostling the passengers along the lengthy travel from their reverie or even their slumber.

Neville remained awake for a good part of the three-day journey. He could have appreciated giving in to more substantial shut-eye, but he simply had too much going on inside his head. Often his brief dozing was rudely interrupted by either another bump in the road or an image invading his consciousness of what might be awaiting him at the end of the trail.

With all that time to think, Neville had definite misgivings by the time the stagecoach deposited him at the country crossroads, from where heading south would lead him toward the old farmhouse. A place he could hardly recall with all that had changed in his life . . . let alone possibly recognize as he proceeded down the dirt trail, his valise clutched in one hand, a single piece of luggage in the other.

As he walked in the late-morning sunshine with sporadic cottonwood shadings providing cool respite from the heat that promised to advance upon the day, punctuating his strides with the tips of his boots digging up and kicking gravel, Neville thought how strange it was that he should be considering this destination as his home. It hardly was when he had lived there, and especially could not hold any such significance today. His pa, always a distant man, would seem even more a stranger to him now—that is, if Pa was still alive. Neville had considered that possibility on the stage ride, that his pa might be dead. He also considered what that would mean to him.

Well . . . in most every way his pa was already dead to him. Neville tried to remember the good in the man, but having experienced something far beyond what he had ever hoped to with Sheriff Dan and Sadie, summoning positive memories proved difficult. He recollected what the sheriff had once said to him when trying to help him cope with his anger and confusion: that a child may be born to a mother and father but doesn't owe them an obligation if one is not earned. At the time, these words went beyond Neville's comprehension, but he'd come to appreciate that wisdom as he gradually accepted Sheriff Dan and Sadie as his surrogate parents. Neville was proud to consider them as such.

Finally, Neville found himself standing on the porch of the little beaten-down house. He stood at the doorway for a long while. He knocked, but the door swung open on its own, broken on its hinges. The silence inside was overwhelming, and in just moments Neville knew that he would not find his pa there. He stood inside the house for as long as he could until the memories from those many yesterdays overwhelmed him and he had to leave. He no longer cared whether his pa was dead or alive. The house was a reminder, and he was more determined than ever to forget.

There were just two final stops he had to make before he returned to what he now truly regarded as his home: a dusty dirtwater town known as Brewer's Gulch. And a good and caring couple he couldn't love more if they were his birth parents: Sheriff Dan and Sadie.

First Neville stopped by his ma's grave, where he stood in respectful silence staring down at a burial mound that now was barely visible among the settling of the earth through the seasons and the proliferation of greenery. Once more he remembered, though he felt no sadness.

Then it was time for him to move on. Now there was only one thing that really mattered to him on this visit. He dug his hand deep within his trousers pocket and pressed his fingers tight around the ten-dollar gold eagle coin.

The opportunity had come for him to return the coin to the man who had given it in the hope that it might bring a poor boy some good fortune: Mr. Caulfield.

It wasn't too far a walk to the house. Neville eagerly anticipated Mr. Caulfield's reaction at seeing him again. Here he was, dressed in neat finery, relatively well groomed—a far cry from what Caulfield would recall the last time he saw him: a scrawny youth desperate in an uncertain ambition, wearing work clothes that had barely seen a day of scrubbing.

Most importantly, Neville had the gold piece to present him. Perhaps it was superstition, but Neville wanted to believe that he'd come through on the luck of the coin.

Yet it troubled Neville when he came to the old man's property and noticed that both the house and the grounds looked nearly as neglected as his own former home.

The old man had taken pride in maintaining his property and would never let it fall into such ruin. It also was unlikely that he would have up and moved off his land. Neville inhaled a breath through parted lips. He understood, and a wave of grief swept through him. During the years that he had been gone . . . the sad truth was that kindly Mr. Caulfield had died.

With this realization, tears glazed Neville's eyes. The emotion seemed to rise up out of nowhere, astonishing the boy, for Neville had endured much pain and upset in his young years without surrendering to tears. He remembered crying only once, briefly, at his mother's burial. But he recalled how his "pa" had taken notice of the boy's weakness and jabbed a stiff elbow into his back to urge him to stand brave. Neville never forgot the sharpness of that bone against his spine, the cruelty of such a gesture at a time when he felt justified in expressing his sorrow, and he'd made it a point to corral his emotions ever since.

But today, at this moment, unconsciously, reflexively, Neville released the reins on what he was feeling. And yet it was odd. Even he recognized it and questioned the reason for his tears. On a personal level Mr. Caulfield really meant nothing to him. His only real contact with the man came that morning at his mother's gravesite, where they'd shared just a brief exchange before Neville set out on his way.

Yet standing back in the country where he grew up, it gradually became easy for Neville to figure. Again, all he had to do was tighten his fingers around the smooth, hard circumference of the coin. It wasn't the man, Mr. Caulfield himself. It was what was represented through the gifting—or, more precisely, the *entrusting*—of that ten-dollar gold eagle. It stood as Mr. Caulfield's belief in the boy, a trust in his future that no one had ever extended toward him. And what he had learned about the coin held even more significance. Despite what Mr. Caulfield had said to Neville about not parting with the gold piece, the old man most likely knew he would never live to see the boy again and wanted Neville to use the coin however it would most benefit him.

Neville determined that even though he could not return the coin to Mr. Caulfield, he would ensure that someone else would gain from it as he had.

He silently made that vow and promised to make every effort to keep it.

FOUR

The next afternoon Neville boarded the stage that would take him back to Brewer's Gulch. He would appreciate the long ride and the return to what he now knew was his home, and he was hoping to enjoy the trip in quiet, sharing the coach with passengers who would not try to indulge him in aimless conversation.

But something unexpected happened. One of the people who stepped onto the stagecoach and seated herself across from him was a lovely young girl to whom Neville found himself instantly attracted. Surprising even himself, Neville promptly but politely introduced himself. The girl was friendly and receptive and likewise told him her name. They soon got to talking and shortly discovered they had a lot to converse about. To Neville it was a wonderful new experience, as he'd never had the opportunity to speak so freely and easily with a girl. Unfortunately the girl would not be traveling all the way to Brewer's Gulch; her destination was a town called Gumption, which preceded his stop by a day's ride and many miles. Disappointed but determined, Neville

hoped to prolong their conversation . . . as he soon also
hoped to possibly continue their relationship.

Her name was Jessica. Jessica Marbury. She was young,
sweet, and, with her blond hair, bright, sparkling eyes, and
charming smile, attractive as all tomorrow. Living in Brewer's Gulch, working at the Grain and Feed most days and
dedicated to improving himself by getting a kitchen table
education by night, Neville had never sought a romantic
relationship. He still had to decide what he was going to do
with his life. Although he enjoyed his job with Sam Grafton
at the Grain and Feed, he could see no future working
behind the counter servicing customers and stocking shelves.
About the best he could figure was taking on a deputy's job
with Sheriff Dan. Partial pay would have to come from
Sheriff Dan's own two-hundred-dollars-per-month pocket,
since Neville had no experience and would have to be hired
on as an apprentice, not to mention that a full-time deputy
was considered an unnecessary expense in a small, sleepy
community like Brewer's Gulch. But if Sheriff Dan was in
agreement, to Neville this could be an acceptable arrangement.

Of course Neville had to ask himself, was working as a
lawman what he wanted to do with the rest of his life? From
what he could see from the free time he spent with Sheriff
Dan in the office, it provided a good life; he'd never get rich
but it was steady work, and relatively uneventful in Brewer's
Gulch. Most importantly, he would have Sheriff Dan to
teach him the ropes, and Neville couldn't ask for a better
mentor.

He found the idea increasingly tempting: not so much as
a career preference, but as a practical consideration for what
he was now envisioning as his future. For as remarkable as
it seemed, in the short time Neville had been with her, he
discovered that his attraction to Jessica was starting to
develop into something more. Something deeper and more
profound. He contemplated what exactly it was that he might
be feeling. Although he had an affection he interpreted as

love for Sadie and Sheriff Dan, he had to admit he knew little about the special kind of love between a boy and a girl; it was an emotion quite foreign to him. But . . . even if it wasn't love, whatever he was experiencing felt totally natural and distinctly pleasant, fairly blanketing him with a warmth and a joy that was exhilarating, and he realized that while she soon would depart from this journey, he did not want to see her gone from his life.

They chatted with a familiarity as if they'd known each other for years, but unfortunately conversation between them was kept to a minimum once their next stop on the second day of the trip brought onboard a rather stern-looking, middle-aged woman who introduced herself as Mrs. Armstrong, a schoolteacher who seated herself next to Jessica, and a bespectacled, hawk-faced lawyer who did not offer his name and quickly engrossed himself in paperwork while he made himself comfortable beside Neville. The lawyer seemed to be of no concern, but the schoolmarm, despite her fussy and obvious attempts at being preoccupied with her own business, gave the distinct impression of being all ears to whatever was being discussed within the confines of the coach.

Neville was displeased by this intrusion, but Jessica, perhaps presenting her playful side, expressed a coy amusement at the interruption. She could see how annoyed Neville was even as he tried valiantly to keep his dissatisfaction to himself.

As the stagecoach rocked along on its journey, Neville's subtle look of disappointment gradually dissipated as his irritation succumbed to Jessica's lighthearted smile and her lively eyes, and soon he was secretly sharing in her humor.

Both were startled when some ways along Mrs. Armstrong focused her gaze studiously on Neville, and then on Jessica, and broke the silence inside the coach when she said:

"I hope you don't mind my saying, but you two make a lovely couple."

Even the lawyer responded to this comment, and he peered up over the rim of his glasses from his paperwork to take his own look at the pair he'd thus far barely noticed.

Neville and Jessica exchanged a perplexed glance. The girl then managed a bashful smile.

"Thank you, ma'am," she said politely.

Neville gave Jessica a more deliberate look, one that he hoped she might interpret as he'd intended. Jessica smiled a little more broadly at him, of a sudden not seeming to care if her telling smile was noticed or not. Neville settled back in his seat, feeling more relaxed. In fact, he found himself suppressing an instant of giddiness. The schoolmarm would never know how grateful he was to her for her remark.

Later that day the stage slowed before coming to a halt at the depot in Gumption, where Jessica was to depart; where, as she explained, she would be staying with her ailing grandmother until her aunt, who was traveling abroad, could return home to be with her. She wasn't expected back for at least a month, Jessica added; then, when Neville tentatively inquired what her plans would be after that, she hesitated before telling him that her parents expected her to return to the family home in the East, where she would attend college. Neville was crestfallen, though he tried to conceal his disappointment. Yet as Jessica spoke, Neville thought he could detect a note of uncertainty in her voice, as if, or so he hoped, maybe she was no longer sure that she wanted to follow through with these plans. He and Jessica shared an affectionate look, one noticed by Mrs. Armstrong. Jessica started to step from the coach. Neville hesitated, then got up from his seat and hastened out behind her.

There was much Neville still wanted to say to her. He knew without question that he wanted Jessica to be part of his life. He wanted to find the right words to say to her, but he felt awkward and there simply wasn't enough time. His words would be hurried, his speech rushed and spoken with other ears listening. It would have to wait, but in the meantime he needed to know that she would wait for him. Their gaze connected only for an instant, but Neville was convinced that what he saw reflected in Jessica's eyes was encouraging.

The stage driver handed Jessica her bag. As she reached

up to take it, Neville's hands likewise rose to assist, and their fingers touched. Together they lowered the bag onto the depot platform; then, instinctively, their hands locked and once more their eyes met.

Jessica slowly lowered her lashes. She didn't speak, just offered a bittersweet smile.

The stagecoach driver cleared his throat to let Neville know he'd best get back onboard as there was a schedule to keep.

"Just a minute," Neville implored. He spoke hastily, clumsily, to the girl. "I gotta get movin', but before I go, I . . . well, would like it if'n we could . . . that we might get together ag'in."

To Neville, impatient, Jessica's answer seemed a long while in coming, but she replied in mere moments.

"There's a long distance between us," she started to say, and Neville felt his chest grow heavy.

Then she added, "But I'd like that, too."

Heartened and encouraged, Neville in the next instant blurted out what he needed to say.

"Look, I figger I got me a plan," he said, speaking hurriedly, noticing the impatience of the stagecoach driver. "A definite plan for the future. Could provide a fine life." He swallowed over a lump in his throat, then went into the homestretch. "What I'm sayin', Jessica, is . . . I know this is real sudden like, but—but do yuh think you might consider sharin' this life with me . . . as my wife?"

Mrs. Armstrong, having been eavesdropping on Neville's sincere but awkward proposal, stunned the couple for the second time when she popped her head out the open window of the coach and spoke in a voice she likely reserved for her unruly pupils.

"Oh, for goodness' sake!" she exclaimed. "Young man, you don't set foot upon this stage until that girl accepts your proposal."

With that, Mrs. Armstrong disappeared back into the compartment, leaving the stagecoach driver to bray his objection and Neville waiting eagerly for an answer.

Neville spoke lowly, hopefully. "Maybe we just got the question answered for us."

Jessica drew out a breath, lowered her eyes demurely, and, with a delicate smile parting her lips, said softly, "Maybe."

Neville felt his heart leap as if he had a jump-toad in his chest—another sensation unfamiliar to him, since he could never before recall experiencing such pure joy. He still regretted having to say good-bye to Jessica, though he could now accept their separation, knowing that it was just a temporary parting. Most encouraging to him was that wedding bells might sound in their future.

It was the start of the bright future he saw for himself—a future that, ironically, never would have happened had he not agreed to make that trip to confront his bitter past. And for that he owed a debt of gratitude to Sheriff Dan and Sadie.

Yet when the stage made its final stop at Brewer's Gulch the following day, Neville's joy became shadowed with a gradual sense of foreboding. He was pleased to be greeted by Sheriff Dan, who was waiting for him at the depot, standing as tall and stoic as always, but concerned that Sadie was not with him.

Sheriff Dan explained that Sadie was feeling under the weather, but in the next instant he assured Neville that she was eager to see him back at the house. These words, while spoken with the sheriff's customary gruff stolidity, held little conviction where Neville was concerned. To him, it sounded as if the sheriff, well aware of Sadie's lengthy and progressive illness, remained in denial—and worse, that there might not be much time left for his surrogate mother. But truth be told, he was surprised that Sadie still lingered, that the strength of her spirit allowed her to cling to life. Neville had harbored the fear that when he came back into town, he would be informed by a graven-faced Sheriff Dan that Sadie had passed on. Such was not the case and Neville was thankful, though he knew, as did Sheriff Dan if he would only admit it, that they both had to be prepared to accept the inevitable.

"Is it what yuh want, Tom?" Sheriff Dan said curiously to Neville when, after reuniting at the depot, the two stopped into the cafe for coffee and a piece of pie. "Work for me as my deputy?"

Neville nodded. "Gave it some thought."

"Maybe not enough," the sheriff remarked as he slowly stirred sugar into his black coffee, lines of concern embedded in his forehead. "Ain't sayin' it's been a bad life, but my missus was never really happy livin' here, think yuh know that. Not much of a place to have a wife and raise a family. She was never too keen on my life as a lawman, either. Even in a place like Brewer's Gulch she confessed her worry each time I'd pin on my badge. And now you're sayin' this is what you want for yourself?"

Neville listened, seriously weighing Sheriff Dan's words. He'd barely touched the pie on his plate. Instead he cast his eyes toward the big window that overlooked the main street and gazed out at the activity. Outside of one or two passersby, the town was as quiet as a graveyard.

"I never expected this to happen, Sheriff Dan," he admitted. "This gal, Jessica, she's . . . well, someone I really wanta be with, and maybe—"

"Maybe think 'bout marryin'?" Sheriff Dan finished for him.

Neville gave a slight nudge of his head. He looked and sounded a mite restless as he gave his answer. "Yeah . . . figger so."

"She feel the same 'bout you?" Sheriff Dan asked as he raised the rim of his coffee cup to his lips.

Neville hesitated with his answer, then offered, "Hope so. Like to think so."

"But ain't certain, I take it."

Neville looked vaguely troubled. "Can't rightly say. She never really said nothin' definite."

"So you *ain't* entirely sure 'bout you two bein' together for the long haul?" Sheriff Dan probed.

Neville glanced across at the sheriff and delivered a deep exhale. "Reckon not. But—"

"Yet 'nuff for you to be colorin' your future as a lawman?" Sheriff Dan interjected.

Neville wore a look of serious contemplation.

"Don't make a decision you might regret because you're in a hurry to do somethin' you ain't even sure of," Sheriff Dan advised him.

"I'm sure of Jessica," Neville said earnestly.

Sheriff Dan dug into the last piece of his pie and chewed with gusto. After he was done he put down his fork, pushed the plate aside, and said, "I think more men have made fool mistakes because they thought they was in love."

Neville snapped his eyes at the sheriff, his features starting to tense but looking not quite offended at his remark.

Sheriff Dan raised his hand in a defensive gesture. "Ain't sayin' you don't got feelin's for this gal, Tom. But near as I can figger, you never really knew no girls before, and just in the coupla days you spent with this Jessica, you've already made up your mind that yuh wanta marry her."

Neville considered his reply before he looked slyly at the sheriff.

"Heard your courtship with Sadie wasn't no long-term affair, neither," he said, not quite impudently.

"True," Sheriff Dan conceded. "But I was a lot older than seventeen. Not a bad idea to first gather some life experience." He paused before adding, "Some advice for you to maybe ponder, Tom. You're only young once. Grasp onto this time and hold firm 'cause it passes all too quickly."

Neville did consider. Sheriff Dan's words did make sense, but Neville remained firm in what he wanted: to be with Jessica, now and forever. And so he shrugged—and then his features lightened as out of the blue he recalled that first morning he had met Sheriff Dan and how he'd disliked him and felt so intimidated by him. And now here he was discussing with the man his first true romantic inclination.

Sheriff Dan kept his focus on Neville before his lips widened under his mustache in a smile that hinted he knew what Neville was thinking.

"I ain't gonna be tellin' you what to do, Tom," he said. "You find what you want outta life maybe just once. How it comes upon yuh . . . well, you can't never tell and maybe it's best if'n you don't question. Sounds as if this trip you hadda make mighta come with an added dividend."

Neville felt relieved. He appreciated the sheriff telling him that. He didn't want to be discouraged from what he knew was right by the man whose opinion mattered most to him.

Sheriff Dan paused to take another sip of his coffee. "And by the way, sorry 'bout your pa."

Neville's response was curt. "I ain't."

He then pulled the ten-dollar gold eagle from his pocket and looked at it thoughtfully, respectfully.

"My only real regret, Sheriff Dan," he said, indicating the coin that he smoothly fingered with his thumb and fore-finger. "Wanted so much for Mr. Caulfield to know I held on to it all this time. Kinda queer, ain't it?"

"No, ain't queer, Tom. And I think he probably knows what you was intendin'," Sheriff Dan said respectfully.

Neville sat back in his chair. He regarded the coin for only a moment longer before he tossed it onto the table in a swift, impulsive gesture of frustration. Then he raised his eyes toward Sheriff Dan—and for just that moment they took on a defensive glare.

Sheriff Dan met the boy's stare easily.

"Reckon don't matter now. This'll pay for our coffee and pie," Neville said, his blood pumping, his control starting to slip. "Maybe you'd like another piece? My treat, ain't gonna cost yuh."

"Settle back, Tom. That ain't the way," the sheriff said calmly.

Other eyes in the restaurant had turned toward their table.

Neville reconsidered. And as quick as his mood had erupted, he regained his composure. He felt ashamed for letting his emotions once again get the better of him. He reached over to pick up the coin, and then he smiled weakly at the sheriff.

"Yeah, you're right," he muttered, gazing thoughtfully at the coin, which he now flipped between the knuckles of his hand, a trick he'd mastered to amuse himself during his long walking journey from his home. "Took me a long way and"—a look of pleasant introspection showed on his face—"it also brought me a long way."

Sheriff Dan was understanding. "And possibly you got a ways to go yet."

"With this?" Neville questioned, lifting his eyebrows from the dancing gold piece.

Sheriff Dan responded straightly to Neville, not acknowledging the boy's neat acrobatics with the coin. "With whatever it takes, son."

Things looked rightly focused in Neville's future, but inevitably an impatience crept into him. He was restless on many counts. His position as a trainee deputy was boring and unfulfilling. As Neville had expected, there was no quick reward to his potential career as a lawman. His tasks were menial, the pay withheld for a month while he put in time as an apprentice—an arrangement insisted upon by the sheriff to determine Neville's dedication to the job. Most troubling was the distance between him and Jessica. It had proven to be a serious obstacle. Neville had desperately wanted to maintain a relationship, but the best he could manage over the next several weeks was writing letters, almost daily. At first Jessica wrote back quickly, her notes expressing affection, but as of late the replies were coming slower and each seemed to be composed more out of a sense of obligation than genuine feeling, and worse from Neville's perspective, Jessica now only *replied*—she had stopped initiating correspondence between them. The day finally came when Neville weakened to desperation and was prepared to cash in his valued ten-dollar gold eagle to pay for stagecoach passage for Jessica to come to Brewer's Gulch, where Neville intended to ask her to marry him, then and there.

Once he got to the bank to trade in the coin for paper money, his singular purpose deserted him and he found himself wrestling with his conscience. It was a difficult decision; he had to find some way to bring Jessica to town and he simply did not have money to provide for her transportation— the gold piece was his only option, and he even tried to make himself believe that old Caulfield would approve, if he knew that it would bring Neville happiness . . .

He got as far as the teller window, where he halted, looked long and hard at the coin—and remembered the vow he made to himself that last time he'd visited Mr. Caulfield's farm: He had to pass on the coin in the same spirit Caulfield had given it to him.

Exhaling a sigh, he walked away from the window, leaving the teller to scratch his head.

He felt ashamed for almost acting so abruptly. It was then that he determined the only way he would spend the gold piece was if there was some way to help Sadie, now completely bedridden, drifting in and out of consciousness and astonishing the town doctor with her will to live. Yet medically nothing could be done for her, and each time the doctor walked from the room after a visit, he shook his head helplessly in what had become a familiar gesture. He reiterated that any day could conceivably be her last. These were tough times for Sheriff Dan, now forced out of his denial, and he spent virtually all of his free moments sitting at her bedside, stroking her hair and whispering comforting words. To Neville this was a revelation. He'd never looked upon Sheriff Dan as a particularly sensitive man, and it was heartbreaking for Neville when he'd pass by the bedroom, faintly shadowed with the curtains drawn, and catch a glimpse of this tender tableau.

Outside their time together in the office, where the sheriff was more quiet than usual, becoming almost withdrawn in his own feelings of helplessness and impending grief,

Neville started to see less and less of Sheriff Dan, and it seemed as if the relationship between them was starting to diminish.

These became difficult days for Neville. Between dealing with his own frustrations with his unsatisfying job and overwhelming desire to see Jessica or at least receive a letter of encouragement from her that they could still plan a future together, and the atmosphere of gloom that had descended upon his once cheerful home, he found himself starting to suffocate under the strain and beginning to think rebellious thoughts that he felt he'd overcome, struggling against the steadily encroaching urge of just wanting to break free and become his own man.

FIVE

Then one day a stranger appeared in town, quietly and unannounced, trotting down the main street on a handsome palomino. The stranger was well dressed, though oddly not wearing a coat or duster, simply a brocade vest over his cream-colored shirt. He dismounted outside the town's hotel/saloon, tethering his pony to the hitching post, and as he walked along the boardwalk he presented himself as an intriguing fellow, though with the suggestion of something suspicious and even mildly ominous behind his intention. He looked perhaps to be in his early twenties but was possessed of a sort of worldliness, suggesting a maturity and a hinting that he was a man one might be wise to keep wary of.

The stranger sauntered into the sheriff's office to inquire whether he should check his sidearms. Sheriff Dan was away and Neville was manning the office. He was still learning the ropes of his apprenticeship and was puzzled by the stranger's query. A rider into town would have no reason to ask such a question unless he might be expecting trouble. Brewer's Gulch was certainly no Wichita or Dodge City, where almost every stranger would be looked upon with suspicion and packing a pistol held the potential for violence. Outside the raucous behavior of trail herders that got out of hand on occasion, requiring the intervention of the sheriff, Brewer's Gulch never had difficulties with people who appeared simply to be passing through.

Neville regarded the fellow peculiarly. "Kinda odd thing to be askin'."

The stranger tipped his black Stetson with the silver band up over his brow, releasing a mop of curly auburn hair that fell over his forehead. He flashed his toothy grin. "Just bein' respectful. Never know the rules of the town you're ridin' into. Seen a man once tossed into jail for refusin' to surrender his Bowie knife. Ain't looking for that kinda trouble. Fact, trouble's the last thing I'm seekin'."

Neville gave a suspicious nod. "Glad to hear it."

"So I can hang on to my side irons?" the stranger said, patting a hand against his silver-beaded holster.

Neville nudged a shoulder. "Don't plan on slappin' leather, can't see no reason why not."

The stranger then did a curious thing. He took it upon himself to make himself at his ease, casually taking a seat and lifting the brim of his hat even higher as he settled back comfortably into the chair next to the sheriff's desk. Neville wasn't sure what to make of this fellow's attitude, which came across as just a little too familiar.

"No," the stranger said with an emphatic sigh. "Truth be told, had my share of run-ins, but that's behind me now." He took another breath and glanced about the office. "Take it the sheriff's not around?"

"Have business with Sheriff Dan?" Neville asked. His tone was guarded.

"Sheriff Dan? No, no," the stranger replied innocently.

Neville ventured further. "For someone who says he ain't got business with the sheriff, you're makin' yourself a mite comfortable."

"Just restin' for a bit. Had a long ride into town. Comin' in here is the first stop I've made in days," he explained. He made a halfhearted gesture to rise from the chair. "But if you'd rather . . ."

Neville hesitantly waved him back into the chair. "No, sit if you have a mind to."

"'Preciate it."

"Stayin' in town for a spell—or passin' through?" Neville asked idly.

"Ain't entirely sure. Likely won't be a long stay."

Neville went about his work, mundane daily duties like organizing the sheriff's paperwork and making sure the rifles in the gun rack were wiped clean of dust.

The stranger's voice rose behind him. "Yeah, pretty quiet town. Heck, I almost rode on by, not even knowin' this place was on the trail."

"Not much happens here, that's true . . . 'ceptin' when the drovers ride in," Neville remarked.

"Drovers." The stranger chuckled inwardly. "Hear they can be a rowdy bunch."

"Can."

"Reckon them boys can blow off a lotta steam."

Neville nodded.

"Hmmm," the stranger sounded.

Neville could detect a strange interest brewing in his visitor. Still he continued going about his duties, now taking a broom from the closet to sweep the hardwood floor, but all the while he could feel those eyes fastened on him, as if the stranger were observing with unspecified interest each detail of his tasks.

Finally, impatient and becoming annoyed at the stranger's presence, he turned to face this man who seemed uncommonly secretive about his business in Brewer's Gulch. The look on Neville's face was rigid and serious. The stranger's expression was calm and relaxed.

"I'm figgerin' yuh want somethin' you ain't too quick to be tellin'," Neville blurted out.

The stranger continued to be vague. "Could be."

Neville began sweeping the floor with an intent mirroring his growing aggravation.

"Well, would help if'n yuh'd just come out and say whatever's on your mind," he said edgily.

The stranger shifted in his seat, crossing his legs and making himself even more at his ease.

"Hear yuh gone sweet on a gal—Neville," he said with a grin that now looked plain devious.

Neville instantly ceased his sweeping. He turned his head slowly toward the man.

"How do yuh know my name?" he wanted to know, his voice quiet but insistent.

The stranger held his grin and ignored the question.

"Sure—and she's a might' nice gal, too," he added. He casually withdrew a switchblade knife from his pocket. He observed Neville from under half-closed eyelids as he flicked open the blade and began digging out grit from his fingernails.

"You better speak plain," Neville said, trying not to appear intimidated. "Don't see what you're gettin' at. But I can tell yuh I don't like it."

"Well, Neville . . . just so happens this gal you've fallen for is someone kinda special to me, too."

Neville could feel his blood pulsing as his face went flush. He suddenly considered that this stranger might be Jessica's beau, perhaps even her husband, and had found out about Neville's attraction to her.

"She's my cousin," the man clarified. "Grew up together."

Neville was relieved, and his head gradually ceased throbbing. But he still didn't understand what this fellow wanted from him. Why he was telling him this.

The stranger went on. "Now don't get me wrong, cousin or not the girl hates me. Plain despises me, in fact. But we share a family bond and yuh hear things and I just happened to hear 'bout you. Yeah, you made quite an impression on her on that stage ride. Fact, well, think maybe if things were different she might not be opposed to takin' yuh on as her husband."

"How d'yuh mean—*different*?" Neville asked carefully.

"You sayin' you can't figger it out?"

Neville didn't care for the direction this conversation was taking. He kept himself quiet.

"Just let's say sweepin' floors ain't nothin' you can plan a future on," the stranger said.

As if in reflex Neville put the broom aside. He listened and remained silent.

"Know it's what *you* want, gettin' married," the stranger said. "And I'm all for it." He lowered his head and emitted a sigh. "Only . . . well, y'see my point 'bout takin' care of a wife on the wages you earn—as a *deputy*, if'n that's what you wanta call yourself." He added slyly, "Might be that I can help yuh out."

Neville blinked. "And why would yuh wanta do that?"

"Maybe I'm a romantic," the stranger rhapsodized.

"Don't think so," Neville said sourly. "And I get the feelin' that by whatever it is you're gettin' at, you'll be helpin' yourself as well."

The stranger chuckled and shrugged. "Share the wealth, as they say."

Neville's eyes crinkled warily.

"After all, family is family, huh?" the stranger added with a deliberately sunny smile.

"Might be I'm the wrong person to talk to 'bout that," Neville scowled.

"Your past ain't what's important. It's your future you gotta be thinkin' 'bout."

Neville felt a knot start to twist in his gut. He felt the urge to sit down but decided it best if he remain standing.

"You seem to know a lot," he said.

The stranger spoke easily. "Make it my business to learn 'bout the people I might be dealin' with."

Neville's patience was reaching its limit. "Speak clean, mister. All you been doin' since yuh walked in here is talk riddles."

"And that troubles you?" the stranger said casually.

"Yeah, it troubles me," Neville said, not hiding his irritation.

"Make it easy on yuh then, friend," the stranger said as

he lifted himself from the chair. "Don't think it wise for us to be talkin' here anyway. Meet me tonight at seven, at Hefton Bend. There's a cutoff from the main trail that leads to Broke Neck Canyon. Once yuh make the turn, ride for 'bout half a mile. You'll come to a cluster of trees on the other side of the ravine. Don't worry 'bout findin' me. I'll be waiting for you."

Neville hesitated before he replied flatly, "Don't think so." He reached for his broom to go back to sweeping the office floor.

The stranger sounded disappointed. "So I haven't convinced you?"

"Convinced me of what?" Neville said tightly.

The stranger frowned. "All I'm sayin' is if you're serious 'bout my cousin Jessica—*Jessie*—you'd do best to be there."

The stranger noticed how Neville's eyes flashed when he mentioned the girl by name. He was satisfied that he now had Neville's full attention.

He went on. "Just so yuh know, there's someone else who's taken a hankerin' to Jessie."

Another sharp reaction from Neville, before his features weakened into a look of upset.

The stranger nodded. "Yeah, happened during all this time you two been apart. Damn shame but can't rightly blame either of 'em. Jessie's a gal that a smart man would do well not to sit too long on the fence for. And my cousin . . . well, despite what she thinks of me, she's entitled to a good life."

The stranger noticed how Neville now looked to be taking him seriously, yet it was also apparent he still had misgivings. That was understandable, so the stranger added a few final words to persuade Neville to reconsider his decision.

"Choice is yours, amigo," he said. "I'll only be waiting 'til quarter past. If'n yuh don't show, I'll ride off and you'll never see me again." His face took on a troubled look. "And probably not Jessie, either. 'Less you can come up with some other way to prove yourself the right man for her. But I'll tell yuh, from what I seen with this fella who's now got his eyes on her, that's gonna be quite a chore. Money, privilege.

Yeah, comes from a good family with plenty of prestige. No girl in her right mind can turn all that down, huh? 'Specially not for someone she really hardly knows whose prospects ain't exactly world beatin'."

The stranger sauntered toward the door to the office. His words were delivered with a calculated arrogance, and he could easily absorb the frustration that was raging inside Neville. He smirked to himself before he opened the door, where he made one final comment, which he issued caustically.

"Yep, don't feel a broom-pusher's gonna be much competition."

Come five minutes to seven that evening, Neville was nearing Hefton Bend, an off-the-main-road dirt-and-gravel trail that led to a steep turnoff into a canyon passage that stretched far beyond and was bordered by rocky cliffs that spread out for miles.

He rode a quarter horse named Lulubell that he'd borrowed from the sheriff, to whom he'd lied and said that he'd been asked to run an urgent errand for his former boss, Sam Grafton. Perhaps Sheriff Dan might have questioned Neville about the errand, but there was a definite and disturbing change affecting his personality. The sheriff had become so distraught over his wife's prolonged illness, which should have mercifully ended months ago, that Neville soon recognized he was numbing his frayed emotions by flask-drinking whiskey. The room in which Sadie lay dying had a permeating odor that Neville could identify from when his own mother was fatally sick, but most times when Neville walked into Sadie's room he could also detect the smell of strong liquor—and always when Sheriff Dan was seated beside her, his head lowered, either in grief or because he could use that time, sitting in a virtual solitude, to deaden his despair. Neville came to comprehend that once Sadie died, it was doubtful Sheriff Dan would ever return to being the good and wise man he once had been. The erosion of the soul of the man whom Neville credited with helping to shape him into the better person he had the potential to become was painful for him to consider. Yet Neville knew in his heart the outcome was inevitable. At the very best, Neville could watch a man merely going through the motions of his life. And what troubled Neville most was that as a lawman, even in a basically uneventful community like Brewer's Gulch, Sheriff Dan, if devoid of passion and commitment, might one day walk into a bullet, through either carelessness or simply not caring.

Perhaps the acknowledgment of these disturbing possibilities had added to his decision to meet with the stranger that evening. As much as he wished it were possible, both in love and repayment, he could not help Sadie—nor would he be able to ease Sheriff Dan's anguish once his wife's illness took its final toll. Both would be gone to him. He tried to fight away the shadow of selfishness, but the truth was that now he had only himself to consider. Himself . . . and the course he would set for his life. Although he had to admit that he hardly knew Jessica, she seemed to be all that was left to him in a life of hurt and challenge that he'd almost overcome.

Yet even that might be taken from him.

He had to find out. It was imperative that he know and, if the stranger indeed spoke the truth, decide the best way to deal with it. The answer might not be what he wanted to hear; the more he thought about it throughout the afternoon, the more concerned he became that he might have a formidable rival for Jessica's affection. He couldn't completely disregard what the stranger was saying.

But he was determined to do whatever it took to turn the advantage in his favor.

The late-summer skies were not quite dark at this hour of the day, though twilight hues were beginning to give hints of their approach through orange-tinged rims breaking across the southern horizon, the deepening shades most noticeable beyond the serrated peaks of the mountain ridge that surged upward and stretched wide across the landscape into the west. It promised to be a brilliant sunset, though one that Neville could hardly appreciate.

He navigated the narrow, twisting trail by keeping his mount at an easy pace. He'd gotten to know much of the surrounding areas during his years living in the territory but hadn't before ventured out to Hefton Bend. It was a desolate, almost foreboding area with a still, gloomy atmosphere that didn't offer much incentive for travel. To complete the eerie scenario he had to ride past an old hillside cemetery, marked with wood crosses, many bent and twisted by the high winds frequent to these parts.

He arrived at the location with minutes to spare. He drew rein, then checked the pocket watch the sheriff and Sadie had given him as a sixteenth-birthday gift. He experienced a pang of remorse as he flipped open the decorated silver case and again read the neat engraving on the inside cover:

To Neville,
In friendship and with pride
Sheriff Dan & Sadie

He felt remorse because he became convinced this rendezvous he had agreed to had something illegal or deceitful attached to it—but if involving himself meant he could win back Jessica before it was too late, he didn't think he could refuse.

He found he could hardly look at the watch and hastened to bury it back in his pocket.

He must have been too preoccupied with his thoughts, for he was genuinely startled when he glanced to his side and saw the stranger sitting atop his palomino next to him. Neville scolded himself, for he should have been more alert; he easily could have been prey for an ambush. He'd never heard the animal approach even though the hooves would have sounded against the crunch of gravel along the trail.

The stranger observed Neville with his mouth stretched into a grin, half of a thin, unlit cigar clamped between his teeth.

"Knew yuh'd show," he said, forming his words around his stogie.

"Just . . . wanta hear what you have to say and be off," Neville replied curtly.

"A man who don't waste words," the stranger said approvingly. "Can 'preciate that."

"Well . . . then 'preciate I want this done and over with," Neville returned.

"Might not be that simple," the stranger said back to him. "Got a few things to discuss and best if we don't rush the matter." His horse started to get restless, rearing back its head, scraping its hoof impatiently into the turf at the side of the trail, and he tugged on the reins to steady the animal.

"The pony's like me," he said. "Don't like to stay still for too long."

Neville didn't acknowledge.

"Let's pull off the road where we can talk," the stranger suggested.

Neville didn't much care for the idea, and he didn't see the point in it. They were alone; it was unlikely anyone would come up the trail and see them together—if that was what worried the stranger.

"Prefer it if we stay put," he countered.

"Think your butt can take it?" the stranger asked with a smirk. "Just tryin' to make our talk a little more comfortable."

Neville considered. He gave a hasty nod, but added, "Just let's not ride too far."

The stranger gave his own nod.

They crossed the narrow ravine and settled where the shade-giving trees bordered the eastern side of the parched hollow. They dismounted and let their horses nibble at the sparse grass, which was mostly yellowed from the dry heat that had blanketed the territory over the past weeks.

The stranger and Neville sat some feet apart from one another, each resting his back against a tree. At first neither spoke, though Neville watched with a curious interest as the stranger spit out the unlit cigar he'd been gnawing on and pulled out a fresh one. He broke the cigar in half, tossing aside the top part and clamping the bottom portion between his teeth, again not lighting it.

"Seems like a waste of a good cigar," Neville said.

The stranger pulled the stogie from his mouth and wore a sour face as he spit out some loose tobacco. "Don't need to smoke 'em, just enjoy the taste."

Neville tolerated the quiet between them for a few moments longer before he said, "Yuh never told me your name."

The stranger looked at him askance. "Never asked."

"I'm askin'."

The stranger sat without answering, his jaws working around the end of his stogie.

Once again Neville felt himself growing impatient with all this mystery. It was as if the stranger were deliberately trying to provoke him. But for whatever reason Neville didn't know.

He spoke abruptly. "Seems only right since yuh claim to know all 'bout me."

The stranger replied, "Not all, Neville. Just what's important."

Neville spoke restlessly. "Like to get back into town 'fore nightfall."

"Won't be dark for a spell," the stranger said, unconcerned.

"Still got a good hour's ride into town and I ain't familiar with these trails," Neville admitted.

"I'll guide yuh back," the stranger said with a condescending edge to his voice.

"I'll manage," Neville grumbled in return. He then spoke with a subtle accusation. "By the way, you was lyin' this afternoon when you said yuh just sorta stumbled into Brewer's Gulch."

"Reckon I was," the stranger said imperturbably.

"Just let's get this done in a hurry," Neville told him.

The stranger sighed. "Neville, I ain't gonna give yuh my name. Thought about it, considered it, but then figgered that might be the worst thing I could do."

"So what do I call yuh?" Neville asked, spewing the words out the side of his mouth.

The stranger thought for a second before he smiled and replied, "Smith. Let's keep it nice and simple. Yeah, Smith'll do fine."

Neville echoed, "Smith," and then made no comment. He waited for the stranger to start explaining the reason for this get-together.

"What I'm proposin' is simple," Smith said. "We're gonna get us some cash we both need, then we ain't never gonna see each other again."

Neville thought how he was fine with the latter part of what Smith was saying, but growing less curious and more apprehensive with whatever it was he was about to put forward.

"You plan on stayin' in Brewer's Gulch?" Smith asked, his face taking on a look that suggested he'd just considered the question.

Neville couldn't see the point of the question and was slow in answering. Smith relaxed his features and said in a low voice, "No matter. Everything goes off and you won't catch no trouble for this."

"If *what* goes off?"

Smith chewed on his cigar. "Reckon it's 'bout time I tell yuh."

They talked for close to an hour, and when Neville rode back into Brewer's Gulch the skies were dark and clear and glittering with stars; the air had a cool, velvety caress that was refreshing after the stifling heat of the day.

But Neville was oblivious to the weather; he was barely aware of his surroundings as his horse clip-clopped into town. He was feeling mighty low. The way this Smith explained it, Jessica had been waiting for some sort of commitment from Neville and as it had not been forthcoming, she was about to accept the courtship of this wealthy lawyer who was hoping to make her his bride, after which, according to Smith, he planned to take her to Santa Fe, where he'd been offered a position with a prestigious law office.

Perhaps Neville was naïve, but until that afternoon when Smith rode into town he never considered that Jessica would do such a thing. He truly believed that he and Jessica had reached an understanding. He felt in his heart that Jessica would remain patient until he could send for her. Yeah . . . he had to have been naïve, as he thought about it. The lack of affection in those later letters, then how she stopped writing unless in response to one of Neville's notes, and then her replies brief and succinct. The signs were there, he was just too blind to acknowledge them.

He couldn't rightfully blame her. He didn't know much about women, but Smith was right when he said they had a need for security—and, his intentions aside, security was not something Neville could provide her with at the present time.

All the same, he needed her, desperately, in his life. He couldn't see himself moving forward without her. And whatever it took to bring Jessica back to him, Neville was prepared to follow through. It wasn't a difficult decision to make. From as far back as he could remember, his life had run into too many twists in the road, most of which tried to run him into the mud. He'd hoped he had finally found stability with Sheriff Dan and Sadie and, while he *had*, for a while, he could sense that period was coming to an end—in a frighteningly ironic way, as for a second time the contentedness he sought would be cruelly snatched from him by the sickness of a woman he had loved as a mother—her death, as with his true mother, sure to result in unpleasant consequences for the husband left behind—and for Neville, who also paid a price . . . and most likely would again be made to suffer a cost.

This Smith character was clever. He was also devious. Neville couldn't say that he trusted him. But he'd listened carefully as Smith laid out the plan.

An overdue payroll due employees of the Treherne Mining Company would be delivered by stagecoach the next day, to await transfer by special guard early the following morning. From what Smith told him, the money would not be placed in the town's one timber-shack bank, but rather would be safeguarded under lock and key in the sheriff's office. This information came as a surprise to Neville; he'd heard nothing of such an arrangement, yet Sheriff Dan must have known of this delivery for several days. Either this duty was to be performed in such secrecy that the sheriff could not even confide in Neville, his apprentice deputy, or perhaps with all of his present concerns with Sadie's fading health, he was not thinking clearly and telling Neville had simply slipped his mind.

Smith, as well, had seemed genuinely astonished when Neville confessed ignorance about the payroll transfer. He brushed his black Stetson up over his brow, wiped away imaginary beads of sweat, and sat back to consider.

He was counting on Neville's participation, and that required him to be in the know of the specifics.

Neville, though, still wouldn't immediately commit. His involvement rested with how he perceived a future with Jessica. And he'd still had his doubts concerning her.

"I—just wish I could talk to Jessica first," he had said. He needed to hear from her directly that she was considering the courtship of another man. Most importantly, he needed to know that if he could arrange it he still had a chance with her. "If I could just hear from her—"

Smith had been quick to respond. "Yeah . . . only she's gone for a few days, some other family business she's gotta take care of. Granny's got a neighbor checkin' in on her 'til Jessie gets back. But . . . thing is, we can't wait for her to get back. We do this tomorrow or we don't do it at all. It's our one shot."

It was a glib and too-convenient reply. But what choice did Neville have but to accept his word against the ticking of the clock?

The strongbox containing the cash money, amounting to thirty thousand dollars, bonuses to workers included for late payment and overtime, would be brought into the sheriff's office through the back way and guarded safely until the next morning's pickup. The exact time wasn't known, but it was planned for around daybreak, when the town would be quiet.

So as not to call attention to the importance of the shipment, only a single armed guard would be posted inside the office. He, together with the sheriff, would be responsible for keeping watch on the strongbox.

According to Smith, Neville's part would be comparatively easy. All he had to do was confirm to Smith through a simple nod at a prearranged spot in town that the strongbox had been delivered and was being held at the jail. When Neville questioned why this was necessary if Smith knew for certain that the payroll was coming into town, Smith explained that there was a slight possibility that the information he received might have been planted deliberately to throw any would-be thieves off track. Smith wasn't stupid enough to break into a sheriff's office and attempt a robbery if there was nothing to steal. Once Neville let him know that the payroll had arrived, Smith and a confederate would take care of the rest. At that point, Neville's main participation would merely be to cooperate, maybe try to keep control of the situation if the sheriff suddenly got a yearning to live up to the three ounces of tin pinned to his chest.

It seemed simple. Almost too simple for Neville to share equally in the proceeds. But Smith assured him that if everything went off without a hitch, ten thousand dollars was his.

Neville looked suspicious. "Seems kinda odd you wanta split even with me when all I gotta do is walk by and nod my head."

"Your part is important, Neville," Smith said with utter seriousness. "Can't afford no mistakes, which is why I need you on the inside."

Neville then expressed a concern. "They'll hold Sheriff Dan responsible."

Smith puckered his lips and gave his head a mild shake. "Man with two guns aimed at him ain't 'bout to give up his life to protect a mining payroll."

Neville was not so certain. Depending on Sheriff Dan's state of mind, he could easily attempt to thwart the robbery.

He also was curious. He wanted to know where Smith got his information about the payroll and the fact that it would be held overnight at the jail. Smith seemed to know every detail.

"You can least tell me that much," he insisted. "After all, I go through with this and I'm just as guilty as you . . . if things go wrong."

Smith yelped a brief laugh. "You? You're just an underpaid apprentice deputy. They won't expect much outta you. Hell, you ain't even packin'."

Neville felt a little embarrassed at Smith's observation. But it was accurate; he had yet to carry a gun. Sheriff Dan had for whatever reason been holding off on that part of his apprenticeship.

"Still would like for you to tell me how yuh found out so much," he reiterated.

"Can't," Smith said abruptly. "If'n things should go bad, no guarantee that under pressure you won't get to talkin'. Or maybe your conscience will get to yuh. All you gotta know is that we split the money three ways—me, you, and this third fella who'll be with me."

"Take it I won't be told his name, either," Neville presumed.

Smith smiled. "Just call him Rafe. Better yet, don't call him nothin' at all." He paused for a moment before he continued. "See, the thing is, this ain't just a simple holdup. More complicated than that. The people who arranged this don't care 'bout the money. They just don't wanta see it get delivered."

By revealing this last bit of information Smith might have told Neville more than he had intended. Neville knew about the mining operation going on in the western region of the state and had heard talk within the town of how a rival company had failed in their claim that it was they who actually held the excavation rights to the site. It was a long, drawn-out legal battle that had resulted in bad blood between the two companies. Neville started to wonder if perhaps the rival firm might be behind this payroll heist to stimulate unrest among the Treherne Company miners and disrupt if not halt altogether the operation. And acquiring the specific information concerning the route, the stopover, and the transfer would not necessarily be difficult if the right people, company spies in effect, were put in place.

Of course this was pure speculation on Neville's part, but the pieces did neatly add up.

What didn't quite add up was how "Smith"—Jessica's supposed cousin—got himself involved in this scheme.

He was a man of secrets. What was the truth behind him?

Neville had a difficult time accepting that he had agreed to participate in such a plan. But Smith was a smooth talker and had Neville convinced that the way the procedure was to be handled, Neville could not possibly be implicated. Smith again added that after the cash was split between them, he planned to ride away and Neville would never see him or his partner again. He was adamant that there was no way Neville could be tied to the theft. He'd be as guiltless as the sheriff himself.

Free of possible prosecution, maybe. But following the robbery Neville knew there was no way he could remain in town. He had made his own preparations. He would have to wait a few days so as not to cast any unwanted suspicion on himself, and then his plan was to board a stage and ride out to Gumption to find Jessica, and ask her to become his wife. Even if that was not to be, Neville could never stay in Brewer's Gulch and live in the same house with Sheriff Dan. He could never look the man straight in the eye again after betraying him.

He knew he would not get much sleep; his mind was racing, his thoughts a jumble. When he returned to town, his quarter horse trotting quietly down the main road, he noticed a dull light emanating from behind the half-lowered window shade in the sheriff's office, cast by the lantern Sheriff Dan kept on his desk. He was probably sitting inside and Neville briefly debated going in to see him, but with all the emotions of the evening still fresh and churning inside his head he couldn't be sure that he might inadvertently act in some curious way that might spark a suspicion in Sheriff Dan. If the sheriff's head was clear, Neville had learned that not much could get past his notice.

He rode the horse to the livery just down the street and stabled it for the night. Then he walked back along the boardwalk and turned in to the alley to enter the house through the back entrance. He unlocked the door with his key and proceeded directly to his bedroom. Neville knew the sheriff would probably ask the next morning why he hadn't come to let him know that he was home. Neville would simply answer he thought he might be with Sadie and didn't want to disturb them. He'd never told an untruth to either the sheriff or Sadie, and with a shiver of guilt he now realized that much of what he was going to say over the next few days would be blunt lies.

The quiet that filled the house that night was so heavy it unnerved Neville and kept him acutely alert. He felt tense, couldn't relax, as if expecting at any moment for Sheriff Dan to burst into the room to confront him with what was to come. Neville kept listening for the slightest sound outside his door. He knew that if he should hear footfalls start down the hallway his heart would freeze—especially if they should keep coming toward his room. It would be Sheriff Dan . . . and even if he didn't know, didn't suspect, which Neville kept convincing himself he *couldn't*, that it was impossible . . . it was his own behavior that still concerned him. He hoped that once he got his thoughts sorted out tonight he could simply be himself come morning and not do or say anything that might raise suspicion. And this was an attitude he would have to maintain over the next several days—days that he knew would be long and tense. And then . . . he would have to find some harmless way to tell Sheriff Dan that he'd decided to move on.

He only hoped the sheriff would accept this decision without too much questioning. As Neville lay in bed trying to come up with a believable reason for his leaving, he knew that whatever that explanation might be, it would be a further perpetuating of lies. He could tell him that following the robbery he no longer felt he had it in him to become a lawman. Sheriff Dan was never that keen on the idea anyway. Or he could come as close to the truth as he could and admit that he was leaving town to ask for Jessica's hand and that he was considering working the land with the prospect of purchasing his own spread. Of course with the ten thousand dollars Neville would have in his pocket after the robbery, he'd be able to purchase outright a fine parcel of land.

He questioned whether Jessica would cotton to becoming a farmer's wife. Perhaps she was more inclined to the society life that the . . . *lawyer* could give her. Neville had no way of knowing, and if he thought too much about it, that could become another worry. And he already had enough concerns to contend with.

Neville tossed about in bed, anticipating a long night.

And an even longer day come tomorrow.

SIX

It was Tuesday. The bright orange sun that greeted the territory come daybreak had not yet completely cleared the eastern horizon, but all indications pointed to a warm and cloudless day. As he had expected, Neville slept nary a wink the whole night and did not pull himself from bed feeling refreshed. He got dressed slowly, then sat at the side of the bed for several minutes, trying to ease the edginess he still felt and to clear the residue of the night's thoughts from his brain and get himself prepared for the day. Now that the new day had begun, he found himself troubled with conflicting thoughts. The way Smith had outlined the plan, it seemed as if nothing could go wrong. Just a quick, clean robbery. Still, Neville had his concerns. He couldn't know how either Sheriff Dan or the guard would respond to the holdup. He trusted that with guns drawn on them, both men would cooperate. But he couldn't be sure. Sheriff Dan took great pride in being a lawman, and being held up—*in his own office*—might prompt him into a desperate decision. Neville thought with a shudder how he had never seen the sheriff pull his gun, let alone slap leather; he couldn't guess

how swift and accurate his skill might be, but he didn't feel
confident that Sheriff Dan could stand up against two armed
men. The likely outcome was so disturbing to him that Neville couldn't allow himself to consider Sheriff Dan attempting such a foolhardy move.

But even if the robbery was carried out without complications, after tonight Neville himself, while maybe neither
implicated nor suspected, would for the rest of his days have
to live with his guilt for his part in the crime. And while
Sheriff Dan would possibly never know of his participation,
Neville would deal with the added burden of betraying the
man who for these past years had treated him like a son.

Neville, of course, knew that there was still time to back
out. Plenty of time, actually. He didn't have to let Smith
know that the shipment had arrived. He could even go further and inform Sheriff Dan of the plot.

Yes, that was what he *should* do. Would earn him a pat
on the back . . . but no reward to compensate for the ten
thousand dollars he would be surrendering. The ten thousand dollars that might win him Jessica's hand.

And that was his struggle. Against every urge compelling
him to reconsider his part in what was to come, he kept
recalling the image of Jessica and imagining the good life
they could share together, with him having the money to
provide her with security and stability. Throughout the long
preceding night, lying in silence and solitude, he became
further convinced that the dream he envisioned for their
future would not happen unless he went along with Smith.
He could not say he trusted Smith, but he also realized it
could be his one opportunity for the happiness he had long
sought.

Sheriff Dan was sitting in his office morosely eating his
standard breakfast of ham and eggs with a side order of toast
lathered with marmalade, delivered from the hotel restaurant
down the street. His wife could no longer cook for him and
the sheriff had neither the skill nor inclination to prepare
his own meals, so the restaurant catered to him. Sheriff Dan
wasn't eating much these days on any account. He rarely

finished a plate of food, and his lack of appetite had begun to show as his once-sturdy physique started to grow thin and his full and ruddy face gaunt and pale. His eyes were tired and pouched, and the suggestion of hollows had ever so faintly become noticeable in his cheeks.

Neville walked over to pour himself some of the coffee brewing on the woodstove, one of the few mundane tasks the sheriff still cared to do for himself. Sheriff Dan looked strained and tired and acknowledged Neville with a weak nod and the slight curve of a smile . . . but no word of greeting.

Neville poured his coffee and pulled a chair over to the opposite side of the desk.

There was an uncommon silence between two men who had grown as close as father and son. Both had their own reasons for not talking. Sheriff Dan had become remote in his despair; Neville was trying to cope with troubling thoughts. Yet Neville kept hoping the sheriff would say something, *anything* to cut through the tense quiet that seemed to cast a pall over the office—at least what Neville was absorbing—but Sheriff Dan just kept his focus on his partially eaten breakfast.

Neville himself was unsure of what to say but quickly realized that if he didn't try to get a conversation going, nothing would be said between them, and he recognized the importance of maintaining at least a semblance of normalcy this morning.

"How did Sadie sleep?" he asked tentatively.

The sheriff took a moment or two before he finally looked up at Neville. It was another moment or two before he could give an answer.

"Don't know how much longer her strength can hold up," he said in a pained voice.

Neville had heard the same answer many times before. He knew that the sheriff would not offer anything more on the subject. The helplessness he felt seemed to overtake every aspect of his personality.

Neville needed to keep the two of them talking, no matter

how meaningless the conversation, for he also had to have Sheriff Dan tell him about the mining payroll expected in town today. He encouraged some inconsequential small talk, with the sheriff expressing himself in as few words as possible, at times almost seeming annoyed with Neville for interrupting his solitude that morning.

Sheriff Dan never provided so much as a hint as to when the payroll would be arriving. This concerned Neville, as it could interfere with the arrangement he'd made with Smith. His other worry was that Sheriff Dan might be so deliberately intent on maintaining secrecy about the delivery that he might find some reason to send Neville away for the day. Keep him away from the office so he'd have no knowledge of the shipment. That would completely foul up the arrangement—and could have consequences for them both, as well.

The morning crept by, slowly. Neville tried to keep busy with menial tasks while keeping one eye on the wall clock: its steady, monotonous ticking sweeping away another minute, becoming a tormenting reminder of what was to come, for Neville had little doubt that whether or not he provided that signal to Smith, the robbery would still be carried out. There was too much at stake for Smith not to follow through.

Another quiet day in town, no interruptions to pull the sheriff away from the office—and still no word from him about the shipment. Occasionally the sheriff would tell Neville to keep an eye on things while he went into the adjoining living quarters to check on his wife. Neville had never been so filled with anxiety. It was the waiting—*the infernal waiting.* By now he was grateful that Sheriff Dan was not in a talkative mood. The silence between them grew heavy, but Neville appreciated it. As the morning became afternoon and Neville's nerves were beginning to fray, he doubted he could engage in any kind of conversation with the man, not without the risk of giving off signs that might alert Sheriff Dan as to what was ahead.

Around three P.M. there was a pronounced knock at the back door. The sheriff had gone to take another check on his wife and so Neville went to answer it, keeping his gait steady and sure, even though his legs were beginning to feel like wet straw. He left the office and walked to the door that opened on the hallway and also branched off to the living quarters. Before he could turn the knob, the sheriff appeared at the end of the corridor and regarded Neville with an expression that indicated he would handle it.

Neville obliged. He didn't have to be there; that knock on the door told him what he needed to know. He turned and started back into the office.

He didn't look back. He heard the door open and the sheriff say in a calm, formal voice, "We'll take it inside the office."

Another voice, which had a doubtful intonation, suggested, "Might be safer if you keep it somewhere inside the house."

A pause, and then Sheriff Dan said abruptly, "No." Then speaking in a gentler tone, "My wife's inside. . . . Don't feel the need for this to intrude upon my home."

"Your choice. Harley here'll be stationed in the office anyway."

Neville tried to remain uninvolved in any of this. He still thought there could be a chance that Sheriff Dan might send him away on some bogus errand to keep him in the dark as to what was transpiring. He watched unobtrusively out the corner of his eye as a large piece of luggage, obviously a disguise to conceal the strongbox holding the payroll, was carried inside the office.

There were two men with Sheriff Dan, one of whom was the guard called Harley. Both were deliberately dressed like cowpunchers so as not to call attention to themselves during the ride into town. Each was an able-looking man who appeared up to the task, so Neville couldn't tell which one would stay on as the guard.

"Have yuh figgered where yuh wanta put it?" the man who had been doing the talking asked. Neville observed that he had a wild mustache that looked to take up the bottom portion of his face.

Neville kept one ear open, but as he sat at the bureau arranging some papers he continued to appear completely uninterested.

"Yeah," Sheriff Dan replied. "We lock it right inside one of the jail cells."

"Kinda obvious, ain't it," the fellow with the mustache said doubtfully.

"Maybe. But I got only one set of keys for the cells. If'n I don't know where the keys are, ain't much chance I can open the door less'n whoever might try to rob us wants to blast it open with dynamite."

"Might'n't that be takin' a bit of a risk? Just supposin'."

The sheriff spoke with confidence. "First off, no one even knows 'bout this delivery. And s'posin' someone does know or finds out. First, that someone's gotta try to get by me and Harley, and not too likely with us waitin' to meet 'em with firepower. Then they'd hafta find out where the strongbox is . . . and then try to get to it. Each of them steps is a fool's move."

"Cells are unoccupied?"

"Only got four and in all the time I been sheriffin' ain't never seen more than two, maybe three occupied at any time, 'course sharin' more than one to a cell if'n it's the drovers sleepin' off a rough one."

The fellow with the mustache seemed satisfied. "Well, that's precisely why we chose Brewer's Gulch for the transfer."

Neville now knew the procedure. More than he needed to know given the arrangement made with Smith, but that was good. The strongbox was removed from the suitcase and placed inside one of the jail cells. There were a few more minutes of small talk between Sheriff Dan and the two men before the one who had been speaking with the sheriff took his leave. Neville cast a furtive glance over at the man, Harley, who would be sharing guard duty with Sheriff Dan and took a quick study of him. He looked formidable and was clutching a twelve-gauge double-barreled shotgun loaded with buckshot that could likely blow a man in half. The thought entered Neville's brain that he wouldn't want to tackle either him or the sheriff, and he questioned the fool-hardiness of Smith and his partner to attempt such a risk.

Even with this uncommon occurrence and Neville a witness to it all, Sheriff Dan seemed to avoid explaining what was going on to him.

Neville experienced another pang of guilt as he realized that whether he was told anything or not, he already knew more than Sheriff Dan.

Neville checked the wall clock. He had to get ready to leave the office, briefly, to give his signal to Smith. That was easy enough. He hadn't eaten lunch, which up until recently had always been prepared by Sadie, and he would tell Sheriff Dan he was going down to the hotel to get something to eat.

Just as he started to rise he felt a hand on his shoulder. He turned and glanced up into the stern features of the sheriff. The look wasn't intended to be cruel or critical, just serious. Sheriff Dan penetrated the boy with his stare, relating through the expression in his brow-heavy eyes that what he was about to say was of mighty importance and that the boy had best listen carefully.

The sheriff had removed a single large key from the cell ring, which he held firmly between his thumb and index finger. He waved it in front of Neville gently, slowly, but with a deliberate intention.

"Tom, I want you to put this key somewheres," he said. "What I'm sayin' is hide it. I don't wanta know where it is. No matter what, until tomorrow morning when I ask yuh for it, you don't tell me. Under no circumstance. Understand?"

Neville understood all right, though he pretended to come across as ignorant to the request, responding to the sheriff's instruction with a puzzled obedience.

"Don't know if'n yuh heard any of what we was discussin'," Sheriff Dan went on, his voice low but speaking with purpose. "That ain't somethin' you need to be knowin' at the moment. Maybe I'll tell yuh later, but for now don't ask questions and just do exactly what I say."

Neville nodded.

And then the sheriff said in a gentler voice, "Remember. I'm entrustin' this to you, son."

Sheriff Dan speaking those words fired a thunderbolt through Neville, almost knocking him off his chair, and he had to call upon every ounce of willpower to keep himself steady. Because hearing the sheriff say that caused Neville's thoughts to flash back to the moment when old Mr. Caulfield had presented him—*entrusted* him—with the ten-dollar gold eagle. Neville recalled how he had honored that trust and how that very special coin had brought him through his wanderings to the home of Sheriff Dan and Sadie. How, if even in the most oblique way, the possession of that coin had gifted him with the family he had sought.

Despite temptations, he'd kept his word to the old man. He could not part with the coin even when he was desperate to send for Jessica. Jessica, for whom he was now willing to turn against the only people who had ever truly cared for him. His thoughts became troubled as he contemplated how he could not betray his word for a man he barely knew . . . yet could betray the love and friendship of Sheriff Dan.

Neville swallowed, and he was sure that Sheriff Dan noticed the bob in his throat. He struggled to keep eye contact with the sheriff. He could still see the personal pain that the sheriff could not hide, but also reflected was the genuineness of Sheriff Dan's trust in him.

"I know I can depend on you, Tom," the sheriff said earnestly. He paused. "Just one thing: I need you to give me your word."

The same words had been spoken to him by Mr. Caulfield, and they came rushing at Neville out of a distant past. Why could he now remember them so clearly when at the time they seemed to pass by him with no real significance?

Neville was taken aback. He never expected to be asked to acknowledge a commitment of trust. By giving his word to Sheriff Dan, he knew he would then have to betray Smith. Because it had been bred into him by Sheriff Dan himself that a man could cheat or steal, but there was nothing more lowdown than going back on one's word. The sheriff elaborated that no matter what a man's circumstances in life, he could feel whole and proud if he stayed true to his word. A man's word was his bond and all that he could really call his own, and therefore not to be taken lightly. This was one lesson Neville recalled that had made a lasting impact on him.

He had no time to think out his decision. Sheriff Dan was looking steady at him and would not release his focus until Neville expressed through his words that the sheriff could depend on him. He had to make his choice now.

And once he made that decision, there would be no turning back. It had to be all or nothing . . .

SEVEN

He accepted the key while trying to prevent his fingers from trembling. Since he wasn't supposed to know the importance of the key, he had to be careful in every way not to give Sheriff Dan even a hint that anything was amiss.

He carried the key with him into the living quarters, taking it into his bedroom where he scoured about for a suitable hiding place. He couldn't think clearly to come up with anyplace clever and finally just buried it deep under his mattress. When he returned to the office, he glanced up at the wall clock. By now Smith would be waiting for him. Neville wouldn't show. He contemplated how that was going to affect what Smith was planning.

He contemplated how that was going to affect *him*.

Neville released much of the anxiety that had been building in him over the past twenty-four hours in a protracted exhale of breath that even caught Sheriff Dan's attention. Neville noticed his slightly quizzical look and explained that he hadn't gotten much sleep the night before. Sheriff Dan gazed at him oddly but nodded just the same.

Strangely, coming to the decision he'd made did not cause

Neville much regret. He still had to consider that maybe all that Smith had told him about Jessica and the lawyer was just a ruse, a sort of subtle blackmail intended to get Neville to throw in with him. Smith was a criminal and certainly not above such a ploy. What he also came to consider was if all that Smith had told him about Jessica truly was a lie, how could he ever face her, offer her his love while harboring the knowledge that he'd participated in a lawless act to win her affections?

Neville realized that his brain had been all over the map, his reason caught in a whirlpool of conflicting thoughts and vacillating decisions. Now, as he allowed himself to slowly relax, he believed he was clearheaded enough to recognize that whatever his move had been, whatever course he'd chosen, it ultimately would have been a gamble. He decided to play percentages, and the cards he had finally laid on the table looked right to him.

What of a sudden seemed of most importance to Neville was his careful observation of Sheriff Dan as he assumed his official duties that afternoon. It became obvious that the sheriff needed this diversion of protecting the mining payroll—a relatively simple assignment but one that appeared to give Sheriff Dan a much-needed sense of purpose. For the first time in weeks Neville detected a spark of the old lawman in the sheriff. The town itself was too quiet to keep the sheriff adequately occupied. He'd make his usual rounds then come back to the office and wait for a complaint to come his way. He had too much time during the dusty and dreary days to sit and worry himself over Sadie, and this had taken a toll. The guarding of the cash strongbox might provide only a temporary solution to his growing despair, but Neville quickly came to see how cruel and unjust it would be for him, the surrogate son, to sabotage what could prove to be a moment of meaning for Sheriff Dan.

The day passed, and it was going on evening. Neville never kept his appointment with Smith and sat inside the office, starting to grow apprehensive and wrestling with himself to keep that worry in check. In his mind's eye he pictured that unnerving grin Smith had stretched across his face, and how he was sure Smith wasn't smiling now.

Neville harbored the desperate hope that maybe the robbery would be called off. That because Neville had failed to keep their appointment, Smith might think that the shipment hadn't arrived. But that didn't really convince him. Neville was expected to show either way. With him failing to do so, Smith would likely take the chance to check out the situation for himself. Of course Neville could have met with him and lied that the payroll hadn't come. He'd considered then abandoned that idea. It was likely Smith didn't trust Neville any more than Neville trusted him, and Smith might still be determined to see for himself. Apparently a lot of preparation had gone into this plan, a major mining interest was involved, and so with or without Neville's involvement, it seemed doubtful that Smith and his companion would not visit the sheriff's office that night.

Throughout most of the afternoon Neville struggled with another dilemma: whether he should inform the sheriff about what he knew. He finally rejected that idea for two reasons: That faint, fleeting hope the robbery might not happen . . . but more importantly—and *selfishly*, he conceded—he was fearful to explain to Sheriff Dan why he hadn't come to him immediately after learning of the plan. Why he had waited until the following day to confide in him. Sheriff Dan would certainly question that.

And how could Neville answer? Again it would come down to his having to lie to the man.

The only explanation Sheriff Dan might accept was if Neville were to say he was afraid . . . There was some truth to that, though a confession of cowardice would almost surely tarnish him in the sheriff's eyes.

Just as unsettling as the long, uncertain waiting was the presence of the man called Harley. He'd positioned himself on a chair just outside the door leading to the jail cells and had sat there the whole time, shotgun placed lengthwise across his lap with one hand resting over the stock, his other hand caressing the double barrels, and all the while not uttering a word. Neville couldn't know whether Harley was employed by the Treherne Company or perhaps was a specially hired private detective. It made no difference, really; his mere presence was enough to discourage bandits. It wasn't so bad when Sheriff Dan was in the office, but later in the afternoon he had to take a lengthy leave as the doctor had come to check on Sadie, and Neville was plain uncomfortable being alone with Harley and his dark, probing eyes.

When Sheriff Dan returned to the office, he once more looked distressed, and some of the spark Neville had noticed earlier had again vacated the man. Neville saw no need to inquire how the doctor's visit had gone. The expression on the sheriff's face was all too familiar and telling.

But Sheriff Dan pulled Neville aside, laid a hand on his shoulder, and looked at the boy solemnly. It was as if he needed to speak what was heavy on his mind. He spoke in a low voice so as not to be overheard by Harley, who it was doubtful was listening anyway.

"Tom," he said, "as much as it's gonna hurt me to lose her, I—I almost wish God would take her."

The sad sincerity of the sheriff's words affected Neville. And he could understand why Sheriff Dan would make such a comment. Sadie's suffering had been going on for too long, and he wanted her to be at rest. But what surprised Neville was Sheriff Dan's mention of God. The sheriff wasn't a churchgoing man; neither he nor Sadie said grace when they sat down at the table to eat their meals. Neville had never even seen a Bible anywhere in the house. Yet apparently there was a spiritual side to the sheriff that he had never revealed. And instead of cursing God for bringing this terrible illness upon his wife, Sheriff Dan merely asked for him to bring her peace.

While Neville himself hadn't been raised with any Christian values and really hadn't given much thought to God or religion, he found it admirable that Sheriff Dan would make this acknowledgment before him in selfless concern for his wife.

Around nine P.M., Sheriff Dan's mood lifted a little. He asked Neville to go fetch them some supper from the hotel. Neville felt a lump form in his throat. He deliberately hadn't left the office all day, lest he chance running into Smith on the street. Neville had kept a wary watch out the front window of the office, frequently yet furtively checking to see if he might catch Smith walking by, seeking Neville, since he hadn't kept their appointment.

Harley merely shook his head when Sheriff Dan asked if he wanted anything to eat. He then reached into a small bag he had beside him and pulled out a large apple, which he began to munch deliberately.

Sheriff Dan pulled money from the pocket of his trousers and counted out some silver, which he handed to Neville.

"Go get us a coupla dinners, Tom," he said.

Neville swallowed, nodded, and then hesitated just a bit too long, raising Sheriff Dan's curiosity.

"Somethin' wrong, Tom?" he asked.

And at that moment Neville found himself tempted to confess all to the sheriff, to prevent his having to walk out into the night, not knowing if Smith and his companion might be waiting for him in some dark corner. He might be thought of as a coward, but the truth was that he *was* scared. Yellow, even.

But Neville still couldn't bring himself to say what he knew, so he answered Sheriff Dan's concern with a shake of his head and left the office for the short walk to the hotel. He heard the inside door latch slide and twist into the locked position. Until the payroll was picked up the next morning, Sheriff Dan looked to be taking every precaution. But for the next while Neville would be locked out into the night.

Neville walked at a steady pace, not hurried so as not to call attention to himself, listening for sounds other than the clip-clopping of his boots across the planks of the board-walk, keeping watchful as his eyes darted along both sides of the dark, quiet street where at this hour few passersby roamed, and taking extra care when he came to shadowed corners between the buildings, where he'd halt, peering into the gloom before once more picking up his step.

He made it to the hotel without incident. He permitted himself the opportunity to relax in the lobby while the kitchen prepared the dinners; tonight's menu was roast beef and beetroot with peach cobbler for dessert, two orders of which were shortly brought out on a tray, the steaming plates protected against the night chill by a towel. Neville paid for the food, took the tray with both hands, and started back to the office, again keeping mindful of his surroundings, especially as the skies had grown darker and the streets now appeared deserted.

Once he reached the sheriff's office he exhaled a relieved if self-conscious sigh. He was starting to feel better and could even feel a little foolish for giving in to his dread. Once the door to the office was safely locked behind him, he couldn't foresee any trouble. Smith wouldn't be able to get inside unless he broke in, and such a move would earn him a bullet.

He forgot the door to the office had been latch-locked by the sheriff when he'd left, and it was only when he turned the knob and stepped inside, beginning to shut the door behind him, that he realized with a sudden start . . . *that the latch was not fastened.*

"Step inside, Neville," he heard a familiar voice say.

Positioned on opposite sides of the office back toward the jail were Smith, with his Colt revolver drawn, and his dirty and vicious-looking sidekick, the man called Rafe, who was leaning lazily against the wall brandishing the twelve-gauge double-barreled shotgun once held by Harley. They had the drop on Sheriff Dan, who had been stripped of his gun belt. The guard Harley lay facedown on the floor, blood pooling from a wound in his back.

At hearing Neville being referred to by name by one of

these criminals, Sheriff Dan regarded the boy with a look of incomprehension. Reflexively, he rose from the chair where he had been sitting and fastened his eyes on Neville.

"He called you by name, Tom?" he said questioningly.

Neville heard the words but was unable to release his gaze from the body on the floor. He'd never seen a man who had been murdered, and it was a numbing sight. From where he was standing he noticed how Harley's eyes had half rolled back into their sockets, glazed and sightless.

"Look at me, boy," the sheriff demanded.

Neville lifted his eyes, trailing them toward the source of the voice, but they could not quite connect with Sheriff Dan.

"He's dead," Sheriff Dan told him straightly. His breathing became heavy as he half turned and pointed to Rafe. "That scum over there, he came up behind him and stuck a knife into his back." He spoke thickly. "What do you know 'bout this, Tom?"

Neville looked for a stall. He became aware that he was still holding the tray with the hotel dinners. His hands were shaking and he hastened to place the tray onto the sheriff's desk before he dropped it to the floor.

"You better talk to me, boy," the sheriff said, his mood heated and his tone no-nonsense. "You tell me how these fellas know who yuh are, 'cause by God I don't wanta believe you have any part in this."

Neville looked nervously from the sheriff to the grinning Smith. He felt sick and weak and wanted to sit down. But he forced himself to keep on his feet to present at least a facade of innocence in front of the sheriff. The situation didn't look good, but he had to stay steady if he stood *any* chance of convincing the sheriff that he had no part in this. His major concern was that he hadn't come through for Smith and knew that the man now owed him nothing. All Smith had to do was start talking. Take his payback by telling the sheriff everything.

Smith looked pleased that Neville seemed to understand his predicament. He chose to prolong his apprehension a mite longer by answering the question that he knew Neville would dare not ask under the circumstances.

"The sheriff's duty is to help the community, Neville," he said sardonically, using his free hand to break another cigar, half of which he rammed into his mouth. "Come to the door sayin' there's trouble and a right honest lawman ain't gonna turn his back on you. And that's just what Sheriff Bridges done."

With troubled eyes, Neville again regarded the dead man on the floor.

"Well," Smith drawled while he sucked on his unlit stogie, anticipating what was going through Neville's brain, "gotta admit we played a little unfair. Y'see, my friend over there can pick locks with the best of 'em. Quiet as an Injun, too. While I kept the two of 'em talkin', my friend snuck his way in through the back, and . . . well, that fella layin' there was dead 'fore he even knew he'd been killed."

Rafe sputtered an obnoxious laugh while he rocked his head, pleased at Smith's acknowledgment of his "talents."

"Anyway, that makes no never mind," Smith said dismissively. "What *is* important is that Sheriff Bridges ain't bein' too cooperative. Won't tell us where that payroll is. Coulda made him talk in our own fashion but knew you was comin' back, so thought we'd wait and see if'n you might be more obligin'." His tone turned deadly serious. "So where is it, Tom?"

Before Neville could even think to answer, Sheriff Dan broke in, bluntly:

"You're in with them, ain't yuh, Tom?"

Neville's face twitched, tellingly. He tried to speak but knew there was nothing, absolutely *nothing*, that he could say to the sheriff.

An expression of sadness shadowed the sheriff's features. Neville had seen that look on Sheriff Dan many times since his wife took ill, but never with such distress as his face was registering now, a troubling combination of sorrow and deep disappointment. Neville couldn't help thinking that his sticking a knife into Sheriff Dan's back, as Rafe had done with Harley, would have been more merciful.

Sheriff Dan lowered his eyes and shook his head.

"Can't believe yuh let me down, Tom," he said, aggrieved. He took a moment, then slowly raised his head, his expression now harsh. He fixed glowering eyes on Neville. "You let us *both* down."

Neville knew that he was also referring to Sadie. Sadie, who was in her bedroom not far from where this drama was unfolding, oblivious to what was happening as she continued to die a lingering death.

Neville just stood there, trying to at least meet the sheriff's eyes for whatever that might be worth—but failing in the attempt. Even if he could find the words, it was too late to try to explain. He was overcome with regret that he hadn't come clean to Sheriff Dan when he'd had the chance. Now there was nothing he could say that would make any difference. Sheriff Dan knew he was a part of this.

Smith was becoming impatient. He shifted his weight from one foot to the other and traded gun hands. "My friend and me don't got all night," he said. "And we ain't leavin' here without that money."

Sheriff Dan spoke boldly. "Then you're in for a long night."

Rafe answered, "Yuh sure talk brave for someone who likely ain't gonna live to see sunup."

Smith turned slowly around to face Neville. The cool, easygoing attitude with which he had introduced himself the day before had become one of frightening menace. His appearance darkened, features baleful, the familiar grin pulled back so that his thin lips all but vanished, revealing teeth bared like an animal gone rabid.

"I'm gonna overlook that you didn't keep our appointment today," he said, much to Neville's dismay. "But you see what my friend done to that deputy or whatever he was. Ain't gonna make no difference now if'n we kill the sheriff. We got the noose 'round our necks. Now I got a hunch you know where that money's at, Neville." He glanced over at the wall clock. "Thirty seconds, that's all yuh got."

Neville didn't doubt that if he did not cooperate, Sheriff Dan was a dead man. Still, he tried to reason with Smith.

"You fire that gun and half the town'll be here," he said, trying to keep the desperation from his voice. "You won't stand a chance."

Smith gave a brisk nod. "Yeah . . . if'n I fired my pistol. But I ain't that dumb. I'm just gonna hold the gun on him while my friend carves him up."

Rafe had the shotgun braced under one arm, and he dramatically withdrew the big, still-bloody knife from the sheath hidden inside his duster. He looked dull and crazed and capable of doing just what Smith threatened.

Neville turned toward Sheriff Dan. The sheriff was still regarding him icily, as if in his eyes Neville mattered no more than these murderers. And Neville now had to accept that regardless of what happened, whatever the outcome, the relationship that had been established between the two of them was over. He would be as dead to the sheriff as Sheriff Dan would be to him if Rafe were set loose on him. Still, he could not stand by and watch the man be slaughtered by a knife-wielding maniac.

"If you got a speck of honesty left in you, Tom, you won't tell that vermin anything," Sheriff Dan said to him.

Neville looked distressed. What he'd dreaded seemed only seconds from happening. The sheriff was prepared to be murdered to fulfill his duty.

"I—ain't gonna let 'em kill yuh, Sheriff Dan," Neville said weakly but adamantly.

Sheriff Dan expelled a breath, but it wasn't an expression of relief. He spoke softly. "Then you're a fool, Tom. They already killed a man and I watched 'em do it. I'm a lawman and I'm lookin' right at 'em. They're loco, but they ain't dumb. They know the minute they walk outta here I'll be after 'em with every good man I can round up. They ain't gonna let me live no matter what."

Smith seemed at a loss. The sheriff had accurately summed up the situation. He was a dead man, and exactly for that reason he could express his bravado. This acceptance of his fate didn't leave Smith with much bargaining power.

The outcome looked hopeless. Neville's brain worked feverishly to try to come up with a solution to this dilemma. Some answer that would spare the sheriff his life.

Finally, he hit upon an idea. A long shot that just might work.

"You're right, I do know where the payroll is," he said suddenly.

Sheriff Dan tossed Neville a sharp, disapproving look, the glare in his eyes warning the boy not to say anything more.

Neville turned away and ignored the lawman's piercing stare.

"The strongbox is locked in one of the jail cells," he said. "I have the key."

Smith wore a lopsided smile. "Well . . . reckon that sorta simplifies things."

Neville drew in a breath as he played his one advantage.

"Depends," he said.

"What d'yuh mean—*depends*?" Smith said skeptically.

"You gotta trust me."

Smith squinted his eyes warily. "Trust yuh?"

Neville gave a slow, precise nod. "Yeah."

"Tom, I'm tellin' yuh to shut up," Sheriff Dan said sternly. "You don't tell him anything."

Smith turned on him. "No, lawman, you better be the one to shut up. Whether you realize it or not, if your boy here hadn't spoke up you'd be gettin' sliced into bacon just 'bout now. That thirty seconds is long past."

Smith focused his attention back on Neville while Rafe kept his glazed and crazed eyes on Sheriff Dan, looking itchy and eager for another kill.

"Okay, Neville, what are yuh offerin'?" Smith asked in a more relaxed tone.

"That you leave here, head out to where we met yesterday . . . and I'll bring yuh the money. Then you just ride outta the territory and don't never come back."

Smith considered. With his stogie clenched between his teeth, he rolled the barrel of his Colt against his forearm.

"You know the sheriff'd still be after us," he reminded.

"No. He won't," Neville assured him.

"And how can yuh be certain of that?"

Neville chanced a glance over at Sheriff Dan, whose expression seemed to indicate that he knew what Neville was up to. And he didn't approve, starting to look angry and tense.

"I'll keep him locked in a cell," Neville answered. "Won't be no one by here 'til morning, when they come to pick up the payroll. Gives yuh plenty of time to get away."

"And I could trust you on that?" Smith said dubiously.

"Yeah, you can trust me. I got nothin' to lose now," Neville responded with pronounced bitterness. "You made sure of that. I'll be on the dodge as much as you."

Smith questioned the sheriff. "That true?"

Sheriff Dan momentarily surrendered his stiff expression and looked wounded, never having expected to be in a position to answer such a question. But he recovered. Once more his features hardened as he locked eyes with Neville and said with intent, "I'll hunt the three of you 'til the day I die."

Neville didn't doubt that. But by the time Sheriff Dan could start tracking him, Neville would be long gone.

Smith considered some more. Then the grin reappeared on his face and he nodded approvingly at Neville.

"Never coulda guessed you was so clever," he said. "But tell yuh what, just to keep me feelin' better, you let me take the keys. Then I know we got our own advantage."

Neville gave a slow rock of his head.

Smith shifted his eyes toward the sheriff. "Y'know, lawman, you owe this fella. For the second time he just saved your hide."

Sheriff Dan refused to acknowledge any gratitude. He looked disgusted. Disgusted and disappointed as both his faith in his adopted son and his own pride had been injured. Still, he walked without protest into the jail and permitted Neville to lead him into one of the far cells. As Neville locked the sheriff inside he thought how he had never felt so miserable in his life, even as he tried to rationalize that his action was keeping Sheriff Dan from being killed.

"Well," Smith sighed as he took the key ring from Neville, "I ain't a killer so's I can't say I'm disappointed. Rafe, on the other hand . . . he don't look too happy."

Smith started to move toward the office door. Rafe followed, though walking backward with slow, deliberate steps, the twelve-gauge trained on Neville.

Smith halted before he reached the door. The look on his face suggested that he'd just got a thought.

"Uh, no, Rafe, might be best if you stay put," he said. "For insurance."

Neville was quick to object. "Don't need him here. Sheriff's locked inside, you got the keys, and I gave you my word I'll bring the payroll."

"Ain't that I don't wanta trust yuh," Smith returned, deadpan. "But seems to me 'til we get that strongbox the odds are still on your side."

Neville regarded Rafe with a miserable look. "By leavin' *him* here I don't trust *you*."

Smith spoke around the half cigar that slanted from his lips. "You sayin' we're at a stalemate?"

"I already told yuh, there ain't no way out for me," Neville stated steadfastly. "I got no plan to try and save that payroll. Why would I? Wouldn't make no difference now. You heard what the sheriff said. Once he gets outta that cell, he ain't gonna be givin' me no pat on the back."

"Reckon that's true 'nuff." Smith thought a little longer. He breathed out, narrowed his eyes in cruel thought, and said, "Okay. Okay, I'll take your word, but only 'cause I need that money and can't afford no stalls. You'll still get your share. But a word of warning, Neville. You don't come through and I promise you'll spend the rest of your days lookin' over your shoulder. Guaranteed the sheriff hot-tailin' yuh will be the least of your worries."

Smith gestured with a swift jerk of his head for Rafe to join him at the door. It was with a noticeable reluctance that Rafe followed. He still craved blood. The man was crazy.

Neville could recognize that and was convinced that had he stayed behind he would have tried to finish off Sheriff Dan—maybe even Neville, too, even at the risk of jeopardizing the payroll.

"You got an hour," Smith told Neville, emphasizing his point with a stiff thrust of his cigar.

The men exited the office and the room fell into a tense, uneasy silence. Neville waited until he was sure Smith and Rafe were gone before he started for his bedroom to retrieve the key to the jail cell that contained the strongbox. He didn't want Sheriff Dan to speak to him; he didn't even want to acknowledge the sheriff's presence. But when he returned to the office and unlocked the door to the cell, Sheriff Dan took the opportunity to talk with him, and his words were blunt and aggressive.

"You gonna leave a dead man on the floor?" he said.

Neville ignored him as he got down on a bent knee and reached under the chain-fastened bunk and felt about for the strongbox.

"No man deserves that kind of disgrace," the sheriff added.

"Someone'll be by in the morning," Neville muttered. "Take care of him and you."

"What 'bout Sadie?" Sheriff Dan then said. "You gonna keep me locked in here 'til morning? You really become that mean not to care what happens to her?"

Neville felt the nerves in his body grow taut as a wave of guilt swept through him. For an instant the pain from this guilt was almost unbearable. He half closed his eyes and said through pursed lips, "All right. Best I can do is . . . I-I'll call on the doc 'fore I ride out. Have him come by. Without them keys it'll be a good while 'fore you get out anyway."

"Reckon you got your own reason for doin' this," Sheriff Dan presumed, speaking quietly.

Neville wasn't listening—to either the sheriff's words or the tone of his voice, the gentleness of which may or may not have been genuine. Neville couldn't know. Circumstances had propelled his life into a new direction where he planned to be accountable only to himself, and that meant doing whatever it took to survive.

He pulled out the strongbox and hurried from the cell, leaving the door ajar.

Sheriff Dan called after him. Neville halted in the doorway to the jail, though he didn't turn around. He could not meet the sheriff's eyes for what would be the last time.

Sheriff Dan said, "Things can't ever be put right 'tween us, Tom, think you know that. But ain't too late for you to do what's right to put your life in order."

Several lengthy seconds passed. Perhaps it was a futile attempt, but the sheriff held a faint hope that maybe his words might make an impression on the boy and that he might reconsider his action.

In the next moment Neville provided the answer . . . when he walked swiftly from the room.

Sheriff Dan's face reflected his frustration, mirrored his chagrin.

"Then you'd best move quick, boy," he said mutedly.

Just before Neville could leave the office, he took notice of what had been tossed across the room and was lying on the floor across from the sheriff's desk. He walked over and took a moment to consider Sheriff Dan's gun belt. While he had rarely given it much thought, it occurred to him that he'd never learned how to handle a firearm. Sheriff Dan had often taken him fishing but never had the two gone out hunting, so even the handling of a rifle was unfamiliar to Neville.

Still, wearing the gun belt, Colt .44 revolver tucked into its holster, would give him a sense and semblance of protection as he rode on to wherever his trail would take him.

He knelt to a crouch and his fingers reached for the gun belt . . . halted. And slowly he drew his hand back.

He stood upright. He felt a slight trembling course through his body. He could walk off with the cash-filled strongbox but found that he could not strap on Sheriff Dan's gun belt. He tried to comprehend why that was and could reach only one explanation. The only explanation that made any sense to him.

He didn't feel entitled. He hadn't the right to take with him something so representative of the type of man Sheriff Dan was.

Not when he had caused him such pain and disappointment.

So before Neville could experience another urge of temptation, he rushed from the office.

With only the moonlight to guide him, Neville rode the sheriff's horse, Lulubell, through the dark, cloudless night toward Hefton Bend, intending to honor his word and keep his rendezvous with Smith. Purple mountain peaks loomed in the distance, against the direction toward which he would turn—where Smith and Rafe would be waiting. Neville didn't know what to expect. On one hand, although a man was dead, everything had turned out as planned. Yet Neville could not forget that he had betrayed Smith that afternoon by not showing up to give the signal to confirm the arrival of the payroll, as had been arranged. Neville had noticed the unpredictable mood of Smith that night, to say nothing of the murderous appetite of his partner. How could Neville be sure that Smith wasn't nursing a grudge and waiting for this opportunity to even the score? At the very least he was under no obligation to share the money with him. That alone provided reason for Smith not to let him leave Hefton Bend alive.

Neville found himself unconsciously slowing his animal's pace. As he rode past the hillside cemetery with its scattered rows of makeshift crosses, unpleasant thoughts continued to cloud his brain. He began to consider that he might be riding into an ambush.

The night air was cool, but he had begun to sweat under his shirt.

He brought the horse to a trot. He was nearing his

destination but knew he could not go on. He pulled rein just a short distance from where the road would branch off onto that lonely trail . . . where Smith and Rafe would be waiting.

Neville had to make a difficult decision—and quickly. If he followed through with his promise to Smith, he most likely was a dead man. If he betrayed him again he'd spend the rest of his life looking over his shoulder, waiting for Smith to fulfill *his* promise.

He considered the strongbox, which he'd placed in a canvas pouch now draped over the saddle. For a brief instant he entertained what was probably the most sensible solution: Return to town with the payroll and face whatever punishment awaited him. That idea passed quickly. He felt convinced that Sheriff Dan would use all the influence of his office to make him suffer the harshest penalty the law would permit . . . and while that was an outcome Neville could not allow for himself, from Sheriff Dan's standpoint he truthfully could not blame him.

He understood he really had only the one option. He could go a long way on the money in the strongbox, far from Smith and Sheriff Dan, who was sure to get on his trail as soon as circumstances allowed.

Neville didn't know where he would go, but he was sure of one thing: he could not follow through with his plan to meet with Jessica in Gumption. Once Smith realized he had been betrayed by Neville, that was the first place he'd search for him.

Before Neville wheeled his horse to ride off, he took a moment to consider the bitter irony. He had committed his first and only dishonest act because of Jessica, and now he had become a criminal—wanted by both sides of the law—about to embark on a life on the run . . . without ever winning the prize he sought.

EIGHT

The years passed quickly and during that time Neville rode from town to town, drifting as a saddle tramp throughout the Southwest and into Midwestern territories where he'd stay for short spells, never establishing roots, until restlessness and the worry of being tracked down by his pursuers got the better of him and he would move on. Throughout those travels Neville remained extremely careful, yet he never carried a gun on his person. He knew that even if the situation warranted it, he could not kill a man. His conscience was troubled enough that he had become a thief; he would not add to his guilt by becoming a murderer. And so as an alternative to such an unsavory proposition, he resolved just to keep on the move.

He'd developed a strong sense of independence. The insecurity and longing for stability that had accompanied him during those formative years all but dissipated like the winds after a storm as he learned through necessity to become his own man. Because he had the advantage of a nice supply of cash to keep him going, he determined never to become beholden to any man.

Circumstances compelled him to keep riding, frequently challenging rugged, uninhabited terrain and enduring altering climates. Yet as time passed Neville also grew weary, and he felt the yearning to find himself a stretch of land and finally settle down. That desire traveled with him through journeys across prairies, flats, and hardscrabble desert surfaces, over hills and through canyon passages, where he endured both blistering heat and bitter cold. It stemmed from the memory he still held dear of the girl who had first touched his heart, Jessica. She remained a strong impression on his thoughts. With little effort, he could picture her as clearly and as defined as when he first sat across from her on that stagecoach ride. He acknowledged that she was gone from his life—if what that criminal Smith had insinuated was truly a fact, Jessica had likely moved on to a more prosperous life with a fellow of better means than Neville—yet that momentary joy she had brought him remained steadfast in his thoughts, accompanying him on his long solitary travels where he could almost physically feel her presence, as though helping Neville to navigate his difficult trails.

At the same time, there were occasions when those memories would fill him with a pain so great that Neville would become reckless. Even before he reached adulthood, he'd taken to consuming alcohol in an effort to numb both his mind and his conscience. Bartenders were generally quick to serve him once they saw the roll of bills he carried on his person. And in that vulnerable state he also became prey for professional gamblers who knew how to spot an easy mark. They would sit at their table and watch as Neville carelessly withdrew large bills from his pocket, which he would slap down onto the bar to pay for another round of drinks for whoever happened to be in the house, and then smoothly, craftily, these card sharps would entice him to participate in a hand or two of stud poker.

Neville would always oblige. Money was no concern to him, and by that point he felt privileged to be asked to play cards with men whom he assumed by their dress, fancy accoutrements, and upper-crust attitude were people of character—never guessing that he was being played the chump.

By the time Neville reached the age of twenty-two, he was all but broke. He'd spent his ill-gotten gains carelessly, buying more than a few house rounds in saloons he'd stopped into along his travels, together with his penchant for high-stakes gambling and soon discovering and enjoying the pleasures of expensive women. The day finally came when Neville took stock of his situation. It was then that he realized he'd intentionally wanted to rid himself of that money. Thirty thousand dollars. It was cash that carried with it a guilt. An all-consuming guilt that he'd tried to free himself of through rash spending.

Finally, all he had to his name was just about four hundred dollars. Meager money. Barely enough to put a down payment on a good stretch of farmland. Yet Neville knew that was what he wanted to do with the cash remaining to him. With little schooling and virtually no training outside that brief spell as a store clerk, Neville saw farming as the only option left open to him as a livelihood. It was the work he'd done alongside the man he once called "Pa," and even though their efforts yielded disappointing results, Neville believed he could succeed provided he purchased the right kind of land. Unfortunately, after steadily checking his cash supply, which continued to dwindle, he discovered he was at a disadvantage in that regard. From discussions he'd had with various saloon patrons with whom his generosity had brought him into contact, he learned that prime land was at a premium, parcels selling at a high price.

Still, this was the direction he had decided upon. He knew he could not go on riding aimlessly forever, and by this point, feeling relatively secure that through his zigzagging and territory border crossings he had eluded both a sheriff's posse and vengeful outlaws, he finally wanted to pull rein.

And there was another consideration. He had the urge to establish roots so that he could marry and start a family.

In a way he was surprised that such a yearning was so

strong in him. Mostly he had bad memories of families. His mother, a weak, fragile woman too soon taken ill . . . the abuse he suffered at the hands of a father who was a cruel, bitter drunkard. While he had enjoyed a respite with Sheriff Dan and Sadie, even that had ended badly.

During his travels he had a lot of time to contemplate. He'd done all of the wrong things a man could do: betrayed, stolen, drank, whored, gambled (badly); now he wanted to bury that past and try to make a new start.

He could regret that it had taken him all this time to come to such a decision, but maybe he'd had to experience all that he had, to cleanse himself of future temptations. At least that was how he attempted to justify those mistakes he had made.

W as it a conscious decision, a hankering over which he held no real control, or was it just stupidity? Those were questions Neville could not rightfully answer as he rode into the county where he would find the town of Gumption, the last place he had heard Jessica had been. He'd traveled many miles following his participation in the payroll robbery. His face was stamped with a maturity that made him almost unrecognizable as the smooth-featured callow youth he had been just several years ago. He didn't know what he expected to find, perhaps an end to the trail, but his life had changed dramatically because of his desire for a girl, and it was as if he needed to know if it all had been worth it.

He doubted that would be the case. But if by chance he should find her in Gumption—or discover her whereabouts—he determined he wanted the chance to talk with her.

When he rode into Gumption, the first thing he took note of was how the small community hadn't changed from how he remembered it, the day he and Jessica had stepped from the stagecoach and had made what he'd believed was a commitment to each other. On one hand, with all that had happened since, that memory seemed to stretch back nearly an eternity, yet recalling the town as it was that sunny day and how it now stood, it didn't seem that long ago.

Neville tethered his horse to the hitching rail outside the coffee shop and walked in. He figured this was as good a place as any to start his search. He took a seat at a window table and, after checking out the patrons, he observed the serving staff. Just two plain-looking youngish girls, and Neville had the distinct impression they wouldn't be able to offer much by way of information. But then he noticed a plump, older woman working behind the counter. She looked to be the mother of the two girls and someone who likely had lived in this one-horse town a while and who might know Jessica—or at least remember her.

When one of the servers came to his table to take his order, Neville idly studied the menu and asked for coffee and a piece of berry pie. He then told the girl he wanted to speak to the woman behind the counter. The girl offered that her name was Rosie: Mama Rosie, the proprietor of the restaurant.

Rosie was given the message and Neville noticed how she glared at him suspiciously, expressing an attitude that was none too friendly. This didn't trouble Neville; by now he was used to it. He'd received similar "greetings" in many of the small towns he'd passed through, where all the citizens knew each other and strangers were regarded warily. The girl came back to the table and told Neville that Rosie would speak with him after lunch was over.

Neville drank two cups of black coffee and had ordered a second piece of pie before Rosie waddled over to him. She maintained that chilly, uncertain look as she stood at the side of the table, her breathing loud and labored.

Neville offered a smile—which she did not return. Her miserable attitude wasn't filling Neville with optimism. He decided just to speak to the point and get this over with one way or the other.

"I'm lookin' for someone," he said, keeping the inflection in his voice moderate. "A girl named Jessica. Jessica Marbury. Some years back she came here to Gumption to stay with her grandmother."

A spark of recognition flashed in Rosie's eyes. Neville was watching her closely and noticed her reaction and instantly felt encouraged.

"You say you know her?" Rosie said straightly as she wiped the palms of her pudgy hands against her soiled apron.

"Well . . . got to know her as well as I could on a two-day stage ride," Neville told her honestly.

"I remember the girl," Rosie said after a lengthy pause, as if first trying to determine if this stranger had a legitimate reason for his inquiry. "Knew her grandmother well. Girl used to come in here for tea and to buy biscuits for her. Name was Edna, the grandmother, that is. Edna Corbett. Died not long after the girl came to town. Maybe a month. Six weeks. Girl moved on shortly after that. Never saw her again."

Neville was disappointed, even though he expected to discover as much.

Still, he asked, "Don't s'pose you know the whereabouts of the girl?"

Rosie shook her head stiffly. "Last I remember seeing of her was at the funeral. Never got to know her real well. More of a nodding acquaintance. Came in, drank her tea, bought her biscuits, then she'd be on her way. Probably never spoke more than a dozen words 'tween us."

"Don't reckon yuh know of anyone in town who might know where she coulda gone?" Neville said further.

Rosie's face took on a troubled look. She started to speak, then stopped herself.

Neville was curious by her sudden hesitation. In his most sincere voice he urged her to tell him whatever she could.

"Maybe you should first be telling me why the interest?" Rosie said. "Askin' a lot of questions when it sounds to me as if you two barely knowed each other."

Now it was Neville's turn to show reluctance. But he relented; he could see he wouldn't get an answer unless he fessed up.

"I—was plannin' on marryin' her," he said.

Rosie looked curiously at Neville; again he could

understand the quizzical expression. From her standpoint, what he was telling her had to sound odd.

She said, "I do know she had a brother. Used to ride into town from time to time. A bad sort from what everyone said. Then he up and proved it. Some years back he killed the sheriff in Brewer's Gulch."

NINE

Neville looked stricken. His complexion paled and his eyes became strained with anguish. For a moment he felt his body weaken and he was grateful he was sitting down. He reached for the coffee cup to steady himself and tried to keep his hand from trembling. Rosie noticed his reaction. She pulled out the chair across the table from Neville and seated herself.

"Are you all right?" she asked with concern.

Neville looked at her, his face set in an expression of disbelief. He couldn't speak. He felt numb. She was talking about Sheriff Dan. Dead. Murdered. And the killer . . . Neville's brain had yet to clear from the impact of this news, but he instinctively knew who was responsible. The man who called himself Smith, who said he was Jessica's cousin, but who lied. Who in truth was actually her brother.

Adding to his shock, Neville was overcome with a devastating guilt. For as he thought back to the day of the payroll robbery, he remembered how he could have prevented it, if only he had informed Sheriff Dan of the plan. The sheriff would have been ready and waiting; he never would have fallen for Smith's deception that night. As if hit with a double load of buckshot, Neville knew that none of this had to happen. But it had . . . and he could hold himself responsible for being too afraid to confess what he knew.

But he had to ask himself, why did Smith go back to Brewer's Gulch? Had he returned searching for Neville? That was the most likely reason. He came back hoping to retrieve the money. Did he gun down Sheriff Dan intentionally in a kind of retribution for Neville's having betrayed him, or had the sheriff tried to arrest him and been shot in the attempt?

"Did you know Sheriff Bridges?" Rosie asked tentatively.

Neville gradually managed to compose himself. Looking straight at Rosie without responding to her question, he asked, "Did they . . . ever catch the man who shot him?" He hesitated, finding his next words almost too painful to say. "Jessica's brother."

Rosie gave her head a rueful shake. "Not that I heard. Know a posse went out after him 'cause a lot of the men here in Gumption rode along. They tracked the hills for almost two weeks but came back empty-handed."

"What—do they figger happened to him?" Neville asked slowly.

Rosie lowered her eyes. "Anyone's guess. Some suppose he got away. Most prefer to think he got himself killed hiding in the hills."

Neville folded his hands across the table and bowed his head, almost looking to Rosie as if he were saying a prayer.

"Sheriff Bridges had a lot of friends," Rosie went on. "He even served as sheriff here for a spell."

Neville was surprised to learn this. Sheriff Dan had never mentioned he'd been a lawman in Gumption.

Neville abruptly got to his feet. He needed to step outside for some air. He pulled some money from his pocket to pay for his coffee and pie and laid a couple of bills atop the table without checking to see the amount, though it far exceeded the seventy-five cents he owed. It didn't matter to him. Now more than ever he wanted to be rid of that money still in his possession. Shame and remorse consumed him as he thought about Sheriff Dan lying dead on a dusty street while he went about spending stolen cash like a drunken sailor.

He started to thank Rosie, but words had become difficult for him and so he merely gave her an appreciative nod.

As Neville climbed up onto his horse and prepared to leave Gumption, he came to understand in a vague way why he had felt compelled to ride into the town. It wasn't to discover what had happened to Jessica. He knew he wouldn't find her. It only made sense that she would have left Gumption a long time ago. He came to the town because he was meant to find out about Sheriff Dan. He might never have learned of his death otherwise, and while such a process went beyond his comprehension, it was what some distant part of him must have suspected . . . and what needed to be confirmed.

Neville rode the trail out of town slowly, his head heavy with troubling memories and disturbing thoughts. As the road forked ahead of him he felt another driving urge: to take the trail that would lead him into Brewer's Gulch. He not only had to find out everything he could about the day Sheriff Dan was killed, but he also needed to know what had happened to Sadie, who he knew with an aching heart must have long since passed on.

It sent a chill through Neville to consider that perhaps she was alive when her husband was murdered. To learn that Sadie, as ill and helpless as she was, had been informed that Sheriff Dan was shot down in the street would be a burden Neville would carry with him for the rest of his life.

But he knew that the uncertainty would haunt him even more.

It wasn't a difficult decision for Neville to make. He would chance going back to Brewer's Gulch. It was a risk, he understood that. The town would certainly remember who he was . . . but he was gambling on them not recognizing who he had become. The years since leaving town had roughened his appearance, and maybe memories in the town were faded. But the one person he would talk to, who could provide him with the answers he needed to know, *would* remember him . . . because if he didn't recognize him, Neville would tell him outright who he was.

And that man was Sam Grafton, Neville's old boss at the Grain and Feed.

Neville tried not to appear conspicuous once he turned off the trail and followed the main street into town. He kept his horse at a steady pace and held his posture straight and his head high, exuding an aura of confidence even as he tried to subdue the tremor in his belly. There were citizens out and about since it was midafternoon when he arrived in Brewer's Gulch. Some curious looks came his way, but Neville had his Stetson pulled low and had assumed a few days' growth of beard, which further altered his appearance. He didn't directly acknowledge any of the glances or the one or two outright stares that reached him, but neither did he look away.

He dismounted outside the Grain and Feed, which was located near the opposite end of the town. He glanced up at the signage, which still read in a bold script: **SAM GRAFTON, PROPRIETOR.** Neville remembered Grafton as a good man, kindly and fair, who had taken a liking to him, and he felt pretty confident that he could trust him. Yet Neville remained aware that his visit could also be risky. It was certain that Grafton, along with the rest of the town, had formed and maintained a much different impression of Tom Neville in the years following the holdup. It was possible that some of the citizenry might even hold him to blame for Sheriff Dan's death.

Neville walked into the store and the bell over the door jingled, bringing back memories of the many times he had heard that sound announcing a customer when he was employed at the Grain and Feed.

Neville didn't see Grafton upon entering; he wasn't tending to business in the front of the store. Still, the door wasn't locked, so Grafton was somewhere on the premises. Neville stepped over to the cash counter and stayed put, and soon he heard footsteps approaching from the back room where the surplus merchandise was stored. Grafton emerged from behind the curtain separating the store from the stockroom, smiling and wiping dusty hands against his apron. The man hadn't changed much over the years except that he had taken to wearing spectacles. As he started to walk toward Neville, Grafton's expression gave no hint that he recognized his former employee. Neville was glad of that. If his old boss didn't recognize him, it was doubtful anyone else in town would.

"Afternoon," Grafton said cordially. "Anything I can help you—"

And then his words cut off, abruptly, as a slow but indistinct recognition did come to him. He tilted his head, lifted his hand, and waved a finger in a frustrated gesture to try to place where he remembered this man.

Neville leaned back against the cash counter and folded his arms, nodding.

"Been a long time, Mr. Grafton," he said.

Instantly, Grafton reacted as if he were looking at a ghost. His eyes grew wide behind his spectacles, his jaw went slack, and he took a couple of reflexive steps backward, for a brief second looking to almost lose his balance.

"Tom," he gasped, his waving finger now pointing stiffly at the man. "Tom Neville."

Neville nodded with a bit more emphasis.

"My God," Grafton whispered. He removed his spectacles, looked through them short of an arm's-length distance, then fitted them back over his eyes. "I—simply can't believe I'm lookin' at you."

Neville asked, "Can't believe that I've come back to Brewer's Gulch . . . or that I ain't dead or in jail?"

"Reckon both," Grafton answered, benumbed.

"Have a reason for comin' back," Neville explained, removing his Stetson and holding the hat at his waist with both hands clutching the wide brim. "I wanta hear what happened to Sheriff Dan. And . . . I need to know what became of his missus."

Grafton needed to recover from the shock. He held up his hand to Neville to permit him that privilege. Neville nodded that he understood.

After a few moments, Grafton appeared more settled and ready to talk.

"Why don't I close up shop and we can go talk in the back?" he suggested. "Never know who might walk in."

"I'd 'preciate that," Neville said.

He felt much better, and the fluttering in his stomach ceased. By Grafton's suggesting they speak alone without chancing intrusion, Neville knew he had nothing to worry about with his old boss.

They sat together at a small desk in the stockroom where Grafton recorded his inventory. Neville noticed how the man still appeared a little tentative being in his presence. He couldn't rightly blame him and tried to ease Grafton's uncertainty by beginning their talk on a light, cordial note.

"Brings back a lot of memories, my bein' here," he said as his eyes drifted about the room. "Good memories."

Grafton opened a side drawer on the desk and withdrew a bottle of whiskey. He poured some into a coffee cup, then offered the bottle to Neville.

Neville reached for it and regarded the amber-colored liquor with an ironic expression.

"Back in the day I could hardly look at the stuff," he said reflectively. "Now I've kinda taken a likin' to it." He took a swallow straight from the bottle.

His own quick ingestions of booze relaxed Grafton sufficiently so that he could broach the most obvious question:

"Why'd you do what you done, Tom?"

Neville expected to be asked this and so didn't react with offense or resentment. He put the bottle down on the side of the desk, adjusted himself in his chair, and looked straight into Grafton's eyes.

"I'm gonna come clean with you, Mr. Grafton, 'bout everything," he said in a straightforward tone. "Doubtful that anyone else would believe what I'm gonna tell yuh, and maybe you won't either. But 'fore you tell me what I need to know, figger it's only fair that I tell yuh what happened. And I'm meanin' the *truth*, Mr. Grafton. The honest truth."

"Never known you to be a liar, Tom," Grafton said. He nodded. "Go on."

Neville told his story, at times halting at particularly painful recollections, at other times speaking too rapidly as his emotions became heated. He'd occasionally stop just long enough to study Grafton's face to try to determine whether the man was accepting what he was telling him.

Grafton had consumed a couple more shots of whiskey while listening, but the liquor had not swayed his impartiality on the matter. By the time Neville was finished, his features pained from reliving the experience of that terrible night and the consequences that followed, Grafton regarded him with an expression of sympathy and even a trace of understanding.

But he also felt emboldened by the whiskey and was critical and spoke bluntly. "You shoulda stayed back and told everything to Sheriff Bridges. Taken your punishment like a man. He might not have gone easy on you, Tom, but he would have respected you."

Neville could appreciate what Grafton was saying. But he doubted that he would have earned any respect; he retained a clear memory of Sheriff Dan's attitude that night. He'd made it plain that Neville was no longer a part of his life. He would have been treated just like any criminal.

Still, he nodded and said pensively, "The funny thing is, today, bein' who I am, what I been through and what I've had to live with these years—the guilt and all else—that's the choice I'd probably make." His lips pursed. "But I wasn't that way then, Mr. Grafton. I was a scairt kid bein' pulled on two ends who didn't know what the right decision was."

Grafton considered, then accepted that reasoning with a slow nod.

He said, "Reckon you should know, Tom, that after it got 'round town what happened and with you runnin' off, Sheriff Dan never spoke your name again—not 'til the day he . . . well, when it happened."

Neville glanced down at the floor, trying to conceal from his old boss the hurt and shame he was feeling. After a bit he lifted his head, drew in a breath, and asked, "What happened that day, Mr. Grafton?" He then quickly raised his hand to halt the man before he could answer. "Wait. 'Fore yuh tell me, I first gotta know: Sadie . . . was she alive when it happened?"

Grafton shook his head sadly. "No. She passed maybe a week or so after that incident with you."

Neville didn't much care for the way Grafton phrased his response; the intention was a little rough. But learning that Sadie never had to know of her husband's violent death was a relief to him, and for that, at least, he could feel grateful. Still, it was small consolation for all that Neville held himself responsible for.

"Tell me . . . 'bout Sheriff Dan," he said gently.

Grafton considered pouring himself another drink but decided against it. After first offering the bottle to Neville, who declined, though he could have used another belt to brace himself for what he was about to hear, Grafton put the bottle back inside the desk drawer.

"Don't forget a day like that," Grafton began, smiling wanly. "Just 'round midafternoon. Wild kid came riding into town. Musta been drunk or just plain crazy. Guns blazin', shouting at the top of his lungs. I took a gander out the window to see what all the ruckus was about. Wasn't 'bout to step outside. Saw people screaming and runnin' off the street, dodging bullets that were flyin' everywhere. That's when I looked down the street and saw Dan Bridges walk out of his office. Don't think he made it three steps outside the door when that killer caught sight of him and rushed toward him on his horse and shot him dead before Dan could even go for his gun. If he'd had it drawn before he stepped outside it might have been a different outcome. But Dan . . . I don't know what Dan was thinkin'."

There was emotion in Grafton's voice as he recounted the story. When he was done he removed his spectacles and wiped the lenses with a cloth he'd pulled from a cubbyhole on his desk.

"Both he and Sadie are buried side by side on the hill," he concluded.

"One question I gotta ask," Neville said. "That cowboy . . . did it look to you that he had it in mind to shoot Sheriff Dan?"

"At first didn't look as if he was gunnin' for anyone particular," Grafton replied. "But like I say, once he saw the sheriff, he went right at him."

Neither man spoke after that. The room fell into silence as Neville considered a disturbing possibility. Maybe . . . Sheriff Dan never intended to draw his gun. Perhaps with Sadie gone . . . along with his *other* disappointments, he no longer cared.

Neville quickly dismissed the idea, reassuring himself that the sheriff took pride in being a lawman and never would have allowed some crazed cowboy to shoot up his town.

Yet Neville knew that if he thought about it much longer, he couldn't be entirely convinced.

"Did they ever find out who his killer was?" Neville asked. Of course he'd already been told; he just needed to hear it again. And perhaps be given a name.

"Some punk named Duke Marbury. Searched all over the territory for him but, from what I hear, never caught up with him."

Neville's face didn't change expression as Grafton confirmed the real identity of the man who had called himself "Smith."

Duke Marbury, Neville thought grimly. He'd come back apparently to even the score.

Again the irony set in, and it left a bitter taste. The killer of the man who once was as close to Neville as a father was the brother of the girl he had wanted to make his wife.

Neville thanked Sam Grafton and rode out of Brewer's Gulch without any of the citizens ever knowing he had been in town. Grafton had assured Neville that as far as he was concerned he'd never seen him. While he wished Neville well, he wanted to forget that the visit had ever happened.

Neville understood. He was appreciative, though as he left the store he was feeling so overcome with culpability and despondency that he almost didn't care *should* a posse be waiting for him right outside the door.

He rode his quarter horse briskly, rapidly upping the pace, as if he had an appointment to keep; though, like the trail he had followed for years, he was heading toward no specific destination.

All he could do was ride.

And ride he did over the next several months, drifting aimlessly, carelessly spending the remainder of his "blood money" on diversions intended to help him forget, such as drinking cheap whiskey and bedding two-dollar whores, until, the same as years ago when as a boy of fourteen he had set off from his home, he found himself broke and hungry.

Oddly, one thought remained constant. He still wanted to purchase a stretch of farmland. The desire heightened as he spent those last few dollars and saw how once the money was gone, so was his companionship with those who had enjoyed his generosity. He decided that he wanted to live his life in anonymity and solitude, away from towns and people and their greed and hypocrisy. He might never escape the memories, but he wanted to salvage what was left of his life his own way.

But he now realized he would have to work, perhaps years, to achieve that goal. And the thought didn't much trouble him. While not long ago he'd had more than enough money to buy the finest pastures, he didn't regret not using the cash for that purpose. It was dishonest money, stained with blood and betrayal. He never would have felt he'd earned the privilege to harvest land purchased that way. And he knew the ghosts would have haunted him. The only way he could feel true accomplishment was to start from scratch.

Neville spent the next weeks searching for work as a farmhand. His efforts yielded disappointing results. Days he went hungry; nights he slept cold. He called on landowners whom he had treated to rounds of drinks during his expansive days, only to be regarded with convenient forgetfulness or simply and rudely turned away.

Discouraged, Neville rode into a town he'd yet to visit during his travels, another small, dusty community called Bakersridge, intending to sell his quarter horse, Lulubell, for eating money. He thought grimly that if he failed in this attempt he'd likely have to eat the horse. The animal was tired and pretty well wore out, and Neville knew he'd see minimal money for her. Still, he rode her to the town livery stable and tried to make a deal. A sadness rode with him. Lulubell was the last connection he had to the years he'd spent with Sheriff Dan and Sadie. It would be a final parting with the past, and while he wanted to move forward with his life, Neville could not deny feeling a sort of melancholy.

The stable owner, an elderly, tobacco-chawin' fella named Bill Fletcher, gave the animal a cursory look, considered, then sighed and, emphasizing the dramatic, shook his head.

"Crow bait," was all he said as he slapped the horse's rump.

"Don't seem to me yuh gave her much of a look," Neville said to him.

Bill shrugged. "Don't need to. Seen enough."

"Ain't askin' much for her," Neville told him.

Bill nodded vacantly.

"The saddle's gotta be worth somethin'," Neville argued.

"Just worn leather," Bill muttered. "Might give yuh a coupla bucks. But I ain't got no use for it."

"Yeah, all right . . . a coupla bucks," Neville agreed miserably.

Bill turned to Neville and cocked an eyebrow. "Rode her hard?"

"Rode her long."

Bill nodded. "Can tell."

"Yeah?"

"Animal's durn near lame," Bill remarked.

"Seemed she was ridin' a little slow," Neville said, shifting his stance uncomfortably. He wasn't about to admit to the old codger that over the past miles the horse had gotten unsteady in her gait.

"Well, she run her course." Bill started to scratch his head and continued on thoughtfully. "Could put her out to pasture, I reckon. Though kindest thing to suggest would be to let the poor animal rest." He turned to expectorate some tobacco juice into a pile of hay. "Could do it for yuh. Only cost yuh five dollars. Ain't a stranger when it comes to puttin' an animal outta its misery."

Neville responded with an insulted growl. "Listen, mister, I come here to sell her, not to have *you* tell me I gotta pay to have her shot."

Bill went on the defensive. "Whoa now. I ain't *tellin'* you nothing. Just suggestin'. Gotta be your choice, naturally."

Neville noticed the man's sudden jitteriness and decided to take advantage of the moment.

"Tell yuh what," he said. "Seein' that you're so intent on takin' my horse out back—or wherever yuh do it, I'll give you my own offer. I'll let you take her to pasture for twenty-five . . . no, make it fifty dollars."

"Fifty!" Bill exclaimed. "Can sell yuh a fresh one for sixty-five."

"Fifty," Neville repeated.

"Could probably work you a deal on a trade—"

"Fifty," Neville cut in again.

"Look, mister, I ain't tryin' to cheat you," Bill said, his jaw working around the wad of tobacco.

"'Course not," Neville said sardonically. "Met a lot of you upright horse traders during my travels. Just wanta fair shake for both of us."

Bill cleared his throat. "And your idea of a fair shake . . . ?"

Neville gave a casual shrug. "Told yuh. Fifty dollars."

"You're forgettin', you come to me," Bill reminded sharply.

"That's right," Neville agreed. "And since I'm givin' you first chance to buy, only fair you should make me a good offer."

Bill looked as if he were getting ready to state another

objection. But a quick glance into Neville's dark, brooding eyes halted him.

"I'll go as high as thirty. No more," Bill said adamantly.

Neville considered the offer. He knew his horse wasn't worth fifty dollars, but he had to have some room to negotiate. In truth he was hoping for twenty-five. He was coming out ahead. Still, he didn't want to seem too eager and gave a reluctant nod.

"Thirty-two," he then said. "You're forgettin' to add in the saddle."

Bill nodded back to him and he hobbled into his office. Neville sauntered in behind him. Bill went straight to the drawer where he kept his cash box. He flipped through the currency and counted out three ten-dollar bills and two silver dollar coins, thrusting the money into Neville's outstretched hand. Bill then hastily closed the lid and returned the cash box to the drawer.

"Much obliged," Neville said, politely tipping the brim of his Stetson.

Their business completed, Bill made it plain he would prefer if Neville left his office. But Neville remained where he was, standing just inside the doorway.

"Would prefer this done nice and legal like," he said.

Bill was flustered and didn't know what Neville was talking about.

"A bill of sale," Neville explained patiently.

"You *rob* me and you ask for a bill of sale," Bill blurted out, suddenly adopting an indignant tone.

"No one's robbin' you," Neville said innocently. "We worked out a fair business deal."

"Fair? You's the one what come out ahead," Bill said miserably. "Shouldn'ta gave yuh more than ten bucks for that broken-down nag."

"Well, you can sleep well tonight knowin' yuh done a good turn," Neville said with a half smile.

"Sleep good 'nuff," Bill mumbled under his breath.

Huffing, Bill pulled out his ledger and began to write out

a receipt. He stopped, looked up at Neville, and asked, "Would help if'n yuh give me your name."

"Smith," Neville replied, still holding the half smile. "Just jot down Smith."

Neville grabbed his saddle pack from Lulubell, brushed her nuzzle tenderly, and walked from the stable, not looking back even as he heard the horse grunt as she watched him leave.

He knew it probably wasn't wise for him to stay around town much longer, but he was in kind of a dilemma with no horse and only thirty-two dollars in his poke. He decided to find a restaurant, get a meal, and figure out his next move.

It proved to be a fortuitous decision.

While sitting at his corner table waiting for his order of baked ham, mashed potatoes, peas, and corn bread drizzled with syrup, he overheard a rather gruff-looking fellow with lion's-mane hair complaining to his companion that he'd recently lost two of his ranch hands, who'd decided to travel north to Colorado and search for gold. The California gold rush had inspired adventurous spirits to seek out the next valuable gold deposit, and rumors had been spreading about an ore discovery at Cripple Creek. Neville listened with interest and considered how that might have been the path for him to pursue back when he still had funds. It would have taken him far from the state and his pursuers and maybe, with luck, he could have parlayed his thirty thousand dollars into a bonanza. Now, though, he would be satisfied simply to find honest work on a farm. The thought of hard work and sweat appealed to him because he could see no better antidote to stave off the guilt that stubbornly and persistently gnawed at his innards, allowing him barely a moment's peace.

He kept one ear attuned to the talk going on at the next table while he ate his meal, barely tasting the food as he decided to ask the man for a job. Finally, when it looked as if the man, whose name Neville overheard was Carter, and his companion were getting ready to leave, Neville stood up and approached their table. He politely introduced himself as Tom Smith. He apologized for listening in on their conversation but said he was looking for a job. Carter sat back down in his chair and with perceptive eyes studied the young man. Having barely eaten over the past weeks, Neville didn't present himself as the sturdiest specimen. He wasn't surprised when Carter almost immediately remarked on that, adding that the work on his cattle ranch was hard labor and generally lasted from sunup to sundown. Neville resisted saying that he'd had no experience working with cattle but did say he'd spent a lot of years laboring those exact same hours. A couple of good meals under his belt and he'd be ready to go. Carter continued looking closely at Neville, his expression doubtful, but after several moments he breathed in deeply and, following a slow exhale, said, "Well, can't afford to be too particular who I hire. Always the risk I could lose more men to this gold fever. All right, young fella, I'm willing to take a chance on yuh."

Before Neville could proffer his thanks, Carter brandished a finger and added, "But just to let you know, it's a trial. For a week. I like your work, I'll keep you on. If not, you're entitled to a full week's pay."

Neville nodded. "Fair 'nuff."

Carter finally extended his hand, and Neville reached out to clasp it.

"Name's Carter Wilde."

"When can I start?" Neville wanted to know.

Carter was impressed with the young man's eagerness. "Could use yuh tomorrow, if'n you're up to it. Get out to the ranch 'fore sunup and you can start the day with a good breakfast."

Neville shifted his eyes and looked a little embarrassed. "Only thing is I'll need a way to get out to your spread. Hadda sell my horse. Had no other way to eat."

Carter thought for a moment. Then he said, "Tell yuh what, Smith. Fetch your belongings and you can ride out with me."

Again Neville seemed uneasy. "Ain't really got no

belongings, either. Just what's in my saddle pack over by the table."

"Well, bring what yuh got," Carter said. "We'll get yuh settled and not only feed you a breakfast but get a night's supper into you, as well."

Neville was now a man, but as the weeks passed and he did his work, primarily raising hay and feed grains for the other ranch livestock yet accepting any chore assigned without complaint, he recognized that he had been given a second opportunity to make good with his life and to earn the respect of a man he admired. Carter Wilde was a widower and childless, but he took to his new worker in a way that was familiar to Neville, as it brought back memories of Sheriff Dan. Carter employed a number of ranch hands since his property was so expansive, stretching far into the valley, but he seemed to take a special liking to Neville. For one thing, Neville worked so hard and willingly that Carter soon didn't see the need to immediately employ a second hand as was his intention, so purely from an economic standpoint Neville earned favor from his boss. Carter also appreciated that, while at first rather taciturn, Neville began opening up to him about certain aspects of his life. For "Tom Smith," however, there remained particular details that Tom Neville was not about to reveal, even as he felt he could trust his boss.

At first Neville's fellow workers were amused by his enthusiasm for his work and on occasion even sloughed off from their own labor knowing that eventually Neville would get around to finishing their chores, but it didn't take long for some of the men, egged on by a bully and belligerent braggart named Dave Crosby, who also happened to be the ranch foreman, to resent the obvious favoritism shown Neville by Mr. Wilde. They also weren't impressed by what they saw as his unfriendliness, demonstrated by his refusing to join the men in town on Saturday nights after being paid their wages. Neville wasn't intentionally being rude. He chose not to go along only because he had his sights on buying his own farm and wanted to save every penny he could. He saw how these men drank and gambled and how some were flat broke come Sunday morning. Often he was approached for a loan 'til payday and Neville never obliged, incurring further dislike from the men. But that wasn't much of a concern. It was more important for Neville to set aside that nest egg than to be liked by his coworkers.

One late autumn Saturday night while relaxing with Carter on the porch while the other men were in town blowing their pay on women and drink, Neville got the urge to reveal a bit more of his past. Carter already knew about his tough years growing up with a brutal man whom Neville had difficulty acknowledging as his pa. Carter had also learned about the special significance of the ten-dollar gold eagle Neville carried with him and why he refused to part with it even during his tough times. Now Neville was tempted to tell him a little about his special relationship with Sheriff Dan and Sadie. He'd never shared his feelings about the couple with anyone and at times wished that he could. He thought that by remembering them in this fashion it might ease a little of the pain that still burdened him. He felt he could speak openly to Carter, though naturally Neville had to be careful not to reveal too much. Though the events were far in his past, he was still considered a criminal—a fugitive who likely still had a price on his head. That was a reality he'd had to carry with him—his own private purgatory. On this night Carter didn't say much, but he listened to Neville while sucking on his pipe, with its aroma of sweet tobacco adding a pleasant fragrance to the still and cool of the country air.

Perhaps what happened was lucky, for Neville was feeling so comfortable talking to Carter that he might have let the secret of his past slip out. In the distance both men could hear hoofbeats rise from the quiet of the valley, rapidly approaching the ranch house. Neville and Carter looked at each other, and then Carter got to his feet and moved toward the edge of the porch. He squinted as the riders slowed their horses as they neared the house. Dave Crosby was at the lead.

"Boys back a little early," Carter observed nonchalantly.

Almost from the first day Neville started work at the ranch, Dave Crosby had decided to hold a strong objection toward him. Looking for any reason to intensify this enmity, he wasn't impressed seeing Neville and the boss sitting cozy on the front porch, and he showed his disapproval by eyeing Neville tightly, though speaking directly to his boss.

"Town's deader than a doornail," Crosby said in a gravelly voice, his breath redolent of alcohol, closing the distance between them.

"First time I ever heard yuh complain of that, Dave," Carter said.

Crosby was swaying unsteadily on his saddle, as were most of the men who had ridden back with him. There were only five; the rest had decided to remain in town to seek out their own individual diversions.

"Well, you boys look pretty well liquored up," Carter commented. "Might not be a bad idea if'n you all head to the bunkhouse 'fore one of yuh takes a tumble." He added, "Lotta work to be done in the comin' weeks. Can't afford no broken legs . . . or necks."

Crosby tossed Neville a look that seemed to say Carter had all the help he needed so long as he kept the new man all cozied up to him.

"Thought we might take in a few hands of cards," Crosby said, shifting to a more agreeable mood. "Like it if'n Smith might join us. Ever do any card playin', Smith?"

Neville stood up from his rocker and walked beside Carter, resting his hands on the porch railing.

"Some," he replied.

Crosby said with a grin, "Well, Smith, don't mean no offense but you ain't been the friendliest cuss since yuh come out to the ranch. Best way to get to know someone is over a friendly hand of poker."

Carter spoke up before Neville could answer. "Seein' the

condition you boys are in, think Tom here might have an advantage."

Crosby massaged the whiskers along his jaw as he considered.

"Could be," he muttered. Then he snapped his fingers with a flourish. "Tell yuh what, then. Since this is just intended for us to get friendly, what say we play for penny stakes?"

Carter spoke to the group as a whole. "You still have some of your pay?"

Grinning, Crosby twisted his head to look at his men, who likewise were smiling.

"Sure," Crosby answered Carter. "And ain't that a helluva thing?"

Neville knew he couldn't refuse the invitation without the potential for trouble, given that these men were loaded up with whiskey and likely quick to take offense, and he gave an affirmative nod.

"All right," he said. "Penny stakes."

Crosby wore a peculiar smile. "Let us get these horses unsaddled and we'll meet yuh at the bunkhouse in, say, fifteen minutes."

Once the men rode off toward the barn, Carter looked at Neville and held his eyes steady until Neville turned his head toward him.

"Tom, I seen what's been goin' on here 'tween you and them," he said with a hint of concern.

"I ain't got no problem with the men," Neville replied with a casual shrug.

"Know *you* ain't," Carter agreed. "But I know some of those boys don't cotton to you."

Neville smiled wryly. "Known that within the first coupla days."

Carter spoke to the point. "Tom, they know they can't start no trouble without riskin' their jobs, so up to now they've kept themselves behaved. But it's Dave Crosby I'd keep a watch on. Seein' how he is tonight, stinkin' of liquor, him wantin' to pull you into a game of poker . . . Well, just be careful, that's all I'm sayin'."

Neville lifted his eyes to focus on the night skies, alive with the brilliance of countless twinkling stars, spread out high over the valley. He thought how he liked it out here and wasn't about to do anything to incite trouble.

He said good night to Carter, hitched up his trousers, and started to walk the short distance to the bunkhouse. Carter's words did generate some concern, but he had no choice but to join the men in their card game; otherwise they might have more reason to harbor hostility toward him. A light glowed from inside the bunkhouse, and already he could hear raucous talk and laughter going on among the men.

As he stood outside the doorway, he tried to convince himself that the men just wanted to be friendly. But he truthfully couldn't be sure that was their intention. They were a hard bunch and they were drunk. He just hoped there wouldn't be any trouble that he couldn't handle peaceably.

Neville walked inside and saw three of the five men sitting at a square table in the center of the room sharing swallows from a jug of corn whiskey. The other two ranch hands were watching from their bunks, one sitting upright, the other stretched out on his side.

Crosby came across as accommodating, inviting Neville to join them at the table with a sweeping gesture of his hand. His voice was loud, boisterous.

"C'mon, Tom, let's see if you can't win yourself some money tonight," he said. "Stud or draw?"

Neville shook his head to indicate that he had no preference. Then he smiled tightly and seated himself in the chair opposite Crosby. He even took a swallow of the corn whiskey once the jug was passed to him. This was a new experience, drinking rotgut with ranch hands. All of his drinking had been in saloons, mainly premium liquor when he'd had the money; he'd never drunk homemade hooch and he couldn't say he cared for the taste of it. Nor the effects that came upon him just moments later. He didn't want to appear unsociable to these boys, not knowing if they might just be waiting for an opportunity to take offense, but if he drank much more of that whiskey he'd likely find himself on the floor staring bleary-eyed up at the rafters.

Keeping a sly eye on Neville, Crosby riffled the edges of the deck and began shuffling the cards, dealing to himself and the other three players. The two men on their bunks continued to watch with interest.

"Now let's have us some fun," Crosby said as he unfolded his hand . . .

About a half hour later, after several hands had been played, Neville was ahead of the game with his penny-ante winnings. The last hand he won with a pair of deuces against an ace high. Not only were Crosby and the others too drunk even to recognize the suits they held, but Neville had learned some tricks of his own after all those years of being taken by professional card sharps.

Neville decided to call it a night. He stood up, pocketed his winnings, and prepared to step outside for some air before retiring.

Crosby, whose head was bowed, lifted his face and glared at Neville through glazed and bloodshot eyes.

"You ain't goin' nowhere, Smith. I got a right to win back my losses," he said, slurring his words so that it came out "losshesh."

Neville was amused. Between the three of them their losses amounted to just five dollars and thirty-eight cents. Hardly enough to get riled up over.

"Not tonight," he said. He stretched and yawned. "Takin' in some air, then gettin' ready for bed."

Crosby looked at him oddly, his features twisted. "What're yuh talkin' 'bout, bed? We don't gotta work tomorrow. It's Sunday. Got the whole day to sleep."

"Makes no never mind. Been a long week and I'm tired," Neville said conclusively.

Crosby grunted and thrust himself aggressively from the table and staggered forward a few steps. His face was mottled, ravaged by excessive drink; his head was lolling and he could barely keep himself upright, holding his body steady by clutching the edge of the table. But he was ready for a fight.

Neville cast his eyes at the other two men seated at the table. Both looked too drunk to want to involve themselves in whatever Crosby had in mind. The two men still on their bunks also didn't make a move. One, in fact, merely rolled over to face the wall; he found the prospect of sleeping off the effects of the night's liquor more appealing than watching another bunkhouse brawl. Maybe these men didn't particularly care for Neville, but it was Dave Crosby alone who wanted to challenge him.

"I been wantin' to knock you on your ass from the first time I saw yuh," Crosby said belligerently.

"Wouldn't advise it, Dave, not tonight," Neville cautioned. "You can't hardly stand."

Crosby spoke with drunken bravado. "Don't worry none 'bout me. It'll be you what's layin' on the ground."

Neville had never been in a fight in his life. Had Crosby been sober he could well picture the outcome, for Crosby was bigger and surely stronger than Neville, but Neville knew he had the advantage tonight. He was just grateful that when that jug got passed around earlier, although he made it appear he was taking generous swigs, he'd prudently taken only the smallest sips.

He sighed resignedly. "Still think you're makin' a mistake, Dave. But if'n you're insistent, let's step outside and get this over with."

He turned to start for the door—and before he knew what was happening he was tackled from behind and thrown with impact onto the floor, twisting his head to avoid slamming his face full onto the solid wood planking. He was then wrestled onto his side. Strong arms held tight around his waist, pinning his arms against his sides; Crosby unfairly had given himself the edge. Neville struggled against the strength of the man's grip, trying to free at least one of his arms so that he could fight back. Even though Crosby was slobbering drunk, Neville was surprised at the power of the man; he felt as if his guts were being compressed as Crosby squeezed a viselike grip around his midsection. Neville's head began to swim. He found that he could barely breathe and was soon gasping for air.

Neville knew that if he couldn't release himself he'd likely pass out and be at the mercy of Crosby, and in Crosby's alcohol-crazed state Neville couldn't guess what the brute was capable of. Neville took a second or two to relax and, as he hoped, by weakening his resistance, he could also feel Crosby loosening, if only just a little, his hold.

Then, summoning every ounce of strength he possessed, Neville flexed his biceps and thrust out his elbows and managed to get his right arm free before Crosby relocked his grip. Because of all the alcohol he'd ingested, Crosby's energy was rapidly fading; he'd put out too much effort at the beginning and couldn't sustain his advantage.

The tables quickly turned. Neville could feel the strength ebbing from Crosby, and in a quick maneuver he was able to flip him onto his back, using his free arm as leverage. He could hear how Crosby's breathing had become labored from all his effort. Neville continued to twist his body until he completely broke free of Crosby's grip, and then, scrambling to his knees, he took hold of Crosby by the shirt collar and tugged him upright into a sitting position. The exertion had sped the liquor through his system and Crosby was totally spent. Still, with his adrenaline pumping and his system fueled with a boiling rage, Neville was prepared to do to the man what Crosby had in mind for him. Unexpectedly his brain flashed back to those beatings the old man had given him, where he never fought back because he thought that to hit his pa would have been wrong. But now he could defend himself, no matter what it took. He steadied Crosby and with one hand closed tightly around his collar he drew back his fist, prepared to pummel Crosby until his fat, semiconscious face resembled a bloody pulp.

He heard a couple of the men in the room, those whom he had assumed were Crosby's "friends," urging him on like eager spectators at a bare-knuckle match.

"Go on, Tom, finish it!"

"'Bout time somebody wiped the floor with him."

"Didn't come at yuh fair, Smith. Give it to him! He deserves it!"

These reactions were unexpected and both astounded and troubled Neville . . . as did his own urge to follow through and beat a man who had become helpless in his grip. Crosby was a bully who showed he was also a coward who wouldn't fight fair. Neville understood that if he hit him now he wouldn't be any better, and he couldn't conceive of lowering himself to Crosby's level.

His fist still aggressively poised, Neville looked at Crosby, who was regarding him dumbly, his comprehension now seemingly numb, gurgles emanating from his throat, traces of drool glistening his chin. Despite his play-dirty tactics, Crosby not only had been defeated, he was a man left without much dignity.

Neville's face reflected his disdain. He shoved Crosby backward so that his torso twisted and he landed flat on his stomach with his legs bent at an awkward angle. He lifted himself feebly and unsteadily onto his elbows. Then he raised his head and his half-closed eyes shifted to search the faces of the others in the room. The two card players, though heavy-lidded themselves, regarded him with disgust. The man still watching from his bunk merely joined his companion and turned his head toward the wall to get some shut-eye.

The next morning Dave Crosby quit. He rode away from the ranch with an aching body and raging hangover before sunup, before even having breakfast. No one seemed to show much regret at his departure.

Later in the day, while the men were engaged in their usual Sunday afternoon pastime of tossing horseshoes, a recreation they indulged in with the utmost seriousness, Neville spotted Carter walking toward the barn, and when the older man saw him he gestured for Neville to come see him.

Neville watched the final toss of the first game before he walked over to join his boss. The horseshoe clanged against the stake and a loud whoop went up among the men who had placed bets on that two-man team. Neville didn't play, but he enjoyed watching, and today no one was teasing him for not participating in the Sunday tournament.

Carter, who worked as hard as any of the men he employed, had just started pitching hay into a sloping pile at the far side of the barn. Neville picked up a piece of straw from the floor, sliding it between his lips, and sauntered up next to him.

Carter kept working while he talked. "Heard 'bout what happened last night. Told yuh they was lookin' for trouble with yuh."

Neville sucked on his straw. "Not *they*, Mr. Wilde. Just Dave Crosby."

Carter stopped pitching hay long enough to wipe the sweat from his brow with a back sweep of his wrist.

"Fact them others kinda sided with me," Neville added.

"Always a troublemaker, Crosby was," Carter said, drawing a breath. "Liked to cause a ruckus. Coupla times I hadda pay his way outta jail when his Saturday celebratin' got a mite outta hand. Kept him on only 'cause he was a good worker. Well, was 'til I made him my foreman. Big mistake. Can't afford to be losin' workers, but won't miss havin' him 'round here tryin' to stir things up."

"Don't seem like any of the men are much upset, either," Neville remarked.

"Doubtful they are," Carter confirmed. He resumed forking hay. "Been my experience that you'll find someone like Dave Crosby at almost every ranch west of the Mississippi. The one who rides in, sizes things up, and with a boast and some outright gall puts himself in charge. Men might not necessarily like it, but most of the time they go along 'cause the fella knows how to pull the right strings, usually by showin' 'em a good time, how best to blow off steam. Then to really show what a big man he is, he finds someone he can turn the others ag'in. Pretty much describes Crosby and the way I saw it 'round here. Yet once you get rid of the bad apple, the others generally all fall back into line. The trick is not to make that mistake ag'in."

"Think you might have trouble with him down the road?" Neville inquired.

"Not likely," Carter replied. He looked straight at Neville, his expression set and serious. "In any case, wouldn't be me who'd have to deal with it." Then he tossed a playful wink. "That'd be your problem."

"Got lucky once," Neville said. "Don't wanta chance it a second time."

"Well, reckon it hadda be," Carter drawled. "The men wasn't ag'in the two of yuh havin' a fair fight, but they lost all respect for Dave when he pulled that dirty trick. Fellas here might be rough-edged, but they seem to follow a principle."

Carter drove his pitchfork into a square bundle of hay stacked against the side of the barn and rolled down the sleeves of his shirt.

"Anyhow, got somethin' else I wanta discuss with you," he said.

The upshot of their talk that afternoon was that Carter wanted to put Neville on as his new ranch foreman. Neville was almost knocked backward into the hay pile Carter had been building when his boss offered him the job. He naturally was enticed by the substantial raise in pay but had doubts that the hands who had worked at the ranch longer than him would accept him as someone from whom they would be expected to take orders. He felt it only fair to express this concern to Carter.

To Carter it was a minor worry.

"An opportunity like this only comes along once, son," he said, his words blunt and direct. "Ain't no spur-of-the-moment decision, either. Been thinkin' 'bout this for a while. Knew that Dave was eventually gonna do somethin' to shorten his stay; saw that maverick nature in him from the start, so I kept my eyes open. Yeah, you ain't been here as long as the others, but you caught on quick and you do the work."

Neville started to interject, and Carter, knowing where he was headed, put up his hand to halt him.

He said, "Know that bein' a ranch hand ain't part of your plans, and I ain't got no problem with that. You got a right to build your own life and I feel privileged to help, I truly mean that. But 'til that time comes, you're the man I want to give me a hand managing this ranch."

Neville was forthright. "Probably can't promise yuh more than a year."

"Can get a lot of work done in that time," was all Carter said.

Neville lowered his head and rubbed the back of his neck. "Still don't know how the others'll take to it. Ain't hardly the type in their eyes to be tellin' another man his business."

Carter draped an affectionate arm around Neville's shoulders.

"Depends how yuh see it, Tom," he said solemnly. "You earned a new respect last night. Not 'cause yuh fought Dave Crosby, but that you didn't hit him when he was down. You fought fair and the men think favorable of you for that."

Neville gave a modest shrug. "Don't take no special pride in that."

"Maybe not," Carter went on. "But I can tell yuh, gettin' that bunch on your side ain't somethin' that comes easy."

"Reckon I can't say no to your offer, Mr. Wilde," Neville said after a few moments' consideration. "If'n yuh think I can handle it, I'll take the job."

With his new responsibility Neville not only earned respect from his men, he also developed respect for himself. He had remained haunted by the crime that blemished his past and the toll it had taken on those close to him. But he learned that he could never go on profitably in his life by forever acknowledging that brand he'd stamped upon himself.

Neville worked hard over the next year, and Carter was

pleased with his effort, never once regretting his decision to make Neville his foreman. Neville took his job seriously and not only oversaw the daily operations of the ranch but pitched in to help whenever necessary, regardless of the task. If manure needed shoveling and no one was around to do it, Neville rolled up his sleeves and literally dug in. He enjoyed manual labor and appreciated how it strengthened his physique and, most importantly, kept his brain free from those troubling thoughts that on occasion would start to resurface.

Neville was careful to save his money. Only on rare occasions would he join the others on a Saturday night jaunt into town, where he'd limit his drinking to a glass of beer and a shot of whiskey. It continued to amaze him how carelessly his coworkers would throw their money around, often spending a whole week's wages on a single night of carousing. Yet Neville remembered it wasn't so very long ago that he had done the same, though the cash that he spread about among barkeeps, thirsty saloon patrons, gamblers, and dance hall girls was money not earned by hard sunup-to-sundown labor.

It wasn't that Neville didn't trust his coworkers—he was just being prudent; so outside of a few small withdrawals, he had asked Carter to hold on to his wages, and Carter was happy to oblige. Neville had figured that by the end of the year he'd have sufficient funds to put a hefty down payment on a fine piece of property. He was especially grateful when Carter had offered to keep an eye and ear open for any farmer wanting to sell his land. Farming was a skill with which Neville knew he would have to reacquaint himself. He wished he could have had more practical experience working at the ranch, but although Carter's ranch performed some farming, its primary function was the raising of livestock, and supervising cattle was Neville's main responsibility since accepting his promotion. He doubted he would be owning a cattle ranch anytime soon.

The year passed quickly, and finally Neville decided the time had come to collect his pay and move on. Carter was

reluctant to see him go, but his queries had secured for
Neville a parcel of land over in the next county. It wasn't
prime land; the owner suffered from rheumatism and had
let the fields grow over and they would have to be cleared
for planting, and the dwelling on the property was just a
weather-beaten shack that provided shelter but not much
else and would need a lot of repair work to make it halfway
comfortable. But the spread could be gotten for a fair price.
No down payment but an outright purchase. Carter had
taken it upon himself to wire the money to the seller,
explaining to Neville that it was more prudent to handle the
transaction that way than to have Neville travel the long
distance carrying so much cash on his person. Neville appreciated his consideration. Still, he would take with him two
hundred dollars, part of which was a bonus given by Carter
in appreciation for all of his work. The ranch had prospered
and had earned a substantial profit during the year that Neville had been foreman.

There was one other show of gratitude provided by Carter. He gave to Neville as a gift the horse he had ridden
during his stay at the ranch—a handsome and sturdy black-
and-white pinto that Neville had named Daniel. Neville had
grown fond of the animal, taking extra care during his off
hours to care for him, and it was evident to Carter that the
two had formed a bond.

And then the night before Neville was to leave, Carter
took him into his house, where they sat in the spacious living
room, which was gaudily decorated in a sportsman style
with trophy heads and stretched animal skins mounted
against the stone walls, and the two shared a glass of brandy.

After a while Carter excused himself, and he rose from
his chair and went into another room in the house. When
he returned he was holding in one hand a rhinestone-studded
gun belt with an ivory-handled, nickel-plated .45 Colt Peacemaker resting inside the holster. Neville gave him an uncomprehending look. Carter stood before Neville, his back to
the flames crackling in the big stone fireplace.

"I remember how you told me yuh had to sell your gun

along with your horse for eatin' money," he said solemnly. "Was thinkin' 'bout lettin' you hold on to the one I gave yuh while you was workin' here. Then decided I'd like yuh to have somethin' a mite more special. A man on his own is wise to carry with him some protection. I'd like for you to take this."

Carter held out the gun belt and revolver for Neville to accept.

Neville hesitated and looked a tad uncomfortable, and he shifted in his seat.

"Mr. Wilde," he said. "Well, sir, the fact is . . . I ain't never fired no gun before. Hell, never even owned a gun. So . . . kinda wasn't bein' truthful when I told yuh what I did 'bout havin' to sell it."

Carter responded to Neville's words with bewilderment.

"Never owned a gun!" he exclaimed. "By God, the saints musta been lookin' out for you, son. Don't know of too many men ridin' overland in this territory who coulda survived without carrying a sidearm."

"Never ran into the kind of trouble where I needed a gun," Neville told him with a shrug.

Carter still expressed disbelief. "If the saints ain't pre-servin' you, you're leadin' a charmed life."

Although Neville didn't voice it, he hardly considered that he'd led a charmed life. Yet as he thought about it, maybe he *had* been awfully lucky. Riding all those miles through uncertain territory, unprotected against Indians or bushwhackers, yet carrying a satchel full of cash in his saddlebag. He must have been a damn fool, yet guns had never been a part of his life—not even during his time with Sheriff Dan. It did of a sudden make him curious why the sheriff never took the time to teach him how to use a firearm, not even when he was apprenticing as a deputy. Maybe those lessons had still been to come, if not for . . .

Neville took a swallow of his brandy to push back an unwelcome memory.

Carter rubbed his fingers along his jaw in a slow, rumi-nating gesture. "Don't feel right, Tom—me handin' over this gun belt and Colt with you not knowin' how to use 'em proper."

Neville lowered his eyes and said nothing.

"Yet . . . don't feel right lettin' you ride off without protection," Carter added with a knitting of his heavy brow, his fingers continuing to massage the faint gray stubble on his chin.

The room fell quiet as Carter gingerly placed the gun belt and Colt revolver on the long center table. He took his brandy and swirled the amber liquor in the snifter as he stepped back toward the fireplace, gazing at the snapping flames and glowing embers in the hearth.

With his back facing Neville, he contemplated how best to handle this.

"Tom," he said, speaking decisively, "I'd like to ask you to stay on for a coupla days. We'll spend that time learnin' yuh how to shoot. Can't teach yuh everything, but so long as you know the fundamentals I'll feel a lot better seein' yuh go." He shook his head and said in wonderment: "Never met a man out West yet who couldn't handle a gun."

Neville swallowed his brandy and held out his glass for a refill. Carter smiled and obliged.

"A man unarmed is playin' against the odds, Tom," he said as he poured brandy from the decanter into Neville's glass. "So far seems to me you've beaten them odds, but a man's luck can't hold out forever."

It proved a whole new experience for Neville, going out into the field and practicing how to handle a gun. His awkwardness was humiliating for Neville at first, but Carter was a patient and understanding teacher. He also proved himself mighty adept at manipulating a pistol, his skill and knowledge impressive. There were also the little tricks. Carter had suggested filing down the sight so that the gun wouldn't catch on the holster. He also mentioned the importance of keeping the inside of the holster lightly lubricated so that the gun could be drawn swiftly, if need be. Speed and accuracy were the two most important elements in handling a gun, Carter had explained. He cited the gunslinging accomplishments of men whose reputations Neville was familiar with. Carter himself had mastered both elements, and he complimented Neville on how quickly he had picked up the basics. He seemed to possess a natural talent, and this realization came as a complete surprise to someone who, in truth, was somewhat timid around firearms. Neville knew he would never win a fast-draw competition, nor did he have the inclination to become a professional gunslinger, but he had matured enough to know the value of carrying a gun. Having a Colt .45 resting at his side and knowing how to use it would allow him to ride along the open, barren trail he soon would be traversing with a certain confidence.

TEN

Neville extended his stay at the ranch by nearly a week, and he rode out on a Sunday morning after wolfing down a hearty breakfast. Until he got himself settled, it would be the last tasty meal he would be eating for a while.

He was sad to be parting ways with Carter, but after all his travels and travails he was ready to finally strike out on his own. Neville understood that if he didn't grab this opportunity now, chances were he never would.

He'd also decided to return to his true name. With the past behind him, he felt he no longer had to deny who he was. Tom Smith would be no more.

The sun rode with Neville that morning, though it took until close to noon for the expanse of warmth to overtake the morning cool. Still, it was a refreshing ride and Neville was eager to see the property that he and Carter had gone out together to survey only a month before—but upon which he would now be settling as its owner. Through his enthusiasm at the time, in his mind's eye he recalled a working paradise.

It was a two-day ride, but since the property had already

been secured and paid for, there was no rush for him to arrive. Neville enjoyed taking the opportunity to savor the clean countryside trail that would lead him into Clarefield County. He hadn't been able to enjoy much solitude working at the ranch over the past year and a half, and he wanted to take advantage of this time alone before setting to work on his land.

His land. Neville never could have imagined how liberating that would sound. As he thought about it, he realized that he had never owned anything that was truly his. Even the ten-dollar gold eagle he still carried with him . . . he was merely the custodian, for he had not forgotten the promise he had made both to himself and to the spirit of Mr. Caulfield that one day he would pass on the coin to someone who might benefit from possessing it, as had Neville. He acknowledged that good fortune as he and his handsome horse Daniel enjoyed the journey toward their new home.

The day he finally arrived, he eased himself down from Daniel and surveyed his property with a much more discerning eye. It was not exactly the paradise that he recalled it to be, and after drawing a breath, Neville muttered to his horse, "Can see I got my work cut out."

The horse nickered.

Neville looked askance at Daniel and smiled crookedly. "Yeah, well, don't think you're gettin' off any easier."

O ver the next several months Neville kept busy. Between work on clearing the weeds and other unwanted growth from the land, then tending to the soil to make it suitable for growing crops, and leftover hours spent fixing up the walls and interior of the deteriorating old shack that he preferred to call a cabin, and which he determined he would eventually tear down to build another house from scratch, his days began before sunup and went clean through to after sunset. He couldn't say the work was easy, but for the first time, working solely for himself, he felt fulfilled.

Unlike the stolen payroll money, which he had spent

carelessly and frivolously, he was prudent with the dollars he had earned from his work at Carter Wilde's ranch. He purchased only the necessities. He ate sparingly and mostly from canned goods he picked up at the store in the town of Still Bend, which was only about a half day's ride from his place.

He generally rode into town once every two weeks to stock up at Ferguson's Emporium (which was a rather elaborate title for what was essentially a general store), starting his ride into Still Bend just after sunrise. One Wednesday, the day he usually set aside for purchasing goods and supplies, he strolled inside the store and was surprised to see a pretty new face behind the counter, busily writing numbers into a ledger. The girl smiled politely at him as he entered and then quickly returned to her work. As Neville found his eyes drawn toward her, a memory was ignited in his brain—one that he didn't know if he should acknowledge or dismiss. He was suddenly reminded of Jessica.

He took his time browsing around the store, idly perusing the merchandise. The shelves were stocked with a variety of goods, from canned food and candy to clothing, tools, and building supplies. He knew precisely what his purchases were to be but he purposely dallied, waiting to see if the girl might ask if he needed any assistance. He tossed subtle glances her way as he walked down the aisles between the shelves, attempting to attract her attention by pasting a helpless expression across his features. To his dismay it looked as if the girl wasn't paying him any attention.

Finally he heard her speak to him from behind the counter. Her voice was pleasant and sweet, if perfunctory.

"May I help you, sir?"

Neville maintained his perplexed expression as he turned his head toward her.

"Is there anything in particular you're looking for?" the girl asked.

"Uh, well, actually . . ." Neville started to say.

The girl closed the ledger, laid down her pencil, and walked out from behind the counter. The first thing Neville noticed as she got nearer was that she carried with her the fragrance of lavender.

Neville was grateful no one else was working in the store at the time, like Mrs. Ferguson, the owner, who would recognize him and know from his previous visits that he knew where virtually every item was shelved in the store. With this girl he could come across as unfamiliar with the stock. He went further and explained that this was his first time in the store, and that he'd be appreciative if she'd help him find the goods he was seeking.

"Do you have a list?" she asked.

"List?"

"Of the items you're looking for."

Neville stalled. Then he said, "Uh, no. But I—know what I need."

He sounded unconvincing, and the girl gave him an odd look.

Neville tapped a finger against the side of his head.

"Good memory," he quickly explained.

On a typical shopping day Neville would have been gone from the store in about ten minutes. He'd purchase his items and perhaps share a word or two with either Mrs. Ferguson or her other helper, an old-timer named Ralph, and then be off on the long ride back to his farm, usually getting there before sundown. On this afternoon, however, Neville prolonged his stay by a good quarter hour while he hemmed and hawed over selections he'd usually just pull off the shelf and basket reflexively, without thought or effort. He frequently asked the girl's advice on which brand of a certain item she would recommend—information that she really could not provide, for, as she timidly explained, she'd just started working at the store and was herself still in the process of familiarizing herself with the stock.

"Well," Neville had said, "then maybe we can muddle through this together."

Finally, when he stood at the counter with the girl totaling his purchases, the door to the store opened and Mrs. Ferguson entered. She was a large, broad woman of late middle age whose moon-shaped face always glowed with good humor. She greeted Neville with a friendly smile, which he tentatively returned. He had hoped to be gone before she came back, and now he was hoping she wouldn't say anything to let on that she knew him as a regular customer. He tried to pass her that message by an obvious shifting of his eyes between her and the girl, but the woman seemed oblivious to his gesture.

"Mr. Neville," she said jovially, addressing Neville with the same exaggerated cheeriness with which she greeted all who shopped at her store. "I trust you found everything you're looking for."

The girl stopped what she was doing. Her eyes lifted and slid crossways from Mrs. Ferguson to a suddenly uncomfortable-looking Neville. At first her expression was hard to read, and then a sort of narrow-eyed harshness appeared on her features. It looked as if she were about to say something—perhaps a nasty comment expressing her disapproval at having been tricked. Neville found himself trying to suppress a telling flush and wished he could simply make a quick exit. Whatever the gal might say, Neville didn't welcome it, even as he knew that he damn well deserved it.

He tried to remedy the potentially humiliating situation by speaking favorably about the girl.

"Yes, certainly did, Mrs. Ferguson," he said. "Your new helper here has been very obligin'."

Mrs. Ferguson was pleased. "Well, I'm glad to hear it, Mr. Neville. Sarah actually just started a couple of weeks ago." Her chubby face became thoughtful. "That's right, you two haven't had the chance to meet."

"Oh . . . Sarah's the name," Neville said quietly, throwing the girl a subtle glance.

"Yes," Mrs. Ferguson said. "Wednesday is usually her day off. She's just filling in this afternoon. I had an appointment with Doc Harmon."

"Ain't nothin' serious?" Neville asked with concern— though it was more an attempt to forestall the embarrassment that might still be coming his way.

"Oh no," Mrs. Ferguson reassured him. "Just the usual aches and pains a person of my age has to deal with."

"Glad to hear it," Neville said. "Uh, not the aches and pains, I mean, but that there's nothin' for you to be concerned 'bout."

Mrs. Ferguson, who prided herself on understanding human behavior, detected something slightly amiss with her customer.

"Maybe I should be asking if *you're* feeling all right, Mr. Neville," she said. "You seem a trifle—out of sorts."

Neville replied with an innocuous look. "Me? No. Just puttin' in long hours at the farm. Lotta work to get done 'fore winter comes."

"You shouldn't push yourself too hard, Mr. Neville. You go making yourself ill and you won't be getting *any* work done," Mrs. Ferguson cautioned.

Neville nodded. "True 'nuff."

Still expecting to be humiliated in front of Mrs. Ferguson, Neville tentatively turned his eyes toward the girl named Sarah. But after a couple of tense seconds she merely let out a little sigh, lowered her face, and returned to adding up his purchases. Neville felt relieved and grateful even as he caught Sarah glancing up at him, a coquettish smile on her lips.

"Mr. Neville," she whispered coyly.

And then her smile broadened.

Neville marveled at how changes in his life seemed to occur so rapidly. He never could have guessed when he rode into town that afternoon to shop for supplies that that very evening he would be renting a buggy to take this shop girl, whose full name he was told was Sarah Tafford, for a ride in the valley.

He frankly was surprised that Sarah had agreed to go with him on this little outing. He suspected that Mrs. Ferguson might have had a hand in persuading her to accept his invitation. The woman didn't know Neville outside his

being a regular customer, but later, when he came by the
store just before closing to fetch Sarah, Mrs. Ferguson was
there, and she looked at Neville with a sly, secretive smile
that, to him, didn't seem so mysterious. Her little smile
indicated to Neville that Mrs. Ferguson had encouraged
Sarah in her decision. While waiting for Sarah to get her
wrap from the back room, Neville offered the woman an
appreciative nod. At the least he felt better that she likely
now understood the reason for his earlier awkwardness.

It was a pleasant evening for a ride out into the country.
The temperature was a tad cool, befitting the season, but
the air was mild and fragrant, the skies clear and beginning
to deepen into twilight shades with the promise of a starlit
night ahead. An autumn moon would soon beam brightly
above the wide-open horizon.

Sarah seemed quiet and reserved as they rode. Although
she barely spoke, Neville caught her casting the occasional
furtive glance in his direction while he manned the reins of
the buggy. Mostly she kept her focus on the road ahead,
which stretched far into the grasslands, the trail bisecting
the vastness of the valley as it proceeded up into the rises of
distant western hills and looking to reach beyond into a hidden horizon. Neville could see that not much would be said
unless he came up with something to say. But it was a little
strange for him, as well. He knew nothing about the girl other
than she'd only recently started working at the store and that
he was attracted to her. He wanted to know all he could about
her, of course, but he also didn't want to start pestering her
with questions that she might not be ready to answer. It had
been a long time since he'd had a significant conversation
with a woman. There was never much talk between him and
the whores he'd bedded during those aimless years when he
had a fistful of dollars and an empty heart.

Off to the far left of the road was a grassy incline that
gently sloped down toward a wide and winding river. Neville
noticed a couple of barefooted boys sitting on a log next to
the water holding makeshift fishing rods. Neville silently
wished them luck, though it was unlikely they'd have much

success bringing home supper this late in the day. Neville looked on a little farther and saw what looked to be a perfect spot for a picnic: a soft carpet of rich green grass reaching farther inland from the water's edge surrounded by a cluster of cottonwoods that provided shade and would afford privacy from the intrusion of any passersby. Neville was tempted to pull in the reins and stop for a spell. Just step out of the buggy and indulge in the serenity of the moment by taking a walk toward the riverbank. Before he could suggest the idea to Sarah, he noticed how she shivered and wrapped her shawl tighter around herself.

"You're cold," he said.

Sarah looked at him meekly. "A little, I suppose."

Neville rode on a little farther, deciding what he should do.

"Might be best if we turn back," he finally suggested. "That is, if you're uncomfortable."

Sarah regarded him with a look of disappointment. "But we haven't hardly gone that far." She smiled reassuringly. "I'll be all right."

Neville shook his head decisively. "No. Ain't worth catchin' cold for."

"Really, I'm fine. Besides, doesn't seem right to turn back after you paid for this buggy."

Neville looked at her with pretend surprise. "I did?"

Sarah lowered her eyes to the small, gentle hands folded in her lap and said quietly, "Well, yes. Of course you did. And Aunt Lilah—"

Before she could finish, Neville shifted his eyes toward her questioningly. "Aunt Lilah?"

"Lilah *Ferguson*," Sarah clarified.

"Oh, *Aunt* Lilah," Neville echoed with exaggerated emphasis. He hesitated, then feigned annoyance. "The old busybody."

Sarah snickered.

They were talking, the two of them—the words starting to come easy.

What Sarah said next took him by pleasant surprise.

"Was just thinking, this would be a nice place for a picnic."

Neville turned his head toward her, briefly, before he shifted his eyes back to the road.

"You know," he said. "Was thinkin' the exact same thing."

He pulled rein and straightened in his seat.

"Miss Sarah," he said, speaking formally. "Would you . . . I mean, do yuh think maybe you might like to picnic with me come Saturday?"

Sarah smiled, a little sadly. "I usually work Saturdays."

Neville's face fell in disappointment.

Sarah then brightened. "But because I came in today I think I might be able to talk Aunt Lilah into giving me Saturday afternoon off."

"I could ride out early morning . . . be in town 'fore noon," Neville said eagerly.

Sarah nodded. "I'll be ready."

"Well, in that case I'd better get yuh back to town," Neville said. "Ain't takin' the chance of you gettin' sick and callin' off our picnic."

Sarah suppressed a giggle, amused as Neville energetically flicked the reins, spinning the buggy off the trail and around in a wide semicircle and rode as quick as the wind back to the quaint little community called Still Bend, determined to get Sarah home and intending for her to head straight into the warmth of her bed.

Neville worked harder than usual around his property the next day, deliberately keeping himself busy so that the time would pass quicker. Yet his mind was so preoccupied with thoughts of Sarah and her sweetness and pretty face that when he surveyed his day's labor as evening approached he was surprised at how much he'd accomplished when he could barely remember physically doing the work.

It was only at night when the day's work was done and he had nothing else to occupy his brain that he surrendered to the vulnerability of his thoughts, and questions and doubts started to make disturbing inroads.

One thing he had determined right from the get-go was that he wouldn't offer his intentions to Sarah as quickly as he had with Jessica. Of course he had been younger then, eager and impatient, and most of all naïve, not having experienced life as much as he had since that terrible night at Brewer's Gulch. He'd learned a bit more about women since then, even if intimacy had not been part of his "schooling." Neville would have to proceed more delicately with her, as Sarah seemed to be of a different character when it came to approach. Her emotions were less accessible. That aside, Neville could not dismiss his hope to ask her to marry him . . . when the moment seemed right. Inexperienced in the propriety of romance, the accepted and perhaps expected ways of courtship and proposal, Neville was a man prone simply to surrendering to the desire of his heart, his yearning to share his life with a suitable partner, who would stand beside him through the hardships and accept him and their life together with an unconditional love. A love far removed from what had masqueraded as a marriage between his mother and his cruel and coldhearted pa.

No, what Neville sought was the love more tenderly and genuinely expressed between Sadie and Sheriff Dan. They stood as his example. What he had witnessed between them during his time living in their home was what Neville perceived as the purest kind of love—yet rarely demonstrative. Until Sadie became ill, Neville could not recall much physical affection between the two beyond Sadie pecking Sheriff Dan on the cheek before he went off to work each morning. Sheriff Dan was not given to displays of tenderness, which, knowing the man as he did, Neville could understand. Still, Neville never doubted for an instant that the two of them shared an enduring love, one that transcended the need for physical closeness. A love that Neville secretly envied and now hoped to find and perhaps enjoy in his own life.

The problem he faced was that he didn't have much to offer. He lived in a shack that, unless reinforced, would doubtful withstand a harsh winter. He hadn't started to earn any money from his farming, and likely wouldn't for a while. His own funds were extremely limited.

Alone with his thoughts, he found his romantic leanings challenged by practical considerations, and he had to halt himself from questioning the wisdom of his intentions.

Neville awoke early come Saturday morning, prepared for his ride into Still Bend. As he rode along the trail with the refreshing morning breeze sweeping against his face, he felt the gallop in his heart begin to keep pace with that of his horse, Daniel.

He slowed Daniel to a trot once he entered the town limits. Neville squinted as he rode down the main street. He instantly spotted Sarah standing outdoors on the boardwalk in front of Ferguson's Emporium, picnic basket in hand, awaiting his arrival.

She looked particularly pretty. She was wearing a yellow cotton dress and had a white ribbon in her hair. Neville surrendered to a smile. Then, with a smooth flick of the reins, he directed Daniel toward the boardwalk. He tipped back the brim of his Stetson in a gentlemanly greeting. Sarah responded with a bashful smile.

Neville lifted his eyes skyward. A few powder puff clouds, but otherwise the day was clear and perfect for a country picnic. He was grateful that no rain looked to be forthcoming to disrupt their afternoon.

Neville had left a deposit to reserve the buggy for their outing after returning it to the livery Wednesday evening. The stable manager proved to be a fair sort. Recognizing that Neville had paid for a full two-hour rental but had returned early, he told Neville he would apply the time remaining against the cost of the rental, thus saving Neville some money. Neville was appreciative. Money was becoming scarce and each nickel saved was considered a bonus.

He maneuvered himself down from the saddle, and then, taking Daniel by the reins, he slowly led the horse down the dry mud roads of the main street toward the stable, with

Sarah keeping pace beside them along the wood planking of the boardwalk.

It didn't take long for Neville to notice that the girl seemed to be in a peculiar mood, as if something were troubling her. The apparent happiness she'd expressed at his arrival seemed to have inexplicably vanished. She now looked pensive, even a mite distressed, if Neville was observing her correctly. He sensed that behind the subtlety of her smile Sarah seemed to be hinting at some disturbing news to come.

Neville went inside the stable to leave his horse and asked the stablehand to give Daniel a rubdown. Then he went around back to fetch the buggy. Sarah waited on the street and once the buggy trotted out around the corner and halted, she permitted Neville to step down and assist her aboard. She thanked Neville by offering a polite smile, then sat quietly next to him.

Neville made small talk as they rode the familiar trail. As before, Sarah didn't have much to say; she continued to appear preoccupied. Neville hoped that once they reached the valley Sarah might relax enough to share with him whatever it was that seemed to be affecting her mood.

He parked the buggy next to the cluster of trees on the slope overlooking the river, which both he and Sarah had agreed was a pleasant setting for a picnic. Since the day was warm, the sun bright, they settled under the shade of one of the large Fremont cottonwoods. Sarah spread out a tablecloth and began setting out the food from the basket: specially prepared delicacies including fried chicken, potato salad, green vegetables, and corn bread. There was also a large jar that contained homemade lemonade. Neville thought how he hadn't enjoyed a picnic lunch since those long-ago fishing trips he'd made with Sheriff Dan. Lunches prepared by Sadie which, he recalled, always contained some special surprise for her men.

"Looks like yuh fixed a fine lunch," Neville said, impressed.

Sarah didn't look up at him when she answered. "Actually Aunt Lilah made the lunch."

"Don't do much cookin'?" Neville asked her.

Sarah was quick to answer. "Oh, I enjoy cooking. But Aunt Lilah insisted on preparing this lunch herself."

While Sarah quietly busied herself arranging the lunch, Neville moseyed toward the river's edge, where he gazed out at the mild currents that broke the stillness of the surface. The whisper of a caressing breeze drifted inland from off the water.

He would be feeling pretty good if not for his concerns about Sarah. He couldn't help pondering what had happened since Wednesday to change her mood so conspicuously. She was responding to him almost as if she regretted her decision to join him on this outing. It was hard for Neville not to feel discouraged right about now.

His thoughts were interrupted when he heard Sarah come up behind him.

He turned and looked down into her soft chestnut-colored eyes, framed by long curling lashes. The smile creasing her lips was faint, her expression difficult to decipher. She merely told him that lunch was ready.

Neville started back with her, and as they walked toward the large cottonwood he had a strange sensation. He couldn't explain it, but it was the discomforting feeling that if he turned his eyes away from her, in the next instant she might be gone. Vanished, like a wisp of smoke, as had happened once before in his life: with Jessica. Sarah had to know he was looking at her, but she seemed to avoid his gaze. Perhaps by not meeting his eyes, she might find it easier to talk about whatever seemed to be troubling her without having to deal with an aftermath of guilt.

"Wish you'd just tell me what it is, Sarah," he said, eyeing her firmly. "Whatever it is that's troubling you."

Sarah sighed.

"Seems pretty clear you got somethin' playin' on your mind," Neville added.

Sarah hesitated before she gave him a quick look. But she didn't seem willing to answer him.

Neville decided to let it rest. He couldn't insist that she

tell him what was troubling her. He didn't know Sarah well enough; it wasn't his right. All he could do was wait and see if she might speak when she was ready. The two sat down to eat. Neville hardly had an appetite and munched on a piece of cold chicken that he barely tasted. Sarah just nibbled at her food, her face set in thought. Neville periodically glanced over at her and thought sadly how this was not the girl whose company he had enjoyed just a few nights before.

They were midway through their eating when an impatient Neville finally could no longer resist his curiosity and spoke up. Although frustrated, he struggled to keep the tone of his voice even and compassionate.

"Whatever it is that's troublin' you, Sarah . . . just want yuh to know that you can talk to me."

Sarah sighed. After a lengthy silence she spoke succinctly.

"Reckon it's only fair to tell you. I might be leaving Still Bend come the end of next week."

"Leaving?" Neville said with a curious tilt of his head.

Sarah breathed out again. "Got a telegram Thursday."

Neville blinked. "Telegram?"

Sarah was quiet.

"A fella?" Neville asked.

Sarah surrendered a very faint nod.

"*Your* fella?"

Sarah nodded once more. "I think . . . he's going to ask me to marry him."

Neville found himself at a loss for words.

Sarah started to speak, but the words also failed her.

"Where do you know this fella from?" Neville asked her with a deliberate mild interest.

"A little town outside Tucson, a place called Bradley," Sarah offered.

Neville thought for a moment, then shook his head from side to side as he didn't know of the town.

"My father died about four months ago," Sarah explained solemnly. "My mother hadn't been well, and she went up to Colorado to stay with her sister. After she died just a month

ago I came to Still Bend when Aunt Lilah offered me a job.
I needed the money and, besides, it gave me something to
do while I waited to hear from Lance. He's been working
in San Francisco."

"Lance?"

"Lance Denning. That's his name."

Neville gave a vacant nod.

"Anyway," Sarah went on, "I . . . hadn't expected to hear
from him so soon."

Although Neville made himself appear to be only mod-
erately interested, he was listening carefully both to Sarah's
words and how she spoke them, and unless he was deliberately attempting to read into something that was not there,
he detected a certain reserve in what she was saying.

He spoke casually. "Been meanin' to ask yuh 'bout Mrs.
Ferguson. You call her *Aunt* Lilah. She a relative of yours?"

"No. Just a family friend," Sarah told him. "My god-
mother, in fact."

"Fine lady," Neville offered.

"She is," Sarah said.

Neville glanced upward, squinting, and watched with
idle interest as the white sunlight filtered through the foliage
and overhanging branches of the cottonwood.

"None of my business, I know, but what does this fella
of yours do in Frisco?"

Sarah looked at him and took a moment to reply. "From
what he tells me he's been working on some business deals."

"From what *he* tells you?" Neville said.

Sarah shot him a defensive look.

"Yes. Not sure exactly what it is he does," she said tersely.
"I know that he travels quite a lot."

Neville scratched at the nape of his neck. "Kinda vague,
ain't it?"

Sarah looked to be becoming agitated.

"Well, can't tell you what I don't know," she snapped at
him. "And really, what concern is it of yours anyway?"

"None, I reckon," Neville said with a shrug.

Sarah didn't know why she found it necessary to provide

Neville with an explanation. Not that she really had one that would adequately satisfy him—or maybe even herself, for that matter.

"From what I gather he helps to start up businesses in towns and communities along the frontier," she said hastily. She huffed a breath and added in a slower tone, "I do know that he wants to settle down, and once he can raise enough money he has plans to open a hotel in Reno. A lot of opportunity there, he says."

Neville pondered. "Imagine so."

"Lance tells me he knows people who might want to be his partners," Sarah said.

Neville gave her a probing look. "Seems this Lance fella *tells* yuh a lot."

The expression on Sarah's face was disagreeable. Neville ignored it.

"Sounds like a mighty enterprisin' fella," he remarked sardonically.

What Neville found curious was the strange sadness he discerned in Sarah. She tried to defend Lance well enough, though her efforts seemed almost too deliberate. Besides that, Neville noted that for someone soon to be reunited with her beau, she didn't seem especially excited—or even particularly happy.

Neville took a few seconds to regard the chicken leg he'd chewed right clear to the bone, then tossed it aside with a flourish. He stood up, brushed himself off, and looked out at the river. He stepped away from the shade and let the afternoon sun warm his face.

Sarah spoke from behind him. Her voice was soft and held a hint of remorse, and the words she spoke perhaps were intended to assuage the guilt she might have been feeling.

"I've disappointed you," she whispered. "I shouldn't have come today. Should have told you about the telegram right off. But Aunt Lilah . . ."

Neville spoke abruptly. "Aunt Lilah? You sayin' you comin' along today was her idea?"

Sarah seemed uneasy.

"Maybe you *should* 'splain why you come with me today," Neville insisted. "Was it to tell me 'bout you and this Lance? If so, I'll make it easy on yuh. You don't gotta say any more. I heard 'nuff."

He stepped in closer to where Sarah was sitting. A shadow fell across his face. Although just a twisted shading from the overhanging foliage, it gave his features a brooding look, further heightened by the darkening of his mood.

"'Less you got somethin' more to say, might be best if we start back to town," he said bluntly.

Sarah raised sad eyes up at him.

"It was my choice to come today. My decision," she told him. And then she paused, debating whether she should say more. Which she did. "Aunt Lilah says you're a good man. But that you're alone and—"

Neville cut off her words. "One thing I don't need is for anyone to feel sorry for me 'cause I'm alone. Might be that's the way I choose to live my life."

He felt resentful and stepped away to collect himself. Sarah watched as he stood with his back to her.

"Aunt Lilah never meant any harm," she said gently.

"No, reckon she didn't," Neville returned after a spell, the hostility fading from his voice.

Sarah had more she wanted to say but wasn't sure if she should. It proved a difficult decision because once she spoke those words, it likely would affect another decision—one over which she'd already felt an uncertainty.

Yet she owed it to Neville—and to herself—to be completely honest, and so she fortified herself with a deep breath and forged ahead.

"Aunt Lilah noticed the way you were looking at me the other day at the store. She . . . well, she also saw the way I kinda looked back at you. She made comment on it . . . and I didn't disagree." Her voice became subdued. "So maybe . . . maybe she meant today just as much for me as for you."

Neville gave the girl an inquisitive look. "The way *you* looked at me . . . ?"

Sarah nodded briskly, then became quiet. She wasn't

quite ready to say more. Not until she explained to Neville precisely what had been troubling her. But this, too, was difficult, awkward, and she had to ready herself for what she was going to tell him—and how she was going to say it.

"Aunt Lilah knows about me and Lance," she began. "And she's never made it a secret that she doesn't approve. She says he's a bad sort and that it's wrong for me even to think about marrying him."

And with those words she fell silent.

Neville was confused—and intrigued. He wanted Sarah to tell him more, but he could see how what she'd already said had pained her. He sat next to her and quietly waited for her to resume.

Gradually Sarah felt prepared to tell him more.

"I knew Lance ever since I was a little girl. We grew up together, fishing in streams and catching tadpoles. I looked at Lance as my best friend. When times were tough he was always there, protective of me. Reckon it was natural that once we got older we'd start courting. Even talk about someday getting married. But eventually we went our separate ways. I went off to finish my schooling and when I next heard from Lance, he'd gone off to San Francisco. He said he'd found work there and that he was going to build us a proper future. To be truthful, I was surprised to hear from him after all that time. Guess he'd never forgot what we talked about."

"Had you?" Neville asked her.

Sarah nodded. "But then he started to come back on visits. It had been years, but it was like nothing between us had changed. Not at first."

Neville gave a nudge of his head to encourage her to continue.

"But shortly I began to see that something *had* changed. He seemed . . ." Her words trailed off and her face became distressed.

"Go on, Sarah," Neville gently urged her.

"Now he wants to marry me, but I don't feel I can trust him," Sarah confessed, the emotion starting to seep through in her voice. "Not anymore. He's not the same person. I notice the difference in him each time he comes back. Just . . . little changes, but . . ." Her words faded off again and, perhaps in an unconscious gesture, she placed a hand across her chest before she continued. "Aunt Lilah only met him the one time and she told me outright that there was something about him that was . . . the word she used was 'sinister.' I remember how she said he cast a dark shadow. I didn't know what she meant, but right after she said it she did something I'd never seen her do before: She crossed herself, like she was saying a prayer. She also said she could tell sure as the sun rises each morning that he was hiding something and that whatever that was, it would only bring me hurt." She exhaled a breath. "Maybe he is keeping secrets. Maybe there is something he doesn't want me to know. No, I don't know what his job is and when I try to question him he changes the subject with promises and sweet talk and all. I keep wanting to believe him when he says he wants to provide us with a fine life and that I have to trust him and it won't be long before we have that hotel. Now I think I might just be lying to myself."

"You are," Neville said solidly.

Sarah looked up at Neville with her features set in a questioning frown.

"Your aunt Lilah told you herself she didn't think the fella's any good," Neville elucidated. "You just said you got your own doubts, yet yuh keep goin' on like you're defendin' him. He wants to provide you with this 'fine life,' you say, still he keeps steerin' away from comin' clean with what he does. That's gotta tell yuh the man's got a right suspicious side."

Sarah shook her head at an unpleasant memory. "I—made the mistake one time of trying to find out about his work, started asking him questions. Just couldn't understand why he was being so secretive. It was the only time I ever saw Lance lose his temper, and that was when I knew he wasn't the man I remembered. Because what he did was something the Lance Denning I grew up with would never do."

"He hit you?"

Sarah gave a hesitant nod. "'Course, once he calmed down he came back to apologize. He even had tears in his eyes. Bought me flowers, took me out for a nice supper."

"Once more you're standin' up for him," Neville remarked critically. "Tossin' oats into the manure pile."

Sarah's face flushed. She knew Neville was right, and she found herself questioning why she remained so determined to defend Lance when she knew in her heart that she no longer had those same feelings for him.

Neville let her work out her thoughts. He had his own to consider. Learning what he had about Lance Denning did not come as much of a surprise. Almost from the moment she mentioned his name, Neville suspected there was something questionable about the man and his motives and that Sarah would be plunging into deep waters if she were to accept his marriage proposal. At first he attributed those suspicious feelings to his own jealousy, and he was relieved to learn that there was a more legitimate cause for his concern. The thought of Denning mistreating Sarah filled him with a rage and there was much he could have said, but for the moment he held his tongue. As tempted as he was to speak his mind about a varmint like Denning, he wasn't sure that it was his place to put forward such blunt and possibly unwelcome remarks when Sarah was clearly struggling with her own emotions. Perhaps wrestling with decisions to be made.

When he did finally break the silence between them, what he said was simple and direct.

"Reckon what you need to be askin' yourself is do yuh still love him?"

Sarah creased her brow at the question, and then her features gradually softened and she lowered her eyes to the tablecloth spread out beneath her, a neutral focal point on which to contemplate her answer. She looked to disappear into her thoughts. Neville was patient but the longer Sarah sat in her deep silence, the more he felt she might not be ready—or maybe even willing—to face that honesty within herself.

The wait grew frustrating for Neville. To him, a simple, uneducated farm boy, giving and receiving affection was a pure and basic emotion, which one either accepted or rejected. Either Sarah still cared for Lance Denning or she didn't. And after what Sarah had told him about the type of person Denning was—what she admitted about Denning violently laying a hand to her—Neville, reflexively tensing his jaw, could not accept that she could still hold any feelings toward him.

Sarah's eyes brimmed and she swiftly wiped away the tears with her fingertips before they could start to streak down her cheeks. She felt embarrassed and hoped Neville wouldn't notice, but he hadn't taken his eyes off her since asking his question and could not help but see the sudden welling of emotion.

He spoke frankly. "From all what yuh told me, you'd be messin' up your life with a man like that."

Sarah tilted her head toward him.

"You asked me if I still love him," she murmured, the glistening in her eyes pooling their chestnut coloring. She'd considered her answer carefully. It was a question she might have avoided even asking herself, and therefore it had proved difficult to answer.

"I don't know," she finally admitted, the pauses between each of her words measured. "I don't know if I ever really did. But—he was the only beau I ever had. How could he have not meant . . . something to me?"

"Don't seem likely that you coulda never had no other fella," Neville stated softly, speaking what he sincerely felt.

Sarah acknowledged the flattery with the flutter of a smile. But then her tears began to fall, flowing freely, running in rivulets down the soft pinkness of her cheeks. Without coming straight out and admitting that she did not love Lance Denning, to Neville's eyes she had answered his question.

Sarah sniffed and looked at Neville with moist eyes. He untied the kerchief from around his neck and reached over to dab the tears.

"I know I haven't been good company," Sarah said apologetically. "I haven't been thinking clearly since I received that telegram."

"Don't feel bad 'bout it. Wrestled with a decision of my own," Neville admitted.

He could not offer Sarah the kind of life she had been led to believe that Lance Denning promised—if there was any truth behind his words, which he doubted. But Neville also understood that if he didn't take advantage of this opportunity, where each was sharing honesty, he might never be given another chance. With her emotions vulnerable Sarah might just go off with Denning and likely suffer a miserable and possibly abusive future. Neville didn't want to see that happen. He couldn't allow it to happen.

He said to her, "You haven't agreed to become his missus?"

Sarah responded with a shake of her head. "He hasn't asked me yet. But I'm sure that's why he's come back."

Neville spoke without compromise. "You don't owe him anything, Sarah. It's your own life yuh gotta be thinkin' 'bout. If after all what you told me you still ain't made up your mind, if you still got doubts, just consider that you could be walkin' into a big mistake. One that it might not be so easy to walk away from."

Sarah sighed deeply, and a slight tremor accompanied her exhale. "But how do I tell him that it's wrong, that I've decided I don't want to be with him?"

"Maybe you don't tell him," Neville suggested. "Maybe yuh just up and move on."

Sarah pondered. Then she slowly shook her head and muttered, "No. That doesn't seem fair."

"He ain't exactly played fair with you, Sarah," Neville reminded her. "Makes yuh fancy promises but won't back 'em up by bein' up-front with you."

Sarah acknowledged that truth with a nod.

"You gotta make the decision, Sarah," Neville said tenderly but with conviction. "Hard as yuh think it might be, it's still gotta be your choice."

Neville now had to speak the words he wanted to say, but they were not words that would come easy. Because he had to know with a certainty that he wasn't acting impulsively. He had to be absolutely confident that deep inside, beyond any doubt, fear, and possible later regret, it was what he truly wanted. Naturally he couldn't be sure that Sarah would accept his offer; that of course would be her own decision, and he realized it might be too soon for her even to contemplate an answer. That aside, he had every confidence he could provide a more honest life than what Sarah could expect from a tinhorn like Lance Denning.

"Sarah," he began, tentatively, "we sure ain't known each other long and I reckon that in itself might hold some concern—and I wouldn't be holdin' that ag'in yuh. What's more, much as I'd like, I can't be buildin' yuh any kind of fancy life, not as it stands right now. But . . . it is somethin' we might be able to work toward, together—if you're willin'."

Sarah was wordless; her reaction did not come as a surprise to Neville, but in that moment he feared that he might have spoken imprudently. He cringed inwardly and of a sudden wished it were possible to take back what he'd said.

"Are you asking me . . . to marry you?" Sarah finally managed to say, delivering her words carefully.

Neville didn't want to have to say it again, so he merely lifted his shoulders in a vague gesture. Then, in an effort to conceal his self-consciousness, he reached inside his shirt pocket for his ten-dollar gold eagle and concentrated on the coin as he flipped it between the knuckles of his left hand, one way, then the other.

Sarah was intrigued by the precision of his finger acrobatics—but only for a moment. Because in the next instant her face took on a look of wonderment, an expression that baffled Neville, one that with his limited knowledge of females he couldn't begin to interpret.

"Aunt Lilah told me this might happen," Sarah said, her voice almost a whisper.

Neville was curious. "That *what* might happen?"

"That you were going to ask me to marry you," she said.

Now it was Neville's turn to be taken aback. So much so that the coin that he had been manipulating so expertly suddenly slipped from between his fingers and rolled onto the ground.

Sarah said further, "I trust Aunt Lilah. She knows people better than anyone I know. Says it comes from working with customers of all types all these years. She's learned to tell the good ones from the bad—those who are honest and those who might not be of the best character." She permitted herself a sigh. "That's why even though I didn't want to accept it—I suppose part of me still doesn't—I trust her with what she said about Lance not bein' right for me . . . and I trust what she says about you."

"Flattered . . . I reckon," Neville said as he stooped over to retrieve his valued coin from the grass. He straightened his posture. "Nice to know you're well thought of. But truth is I hardly know your aunt. Just shop in her store to get supplies. Maybe we share the occasional word, but nothin' more. Sure not 'nuff for her to judge the kind of person I am."

"You can't fool Aunt Lilah, and she's formed a pretty solid opinion of you," Sarah told him. "She says you're honest, trustworthy." Her voice became soft when she added, "Even went so far as to say a man like you is rare to find."

"Yeah, I'm a bargain all right," Neville said kiddingly, to ease his awkwardness.

But the truth was that he wanted to think of himself as a decent person at this juncture in his life. He was glad that Mrs. Ferguson felt favorably toward him. But he also knew the old woman's judgment was not as foolproof as Sarah seemed to believe. He could neither forget nor deny that he had a past. A past that perhaps was even more shadowed and dishonest than what Mrs. Ferguson suspected about Lance Denning.

Neville phrased his words precisely, wanting to make sure he was clearly understood. "You knew what I might be askin' today . . . what Mrs. Ferguson told yuh, and you still came along?"

Sarah spoke surprisingly straightforward. "I did."

Frown lines embedded themselves into Neville's forehead. "And you knew if I was to ask yuh what she said I might . . . that you was gonna say yes?"

Sarah looked at him with an inscrutable expression. "I haven't said yes."

"No, you ain't," Neville said with a twitch of his mouth.

Sarah's eyes wandered off into the distance, leaving Neville guessing as to what she was going to answer. He began fiddling with his coin again, in an attempt to conceal his impatience.

When Sarah finally spoke, she maintained a proper dignity so that Neville would not think wrongly of her.

"It wasn't *that* quick a decision," she said primly.

Neville nodded with an accepting smile. But almost in the next instant his face took on a look that hinted at another doubt. Sarah responded to what she interpreted was his concern.

"No. It's not because of Lance," she said, speaking with firm reassurance. Then her tone softened. "Wouldn't make no difference if you'd asked me to marry you or not, I reckon I made up my mind that I couldn't go back to him. But . . . I had to know if what I told you made any difference to you."

Neville appreciated her being forthright with him, and he believed what she told him. Now he had to reciprocate, and he spoke with equal honesty.

"No, doesn't," he said. A melancholy expression formed across his features. "'Cause there once was someone in my life, too. We made a sorta commitment to each other. Least that's what I thought. But something happened that I still don't know the truth of. Carried the hurt with me for a long time. Fact, Sarah, I'd be lyin' if I said there still ain't a bit of that hurt in me. And we're talkin' a lotta years gone by."

Once he finished speaking he cast his gaze off to the side, away from Sarah so that she could consider what he had just told her without having to meet his eyes. He wanted nothing to influence her decision. It had to be pure. Honest. After many moments had passed and she simply remained silent, he turned his eyes back to her. The look on her face was a blending of compassion and understanding, and he felt encouraged to voice what he intended as his final say.

"Reckon you can tell I ain't much schooled in this. Ain't one for necessarily followin' proper—" Here his face took on a thoughtful look as he tried to find the correct word, finally settling on: "—etiquette. Askin' you to consider becomin' my wife without us first havin' a courtship. So maybe that's the first thing you gotta give some thought to 'fore you decide. Don't want yuh to be havin' no regrets. I want this to be somethin' you're sure of. And if you ain't . . ." His words drifted off and he became quiet to once more give her time to think over his proposal.

"I ain't like Lance Denning," he added. He spoke softly but with intention. "Won't . . . no, *can't* be makin' you no gilded promises. Fact, things may be rough for a while since I'm still bustin' sod. Still tryin' to fix up a house that by all rights I should just be tearin' down. But what I will promise is that I'll work hard for yuh. From as soon as the sun rises 'til it sets at night I'll be bustin' my back to build us a better life." He stopped to take a breath. "Anyway, that's sorta the picture I'm paintin'. Won't be lyin' to yuh. If'n you agree to what might not be the life you saw for yourself . . . I'd be pleased and honored to have you as my bride."

Sarah felt her eyes start to tear. She had never had anyone speak to her with such heartfelt honesty. The promises she had heard from Lance, which she had desperately tried to make herself believe were true and sincere, she now could see were shallow and artificial. But every word Tom Neville spoke was genuine and hard to reject, and she knew that even if the hardships he predicted were in their future, she could depend on him.

What he'd said was true: The wife of a sodbuster was not the future she had pictured for herself. But as she thought about it, the idea began to appeal to her. She could appreciate farming as a clean, satisfying life; whatever they accomplished would be the reward for their own labors. Working together, side by side.

Neville reached out his hand and gingerly laid his

fingertips against her cheek. The smile on his face was gentle, yet at the same time strong and reassuring.

He had the urge to lean forward and kiss her. He'd just summoned the courage—

When at that moment a sudden honking sound from above caught their attention. Neville and Sarah raised their eyes skyward past the glare of the sun to see a pair of geese flying overhead. Crossing the wide valley skies together, side by side, separated and distanced from the flock that followed behind in typical V-formation.

Neville rose to his feet and shook his head in astonishment.

"Would yuh look at that," he muttered.

Sarah stood up, stepped next to Neville, and, impulsively, hooked her arm around his forearm and gave a squeeze.

While neither voiced it, each considered this uncommon sight a sign, perhaps a reinforcement of the commitment they had just made to each other on this strange yet satisfying Saturday afternoon.

They watched in silence as the two geese, partnered in their journey, disappeared into parts unknown.

Book 2

ELEVEN

Commercial City
Many years later . . .

The man from Tucson who'd received the telegram urgently summoning him to Commercial City rode into town on horseback. That was the way he preferred it. He never entered a town in a way that might attract unwanted attention to his presence, and in larger communities he was less likely to draw the stares of onlookers if it appeared he was just one of many passing through the street rather than departing from a stagecoach. He dressed inconspicuously in ranch hand wear, his horse a neutral-colored nondescript gelding, and there was nothing about him from his Stetson to his spurs to raise anyone's suspicions.

Once he arrived by train in New Mexico, departing at Freshwater Junction, he boarded a stage and traveled as far as he felt comfortable before he purchased a horse not from a livery stable but from some simple farmer—an animal that he would buy cheaply with cash and later sell at a substantial profit; the negotiations, if they became difficult,

settled at the point of a gun. He completed the several days'
ride to his destination on horseback.

His line of work, at which he considered himself a professional, had taught him to practice caution, so there were
routines that he followed, procedures and techniques that
had not failed him as he traveled across green valleys and
through desert landscapes, over hilly terrain and through
vast canyons when called upon to perform his specialized
services.

He had received all the necessary information through
a coded telegram that was wired from San Francisco. The
operator at the telegraph office scratched his head upon
transcribing the esoteric message, the wording nonsensical
with no apparent meaning. But it wasn't his privilege to
question. Yet he noticed that the man for whom the message
was intended seemed to understand it perfectly, as a slight
smile curled the corners of his lips as he read it.

Another assignment.

The man was a professional gunslinger.

His name: Lance Denning.

It had been almost two months since the agents sent from
San Francisco had visited Commercial City with their
proposal to introduce gambling parlors to the community—
and whose offer was firmly rejected by the town's dedicated
mayor, Thaddeus Ford.

Soon, the small, three-person committee led by the man
called George Stadler was forgotten. They had departed
town, and within days their presence and their distasteful
proposal were scarcely a memory. Thaddeus Ford returned
to busying himself with plans for economic growth that were
of a more positive value to the town and its people.

Only Sheriff Tim Rawlins remained wary.

After watching Stadler and his associates ride out of Commercial City on the afternoon stage the day after their arrival,
Thaddeus had invited Tim to lunch at the Dominion Hotel
restaurant, Le Chef, where the mayor dined elaborately on

a first course of imported oysters while detailing the San Francisco proposal to the sheriff.

Rawlins listened carefully, all the while with his stern features set in a look of uncompromising concern.

Thaddeus digested another oyster straight from its shell. He took notice of his sheriff's expression.

"You look troubled, Tim," he said good-naturedly. A fine meal always made him content and put him in a relaxed mood.

"Can't say I'm disappointed you turned down their offer," Rawlins replied. "Reckon my worry is if that'll be the end of it."

Thaddeus creased his eyes questioningly over the napkin that he wiped along his mouth.

"Are you suggesting there might be trouble?" he asked.

Rawlins shrugged and sat back in his chair.

"I made my point clear, Tim," Thaddeus said, speaking with conviction. "They rode out on the Concord today knowing that nothing is going to change my position."

Rawlins wore a look that conveyed to the mayor his own doubt.

"I've kept myself in the know as to what's been goin' on with this Frisco syndicate," he said. "But I didn't know they were the bunch behind this visit."

"Either you're worrying too much or I'm not concerning myself enough," Thaddeus said, his eyes shifting toward the kitchen in anticipation of his lunch order.

"Could be," Rawlins didn't hesitate to say. He leaned forward in his chair and spoke directly. "The point is I don't see 'em givin' up so easy, Thaddeus. They're makin' their crooked inroads throughout the territories by not takin' no for an answer. They don't run into fellas like you too often. Someone who gives 'em an outright refusal. Which is why just because they left town I ain't feelin' too reassured that's the last we'll hear of 'em."

Thaddeus settled back into his chair and lifted his wineglass, admiring how the burgundy liquid seemed to sparkle through the expensive crystal.

"Tim, I did battle with Confederates during the war. Fought against redskins, ofttimes in hand-to-hand skirmishes,"

Thaddeus boasted. "And it was through grit and strength that I helped get us through the hardships we faced to build Commercial City into what it is today. I won't allow myself to be intimidated by these gentlemen from California."

"Wouldn't necessarily refer to them as 'gentlemen.'" Rawlins spoke frankly. "Yeah, you still have the purpose, Thaddeus—even the courage—but you're not the man you were twenty years ago."

Thaddeus tried not to take offense at the comment. Neither could he truthfully argue with what Rawlins was saying, because he was right. It was difficult for a man of Thaddeus Ford's pride and spirit to admit that he was past his prime, but not only had he slowed with age, he'd also let his culinary excesses get the better of him, which he justified as rewards he had earned.

He said, "Are you proposing that the town prepare itself in the event they plan their next visit more aggressively?"

Rawlins's eyes met the mayor's. He smiled faintly and shook his head. "Don't think that's how it would work with them. Wouldn't be like Dodge City or Tombstone where a gang of 'em come ridin' into town with six-shooters blazin'. These men are crooked, but they operate like businessmen. They'd plan their move in a more clever fashion."

"Or they just might stay away," Thaddeus countered.

Rawlins's slight lift of a shoulder held little conviction.

Thaddeus remarked, "But you don't think so?"

"I think we have to keep watchful," Rawlins offered. "Because if we do hear from them again, they'll appear out of the dark. Not literally, but in their approach."

Of a sudden Thaddeus Ford's attitude seemed to change as he appeared to give serious thought to what his sheriff was saying.

"I'm just being cautious," Rawlins said. "Which is my job, what I'm paid for. No sense letting ourselves become careless. After all, we have a responsibility to the town."

"Yes, of course," Thaddeus affirmed, starting to regain his professional demeanor.

There was no guarantee that the sheriff's concerns were

founded. But if Tim Rawlins was a betting man, he'd wager on there being trouble in the not-too-distant future.

Lance Denning passed quietly and unobtrusively down the main street of Commercial City to check out the town and compile strategic notes. He was not going to give any of the yokels the opportunity to take a good look at him so they could provide a description later. Once he departed the town he rode some miles west, where he set up camp within an outcropping of bedrock. There he settled down to rest to be ready for the next day.

Come tomorrow and Mayor Thaddeus Ford would be dead.

But that would not be the end of it.

He had an additional task to perform.

Only this killing had a personal stamp attached to it.

Lance sat out in the open, protected from a chilly night breeze by the rugged border of rock against which he huddled, trying to keep himself warm next to the small fire he'd built, a pot of coffee and a can of beans heating over the flames. He was miles away from where anyone outside an unexpected traveler could notice the light of his fire. He couldn't say he was comfortable in this environment, but he was used to roughing it. A nice warm bed in a hotel room certainly would have been preferable . . . only Lance knew that came with a risk. One night's comfort could lead straight to a noose. Hotel clerks were known for having good memories.

His horse was not far from him, tethered and fed and likewise seeking pockets of warmth from the campfire.

Lance pulled out a flask of brandy and added a splash to the coffee that he'd poured into a tin cup.

Alone with his thoughts, he sipped his brandy-laced coffee and reflected. For years his mind had been beset by a memory he had not been able to eradicate. The memory of a betrayal. It had taken him a long time and had cost him plenty of money to find out what he needed to know, because it seemed as if she had simply vanished off the face of the planet. For reasons known only to herself, she did not want to be found. But he couldn't leave it at that. And she should know that he would use his every resource to track her.

Neither the time nor the money had proven a needless expenditure. His persistence had finally yielded results. What he'd found out was unexpected and at first had fueled him with a violent rage. But once his mood settled, he decided not to act impulsively. Instead, the situation might prove a benefit that he could manipulate to his own advantage.

Not only would he fulfill his assignment, he had devised a plan where another man would confess to the crime—a man he had never met but to whom he owed a personal reckoning. A poor dirt farmer, no less. Someone who had taken from him the girl he had loved since childhood and had now subjected to a life of penury. And because she had failed in her promise to wait for him . . . by not honoring her word, she was as guilty in his eyes as the man she chose over him to be her husband.

For that insult to his pride, there was a debt to be paid.

Lance rose early the following morning, drinking the drips of cold coffee left in the pot from the night before and cleaning up his campsite, thoroughly, so that no one who might come upon the spot would ever know he'd been there. His plan was set. He was going to ride into town as casual as could be and take care of business in broad daylight, when no one would be expecting it and he could make his escape in the panic and confusion sure to follow. He knew from the details outlined in the telegram he'd received that the mayor followed a precise-as-clockwork routine, which included a daily stroll from his office to the Dominion Hotel restaurant at eleven forty-five. Occasionally he was accompanied by the sheriff, but if that happened to be the case today, Lance didn't consider it much of a concern. He'd yet to meet a lawman he couldn't outdraw.

Lance rolled himself a cigarette and struck a match against his boot heel to light it. Then he leaned back against his saddle pack, which was perched against a rock, and absorbed the clean, crisp morning air. As he drew on his smoke and viewed

the natural calm and beauty of the open country that surrounded him, he recalled how it used to be for him and his
gal Sarah, the fun they shared as kids, spending hours in just
such an environment, especially during the summer months
when school was out and they played together virtually from
dawn to dusk, exploring nature and enjoying silly games. He
remembered as vividly as if it were yesterday her contagious
giggle, her dancing brown eyes, and her straw-colored hair
tied in pigtails, straight-cut bangs sweat-plastered flat across
her forehead. He knew even back then that he wanted to spend
his life with her. He recalled that moment when they sat under
their favorite old cottonwood tree and he was brash and tried
to kiss her. He remembered his disappointment as she shied
away from his puckered lips and how he tried to ease his hurt
by rationalizing that she would have recoiled from any boy's
attempt to kiss her. It wasn't until she was in her early teens
that she stopped being the tomboy. She became a young
lady—a beautiful young lady who started to favor dresses
over flannel shirts and denim coveralls, and she began to
smell nice as she freshened herself with fancy fragrances.
The change astounded yet pleased Lance as, through his own
maturity, he looked at her much differently than simply his
frog-hunting playmate. But that presented complications that
Lance found difficult to deal with. After so many years of it
being just the two of them, kids inseparable in their imaginary
adventures, he noticed how of a sudden other boys were
beginning to share Lance's admiration of Sarah. Lance grew
resentful, and, to his way of thinking, with good reason. They
seemed to come out of nowhere, seeking her attention,
whereas *he* had always been there for her.

There was one boy in particular: Charlie Ritchess. He
always seemed to come around whenever Lance and Sarah
were together sharing time by their favorite spot, which was
known as Misery Creek. And Lance noticed how Sarah wasn't
exactly discouraging Charlie's attention, especially when
Charlie would start with his smooth-voiced flattery. Charlie
could speak well; he was educated. His parents had wealth
and had sent him away to a fancy boarding school where he

learned poetry and languages and other lessons that would cultivate a gentlemanly image. At age fifteen he let it be known that he preferred to be called Charles and was proudly arrogant in his display of his newfound manners and culture.

And to Lance's dismay, Sarah seemed impressed by it all.

While Lance seethed inside, he wasn't an aggressive lad and never interfered and let Charlie play his little game with Sarah. He listened to those special giggles that he'd always believed were meant exclusively for him as Sarah responded coyly to Charlie's flowery blandishments—and Lance would catch those sly glances Charlie would send his way as if he were challenging him in a private game of one-upmanship. Just to let Lance know that he had competition for Sarah's affections.

Over the next two summers, when Charlie would return from school, Lance noticed how Sarah was becoming a little more taken in by his fancy talk and fine manners. But summer would end, Charlie would go back east, and Lance would once again have Sarah all to himself . . . until the next year when the pattern would repeat itself and Charlie would have acquired even more fancy attributes with which to impress and endear himself to Sarah.

Finally came Charlie's last year at boarding school. He would be graduating that spring. There was every possibility that when he returned home for summer, it would be for good. Lance heard talk around the town that Charlie's father was going to bring him into his haberdashery business, which guaranteed the boy a prosperous future. Lance, whose own prospects were nowhere near as promising, spent many sleepless nights contemplating the dismal future he saw for himself should Charlie decide to stay on in Bradley, which, to his reasoning, would likely be the case. The imaginings he conceived were unsettling, and finally he became so overwhelmed with jealousy and the too-real fear that Sarah would soon succumb to Charlie's embellishments that he determined Charlie Ritchess would not enjoy riches in his future. For once "Charles" arrived back in town, Lance would see to it that he would have no future, period.

The community of Bradley was stunned the day Charlie Ritchess's body was pulled from Misery Creek. Apparently he had gone for a walk along the water's edge and had slipped, struck his head against a rock, and drowned. A tragedy, but one that a coroner's inquest ultimately ruled an accident. What troubled Lance was how distraught Sarah became over learning of Charlie's death. He naturally expected her to be upset since he was a friend, but she was near overwhelmed with grief. Maybe her feelings for the boy went deeper than Lance had thought, and that disturbed him. Nevertheless, he was there to comfort her and hoped that the compassion he demonstrated during this delicate time might bring them closer together.

Of course, if Sarah ever were to discover the truth about how Lance had quietly lured Charlie out to the creek that afternoon for a friendly talk . . .

Lance had spilled more blood since that day. His first murder had generated a thrill that made a lasting effect on someone who up until then had been a quiet, sensitive lad. Once he'd killed a man and discovered, perhaps even to his own astonishment, how the wash of his conscience came as effortlessly as cleansing the blood off his hands in the running water of the creek, Lance Denning had no difficulty committing future kills—especially if he was paid for the effort. His professionalism soon provided Lance with a rewarding occupation.

All the while Sarah remained ignorant of the lawless escapades on which Lance had embarked (including the killing of a sheriff and his deputy during the plundering of a bank in Utah, a two-man slaughter of which Lance was particularly proud). These exploits and the need for protection eventually brought him to the attention of the right people and he was hired to work as an "enforcer" for the San Francisco gambling syndicate. It was an arrangement not always to his liking, as he preferred to keep active and his services were generally not much in demand, since most often negotiations handled by agents proved an effective persuasion. But he was kept on a handsome retainer, which allowed him to partake of the gambling parlors along the Barbary Coast, as well as affording him trips back to

Bradley—and a good portion of which was stashed away into a special fund intended for his purchase of a hotel—for his and Sarah's future.

A future that Sarah had chosen to forfeit.

Lance was a practical man. He accepted that circumstances dictated he could no longer have the life he had wanted to share with Sarah. Too much had changed between them. While she had kept up the illusion that the two of them could enjoy a future together, Lance was no fool. He recognized that the distance between them had widened into an insurmountable gap. She remained innocent and pure. He had become cynical and cold-blooded.

Lance ground out his cigarette. He was done with his introspection. Each time he reviewed his past, the hurt subsided a little more. That pleased him. He almost could let things be, let Sarah struggle along in her life with her dirt farmer. He smirked as he contemplated how that would be punishment enough.

But Lance needed something for himself. A personal satisfaction.

His pride and self-esteem demanded it.

By eleven A.M. Lance was seated atop his horse on a small rise overlooking Commercial City. From his vantage point he could observe the activity that went on in the town at this time of day, the people mostly partaking of mundane duties, with the exception of the construction of the theater that the mayor had boldly proclaimed would bring entertainment ranging from comedy to drama to specialized acts into the town.

Lance smirked as he flicked aside the cigarette he was smoking. He thought with sardonic regret that it was unfortunate the mayor would never live to see the theater's grand opening.

He clucked his horse into the slow ride down from the hill slope and then proceeded toward the town, timing his arrival as close as possible to when Thaddeus Ford would leave his office for his daily stroll toward the hotel.

A check of his pocket watch: eleven forty. Good. Lance was just entering the town limits, riding his pony at a leisurely pace, those citizens out and about not paying him the least attention. Townspeople, merchants, and farmers, going about their business as they focused on the routine of their everyday lives. A destiny Lance once could have seen for himself had not an impulsive act set him on a different trail.

His horse trotted through the main street of town.

The streets were emptying as citizens began entering the town restaurants for their noon meal. Just a scattering of men and some womenfolk still out on the boardwalk. Certainly nothing to cause Lance worry.

He pulled his horse off Archer Street into an intersecting alley, where he dismounted and made himself look as if he were inspecting his animal's front shoe, though with the brim of his hat pulled low he frequently lifted his eyes to gaze out onto the front street, in anticipation of spotting the mayor.

It wasn't long before he saw a corpulent but very well-dressed man walk along the boardwalk on the opposite side of the street. There was no mistaking that it was Mayor Ford. He had a look of confidence about him that was reflected in his gait. Lance slowly mounted his horse . . . but he had to hold steady for a moment as the mayor stopped to chat with a couple of ladies he'd met along the way. They spoke briefly, and then the mayor politely tilted his derby and carried on toward the hotel. With a soft clucking sound, Lance directed his horse out onto the street, maintaining a slow pace to keep steady with the mayor's surprisingly brisk steps.

He pulled the black kerchief he wore around his neck up over the bottom half of his face, concealing all but his eyes.

"Mayor Ford," he called, his voice muffled under the fabric.

The mayor stopped, turned to his right. He was smiling.

Then . . . Lance withdrew his Colt .44 and in a rapid, fluid movement twirled the gun and drew a bead on his target, firing two bullets into the mayor's chest, dropping him face-flat onto the boardwalk. Thaddeus Ford was dead before he hit the ground.

Lance whipped his horse into a dead run and was gone from the main street before the suddenness of the shooting could register with any of the startled pedestrians.

TWELVE

For the first years of their marriage, Neville and Sarah worked alongside each other and enjoyed a small measure of success with their farming. Money was always tight, but Mrs. Ferguson was generous when it came to extending credit at her store.

But the situation would soon become difficult. First came the children—daughters Rose and Penelope—and besides the added expense of feeding and clothing the girls, Neville could no longer depend on Sarah to help him with all that needed to be done around their property. Although he labored throughout the day and often late into the night, it seemed there was always something that needed tending to. He'd wanted to do so much more to both repair and expand the "cabin" into a house replete with comforts such as separate bedrooms and a stone fireplace, but his efforts were minimal, since taking care of the needs of his daughters had become a priority and to meet those demands he had to concentrate most of his energies on harvesting cash crops. Although the vegetables he grew were of a lesser quality, Mrs. Ferguson would usually pay him a few dollars for the bushels he would cart into town on the back of his wagon. It was more a gesture of generosity, for there was little market for his produce, and often, without Neville's knowledge, she would merely give the vegetables away to hungry families in the county.

And then one day Mrs. Ferguson up and died. She simply keeled over behind the counter while filling a customer's order. Neville had taken notice of her frequent headaches and of how the woman had become increasingly forgetful when he'd come to her store, misplacing items he'd previously placed on order or adding an extra expense to his account, which he was embarrassed to have to point out to her to correct.

The store was taken over by a more ruthless individual who firmly believed that business was business and who demanded payment on any debts owed. Moreover, no further credit would be extended and he expressed no interest in purchasing Neville's vegetables.

The timing could not be worse. The girls always seemed to be sick, especially during the cold months leading into winter. The year Mrs. Ferguson died was particularly harsh. Neville did whatever he could to reinforce the cabin to keep the interior warm, but the bitter chill always seemed to seep through. Each winter when the sniffles started, Neville would brace himself. The girls, thankfully, both possessed a resiliency that carried them through those precarious times when bed rest and hot liquids seemed all Sarah could do to combat the fever and congestion, but this year as winter edged into a damp and chilly spring, five-year-old Penelope had fallen desperately ill, and both parents feared that neither Sarah's care nor the child's own fight would cure her.

It was a blustery day, late morning, and the southern winds whipped outside and whistled into the cabin through the many penetrations in the wood. It was a sound Neville had listened to too many times, and one that taunted him as if to remind him that his efforts in providing adequate shelter for his family had been in vain.

With Neville once again nearing surrender, physically

and mentally exhausted, all of a sudden he remembered something long forgotten, strangely removed from his memory
through all the years of concentrating on trying to build a
home for his wife and children. When the thought came to
him he'd been sitting at the small table with Sarah, trying
not to share his wife's despair while Penelope moaned,
tossed, and sweated in her bed.

Sarah noticed the sudden change in his features, his look
of worry becoming one of a vague hope. She regarded him
quizzically. Neville did not respond to his wife's expression
with words, though a smile started to inch across his lips.
Then he thrust himself up from his chair with such suddenness that the chair toppled backward, startling both Sarah
and elder daughter Rose, who had been sitting at her sleeping
sister's bedside, pressing a cold cloth against her forehead.

Neville went over to a bureau he'd purchased at an auc-
tion and struggled to open the top drawer. Once he yanked
it out he withdrew a small packet. He considered the packet
before he carefully shook out what was inside. He turned to
Sarah, who was still gazing at him with a peculiar expression, and he held forth the coin. The ten-dollar gold eagle.

He sighed. "Won't pay off our debts, but it'll cover some
of what we owe now. Might even give us some extra cash,"
Neville explained to his wife, his voice taking on a solemn
cadence.

Sarah didn't speak, but she intuitively recognized that
the coin held a special significance for her husband.

Neville heaved a breath and spoke reproachfully.
"Shoulda parted with this long ago when things got rough."
Then, gazing at the coin and slowly flipping it over between
his thumb and forefinger, he settled his attitude and became
philosophical. "But maybe a reason for that. Maybe 'cause
it's needed now."

His wife and daughter were observing him quietly, specu-
latively. Neville looked at Rose, then at Sarah, and, waving
the coin in front of them, he said decisively, "This ain't doin'
none of us no good growin' dusty in a drawer."

Without saying another word he started for the door, with

each step aware of the silence that followed him and feeling his wife's eyes tracking him. He turned around.

"You ain't sayin' it's wrong for me to be partin' with this?" he said to Sarah.

Sarah gave her head a slow shake. "How can I tell you it's wrong?" She paused and glanced down at her hands folded on the table. "But if that coin has some particular meaning to you, whatever that might be . . . I don't want you to be doing something you might later regret."

"We're talkin' 'bout our daughter, Sarah," Neville said, his words strong and determined. "Nothin' from promises to intentions matters a damn now."

Neville glanced at Rose, who had cringed slightly at his usage of a cuss word. He winked at her and gave her an apologetic smile.

"This is what I gotta do," he said with finality.

Neville would have been lying if he'd told Sarah it wasn't a difficult decision to part with his coin. He could never admit it to anyone, but the gold piece represented so much of who he was, what he had become, for better or for worse. It had traveled with him through good times and especially bad, and now to spend the coin without its fulfilling the destiny he had intended seemed almost like a betrayal.

He wished there were some other way, but practicality took precedence over sentimentality. The family needed food, and Penelope needed medicine from the town doctor.

He pocketed the coin and walked outdoors to ready the buckboard.

THIRTEEN

L ance Denning was miles away from Commercial City. He had traded off his horse along the way, put on a new change of clothing that gave him the appearance of a dude, a tenderfoot, and he could feel comfortable hanging his hat for a short time in Still Bend, taking a cheap room in the town's only hotel and waiting for the day when the man who had taken away his woman and fathered her children was to ride into town.

He bided his time quietly and uneventfully, laying low and resting for a couple of days before going outdoors and sauntering along the main street of the town, dropping into the few shops and meager business establishments along the way and introducing himself as a fabric salesman on a stop-over, and in the most innocuous manner finding out whatever he could about the people in and around the community, inevitably learning about Sarah and her husband. Of course it worked to his advantage to discover that Sarah's aunt Lilah had passed on; otherwise that could have presented a problem Lance might not have been keen on solving, yet one that he would have had to address to maintain his deception. He remembered how Aunt Lilah had held him in low esteem. To recognize him and see him back in town after all these years would only raise her suspicions . . . and that would never do.

The new proprietor of what previously had been known as Ferguson's Emporium, a man named Curtis Marsh, told Lance much. He was a miserable though talkative cuss who seemed to hold a strong dislike toward county people who owed him money. As this Mr. Curtis told it, he'd not only purchased the store from Mrs. Ferguson's estate but had also obtained the debts. And chief among the debtors was the man called Tom Neville, who just happened to be married to Mrs. Ferguson's goddaughter.

"That a fact?" Lance had said idly upon learning this information.

Curtis nodded vigorously, and his attitude reflected the disdain he felt toward Neville.

Lance was leaning against the counter, casually building a cigarette.

"This Neville fella come into the store much?" he asked as he slid his tongue along the rolling paper.

"Not for a spell," Curtis said, frowning. "Why would he? Comes in here he knows he can't buy anything . . . I'd just be after him to pay what he owes." Now he gave Lance a suspicious look. "Y'seem to be more interested than a bystander should."

"Not exactly a bystander," Lance returned with a slow stretching of his lips.

"No?" Curtis said with a twitch in his voice. For the first time he detected something disturbing about the stranger.

Lance didn't elaborate. He struck a match against the side of the counter to light his cigarette. He drew a deep puff. Curtis grimaced as Lance blew a plume of smoke out the corner of his mouth in his direction. Lance looked askance at him. Then he gave Curtis a wry smile and started for the door. Halted. He turned and looked as if he were about to say something but then apparently changed his mind. He tipped the brim of his derby and walked outside.

Lance now realized there was little chance of him running into Neville in Still Bend, given that the man was so
heavily in debt with the town's leading merchant. He stood
next to his horse, fastened to the hitching post outside the
store, finishing his cigarette and deciding what he should
do. A look at the sun's position told him it was around
midafternoon. It seemed his sole option was to travel out to
the farm. He wasn't keen on the long, dusty ride, but it would
prove interesting for him to face Sarah again after all these
years. While he held special, specific memories of their time
together, he felt certain those had been far removed from
Sarah's thoughts. He doubted he would recognize who she
was today. Likely it would be the same for her.

But as it turned out, he was spared the travel and his reunion
with Sarah. As he rode his horse at a canter along the road, he
noticed in the distance a solitary driver heading in the direction of Still Bend, piloting a rickety old buckboard.

Lance slowed his mount and gave a wave of his hand,
requesting that the buckboard come to a halt. The driver
pulled rein with an audible "Whoa."

Lance's horse trotted up alongside. He studied the man
seated on the buckboard. He couldn't know for sure, but he
was betting it was Tom Neville.

"Howdy. Anything I can help yuh with?" Neville asked
cordially.

"Well, I thank yuh for stoppin'," Lance said, likewise
amiably.

Neville gave a deliberate nod. Taking note of the stranger's
sharp apparel, partially visible under an open overcoat, he
was curious what he would be doing on this stretch of road.

Lance, too, was studying Neville and wasn't quick with
his words, and Neville started to look a trifle impatient.

"Your name wouldn't happen to be . . . Neville?" Lance
asked, cocking an eye.

Neville looked more closely at the stranger. He tried to
determine if he knew him, since he'd come across many
people in his travels. But in this instance he was unable to
place who this fellow might be.

"Tom Neville?" Lance queried a little deeper.

"Seems you got me at a disadvantage," Neville said warily.

"Might be," Lance replied, controlling the reins on his suddenly restless horse.

"Look, friend, don't wanta seem rude but I gotta get to Still Bend," Neville told him.

"Just came from there," Lance offered smoothly. "Fact, was there specifically waitin' to see if you'd show up."

Neville wore a troubled look. Because in that moment the crime of his past and its aftermath came rushing back to him; dark recollections he'd tried to bury under the responsibilities and demands of his new life. But as if released from the bottomless depths of a lake, those terrible memories resurfaced. Who was this stranger? What did he know? What did he want from him? One thing Neville quickly determined, much to his dread: Whether this fellow was a lawman out for reward or an outlaw seeking the stolen cash that he'd long ago parted with, he seemed to have a purpose that spelled trouble for Neville.

At the same time, Neville had to contend with a priority. He had to get into town to pick up supplies before nightfall, for it would be a longer drive back to the farm once it got dark. The trail could be treacherous once the sun set, and the bends and weaves had to be traveled slow and with caution.

"Hear tell why yuh ain't been in town much," Lance said with a deliberate sigh. "Kinda unfortunate set of circumstances as I understand it."

Neville settled the reins on his knees while still holding on to the leather. His features grew taut with impatience.

"Don't know who you are, mister—" he started to say.

"Reckon yuh don't," Lance replied abruptly.

"There's somethin' you wanta be sayin', tell it quick," Neville said, his eyes shifting from the stranger's steady gaze.

Lance nodded amiably, his words oddly dismissive. "We'll talk."

With that, he inexplicably whipped his horse into a run,

down the road whence Neville had come. He'd found out
what he needed and was prepared for the next step of his
plan, counting on Neville's unwitting cooperation.

Neville sat perplexed—and admittedly relieved. If the
stranger had been a lawman or bounty hunter, he'd have
been arrested; if he had been an outlaw with knowledge of
his past, chances were he'd be dead. But along with the relief
he felt, Neville also experienced a strange uncertainty—a
sudden trepidation, and he found himself debating whether
he should carry through into town or maybe turn back. The
stranger's ambiguous attitude concerned him; he was too
quick to ride off without revealing why he had been waiting
in Still Bend to see him. A disturbing thought occurred to
Neville that perhaps the stranger had hoped to catch him
alone, and seeing that his wife and daughters were left
unprotected . . . he might be headed toward his place.

One thing that Neville could not ignore: The stranger,
whoever he was, seemed to know more than he should.

It might be the wrong decision, his concerns could be
unwarranted, but Neville couldn't take the chance that the
stranger might pose a threat to his family, and he maneuvered
the buckboard around and started back toward the farm. By
the time he was heading down the homeward trail, even the
dust had settled from the stranger's rapid lead. If he truly
was riding toward the house, he would arrive there at least
a good hour before Neville could pull up in the buckboard.
A lot could happen in that hour, though those were thoughts
he would not allow himself to consider. Still, he was anxious
and decided it would be a better move to unhitch his horse
from the wagon and ride bareback to the cabin.

Before Neville could get any farther down the road, he
was surprised again. Lance had correctly anticipated Neville's decision and had pulled off the trail not even a quarter
mile ahead, camouflaging his horse and himself behind a
high covering of trees and a dense profusion of brush bordering the left side of the road. Lance waited patiently until
he heard the buckboard approach, then urged his horse out
onto the road to block its passage.

Neville drew in the reins to bring the buckboard to a slow halt. He made himself not react at seeing Lance, whose features were shadowed in a shifting gray, an odd sort of shading, perhaps resulting from the thick cloud cover that was starting to pass overhead. But to Neville, the darkening on Lance's face appeared to be the physical manifestation of something deep and sinister within the man. Seated upright on his horse, the stranger looked to hold the portent of doom.

Neville edged the buckboard in a little closer. The wagon slowed . . . then halted altogether. Then just a soft stamping of a front hoof against the hard ground.

"Was waitin' to see if'n you might turn back," Lance said as he adjusted an easy movement with his horse. "Suspected you would."

Neville held himself silent, keeping both hands steady on the reins. If need be, he was ready at any moment to whip his horse into a run and knock the stranger and his pony clear off the road, as it was apparent the man was not about to clear the way for him.

"Could speak here off'n the trail," Lance suggested. He looked skyward. "Or judgin' by the look of them clouds we might do best to move on."

Neville said nothing. He was struggling to control the uncertainty rising in him.

"Far ride to your place?" Lance asked.

"Ain't hardly likely we'll be headin' there," Neville told him flatly.

"S'pose that might be a wise choice," Lance commented.

Neville pulled himself upright in his bench seat. "Meanin'?"

"Meanin' not a damn thing," Lance replied.

Neville spoke in his growing frustration. "Better just tell me what it is yuh want so I can be on my way."

"Gonna *give* yuh what you want . . . Neville. Rather, what it is yuh need right now," Lance answered ambiguously.

"What I need is for you to clear the road so's I can get back to my family."

"Thought you was headin' into town?"

"Don't see how that hardly matters to you," Neville retorted.

"Don't," Lance said woodenly. "Don't at all."

"Then I'd suggest yuh let me pass."

Lance gave a swift jerk of his head toward the horse pulling the buckboard. "Not much of a future for that ol' mule."

"Can't waste no more time," Neville said bluntly. He didn't want the stranger to know of his intention, but once he was rid of him he planned to continue on into Still Bend. But he couldn't be sure he'd make it to town before the store closed.

Lance gazed up at the clouds gathering overhead, darkening the sky. A distant rumble of thunder ruptured the stillness.

"Weather changes fast in these parts," he commented. "Damn little chance you'll get your business in Still Bend done 'fore them skies break."

Neville determined that whoever this stranger was, he had a deliberate motive for intercepting him. He wished he had thought to bring his sidearm along. But he'd left his gun belt with the Colt revolver resting in the fancy holster hanging on a peg back at the cabin. He took notice of how the stranger was heeled, while he was defenseless. Not a good situation to be in.

Yet it seemed obvious that the stranger had come to talk, even if his shifty behavior and ambiguous comments left Neville guessing as to his intent. If the stranger had intended to bushwhack him or provoke him into gunplay, Neville figured he'd be lying facedown in the dirt by now.

Once again Lance had to steady his steed, which now appeared to be reacting to the ominous change in weather.

"Damned if you can figger an animal," he remarked.

"They can sense what's comin'," Neville said.

Lance tensed his grip on the reins to control his horse, which remained agitated.

"Could be," he agreed.

"Met someone like you once before," Neville said. "Lotta talk, not much to say."

"Don't know nothin' 'bout that," Lance replied. "Fact, don't know much 'bout you and damn less 'bout your life." He spoke slyly. "That is, not 'til a certain point when I made it my business to find out more."

The more the stranger spoke his peculiar talk, the more perplexed and anxious Neville became. Did he know about the events in Brewer's Gulch? As Neville saw it, there was nothing else about his past that would cause a man to go to the trouble of tracking him all the way to a hole-in-the-wall community like Still Bend.

"Things ain't been goin' so good for you and your kin on that farm of yours," Lance stated.

Once again Neville was startled—both by the bluntness of the remark and this stranger presuming to know what was going on in his life. How could someone he'd never met know about the hardships he and his family were experiencing?

He was frustrated in his attempt to make sense of it all. The overhead gloom and what it forecast hardly improved the uneasiness of his mood. The sky was slate gray, muting the sunlight, and a light misty rain had begun to fall. Lance pulled his fancy overcoat tighter around his shoulders and lowered the brim of his derby. Neville, who was not clad as protectively, dressed merely in a faded denim jacket, sat motionless as the rain pattered about him.

Lance peered up at the sky. "Gotta hope this weather don't get much worse. You still got that ride back to your farm."

Neville fired him a tight, hard stare.

Lance ignored the intensity of his look.

He said, "The thing is, Neville, you got a family to take care of. You go gettin' yourself sick and end up with one of them fevers I hear has been spreadin' 'bout these parts, makin' people bed-ill, and . . . well, don't think I need to spell it out for yuh."

Neville wasn't interested in his shallow concern. But his words still hit a nerve. He thought about his daughter and the sickness that had befallen her. Again it became disturbingly evident to Neville that this stranger knew more than he was letting on.

He said, "Just tell me outright: Why is the welfare of my family so important to you?"

"There's a reason," Lance said after a lengthy, deliberate hesitation. "One you'll understand. But I don't aim to be talkin' under a downpour."

A cold wind had whipped up, leaving Neville vulnerable against the elements.

Lance offered a suggestion. "You ain't never gonna make it back to your place 'fore this weather turns real nasty. Might be better if'n you swing 'round and carry through to Still Bend. We can grab some supper, have our talk, and you can get done whatever your business first thing in the morning."

Except for the distasteful prospect of sitting down to share a meal with this stranger, Neville had to admit that it was probably the best idea. His only concern was for Penelope and his knowing that Sarah would grow anxious if he didn't come back to the farm tonight. He didn't want to place an extra burden of worry on her, dealing as she was with their daughter's fever, but he had no other alternative since if he dared to chance riding home through the dark and the troubled weather, he might not get back at all.

"All right," Neville said. "Let's head into town."

Lance glanced upward, blinking into the rain. Then he lowered his face and said to Neville, "Smart choice."

By the time they arrived in Still Bend, Neville was soaked clear through. Once he walked into the lobby of the Liberty Hotel he removed his sopping wet denim jacket and tossed it over his arm. The hotel was a drab and dreary establishment, a stopover for those merely seeking shelter instead of a warm and welcoming atmosphere, yet the Liberty was the only hotel in Still Bend and was where Lance had taken a room while he'd waited for Neville to come into town. Neville wasn't keen on having to pay for a room—which meant parting with his gold piece, the only currency he had in his possession. Lance took notice of Neville's coin once he reluctantly removed it from his pocket and determined by the way he massaged its surface that the piece might be the only money Neville had to his name.

Lance gestured for Neville to put the coin back into his pocket, then pulled out his billfold and withdrew sufficient cash for one night's lodging, which he slapped with a flourish onto the desk clerk's counter.

Neville turned to Lance, intending to refuse this gesture of generosity. But before he could object, he stopped himself. He needed every nickel he could squeeze from his coin, and so he swallowed his humiliation and instead merely nodded his thanks.

"Times are tough," Lance commented. "Even proud men gotta get by on what they can."

The hotel restaurant was empty of customers. It was apparent the place rarely did significant business even at peak hours, much like the hotel itself which, while boasting eight rooms, rarely had even half of those occupied—and two of those were rented outright by a couple of old prospectors who'd made sufficient profit from selling their interest in a copper mine to retire to an alcoholic anonymity in Still Bend.

The only featured item on the menu was venison, which neither Neville nor Lance had a particular hankering for but was the dinner they chose. The selection was not so much a concern to Neville since he couldn't claim to have an appetite. His companion, however, looked the type to enjoy the finer offerings in life. His clothing was fashionable, highlighted by a Galloway striped vest and black cravat. Neville couldn't help feeling somewhat inadequate in his presence, as he was dressed in unlaundered just-off-the-field wear.

The waiter came to light the center lamp on the table, which set off a subtle glow and only slightly relieved the dreary atmosphere of the dining room. Lance ordered a bottle of red wine, the best the hotel had to offer, which, not surprisingly, was not a particularly fine vintage, though the cost was high for its mediocre quality. The waiter brought the wine to the table and presented the label to Lance, who dismissed such formality with a shake of his head, and then he uncorked the bottle, pouring a small amount into Lance's glass to taste, which he again brushed aside.

Once the waiter walked off, Lance took the bottle and poured a generous portion into the glass, which he then passed over to Neville.

Neville noticed that the stranger hadn't taken a glass for himself, but, given the curious circumstances, he didn't feel such restraint and quickly downed a swallow of wine.

Lance looked at him, quietly amused.

Neville finished off his wine, reached over for the bottle, and poured himself a full glass.

Lance glanced around the dark and empty surroundings and expressed his disapproval by exhaling, "Place has all the charm of an undertaking parlor."

Neville's eyes did their own wandering throughout the dining room, and though he didn't voice it, he had to agree about the depressing decor.

Lance then spoke more brightly. "But an appropriate place for us to have our talk."

That was an odd comment, and Neville squinted curiously. He tossed back another swallow of wine.

"Yeah," he said, the wine emboldening him. "'Bout time we had this talk of yours."

Lance prudently pushed the wine bottle aside. "Wanta keep our talk friendly. Seen a lotta friendly talk turn bad after too much liquor."

"Ain't sure I'd call this a 'friendly talk,'" Neville returned, lifting a suspicious eyebrow.

"Depends. Might consider it differently after I'm through," Lance said.

Neville leaned back in his chair. He sat quietly and waited for his companion to speak. Once more it seemed as if Lance were stalling. Neville struggled to keep his head clear against the inroads of inebriation. He wanted to be able to understand whatever it was the stranger would be telling him. Up to now he had been speaking cryptically, talking without making his point, offering hints but providing no answer to the riddle. Neville had just barely controlled his frustration with talk that simply made no sense and appeared to be heading nowhere.

"I think 'fore you say anything more, you'd best tell me who yuh are," Neville said determinedly.

Lance smirked and flickered his eyes off to the side. He didn't answer. There followed a long period of silence between them.

And then Lance said, "You ever kill a man, Neville?"

The unexpectedness of the question startled Neville. He didn't answer.

"Well, Neville, I have," Lance said, speaking matter-of-factly. "Wasn't necessarily something I wanted to do . . . but sometimes you got no say over how things turn out in life."

Even with the wine dulling his comprehension, Neville felt his nerves grow taut. He experienced a sudden dread at just the two of them sitting alone, the stranger's eyes now raised and his gaze boring into him.

Lance was receptive to Neville's discomfort and resumed what he was saying, seeming to savor the words he spoke, almost relishing the grisly memories they evoked.

"Killin' the first one is what proves your mettle," he said. "That's when there ain't no real decidin' on whether you end a man's life quick or slow. 'Cause usually that kinda killin' ain't planned. Mostly depends on the circumstances. Sometimes it happens quick, like in the blink of an eye. Then there's where you're watchin' someone struggle to take those last gasps of breath like if you had your fingers closed tight 'round his throat and you squeeze. Or might be as a bullet from your gun burns a hole deep in his belly, and that dyin' takes a mite longer, maybe even days. Seen that happen once. No, ain't particularly pleasant. The thing is, after you kill that first one it's like . . . you gotta do it ag'in. To know for sure the kill felt like it did. It gives yuh a sense of power when you watch a man die by your own hand—fast, slow, makes no never mind. 'Cause you was takin' part in cuttin' short a man's destiny."

Neville looked at Lance with mounting apprehension. His mouth felt dry—and it wasn't from the cheap wine.

"Why're you tellin' me this?" he wanted to know.

Lance shrugged. "Thought by now it might be obvious."

"Ain't obvious."

Lance cast his eyes about the room, checking in case there might be someone hovering in one of the dark corners, overhearing their talk. Satisfied they were alone, he hunched across the table and spoke in a quiet yet defined voice.

"Might make a difference 'cause I'm now gonna tell yuh who I am," he said. "I s'pect it *will* mean somethin' to yuh."

Neville gave a tentative nod. He wanted to know who this man was, yet at the same time he was apprehensive.

"Go on," he finally muttered.

"Name's Denning, Lance Denning."

Neville tried not to react. But there was no way he could not express recognition at the name. It was subtle but showed by the quick flashing of his eyes. Lance noticed and was pleased.

"Figgered you'd know," he said.

Neville neither spoke nor gave a gesture to confirm what he knew. Lance was accepting of that. In fact, he expected no more from him.

Yet Neville's blood was pumping. He reached across the table for the wine bottle and poured himself another glass.

Lance watched with a satisfied smile.

Before any more could be said the waiter brought out their dinners and, noticing how the wine was nearly empty, asked if they would like him to bring out another bottle. Without looking up at the server, Lance slowly and deliberately pushed the bottle across the table toward him, his gesture indicating that they'd had enough. The silence between the two diners had become so heavy that even the waiter could absorb the tension, which made him uncomfortable. He took the bottle, hastily expressed his hope that the two men would enjoy their meals, and hurried back through the swinging doors into the kitchen.

Neville glanced down blankly at his food before pushing the plate aside.

"Not hungry?" Lance asked him.

Neville could not answer. Even if he'd been completely

sober, words would not have come easy. He was having difficulty comprehending the reality of this situation. It had been years since he'd heard Sarah speak of Lance Denning. The name belonged to a distant past. Lance Denning was a man Neville knew, yet didn't know. A man about whom he'd formed a strong, negative opinion—an opinion that, sitting with him now, he was not about to revise. He was someone Neville never expected to encounter . . . yet here he was, and here was Neville, listening to him talk of past murders he'd committed while partaking of his hospitality.

And he didn't know *why*. He didn't know why he was here, or what Denning wanted from him.

"I ain't come here to raise no fuss, Neville," Lance assured him. He settled back into his chair and spoke openly. "I s'pect, though, that you might think otherwise."

"Reckon what I gotta know is why you went to so much trouble for us to meet up," Neville finally said, a weak strain in his voice.

Lance rubbed the fingers of his hand along his jaw. He hadn't bothered to shave for the past couple of days and had the beginnings of a salt-and-pepper beard.

"You know who I am . . . and you can still ask me that?" he said.

Neville nodded slightly. "Yeah."

Lance smiled indulgently.

"Well, then let me do my own talkin'," he said. "'Cause I don't know what *she* mighta told yuh, but I got my side of the story, too—and 'fore we get down to what I plan to propose, only right that you hear it. Give yuh a fair perspective. 'Cause when all is said and done, it's you what's gotta make the decision."

Lance waited for a response, a word, or even a simple gesture from Neville. But Neville sat silently and barely moved a muscle, his expression vacant, yet purposely ensuring that his gaze did not waver from Lance. That was important—and difficult: maintaining eye contact with a confessed killer.

Lance began. "My gal, Sarah, went and ran off on me. That hit hard, Neville. Right hard, like a round of buckshot to the belly. Maybe that's somethin' you can relate to in your own life, I don't know. But no matter. Y'see, I'm a man who's got pride. Don't take it well when my pride gets injured. I don't 'spect to get Sarah back. I come to grips with that. But what *you* gotta understand, Neville, is I got a need—a desperate need to regain my pride. 'Cause a man can't go no further if he ain't got somethin' to hang on to. She run off on me, Neville. She run off and married you. And where it pains me is that she chose someone with nothin' like what I coulda offered her. Then yuh went and fathered Sarah's kids, and you ain't givin' 'em any kind of a life. Yeah, I know all this. Took me a while—a long while, which is why I ain't been 'round sooner. But I got it all sorted out, and that's the reason I come back now."

"You come back . . . ?" Neville started to say in question.

"To set things right," Lance said conclusively.

Neville could feel the blood pulse inside his skull.

"Ain't ag'in you personally, Neville," Lance said in an effort not to sound condemnatory. "Coulda been anyone who come along. Just happened to be you as random as the number that comes up on a gamin' wheel." He paused to consider his comment. "And maybe that ain't a bad way to compare it."

When Neville finally spoke, there was a slight incredulous edge to his voice. "You ain't forgot after all this time?"

Lance nodded, and in the gloom of the restaurant, with his face lighted by the shifting flame inside the table lamp, his features took on a malevolent cast.

"No, I ain't," he said in a voice of equally dark inflection.

Neville found the whole conversation unsettling, and he wanted just to up and leave. He didn't care to hear the rest of whatever Denning wanted to say to him—why he had put out the effort to track him after all these years. It was only his concern for Sarah and his daughters that kept him fastened to his chair. Learning what he had from Denning, he understood there might very well be a reason to be worried for their welfare.

"You care for your family, Neville," Lance said, a statement rather than a question. "You want the best for them, but you ain't never gonna provide it."

Neville didn't say anything.

Lance pivoted his head to again take a quick glance around the dining area, then pulled his chair in closer to the table. He leaned forward, pointed a finger at Neville, and spoke in a conspiratorial tone.

"Supposin' I was to give you my assurance that your family—your wife and your two kids—would be well looked after, that they'd never have to worry 'bout bein' poor no more."

Neville avoided answering directly and said instead, "You can't make no promise like that."

"I'm givin' you my guarantee," Lance said with utter seriousness.

"*Your* guarantee?" Neville said with incredulity. "What's that worth?"

"Maybe more than yuh think," Lance said straightly.

Neville felt a strange sensation creep over his body. Whatever Lance was telling him, it wasn't a joke.

Lance smiled patiently. "You got no reason to accept my word, true 'nuff. But given your circumstances, ask yourself if yuh really can afford not to."

Neville wore a strained expression, though he kept his voice even. "Not to . . . *what*?"

Lance held his smile. "Offer your family a better life."

Neville again went silent.

Lance's smile stretched into a grin. He slid his dinner plate back toward himself. He lifted his fork and picked around at the food. Then he gave his head a shake and spoke with disappointment.

"Just as I figgered, this deer meat looks like it's still got a life to it."

Still, he dug in and began to chew at a piece of meat, halting in his talk and further stretching Neville's patience.

"You still ain't makin' sense," Neville said tautly. "Just get on and make your point."

"Made yuh my offer," Lance said simply, lifting a forkful of greens to his mouth.

"You ain't made no offer," Neville responded with a stiff jerk of his head. "Just talk that's goin' nowhere."

Lance wore a somber expression while he chewed and then swallowed his vegetables. He picked up his napkin and wiped around his mouth.

Finally he made his point. "Simple exchange. The guarantee of your family's bein' well cared for and you confessin' to a crime."

With his sobriety compromised by the glasses of wine he'd consumed, Neville couldn't be sure he had heard him correctly. He regarded Lance with features framed in doubt.

Lance responded to his dubious look with a smile and a nod. "Mean just what I said."

Neville's words were couched in skepticism. "You want me . . . to confess to somethin' I had no part in? Somethin' . . . I don't even know 'bout."

Lance's lips slowly parted, exposing his teeth, though the expression he wore was not intended to be humorous. Neville could instantly detect the shrewdness behind his smile.

"That's what you're sayin', ain't it?" Neville said with emphasis.

Lance didn't reply. Yet to Neville, his silence was more telling than his words.

Neville needed to pull himself together. He felt as if he were suffering from some fever.

But it was real. All too real.

"A man that cares for his family . . . well, ain't much he wouldn't do for 'em," Lance next said.

Neville swallowed past the lump he felt bulging in his throat.

"Might even be willin' to give up his life?" Lance added somberly.

Neville had no reply.

Lance eased back into his chair. "I killed a man in Commercial City," he said reflectively. "An important man. Happened fast, on the street, right around noontime. Why I did it. . . . Weren't nothin' personal. Never even met the man. Was an assignment. A professional arrangement where you're hired to do a job but don't ask questions. While it ain't likely, there's the chance that this killin' might somehow be tied to a business deal that some friends of mine are involved in. These friends would like it so no future problems might come of this so that their negotiations can carry on without any interference."

Neville's words came heavily. "I still don't see what you're gettin' at, other than confessin' to cold-blooded murder."

Lance spoke contemplatively. "What's murder, as you call it out here in the West, Neville? They hand out guns like they was givin' away candy. Life goes cheap on the frontier."

"Don't see it that way. A killin's still a killin'," Neville argued.

Lance wore a dismissive expression. "Well, I ain't gonna be debatin' that. But if someone was to claim responsibility for what was done in Commercial City, it'd make it easy for my associates to move forward with what they're plannin'. And if that *someone* was willin' to accept the consequences, these people might be prepared to pay out a sum of money in appreciation. A mite handsome sum that could see someone's family go a long way."

It was slowly becoming clear to Neville what was being proposed.

"And that someone's reward would come at the end of a rope," he stated grimly.

"We ain't talkin' 'bout *him*," Lance reminded curtly. "We're speakin' 'bout the good life that could be provided for his family."

"And that's all of it?" Neville said brusquely.

Lance hesitated before he said, "No. That ain't all of it. There's also what yuh might call a dividend."

Neville regarded him questioningly. "Dividend? For who?"

Lance had a serious gleam in his eyes. "For myself, Neville. The reason I'm proposin' this offer to *you*."

Neville nudged his head, tentatively, for him to go on.

"I get back my pride," Lance said.

Neville chilled. He understood.

"You get your pride . . . and I get my neck stretched," he muttered.

"That is the likely outcome," Lance confirmed. "But your widow and kids go on to a life free of worry. I don't call one life in exchange for three a bad deal."

A morbid yet valid argument that Neville was not quite ready to acknowledge.

Neville scrutinized Lance carefully, observing every slight shift of facial expression. Trying to discern if he really was serious.

"And supposin' I was to go along with this. What else do you get from it?" he asked bluntly.

"You mean Sarah?" Lance presumed.

Neville nodded. "Yeah. Sarah."

Lance looked momentarily thoughtful before he said, "Sarah made her decision."

"So you ain't holdin' no grudge ag'in her?" Neville said.

"Maybe at one time," Lance replied in a neutral tone.

"And now . . ."

Lance shrugged. "Not much point, is there?"

"How would I know, I'd be dead," Neville said wryly.

"I ain't got no hard feelin's," Lance told him.

"Sounds like you're bein' awful fair to her," Neville said. He hesitated with what he was going to say next because even though his words weren't intended the way they would sound, Lance could likely take them as a bitter reminder. "Considerin' if you wanta be truthful, she's the one that let yuh down."

Surprisingly, Lance didn't so much as raise an eyebrow.

"Sure, I know," he drawled. "But I look at it this way: She'll have her own cross to bear, goin' through life believin' that her husband is a murderer. That satisfies me. I don't need anything more."

Neville's features twisted into a grimace. "So will the girls, rememberin' their father was hanged for a killin'."

"Kids grow out of memories," Lance replied matter-of-factly. "And besides, I figger with the money they'll . . .

let's say *inherit*, your family will go start a new life far from here."

Neville could hardly believe he was listening to such a proposition. He could accept even less that he was actually considering the offer by having this conversation. He had to be drunk. Drunk, crazy . . . or just desperate enough to take it seriously.

"Y'gotta ask yourself, Neville, is life really worth livin'?" Lance said. He spoke almost with a compassion in his voice. "I'm talkin' 'bout the way it is for you now. How it is for your family. Scroungin' out an existence."

Neville didn't answer. Because the "honest" answer—the one he would provide if he were to be completely truthful—was painfully obvious. Regardless of how much he loved his family, his constant worry over their welfare had turned his life into an ongoing turmoil.

"No one can blame yuh for tryin'," Lance said as he looked directly into Neville's eyes. "You took a shot. If your efforts had worked out I wouldn't even be here talkin' to yuh. But the way things turn out in life . . . Well, let's say your situation provided me with an opportunity too good to pass up. A benefit to us both, if yuh open your head to it."

A cunning look instantly crossed Neville's face.

"On the other hand, maybe your situation has given *me* my own opportunity," he said in return. "You just admitted to killing a man—someone important, you said. Might be there's a reward in that. All I gotta do is ride into Commercial City and give 'em your name—Lance Denning."

Neville was surprised that Lance didn't appear the least bothered by his implied threat. His demeanor remained confident and assured.

"Yeah, you could do that," Lance finally said with a contemplative nod. "Only . . . wouldn't be wise. 'Cause if you was to be taken at your word, wouldn't just be me you'd be informin' ag'in." His voice rose and he spoke with a sudden surge of irritation. "Dammit, Neville, ain't you been listenin'? The people I work for have influence. They regard folks of your kind as no more than chicken droppings. They wouldn't take kindly to you playin' hero. Makin' accusations that might put them and their business plans in jeopardy. And I can tell you this, Neville, whether you wanta hear it or not, they can be downright ruthless. Wouldn't be just you . . . but your family that would suffer if'n you was stupid 'nuff to start speakin' outta turn. So 'fore you even think 'bout goin' down that trail, I'd reconsider the idea pronto."

Neville fell silent. Point made, bluntly. Neville was exhausted. He both felt and appeared deflated and defeated. And his defenses were weakening ever more.

It was a mad proposition, but if Denning was true to his word and his offer was genuine, it also made sense. Neville's guilt and despair over what he was subjecting his family to was at times so overwhelming that he had seriously been tempted to walk out into the field to fire a bullet through his brain. Other times he just wanted to hop onto old Daniel and ride far away, selfishly escape, but attempting to justify his move by convincing himself that by disappearing it might encourage Sarah to pack up the girls and go on to start a better life.

Perhaps his ongoing fight against the odds to hold on to his family was the "true" selfishness. With a shudder he considered that he could ride back to the farm tomorrow and find his daughter Penelope dead. Because in his stubborn attempts to hold his family together in a wretched environment, he'd failed to sufficiently provide for her. Both of his girls were weak and ill from poor eating and the cold that seeped relentlessly into the cabin during the winter season. That either child had survived this long was nothing short of a miracle.

But he couldn't go on depending on miracles.

And even Sarah wasn't as strong as she once had been. Where not long ago she had been pretty and vibrant, her constitution admirable, now her face was aging as her energy ebbed. The liveliness in her eyes had dulled and where once they sparkled with a determined love and belief in her husband, now they were tired and pouched and on occasion glazed with despair.

All of these memories penetrated Neville's brain with a painful persistence, and the more he let these thoughts swell in his consciousness, the more he began to regard himself with revulsion.

So . . . the extreme solution that Lance Denning was proposing was not one that he could completely dismiss.

In fact, it might be the only way to set things right.

"Go to my grave a marked man," Neville said musingly. "Probably won't even give me a decent burial."

"That so important . . . when you're leavin' behind somethin' that matters more than a mound of dirt?" Lance countered.

Neville spoke forthright. "I still gotta know if I was to go through with this that I can trust you. That Sarah won't—"

Lance interjected by lifting his hand to silence him, then closing his fingers 'til only his index finger remained upraised. He reached into his trousers pocket and withdrew his billfold. With his eyes fixed on Neville, he slowly withdrew all the folding money inside the billfold and laid it flat under the palm of his hand onto the table, sliding the cash toward Neville, who regarded it with a temptation demonstrated by a reflexive wetting of his lips. Lance offered a knowing smile.

"A thousand dollars," he said. "Cold hard cash. Once they hang yuh, your family gets another five thousand. As I told yuh, my associates will be mighty 'preciative, and they know how to reward a good turn. Six thousand dollars, Neville. More than enough for your family to get by on—for a long time. New start for 'em, fine things for your wife, maybe presents for your kids. Everything you been wantin' to provide 'em with but ain't been able to. I think that money sittin' there on the table shows yuh my offer is genuine." He paused and his face turned serious. "'Course I can't make no guarantees how Sarah's gonna wanta deal with money she knows nothin' 'bout all of a sudden just comin' to her."

Neville himself had already considered that possibility. He rocked his head in acknowledgment.

"But so far as them gettin' the money . . . on that I give yuh my word," Lance said as a promise.

He pointed to the cash still sitting untouched before Neville. "All you gotta do is pick it up and that seals our bargain."

Six thousand dollars. Neville saw the irony and almost could have laughed. At one time he'd had—and squandered—five times that amount, and thought nothing of it, spending it frivolously and having nothing to show for it. Now he was looking at his family's future, where six thousand dollars was like discovering a gold mine. It would guarantee his wife and girls a security that Neville simply could not provide them by any other means.

Neville found that he could barely utter his words. "Don't know why . . . reckon I still don't understand all of what's behind this, other than you wantin'—"

"And that's all yuh really gotta know," Lance interjected.

"But what you're sayin' . . ." Neville was unable to finish.

Lance made himself sound sincere. "Man's done all he can, can't find no other way out, sometimes yuh gotta see the solution as it stands. I been around, Neville. Seen people goin' through rough times. A lotta families ain't gettin' by. Children, kids like your own, fallin' sick, starvin' to death or walkin' 'round with skin hangin' offa bone. The lucky ones . . . they're chowin' down on a diet of grease and fried dough. Your kids even that lucky, Neville? You really gotta look at this as good fortune. Not many people get the opportunity you've been given."

Neville swiftly raked his fingers through his hair in a tense gesture.

He said hastily, "If I agree to this . . . or if'n I don't, when do I give you my answer?"

"This ain't somethin' you can sleep on," Lance told him bluntly. "Fact, yuh gotta make your decision 'fore we leave this table, keepin' in mind this is a onetime offer. You won't be gettin' no second chance. That's the way it's gotta be. All or nothin'." He waited for a reaction that didn't come, and then he added, "Understand it's a big decision. That's why I also know there's that slim chance you might be tempted to pocket that money, gather up Sarah and the kids and try to run off. Wouldn't recommend that, Neville. My associates wouldn't take kindly to a man without honor."

"So . . . there ain't no backin' out," Neville said tenuously.

There was no need for Lance to reply. His lengthy silence and penetrating stare provided the answer.

Neville again ran his fingers through his hair as he regarded the money on the table with a look combining longing and contempt.

"Blood money," he muttered miserably. "Only it'll be my blood."

"That how you wanta see it?" Lance said, eyeing Neville intently. "Or d'yuh wanta look at it with more favorable intent?"

Neville's face gradually became a study in thought.

He spoke uncertainly. "I dunno." After a few seconds of thought: "S'pose . . . maybe." And then he added in a voice of resignation, "But—if it promises a better life for my family."

"I'd call it an opportunity any husband and father in your situation would be grateful for," Lance said. He frowned a bit, considering. "Well, any man that gave a damn 'bout his kin, that is."

Neville took insult at what was insinuated by his remark. Lance Denning knew nothing of how he felt about Sarah and his daughters, to what extent he would go to provide them with a good life. Then his attitude mellowed as he realized how under any circumstance he would freely give up his own life for each and every one of them.

"If it promises my family a better life," he repeated soberly.

"It will," Lance assured him.

Neville blew out a long breath and summoned all of his reserve to keep himself from trembling. There was no more time for talk, argument, or debate. He looked like a man consumed, confused, and conflicted. His face exposed each of these expressions while Lance sat patiently and waited for him to work out his decision.

He did not arrive at his answer quickly, temptation be damned. Neville again stared at the cash on the table, money that with a simple acknowledgment represented his family's future. Not just their welfare but likely their very survival. He again breathed out heavily, but his fingers remained fastened, locked together, tightly, on his lap under the table, as if he were physically trying to restrain himself from making that definitive gesture.

Lance gently prompted his decision with the reminder:

"What's there is just a taste of what's gonna come to 'em, Neville. That money is just to bind our agreement."

Neville still hesitated.

"And one more thing for you to keep in mind," Lance added soberly. "I hafta trust you as much as you gotta trust me."

Neville's fingers pulled apart. Both hands were clammy and they separated without effort, almost of their own will. His right hand rose from his lap and slid toward the bills laid out on the table. Lance watched his movements with interest. But then Neville's hand halted its progress as he instead lifted his left hand, picked up the napkin set before him, and wiped dry the palms of both hands.

Lance gestured with a deliberate pointing of his finger toward the "prize" that was his for the taking on the tablecloth.

Neville met Lance's eyes, briefly—and then in a swift, abrupt motion, as if refusing to surrender to further doubt, he reached out and wrapped his fingers around the cash, crumpling the bills in a fist and drawing the money toward him.

Lance looked pleased.

"Gonna count it?" he said.

Neville didn't answer. There was no need. Instead he fixed Lance with a solid stare, which said in effect: *Decision made. Fate sealed.*

Neville rode back to his farm the next morning. He would check in on his daughter, drop off the supplies he'd purchased—and tell a falsehood to Sarah that he had been offered a job during his stopover in Still Bend.

Most of all, he had come to say good-bye to his family.

When he rode the buckboard onto his property, he was fearful. The "blood bargain" he had made with Lance

Denning, which had consumed his thoughts during much of his ride, took on a lesser significance as he now had to consider what he might find at the farm.

Had Penelope rallied . . . or perhaps had her illness worsened?

Upon hearing the familiar sound of the wagon pulling into the yard, an anxious Sarah emerged quickly from the house with a strained look on her face—a troubled expression that instantly filled Neville with dread.

Neville leaped down from the buckboard and Sarah hurried into his arms. They embraced tightly while Neville prepared himself to receive news that he prayed he would not hear.

"Penelope," he just managed to get out.

Sarah lifted her head from his shoulder and gazed at him with moist, grateful eyes.

"She's better, Tom, thank God!" she told him. "She slept through the night and even got up this morning asking for breakfast."

Neville expressed his relief with a prolonged sigh. The tension that had corrupted his features began to ease.

"But you, Tom . . . why didn't you come home last night?" Sarah asked with a concern that was touching.

Neville nodded, not answering directly. "Gathered up supplies from town. Stopped by the doc's office and picked up medicine for Penelope. Let's go inside, have some coffee, and I'll tell yuh all 'bout it." He hesitated, then made his voice sound excited and confident. "It's good news, Sarah. Real good news."

"You look so tired, Tom," Sarah observed.

Neville wasn't about to tell her that he hadn't slept a wink the previous night. He merely brushed aside her worry, wrapping his arm around her waist, and the two of them walked toward the little cabin.

After each of the packages was brought inside, Neville spent a few minutes with his daughters, overwhelmed with gratitude that Penelope did seem to be improving—and now most certainly would be on the mend with the medicine he'd gotten from the doctor in Still Bend. He then sat at the table while Sarah prepared his coffee. She was surprised and delighted when she discovered Neville had bought her a tin of tea, which she preferred as a beverage but had become a luxury in recent times. Neville enjoyed watching as she brewed her tea with great care and with a look of pure pleasure.

They sat with their hot drinks and talked. Little Rose sat on the floor next to her daddy, and he kept his hand resting affectionately on her head, fingers gently massaging her scalp.

He tried to keep enthusiasm in his voice as he lied to Sarah and told her about the job offer he'd received.

"Just got to talkin' with this fella I met in town," he said. He'd already worked out the details in his mind; he just had to present them convincingly. "One of them chance opportunities where I off-the-cuff mentioned I was lookin' for work and he said he needs someone to be helpin' on a cattle drive. Says he found himself shorthanded . . . seems some of his drovers up and got gold fever. That's why I didn't come back last night," he added. "We ended up talkin' well into the night . . . and got to havin' a few drinks."

"How long would you be gone?" Sarah asked tentatively.

"Oh, probably least six months," Neville answered. "We'll be drivin' cattle to a railhead up north."

Sarah frowned. "But it's still early in the season."

"Not so much," Neville answered. "There's preparations to be done. Means extra pay."

Sarah tried to look happy, share her husband's enthusiasm, support this decision, but her expression betrayed the sadness she couldn't help but feel. It troubled her to think of Neville being gone for such a long stretch.

Neville detected the transparency of her joy. He forced back a swallow and then resumed. "I worked it out with this fella not only to get an advance on my pay but to have all my wages sent directly to you. Won't be needin' nothin' for myself on the trail. But with me bein' gone, first thing I want you to do is sell this property. Pack up whatever you wanta bring and you and the girls move away from here."

Sarah looked astonished at what her husband was suggesting.

Neville reached across the small table and gently laid his hand over his wife's arm.

"We done the best we can here, Sarah, but we both know it ain't no good," he said tenderly. "This ain't no life for you and 'specially not for the girls. Look . . ." He pulled out a handful of crumpled bills that he pressed into Sarah's fingers, which she seemed strangely reluctant to accept. "Almost a thousand dollars, Sarah—minus what I spent in town. Cleared up our account with that shopkeeper Curtis and nearly gave him a heart attack. And there'll be more a-comin' with this opportunity I got."

She didn't acknowledge the money; almost seemed not to notice.

"But . . . if we leave, how will you know where to find us when you come back?" Sarah asked with concern.

"That's all been taken care of," Neville told her, attempting to brush aside her concern with a reassuring smile. "'Fore I leave, I'm gonna be givin' yuh an address in San Francisco. Don't understand all the business details, but they have an office there that'll be handlin' the payroll. You let 'em know where you're at. They'll wire yuh the money . . ." Here his voice started to slip and he quickly collected himself. Sarah seemed to be watching him closely, and she was not a dumb woman.

"And when I come back from the drive, they'll let me know where you and the girls are at," he finished.

Penelope was asleep, but Rose heard all of what her daddy was saying and understood it as best she could in her childish way. Neville became aware of her stifled sobs as her little head began to bob. He reached down for her and pulled her onto his lap.

"I don't want you to go away, Daddy," she said.

Neville smiled at her. He gingerly brushed away her big tears with his index finger.

"I know, honey," he said, mustering all of his self-control to keep his voice from trembling. "Daddy doesn't want to go, either. But sometimes we gotta do things we don't really wanta. A good daddy needs to take care of his family."

Neville hugged her tightly, nuzzling his face into her tiny chest, and then he lifted his head to look back at Sarah.

"It's what I gotta do, Sarah," he said firmly, maintaining the pretense of honesty in his voice.

Sarah struggled with her own conflicting emotions. She knew her husband was right. He couldn't pass up an opportunity to make some real money when they had been working so hard at keeping the farm going with so little success. But the thought of Tom being apart from her and the girls for half a year—maybe longer—distressed her.

Her voice was halting. "When—would you have to be leaving?"

Again Neville worked to keep himself steady. "In a coupla days. Wanta make sure Penelope is all the way on the mend 'fore I go. Hate to be leavin' you with all the details of sellin' the place. Don't expect much for the property; settle for whatever you can get. Money ain't gonna be of a matter. Just know you're headed for better days." He swiftly adjusted his words: "*We're* headed for better days."

Sarah's face lowered. Neville reached over, took her gently by the chin, and tilted her head upward. She gradually raised her eyes and met his gaze.

Neville fixed her with the most genuine smile he could manage.

"That's a promise," he said.

There was nothing else for Neville to say. He only hoped that he had convinced Sarah. He could never remember feeling such an aching in his gut—outside that day when he betrayed Sheriff Dan. And here, again, he spoke a lie, but a necessary one. The last falsehood he would ever tell.

No . . . that wasn't so. There would be one more. He'd be telling his final lie to the sheriff in Commercial City when he came in to confess to a murder.

After that, he would say nothing . . . wouldn't utter a sound . . . not even as they led him up the steps to the scaffold.

FOURTEEN

They'd ridden together for many years and across many miles, and tonight Neville would finally say good-bye to his horse Daniel once they entered Commercial City. He'd have no further need for the loyal old mount, which fairly limped into town, and so he worked out a deal with the livery stable owner. The man named Fred was just getting ready to close up for the night and eager to get home to supper and so was not in the mood to haggle over price. He was prepared to tell Neville to come back in the morning, but Neville surprised him. All he said in a weary voice was just to take the best care of Daniel and accept the horse, and saddle, without any kind of payment. Fred checked the horse over and said he couldn't argue with those terms even though the horse's front right leg needed tending and that he would have to prepare a bandage and salt pack to reduce the swelling. That aside, the horse could still serve some purpose, provided the activity wasn't too strenuous. The two men shook hands on the deal, and then Fred went into his office to prepare the bill of sale. Neville halted him. He said that wasn't necessary. The animal was now his, no need for a paper transaction. Fred looked a tad puzzled—suspicious even. Neville smiled and assured Fred that he owned the horse free and clear. It was just that he wouldn't be needing him anymore. Fred shrugged and nodded, and then Neville went to spend a few minutes with his animal.

"Well, fella," he murmured to Daniel with a grim smile, stroking his muzzle affectionately. "Yuh took me as far as I'm gonna go. But leastwise yuh still got a few miles left in you."

He then nodded good night to Fred and started on foot along the raised planking of the boardwalk toward the sheriff's office. Fred stepped outside and watched him go, perplexedly rubbing the whiskers on his chin.

Neville started his walk slowly but gradually picked up his pace. He knew what he was going to say to the town lawman. All the details had been worked out between him and Lance Denning.

There wasn't much he'd say anyhow. He'd speak his piece once and then say nothing more.

It was nightfall and Sheriff Tim Rawlins was sitting in his office nursing a cup of strong coffee, relaxing as best he knew how and rocking slightly on the swivel chair behind his desk. It had been almost three weeks since his friend, Mayor Thaddeus Ford, had been shot down in broad daylight on the street, and he remained frustrated that there had been no break in the case. The killing had happened so fast and unexpectedly that the gunman was long gone before anyone could recover sufficiently from the shock to attempt a pursuit or even provide a description of the culprit. Still, the citizens had started to put pressure on him. They demanded that this killer be brought to justice.

No one in town wanted the crime solved more than Sheriff Rawlins. The sheer brazenness of the murder provided Rawlins with his main lead. He had his own definite suspicions of who had masterminded the bloody ambush. But how to prove what he suspected was the problem he faced.

The gunman had been hired by the San Francisco gambling syndicate—on that he was willing to stake his badge.

It was a professional killing, made to appear personal—
perhaps committed by a disgruntled citizen seeking ven-
geance against the mayor for some perceived wrongdoing.
But that conjecture didn't hold water with the sheriff. He
knew the mayor intimately and couldn't think of anyone
within the community who would want to see him dead. In
fact, Rawlins had never known a man so respected.

Rawlins had just one opportunity to prove his case. He
was certain agents would again be sent to Commercial City
with the intention to conclude the business that Mayor Ford
had abruptly terminated. They would bide their time so as
not to draw suspicion to themselves. But they would be back.

And Sheriff Rawlins would be waiting.

The sheriff was considering their next play when a tired
and disheveled-looking man walked into his office—a fellow appearing a mite nervous and uncertain.

Rawlins regarded the man without greeting. He didn't
rise from behind his desk. Instead he settled back into his
chair and waited for the stranger to state his business.

Neville's weary eyes shifted about the office before they
settled on the sheriff. He observed the man at the desk, and it
took scant seconds for him to identify Rawlins with the only
other lawman he'd known: Sheriff Dan Bridges. It wasn't so
much a physical resemblance other than both were large, pow-
erfully built men. Nor was it a specific facial expression or
mannerism that he could determine, since there hadn't been
the time to recognize any such similarities between the two.
Neville couldn't define exactly what it was. And then it dawned
on him: This lawman exuded the same formidable presence
as had Sheriff Dan. A no-nonsense approach to his duty. The
badge he wore on his chest was no mere decoration.

Now that the moment had come, Neville felt his resolve
start to weaken. He reckoned that was understandable. Any
man faced with what he was about to experience could not
help but feel trepidation. But he had to fight against his fear,
as he'd made a commitment that decided not only his fate
but that of his family . . . if he should betray his obligation.
Therefore it was imperative that he proceed cautiously,

precisely, with the sheriff. Neville sensed that he was a man
who could not be bamboozled, one who would see through
any deception.

He freed his gaze from Rawlins and almost at once his
eyes connected with the reward poster pinned to the bulletin
board off to the side of the sheriff's desk. It read:

$5000 REWARD FOR INFORMATION
LEADING TO THE CAPTURE AND CONVICTION
OF THE COWARDLY MURDERER
OF MAYOR THADDEUS FORD.

Focusing on the reward money gave Neville momentary
pause. Five thousand dollars. An amount near to what Lance
Denning was going to pay his family for agreeing to getting
his neck stretched. And here he stood, looking at all that
money printed on the poster and him in a position to collect,
since he knew the name of the true killer of the mayor. A
confession made to his face. The temptation was strong, but
again he faced the reminder of what Lance had told him.
The threat might have been subtle, but the promise was one
Neville could not ignore.

Finally Sheriff Rawlins rose from behind his desk. As
he watched the sheriff present himself at his full height and
girth, Neville felt an old intimidation start to surface.

"Stranger walks into my office at this hour, figger he's
got somethin' to say," Rawlins said in a coarse voice. "Else
he's drunk and lookin' for a place to lay his head, and you
don't seem like you been drinkin'."

"I ain't drunk," Neville mumbled.

"Little worse for wear, though," the sheriff observed.

"Been on the trail," Neville replied faintly.

"Ridin' with a herd?"

"No. Just ridin'."

Gradually Neville pulled himself together, though he still
appeared hesitant, tentative. He pointed to a chair next to
the sheriff's desk, and Rawlins nodded and gestured with a
wave of his hand for him to sit himself. Neville took slow,

deliberate steps over to the chair. Rawlins watched him carefully, with a look of interest—and a lawman's suspicion. The stranger appeared a little unsteady on his feet.

"You want a cup of water?" Rawlins offered.

It had been a while since Neville sipped his last drink, but he shook his head no.

Rawlins walked over to him. Neville gazed up at the man, and his lips, chapped and dry from his days in the sun, formed a peculiar smile, just a faint creasing at the sides of his mouth. He noticed how the sheriff regarded him with an expression hard to define.

"You got a drink?" Neville said.

"Offered yuh some water," Rawlins replied.

"No—a *drink*," Neville snapped. "A shot of whiskey."

The lines in Tim Rawlins's face deepened. Wordlessly, he ambled over to a side cabinet, withdrew a bottle of rye whiskey, and poured Neville about a quarter of a glass. Instead of replacing the bottle back inside the cabinet, he brought it with him over to the desk. He handed Neville the glass and noticed how he suddenly hesitated to accept it. He stared at the whiskey contemplatively . . . and then he finally and firmly placed the glass on the desk without taking even a taste.

Rawlins appeared perplexed at this odd behavior.

"Just put it away," Neville told him.

Rawlins prudently pushed the glass aside, away from Neville's reach. He set the bottle on the floor at the side of the desk.

"You got a name?" he said curtly.

After a brief hesitation: "Neville."

"That's it? Neville."

Neville nodded.

"All right, Neville, now why don't yuh just state your business?" Rawlins said in a more friendly manner.

Neville breathed out a sigh. "I do have a matter to talk over with you, Sheriff. But—I'd suggest you handcuff me 'fore I say anything more."

Rawlins regarded Neville with a deliberate look and folded his arms across the width of his barrel-like chest.

"Now why would you be askin' me to do that?" he said.

Neville hesitated, then focused his eyes solidly on Rawlins and spoke outright the words he'd come to say. "'Cause I'm the man that killed your mayor."

For just a second or two Sheriff Rawlins didn't respond, just continued to meet Neville's stare while he held his pose. Then he cocked his brow.

"*You* killed Mayor Ford?" he finally said.

Neville gave a hurried nod.

Rawlins then stepped away. His back was facing Neville. An intentional and calculated move on his part.

"So you're confessin' to murder?" he said.

Neville responded with a whispered, "Yeah."

"And you wanta give yourself up?" Rawlins's tone held a slight sardonic edge.

Neville didn't care for the way the sheriff spoke those words, but he repeated, "Yeah."

Rawlins turned back around to face Neville directly, and he had a peculiar look on his face.

"You walk in here, admit to gunnin' down our mayor, ask to be handcuffed even . . . and yet you don't first turn in your gun," he said.

Neville's eyes slid down to his side, to the Colt revolver resting inside his holster.

"Wasn't the first thing on my mind," he said in reply.

The sheriff didn't say anything.

Neville spoke heatedly. "I wouldn't come to turn myself in if'n I was plannin' to shoot yuh."

"Would seem a mite peculiar."

Neville got to his feet, unbuckled his gun belt, and tossed it onto the sheriff's desk. He then slid back into the chair. He was so tired he just wanted to be put inside a jail cell so he could grab some shut-eye and deal with the situation in the morning. But to his dismay the sheriff did not seem ready to accommodate him.

Neville spoke with an irritated impatience. "Seems you're more concerned 'bout the way I came in here than findin' out why I did it."

"Why you killed Mayor Ford?" Rawlins said.

Neville rocked his head.

Rawlins began to pace slowly around his office. Neville watched his movements and waited for him to say something—*anything*. He felt himself being swallowed whole in what he perceived was a deliberate silence. A silence perhaps intended to make him unsettled enough to admit the truth.

"What're yuh waitin' for?" Neville bellowed. "Whyn't you lock me in a cell? Arrest me."

Rawlins halted his steps. He turned to him. "'Cause I don't think yuh did it," he said simply.

Neville hadn't expected this. He didn't anticipate the sheriff doubting his confession.

"A man don't admit to a killin' he didn't do," he argued.

"Ain't usually the case."

"What sense is there in a man admittin' to somethin' he ain't guilty of when he knows he's got a noose waitin'?" Neville said tersely.

"Why would a man that done the crime confess to it knowin' he's got the same fate in store?" the sheriff asked him back.

Neville struggled to add conviction to his words, speaking pensively. "Maybe . . . maybe 'cause he done it just for that reason. He can't live with the guilt no longer. Not with his conscience gnawin' at him, givin' him no rest. He wants to get hanged to rid himself of that. Death can relieve that burden a man has to carry."

"Is that what brung *you* in here?" Rawlins asked without compassion.

Neville didn't answer.

"Man shoulda thought of that 'fore he pulled the trigger," Rawlins presented.

"Sometimes . . . a man acts fast, without considerin' the consequences," Neville replied in a low, weary voice. "And maybe it gets to a point in a man's life where nothin' else matters. You can only go so far and then yuh look for a way out."

Before Neville could say more, Rawlins interrupted with words that were intentionally harsh. "Things get that desperate for a man, he has to be a *man*. He don't put a gun to his head or maybe go ridin' his horse off a cliff. And I ain't ever yet heard of someone deliberately shooting down a man with the intention of wantin' to get hanged."

"Situation gets desperate 'nuff, a man'll do whatever it takes," Neville replied bleakly.

"Not a man with a conscience."

"Desperate men can't afford a conscience," Neville returned bitterly, wiping away perspiration from his upper lip.

Rawlins gave his head a shake. "That's a sorry attitude."

"Best I can give yuh."

Rawlins leveled skeptical eyes at Neville.

"'Fore we go any farther, I got my own suspicions who's responsible for this crime. And I know whoever pulled that trigger wouldn't come waltzin' in here plumb ready to confess." He paused and breathed out slowly. "Still, I've got a duty to uphold. You came in here of your own free will and confessed to killin' Mayor Ford, and so I'm obliged to hold yuh. First thing tomorrow I'll send a telegram to the U.S. marshal. You'll stand trial in a federal court." He waited a moment before saying, "'Less you decide to come clean 'fore that . . . well, you'll get that hangin' yuh seem to be after."

Neville jerked a thumb at the reward poster. "Reckon you can take that off the wall. Save the state some money."

"That's a federal reward," Rawlins explained. "And think I'll leave it just where it is."

Neville gave the sheriff a bewildered look.

Rawlins smiled thinly. "People in town come into the office regular wantin' to know how things are progressin' with the case. They're an eager bunch after what happened here. Poster comes down . . . they see you sittin' in that cell . . . well, you figger out the rest."

FIFTEEN

Neville had plenty of time to think while sitting in the jail cell awaiting the arrival of the U.S. marshal, which, Rawlins informed him, should be within the next day or so.

It was as if he were backtracking on a desolate country trail approaching the same shadowy destination. So much of what had happened was like reliving his earlier years when he'd made that hasty decision for quick cash and had gone astray. He found himself contemplating if perhaps that was the design of whatever higher power was orchestrating his life—for him to once more find love with someone only to have that opportunity for happiness snatched away, the result of his unexpected introduction to a man with a sinister agenda. He considered the irony of how his life had been dramatically altered by two strangers whose attitudes and motives were strikingly similar, each with a dark connection to the girl in Neville's life. And now here he was locked in a cell by a lawman who in indefinable ways reminded him of Sheriff Dan. The sheriff who had vowed to one day bring him to justice.

Had that delayed day of reckoning finally arrived?

If so, Neville recognized and could even accept that he

had earned a punishment. He'd been long in eluding it. In
selfish, ultimately insignificant ways he'd even been able to
profit from his crime. Momentary joys and satisfaction—all
shallow and unfulfilling—nothing with which to leave a
legacy. Now, he reasoned, at least he had the comfort of
knowing that something good, something positive and
potentially permanent would come from his sacrifice.

The security of his family.

But there was a complication that he had not counted on.
The sheriff. He remained steadfast in his belief that Neville
was innocent. He didn't accept Neville's story that he'd shot
down the mayor in a drunken rampage. No motive, just
looking for someone to kill in an inebriated state. To Rawlins, who possessed a long and solid career in law enforcement, both as a detective and investigator in big cities in the
East and now as a frontier sheriff, what Neville claimed
simply did not seem plausible given what he had been able
to discern in the man's character. Drunk or sober he didn't
possess a killer instinct, regardless of how desperately Neville tried to convince him otherwise.

That was another reason that once Neville was confined
to his cell, he simply ceased talking. Tim Rawlins was a
clever man, much like Sheriff Dan, who, while generally
taciturn, talked a lot when he felt it necessary, and Rawlins's
attempts at genial conversation subtly introduced a lot of
questions. It would be easy for Neville to slip up, say the
wrong thing. Stubbornly maintaining his silence ensured
that he would not accidentally compromise his admission
of guilt, regardless of what tactics the sheriff tried. So when
Rawlins tried to engage him in conversation, Neville would
simply remove his ten-dollar gold eagle from his breast
pocket and start flipping it between his knuckles. He would
concentrate on his little trick, not on the sheriff's words.

And so, on his own, Sheriff Rawlins tried to find out
whatever he could about the man who simply called himself
Neville. But his efforts proved fruitless and downright frustrating. There wasn't any specific course he could pursue
with such a slim lead, and Neville merely sat there on his

bunk, hour after hour, consumed in a damnable quiet, playing with his coin, taking a bite of his meals now and then, but seemingly lost in whatever mystery occupied his mind.

What Rawlins purposely did not do, however, was release to the community that he had in his custody the man who claimed to have shot their respected mayor. If a visitor happened to drop into his office and question him about the man sitting in the cell, Rawlins would merely answer that the prisoner was being held on another charge. It was a necessary precaution. Not only because Rawlins was convinced Neville was innocent, but he also was acutely aware that by revealing Neville's claim he could incite a town riot that most likely would result in vigilantism.

Yet . . . as Rawlins looked for a way to get at the truth, he saw a possible solution. Perhaps instilling in him the fear of a lynch mob might encourage Neville to come clean.

It was an extreme measure, but Rawlins also rationalized he had nothing to lose.

And whether he recognized it or not, neither did his prisoner.

Come supper one evening, Rawlins dragged his chair close to the jail cell and settled down with his meal. Neville's dinner sat untouched on a plate next to him on his bunk.

Rawlins looked approvingly at his supper and forked around his beef and watery bean concoction. He spoke while he chewed, eyes focused on his plate, his voice suggesting no worry or concern.

"Some stirrin' up in town," he said. "People gettin' curious. Startin' to raise the suspicion among one 'nother that you might be the one that gunned down Mayor Ford."

Neville didn't respond. His face maintained a vacant expression while he flipped his gold piece.

Rawlins gave him a slanting glance.

"I didn't say nothin' myself," he assured Neville. "But surprising how gossip 'round town can spread. Yeah, almost like a brushfire. Starts off as a rumor but grows into what people wanta believe. Citizens seen you sittin' in that cell and they start drawin' their own conclusions."

Neville stayed quiet, the look on his face unflinching. Rawlins, however, noticed just the faintest flickering of his eyes in his direction.

Rawlins scooped up another mouthful of food, which he both slurped and chewed with pleasure.

"Yeah," he said, sighing for emphasis, "with feelin's bein' what they are, the citizens get a bit anxious and are apt to reach any conclusion."

Still not a word from Neville.

"S'pose my concern is that the U.S. marshal gets here soon," Rawlins added largely. "Always seen Commercial City as a peaceful place . . . but I can't guarantee how much longer that'll be. I been sheriff here since when the town was first built and I ain't never had to hold a murderer in my jail. Nope, and 'cause of that never seen how people here would react to havin' a killer in their midst. And not just a killer, mind you, but the man who says outright that he murdered the most respected person this community has ever known." He slyly eyed Neville.

Neville refused to acknowledge what he could see was the sheriff's ploy. Hell . . . the lawman couldn't have been any more obvious.

Still . . . Rawlins was most likely right on the money, describing how the citizens might react if their suspicions about the man sitting in their jail reached a fever pitch. They might not be so patient and law-abiding to await the arrival of the federal marshal to safely escort the prisoner to a proper trial. From what Neville had been able to discern from Sheriff Rawlins's one-sided conversations, these townspeople still embraced a pioneer spirit—and possessed the basic right-or-wrong mentality, the latter of which demanded swift, severe punishment. As a lad Neville recalled hearing of pioneer treks where even the stealing of food could result in a whipping or even a hanging, even if the taking of those morsels meant that a child might not starve. A crime had to be dealt with harshly—if not necessarily justly. Neville could not know whether these citizens still held on to their practices of frontier justice.

The plain truth was that Neville had yet to fully accept that he might die legally through the decision of a court. And Sheriff Rawlins had made him aware that there could be an even swifter and more cruel justice. One whose immediacy and violence instilled in him a very real trepidation:

The too-real possibility that he could fall victim to the fury of a lynch mob.

Rawlins finished his dinner. He suppressed a belch and pushed the tin plate aside. He turned to Neville.

"Can try to hold 'em back if'n they decide to charge the jail," he said, though speaking with little conviction. "But I'm one man ag'in a town. And I ain't gonna be beaten down or even killed to protect someone who won't even protect himself."

At hearing those words Neville leaped to his feet and moved swiftly toward the edge of his cell, gripping the iron bars tightly. He finally spoke—and there was desperation in his voice.

"But that's your job," he said tensely. He pointed to the tin star fastened on the sheriff's chest. "Why yuh wear that badge."

Rawlins stood up, his expression rigid, but inwardly pleased that he'd finally stimulated Neville into talking.

"Yeah," he said. "But there are things that gotta be considered. If'n you was guilty, if the law was to proceed as it should given there was truth in your confession . . . yeah, in that case I'd have a sworn duty. To protect the accused 'til justice could have its say. But there simply ain't no truth in you. And I ain't fool 'nuff to be riskin' my life for no liar."

Neville spoke deliberately. "Why won't you believe me?"

Rawlins replied loudly, "'Cause you don't believe it yourself."

"You're sure of that, huh?" Neville challenged.

Rawlins nodded confidently. "That shootin' was the work of a coward. Cold-blooded but still a cowardly act. And from where I stand, any man willin' to stick his neck into a hemp noose can't be no coward."

Neville was starting to look sweaty; his bravado appeared to be fading.

"I don't condone murder," Rawlins said. "I'll do whatever is in my power 'fore the U.S. marshal gets here. But should things get outta hand 'fore that happens . . . I can't give no guarantees."

Neville's lips twisted.

"You're a damn fool," Rawlins said shortly.

"Been called worse."

Rawlins gave a sigh. "What I can't figger is why yuh can't see no matter how it turns out—either with vigilantes breakin' in here to string yuh up or with you swingin' from a rope after the courts judge yuh guilty . . . on your own confession—the outcome is gonna be the same. Yet yuh seem more fidgety 'bout the quicker hangin'. Kinda looks to me that you're lookin' for a reason for a stall. And if that's the case, I'd say you don't really wanta die."

Another day passed. Neville remained steadfast in his decision not to say anything that might clear him of his false confession. It was likely the U.S. marshal would be arriving at some point today. Neville didn't know how he felt about that. His immediate concern had been falling victim to a lynch mob. But now it seemed as if that threat had faded; at least the sheriff had said no more about it and things had remained quiet. Yet once the federal marshal rode into town, Neville's fate was likewise sealed. There could be little doubt as to the outcome with him pleading guilty at the trial.

Sheriff Rawlins dealt with his own frustration. Neville had sentenced himself to the hangman's rope and he still didn't know why. What Rawlins *did* know was that it could be a terrible death. He'd witnessed his share of hangings while a lawman in the East and admittedly cringed at each one. The condemned twitching at the end of the taut rope, slowly suffocating to death if he wasn't fortunate enough to have his neck snap on impact. He recalled one particularly gruesome hanging where the noose was improperly knotted and a man's head was severed clean from his body when the trap opened. The technique supposedly ensuring a swift and relatively peaceful descent into unconsciousness followed by death was by no means foolproof.

Yet Rawlins felt he'd run out of options to encourage Neville to come clean and spare himself such a fate. Rawlins not only wanted to save an innocent man's life, he'd also come to suspect that Neville might know the identity of the actual killer of Mayor Ford.

And whoever that person was . . . if Rawlins could persuade Neville to tell him the truth, it might put the sheriff on the trail that could lead to the identities of the true masterminds, those men safely concealed in their shadowed respectability in San Francisco.

"I s'pect you'll be seein' the federal marshal today," Rawlins said resignedly to Neville.

Neville appeared unconcerned. He hadn't eaten much since he'd been jailed and already looked thin and gaunt with eyes that seemed to have become as gray as the strands that now swept in a contrast through his brownish-yellow hair. Rawlins thought with astonishment how he had never seen a man age so rapidly as Neville had over these past days. But then . . . facing the fate ahead of him, that wasn't difficult to understand.

"Could get yuh breakfast," he offered.

Neville didn't answer. He looked to ignore the sheriff completely.

"Well, all considered," Rawlins said in a neutral tone, "s'pose you wouldn't be worse off starvin' than takin' the rope."

Neville's jaws clenched so tightly Rawlins could almost hear the grinding of his teeth.

As the day moved forward Neville was starting to experience a sort of conflict with himself. He stood for long periods gripping the bars of his cell, his nervous eyes veering toward the clock on the wall. Before today he'd hardly considered the passing hours. It seemed of no matter with plenty of time still remaining to him. But first the minutes ticked away. Then half hours . . . hours themselves. Rawlins took note of the anxiety taking hold of his prisoner.

He decided on a final attempt to reason with Neville.

He said, "Once you're in the custody of the federal marshal, it'll be outta my hands. Little I can do other than keep on the hunt for the real killer. But might not be time 'fore you're given the rope." He paused before adding: "'Course, doesn't matter to you, shouldn't matter to me."

Just a narrowing of Neville's eyes in response.

"And that in itself is a crime," Rawlins continued. He walked over to the stove to pour himself a cup of coffee. He halted abruptly and half turned toward Neville with a crafty expression.

"Somethin' I was meanin' to ask yuh. Your revolver. That the only sidearm yuh own?"

Neville looked at the sheriff uncertainly before giving a slight nod.

"What I figgered," Rawlins said. "What's interesting is your gun is a .45 Colt. The slugs the doc dug outta Thaddeus Ford came from a .44."

Neville looked startled—but only for an instant before he regained himself. At first he said nothing, but then he devised a quick answer.

"Didn't use *my* Colt," he said firmly. "Got ahold of another gun. Dropped it on the trail after I hightailed it outta town."

"You sure got all the answers," Rawlins responded.

Neville went to sit back on his bunk, then abruptly pulled to his feet and started to pace his cell.

"One last thing I need yuh to know, Neville," Rawlins said, and his words expressed irrevocable purpose. "I *am* gonna bring in Mayor Ford's killer; that's a certainty. Why he murdered the mayor, that I've known from the start, which is another reason why what you're tellin' holds no weight with me. Whether I put the cuffs on that coyote or if'n I'm forced to shoot him dead, that I ain't so sure. By then, you'll be buried somewhere. Buried and forgotten. Hell of a thing, givin' up your life for nothin'."

And then it looked as though Neville was about to say something, but resisted.

"Go on, Neville, talk to me," the sheriff urged him. "Say what it is that you want to."

"It ain't as you say: *nothin'!*" Neville exclaimed. Then, seconds later, it all spewed out of him, with a barely contained rage. "How can yuh call it *nothin'* when a man's got a family to feed? When you see your kids sick all the time and yuh can't do nothin' 'bout it. Fearin' they might be dyin' 'cause you can't take proper care of 'em. Can't get 'em the medicine they need. All you can do is hope and maybe pray that they get better. And a wife hangin' on to her belief in you even when yuh both know the promises you made ain't never gonna come real. When all that's ag'in yuh, it's hard to feel you're a real man. So you can't say it's *nothin'* when a man's gotta make a decision 'cause he's got a family to consider."

By the time Neville finished his tirade it was as if the emotional exertion had expelled all the breath from his lungs. He held himself tight against the bars of his cell, looking spent from venting a bitter frustration he'd kept dormant.

Yet Rawlins wore a satisfied expression. He felt that he had finally started to get through to his prisoner. With his outburst Neville had revealed something about himself that might provide a clue as to why he'd confessed to a killing for which he was not responsible. Only the sheriff didn't know how much more he could persuade out of Neville. The marshal could be riding into town at this moment. Time was running out.

"That why you're doin' this, for your family?" Rawlins prodded gently. "You sayin' you got a wife, Neville? Children?"

Neville didn't answer. He appeared upset with himself for allowing the sheriff to provoke him to the point where he'd said things he shouldn't have.

The sheriff was stern. "You was talkin' 'bout *yourself*—and don't go denyin' it. What's tragic is that I don't see how gettin' yourself hanged is gonna do much for your family. Your missus loses a husband, your kids a daddy. At what price, Neville?"

Rawlins noticed how his words looked to hit a nerve with

Neville, a sharp expression of pain that Neville was again quick to conceal.

Rawlins sighed. "Think you've come 'bout as clean as you're gonna for now. Still . . . if'n I was you, while there's still time, maybe I'd dig a little deeper into my conscience. What *really* matters most."

His words might have had an effect. Neville looked to absorb himself in a sort of contemplation. The false bravery of men often dissipated once judgment or punishment was near. Maybe Neville was realizing for the first time that hope lay here, with the sheriff. As Rawlins had plainly noted, once Neville was taken out of his hands by the U.S. marshal, to suddenly plead his innocence would likely make little difference. Many men facing the gallows had suddenly rescinded their confessions only to be ignored. The court alone would determine his fate.

But if Neville had allowed himself that thought, it faded fast as he turned away from Rawlins with an expression of what might have been self-disgust and sat back on his bunk. Once more he looked to close himself off from the sheriff.

"I ain't unfamiliar with those conditions you're describin', Neville," Rawlins said to him, quietly. "Neither was the man you insist you killed. When we crossed the country to settle here, hardly none of us had more than the clothes we was wearin'. Always seemed to be in short supply of essentials. Ridin' trails that were ofttimes treacherous and with the weather sometimes blowin' up a storm that we'd think we'd never see ourselves through. Then there was sickness, where men died, women, children. We dug a lot of graves along the way. Fact, one could almost follow the trail of our journey 'cause the landscape is dotted with the wood crosses we pushed into the dirt. Yeah, Neville, maybe I can find it in myself to understand somethin' of what you're feelin'. 'Cause I been there and seen my share of hard times. A lot of heartache and sadness. But I also seen just as much grit and determination, and that's somethin' I don't see in you. 'Cause you just wanta give up. You wanta use your disappointments not only to bring pain to your kin, but to protect a real killer. Someone even less a man than what you're pretendin' to be."

Neville sat with his eyes cast down to the floor of his cell. He listened, but Rawlins couldn't know if he'd *heard* any of what he had said. At any rate there was nothing more for him to say, and so Rawlins spoke his final words as a blunt acceptance of Neville's decision.

"So go 'head and do it, Neville. I ain't gonna stop you. Fact, I'm through talkin'. Y'got anything else to say, you can speak it to the judge when yuh get to court."

Rawlins had made his point. He'd spoken with all the conviction he could muster. His attempts might have failed, but at least the sheriff could let the prisoner be led away to his fate with as clean a conscience as he would permit himself.

Once the U.S. marshal showed up, Rawlins would simply execute his official duty and turn his prisoner over to him, and there would be nothing more he could do. Not for Neville. But Rawlins still had a duty to perform. To round up the true culprit to the crime and bring him to justice. And through that arrest, to do all in his power to expose the corrupt and murderous machinations of the West Coast gambling syndicate and permanently halt their snakelike penetration into frontier communities.

It was a debt he owed his friend, Mayor Thaddeus Ford. A debt he intended to honor.

He wasn't sure exactly what prompted him. Perhaps the temptation was too great. Maybe the abruptness of her leaving, what he still considered her betrayal, had left a wound yet to be healed. Even Lance Denning wasn't sure of his motivation. But not a week after Neville rode away from his family and farm to turn himself in for a murder he did not commit, the man who initiated his bogus surrender rode up the trail to the desolate homestead. What he saw made him question his own eyes. He knew the family was living in penury, but he couldn't imagine how bad it really was. Glancing about the property, he felt no surprise that Neville had accepted his offer to forfeit his life for a better chance for his family.

It just so happened that Sarah was out in the yard, dressed in denim overalls, a wide-brimmed straw hat perched atop her head to protect her eyes from the glare of the sun. It appeared as if she were tending to some gardening—which Lance could not understand, given that there looked to be nothing of substance that could be produced from the soil.

He made it a good distance up the dry mud trail before the clip-clopping footfalls of his horse alerted Sarah to his presence. She turned in his direction but could not immediately identify the visitor, since the midday sun was bright and all she could make out was the silhouette of a horse and its rider. As he rode in a little closer Sarah shielded her eyes with a cupping of her hand over her brow. The rider was more distinct—it was a man—but she still couldn't determine who he was.

Not until she heard the voice—unmistakable even after all these years.

"Howdy, Sarah-gal."

Instantly she knew. She could forget neither the voice nor that individual way he always referred to her: *Sarah-gal*. The horseman trotted closer toward her. Soon she recognized the face behind the voice. Features that hardly had changed in the years that had since passed. She stood with her mouth agape.

"Lance. Lance Denning," she said in a gasp.

Lance nodded politely, tipped the brim of his hat, and reciprocated. "Sarah Tafford."

Sarah prevented herself from revealing that she now had a married name. Not knowing why Lance had suddenly shown up, she figured it was better not to say too much.

But in the next moment the truth of her situation became apparent when daughter Rose came rushing from the house. Lance observed her closely, with a smile. He could tell immediately that the child was Sarah's daughter. She was the spitting image of the girl Lance remembered playing with when they were both children.

Rose halted when she saw the stranger on horseback. She tilted her head and regarded him with a questioning look.

"Mama," she started to say.

Sarah looked down at her. "Yes, honey?"

"That's not Daddy," Rose said petulantly.

"No," Sarah replied gently. "No, he . . . he's a friend of your daddy's."

Lance grinned broadly and removed the Stetson from his head, wiping back the hair from his brow. He spoke directly to the child.

"That's right, little miss," he said kindly. "Know your daddy well."

Sarah's eyes lifted sharply, and she regarded Lance puzzledly. He spoke as if there were truth behind his words. Yet Sarah knew there was no way he could be acquainted with Neville. No way . . . that she knew of.

With the purity of a child's perception, Rose instantly decided she didn't like this man. A voice that tried to sound friendly, but really wasn't.

Lance ignored her timidity and refocused his attention on the woman. "Been a long time, Sarah."

Sarah hesitated, then nodded.

Lance studied her. She was still attractive, but the hard, desperate life she had been made to endure had settled upon her features. Her eyes were fatigued and her smooth pink skin had become pale and coarse. Yet seeing her again after all these years reignited in Lance an old passion.

"Been ridin' for a spell," he said. "Would be obliged if you might offer a thirsty man a cold drink."

Sarah seemed reluctant to accommodate him. But finally she gave a hasty nod and Lance prepared to dismount. Sarah turned to him and said bluntly:

"No need to get off your horse. I can bring you out a cup of water from the house."

Lance wore an ironic expression as he settled back into the saddle.

"Not exactly what I'd call hospitable," he said wryly.

Sarah didn't answer. She looked tense, and as she started toward the cabin she pulled her daughter close to her.

Lance called after Sarah before she reached the door. "Ain't gonna make it hard on yuh, Sarah."

Sarah considered for several moments. Finally she turned toward him.

"I'll get you your water," she said. "But after I . . . I'd like it if you'd leave."

Sarah went inside. A minute or so later she emerged from the cabin holding his drink. Rose followed her mother, but keeping her little body at a distance.

"Wet, but it ain't cold," Sarah said vacantly as she handed Lance the water.

Lance took the cup from Sarah's fingers in a slow, almost deliberate gesture, keeping his eyes on her while she tried to avoid his gaze. He sipped at his water, slowly, in no hurry to rush off even though Sarah made it plain she'd prefer if he was off the property. He wasn't particularly offended by her rather rude behavior, though he was troubled at her seeming to regard someone she had grown up with and knew intimately for many years as someone she should be wary of. Yet given circumstances that she had no knowledge of, he could find a strange, dark humor in the situation, which he chose to do.

He steadied the restlessness of his horse. He smiled a sardonic smile as his eyes studied the weathered dwelling that didn't look as if it would survive another strong gust of wind, and then he once more surveyed the expansive but unproductive property.

"Looks like yuh mighta found some sorta happiness," he remarked. He glanced at Rose, who had walked up to her mother and now nuzzled close to her. "S'pose riches ain't so much in what yuh own but what yuh have."

Sarah stood wordlessly, brushing her daughter's hair with the palm of her hand.

Before Lance swung his horse around back onto the trail, he uttered with a wry undertone:

"Know y'all do well."

He snapped his horse into a gallop down the path back onto the main trail, leaving behind a cloud of dust beyond which, to Sarah's eyes, he looked to vanish, disappearing with the swiftness with which he had arrived.

Soon . . . just the distant and fading tramping of hoofbeats against the hard earth.

As Rose continued to hug into her, Sarah sighed. She wondered why after all these years Lance had suddenly chosen to make an appearance—and how he even had known where to find her. Aunt Lilah was the only one who could have told him where she had settled, and she was long dead—and she would never have told him in any case because of her distrust and plain dislike of the man.

While she had nothing on which to base her suspicion, a queer intuition made Sarah question if Lance's unexpected showing up at the farm had anything to do with Neville's "job offer."

Although she would not have confessed her doubts to her husband, Sarah couldn't bring herself to completely accept Neville's sudden stroke of luck.

Instantly, she wished it were possible for her to ride out after Lance and confront him. Ask him why he *really* had come to see her. Perhaps her doubts were unfounded. But . . . maybe she did have a reason for her uncertainty.

All of a sudden she felt worried. Worried and helpless.

She had a great concern for the well-being of her husband.

SIXTEEN

———

Sarah's concern would have been justified beyond her most fearful imaginings had she known that just short of a week after Lance Denning rode away from the farm, the U.S. marshal was riding into Commercial City to take her husband into federal custody, to be tried for the murder of a city official.

Marshal Elias Schaeffer presented an imposing figure who caused heads to turn as he rode his bay horse at a steady pace down Archer Street. He sat tall and erect in his saddle, exuding what some might interpret as a dangerous confidence. He was aware of people halting in their stride along the boardwalk to gaze at him, but he coolly ignored the attention as none of these folks concerned him. He was a man of singular purpose and had a specific duty to perform.

Elias Schaeffer was pale-complected. His face was long and narrow so that his jaw was taut and his cheekbones so pronounced almost to appear skull-like. His hair appeared short and trimmed under the wide gray Stetson he wore, though his auburn mustache was full and flowing, the long bristles concealing most of his mouth. He wore an open duster revealing a vest upon which his badge was pinned. Resting inside his holster was an 1873 Colt Peacemaker. Inside the scabbard at the side of his horse was fitted a Henry repeater rifle.

No one who watched the stranger ride into town knew why he had come. Some of the more timid citizens held the hope that he was just passing through. Lawman or not, he was an intimidating presence.

Tim Rawlins happened to be peering out the window of his office when he saw the marshal start to veer his horse over toward the building. Rawlins heaved a sigh, then turned slowly to Neville. He was about to tell him that the marshal had arrived, but just the look on his face seemed to be all that was necessary as Neville nodded that he understood.

Schaeffer tethered his horse to the hitching post outside the Municipal Building and walked with long, brisk strides toward the sheriff's office. When he stepped through the door to the office he did not introduce himself, nor did he utter a word of greeting. Instead he took a slow, inspecting look around the premises and peered into the jail, with its one occupied cell. His face was set, his expression unfathomable. Only then did he announce his name to Sheriff Rawlins. Rawlins instantly detected the no-nonsense attitude and approach of this man. He was someone who tackled his job with the utmost seriousness. Therefore he was somewhat taken aback when Schaeffer removed his Stetson and a bushel of hair came tumbling out, cascading over his shoulders and down his back. The length of the hair now framing his head made Schaeffer's face appear even more raw-boned.

Rawlins found the marshal an intriguing specimen. He looked about as lean as they come, but Rawlins determined he was a man one would be wise not to tangle with.

Schaeffer kept his beady eyes steady on Neville, who was standing with both hands gripping the bars of his cell. Both men had rigid expressions and eyed each other wordlessly.

Finally Schaeffer nodded. "All right, Sheriff, I'll take him off your hands."

Rawlins took the key ring from the wall peg behind his

desk and walked with his head lowered toward the cell. As he opened the door, he glanced up at Neville with a look that urged him to tell the truth before he signed the papers officially turning him over to the custody of the federal marshal.

As it was, it was already too late. Marshal Schaeffer would not be returning without a prisoner.

Neville gave a slight nod in appreciation of Rawlins's efforts but remained silent as he was led from the cell and slapped into the handcuffs that Schaeffer swiftly produced.

"You're either the bravest man I ever met or the stupidest," Rawlins muttered, his comment arousing the marshal's curiosity. But Rawlins saw no point in elaborating. Not as long as Neville understood what he meant.

Rawlins concluded with, "In any case, you're the most mule-headed stubborn."

Neville responded only with a wry smile.

Rawlins had made arrangements with the livery stable to have the secondary horse saddled and ready to transport the prisoner. Out of added caution it was waiting out back.

"Got 'bout a two-day ride ahead of us," Schaeffer said, talking past Neville to the sheriff.

Then he spoke directly to Neville, his voice flat, his eyes empty, demonstrating that he was a man with little compassion for criminals.

"Can't make no guarantees but I'll make yuh as comfortable as I'm able," he said.

To Neville, now smiling secretly, such an accommodation held little importance.

Because he had already made his decision. He'd weighed it out carefully during his long hours sitting in the jail cell, fiddling with his gold piece to block out the sheriff's entreaties . . . and occupying himself with thoughts of how he could cheat the hangman.

The way he had it figured, he'd fulfilled his part of the bargain with what was expected of him by Lance Denning. He'd confessed to a murder he hadn't committed, and maintained his guilt; everything that would now follow would purely be a legal formality, each step leading to a predetermined end. The

trial. The verdict. The hanging. Three neat, simple steps. There
was only one thing that concerned him: the waiting. Sitting out
the wait in virtual solitude until the rope was placed around
his neck and the trapdoor flung open, his body to be dropped
into space, his neck snapping. Or maybe a slower death, like
those he had read about as a wide-eyed youth in those forbidden
penny publications he would occasionally, secretly, acquire
with their graphic descriptions of a condemned man strangling,
gasping for air, before his soul was either sent to eternity or
sucked into the black void of oblivion. That wasn't how he
planned to go. Nor could he endure sitting out those final days
tormenting himself with thoughts of Sarah and the girls and
never seeing them again . . . and of them never knowing what
became of him. Likely believing he had abandoned them. Sitting, waiting, with such thoughts corroding his brain, would
be too much to bear. Already it had taken a grip on his body
and soul that seemed to knot tighter by each passing hour.

No . . . he didn't intend to prolong this. He wasn't going
to lengthen his agony by days, perhaps weeks.

If he was going to die, he wanted it to be on his own terms.

His hands were manacled; the procedure had been done
quickly, efficiently, with no time for him to make the move
toward the lawman's gun that he had considered . . . the
holstered revolver that he could have made a grab for if he'd
acted just an instant sooner. Hold the gun on them, attempt
a run for the street, and wait for a bullet to slam into his
back. Because what was most important was that he had to
be killed. If he didn't die, his family's welfare if not their
very lives were in jeopardy.

His only option now was just to make a dash for the door
and hope that such an impulsive move would catch Sheriff
Rawlins by surprise. Ignore the warning to halt and keep
running—out of the office and onto the street until a well-
placed bullet downed him. And then it would be over. Quickly.
He doubted he would even feel the impact of the lead.

A death preferable to the alternative.

Neville's eyes kept veering toward the door to the office.
He had to move swiftly—and maneuver well to guarantee

that he made it outside, because whatever else happened, he could not be tackled to the ground and subdued. He had to be shot—and the bullet had to be fatal.

There was no talk going on between the marshal and the sheriff. But soon either Rawlins or Schaeffer would leave the office to bring the horse standing out back around to the front, and that was when Neville would attempt his move. All was set, except he worried that he might telegraph his intention. He was conscious of every breath he took, every slight motion of his body. With each twitch of his face he feared the lawmen might become wise to what he was planning. Worse, in his anticipation he had begun to sweat. He struggled to keep himself steady, holding his head low to avoid even the most minute eye contact with Rawlins or the marshal.

Just seconds . . . but each moment that passed took on a greater urgency.

"I'll bring the horse 'round front," Rawlins finally said to the marshal.

Schaeffer sipped at the coffee he'd poured for himself. "Fine."

Neville held himself at the ready and once Rawlins's back was to him he started to position himself for his break—

Then, as if out of nowhere, a fist slammed against the side of his face, sending Neville reeling. He wound up with his butt on the floor, a dazed expression smeared across his face. He heard, numbly, the heavy sound of footsteps, and when he glanced up Sheriff Rawlins towered above him.

"Saw that comin' the minute yuh stepped from the cell," Rawlins growled.

Marshal Schaeffer remained stolid as he moved beside the sheriff and cast his black, beady eyes down at Neville.

"He was gettin' ready to make a break," Rawlins explained to the marshal. "A damn desperate fool's move."

Schaeffer spoke to Rawlins, his words filtering through the long, coffee-glistened hairs of his mustache. "Tries somethin' like that along the trail and he won't make it to trial."

Rawlins turned his eyes toward Schaeffer and bit down on his lip. And then he understood. What Neville had planned was not a "fool's move" at an escape he would never manage but an attempt to get himself killed and thereby avoid the noose. But Rawlins didn't need that burden added to a conscience already weighed heavy with guilt. A guilt he carried because he was thwarted in his efforts to prevent a needless death. And it troubled him as much as his inability to protect his friend the mayor from an assassin's bullet.

He spoke with conviction. "Marshal, just that you should be knowin', this man ain't no more guilty of killin' Thaddeus Ford than I am."

Marshal Schaeffer's face took on a critical look, which he directed at Rawlins.

"You sayin' yuh got me out here to bring in an innocent man?"

Rawlins's eyes stayed focused on Neville, as if waiting for him to finally speak the truth.

"Maybe you'd better 'splain," Schaeffer said, his disposition slightly ruffled.

"Didn't send for yuh unjustly, Marshal," Rawlins told him straightly. "This man confessed to the killin'. That's what he claims, can't get him to say otherwise. He wants to hang." He turned to Neville, just starting to scoop himself up from the floor. "Ain't that so?"

Rawlins then stooped over and hooked his hands around Neville's shoulders, drawing him roughly to his feet. When Neville was fully erect, the sheriff shoved him against the far wall, pinning him there with his forearm pressed against his throat.

"But the game-playin' ends now," he glowered.

To Neville, still recovering from the blow the sheriff delivered, a glint of madness appeared in the man's eyes, hinting at an uncertainty about what Rawlins might be capable of.

"I don't care 'bout you, Neville," Rawlins went on. "You could walk outside and get hit by a stray bullet and I wouldn't shed no tear. But I take serious my responsibility both to this town and to my badge . . . and that sure as hell don't include takin' part in this farce . . . standin' by and watchin' some damn fool idiot get hanged for somethin' he didn't do."

Neville tried to struggle free from the arm held firm against his throat. Rawlins loosened his grip—just a bit. But once it appeared Neville was going to talk, Rawlins slammed his forearm back against his windpipe, gradually increasing the pressure.

He spoke in a tense growl. "Don't want no more of what I been hearin' since you walked in here. Ain't lettin' go 'til you tell me what you *know* I wanta hear. You don't . . . your stranglin' comes now."

Schaeffer wore a concerned look, and he took a tentative step forward. But then he held himself back. He questioned the sheriff's conduct but decided to give him the benefit of the doubt.

Neville's face started to turn a pale shade of blue. A faint froth formed at the corner of his lips. Despite his efforts to free himself, Neville was unable to break the sheriff's grip; Rawlins was a powerful man—and he was determined.

Finally Schaeffer advanced to pull the sheriff away. But before he could intercede, Neville forced a stiff jerk of his head, indicating that he'd had enough and was ready to talk. Rawlins only slightly relieved the pressure, making it clear that unless Neville spoke the truth he'd ram his forearm back against his throat and this time hold it there all the way.

When he finally let go, Rawlins seemed almost as short of breath as Neville. To him it was an emotional exertion, a discharge of the frustrations he'd been made to endure since the night Neville walked into his office. For a moment he had to wonder if he might have carried through on his threat and choked the life out of Neville. He could never remember feeling such a release of rage. It frightened him, and he had to push from his mind what might have been the possible outcome.

Marshal Schaeffer stood looking unsure of what he had just witnessed.

"All right," Neville gasped. "All right . . ."

His body surged forward as he attempted to catch his breath. Rawlins helped him over to a chair.

With his head bowed Neville sputtered, "I—I can't do this . . . not to Sarah . . ."

"Sarah? That your wife? So you admit you got a missus?" Rawlins said, demanding confirmation. "Or the way you was plannin' it—a soon-to-be *widow*."

Neville didn't acknowledge the insensitivity of the remark. He went silent as the steadiness of his breathing gradually returned. And during that time he kept his face lowered and his eyes directed to the floor.

"I—got a wife," he said in a whisper. "And two daughters."

"Now you're startin' to make sense, Neville," Rawlins said, adding with a cynical edge, "and all it took was almost chokin' the life outta yuh. But still a lotta questions gotta be answered."

"Might be to my advantage if you filled me in," Marshal Schaeffer suggested.

Rawlins pointed to Neville and said austerely, "Like I told yuh, Marshal, this man ain't guilty of what he claims."

"Reckon by now I figgered that," Schaeffer concurred.

Rawlins kept a tight, penetrating stare on Neville. "The point is, he mighta not done the killin', but I'm wagerin' he knows who did."

"That a fact?" Schaeffer said with interest.

Neville lifted dull, hooded eyes up at the sheriff. The color was coming back into his face, but his expression reflected his exhaustion. He felt both physically and emotionally drained.

Rawlins went to unlock the handcuffs. Once his hands were free, Neville started to massage his wrists in a steady and reflexive gesture.

"Ain't gonna see yuh hang," Rawlins said. "'Cause that's what yuh want . . . and I ain't gonna oblige." He turned back to Marshal Schaeffer. "Hoped it wouldn't go this far, but once you got here I hadda see it through 'fore this fool made a mistake." He glared at Neville. "An even bigger idiot with him havin' a wife and kids."

Schaeffer blinked. "You knew he might try to escape?"

Rawlins nodded. "Yeah, had a pretty strong suspicion. Fact, sorta counted on it . . . once you showed up. Never knew a man yet who'd stand still for a noose, no matter how tough he pretends to be."

Schaeffer nodded solemnly.

Rawlins walked over to the cabinet where he kept his bottle of whiskey and brought it over to Neville. The look in his eyes insisted that he take a drink. Neville obliged him—without hesitation. Before Rawlins could even offer him a glass, Neville had twisted open the cap and swigged back a couple of good swallows.

Feeling a little more relaxed thanks to the swift effects of the liquor, Neville was finally prepared to talk. Yet he still faced a dilemma: He wasn't sure how much he should say. There remained the consideration of what Lance Denning had said about the people he worked for . . . and the cunning threat of how they wouldn't take kindly to being betrayed. It wasn't that Neville had much worry for himself—he'd already come as close to death as any man. It was his concern for Sarah and the girls. Alone out on that lonely stretch of land. Miles from anyone. Vulnerable.

Neville drank a bit more whiskey before Rawlins prudently put the bottle aside. Marshal Schaeffer declined the offer of a drink and stepped off to a corner of the room, leaning against the wall with his arms folded across his chest, listening but not saying anything, curious to hear what Neville had to say.

"Okay, Neville," Rawlins said. "Time for you to free up your conscience."

SEVENTEEN

The story came out as best as Neville could recount it, and when he was finished the lines of strain etched into his features and the rattle in his voice left little doubt that he was telling the truth. Sheriff Rawlins and Marshal Schaeffer looked at each another without speaking. It was a strange silence that followed. Schaeffer walked over to the stove to add more coffee to his cup. It had gone cold, but he drank it just the same.

It was Rawlins who finally broke the quiet, but his words offered neither sympathy nor compassion. "Yuh made a deal with the devil, you know that, don't yuh?"

"What choice did I have?" Neville tried to argue. Yet he realized that from the sheriff's standpoint, there was little he could say that would justify his actions.

"Yeah," Rawlins said, barely choking back the contempt he felt for the man's blatant stupidity. "You hear outright how a varmint killed a good, decent man and yuh play right along with him. For your own benefit."

Neville straightened in his chair and tried to keep calm against the sheriff's strong accusation. Rawlins had to be made aware that he hadn't agreed to the bargain with Lance Denning for his own gain.

His voice was level, his words pronounced. "He gave me his word my wife and girls would be taken care of. He paid me money up front—a thousand dollars."

Rawlins spoke cynically out the side of his mouth. "Cheap at the cost."

"I—hadda take him at his word once I saw that money," Neville said. "It'd give Sarah and my daughters the life they deserve. What I couldn't give 'em."

"A noble gesture," Rawlins sneered.

Neville scratched his scalp with a furious intent. His face was screwed into an expression of frustration. The sheriff wasn't giving him much slack.

"I—was drunk, dammit," Neville finally admitted. "Drunk and I reckon lookin' for a way out. Yeah, and when I heard all he had to say, I agreed to it. Didn't much care anymore—'bout what happened to me. He told me right out our bargain was sealed once my hand picked up that money. I lived up to my end, turnin' myself in to yuh. Took him at his word he was gonna keep his part of the deal."

"And yuh bought into it," Rawlins said. "You trusted the promise of a murderer. Why would he have to honor his word? Think 'bout it, man: Once you're hanged he owes you no obligation. A man who would come to you with such an arrangement. . . . You so blind yuh can't see his word ain't worth coyote spit?"

Blind? The word resonated with Neville. For the first time the truth had been presented, bluntly, painfully, and with humiliating impact. He'd been made to recognize that he had been so blinded by his desperation that he hadn't considered the very real possibility of what Sheriff Rawlins was saying. It was true, there was no reason for Lance Denning to come through with the promised five thousand dollars after he was dead. Why should he? The only person who knew about the deal was Neville, and he'd be cold in his grave. And Denning surely must have known that Neville would never reveal such a desperate plan to his wife, so he was under no obligation there, either, since Sarah would know nothing about their arrangement. Only a man of honor would fulfill his end of such a bargain . . . and Lance Denning was a confessed killer who doubtless didn't possess a shred of integrity.

Neville felt overcome with shame, both for his misplaced trust . . . and for what he now perceived as his weakness, the lessening of his measure as a man. But most of all he was fearful for the safety of his wife and daughters.

He shot up from his chair.

"Sheriff, I gotta ride back to the farm," he said suddenly, urgently. "Gotta get back to Sarah and the girls."

"First sensible thing you've said," Rawlins told him.

"No, I gotta go," Neville said imploringly.

Rawlins couldn't hold him. He wasn't guilty of any crime . . . outside of his own stupidity.

"Yeah, you can git," he said.

"Might be best if I ride out with him," Marshal Schaeffer offered as he put his tin cup aside. "Territory is still within my jurisdiction. Don't wanta chance trouble along the way. Maybe runnin' into this Denning character."

Rawlins looked at him, hesitated, then nodded grimly.

Neville put out his hand and said to the sheriff, "My revolver."

Rawlins went to the cabinet where he had stored the pistol and unlocked the glass door, removing the Colt .45 and handing it to Neville, along with a subtle look cautioning him not to be trigger-fingered.

Neville nodded in understanding.

Rawlins said, "Any way we can reach your family by wire? Have someone close by ride out to your place and let 'em know you're comin'?"

Neville shook his head. "Ain't a telegraph office in a hundred miles. Best if we just to ride out."

Rawlins spoke forthright. "Understand your concern, Neville. But seems doubtful any harm's come to your family. If Denning and them others was planning such a move, they'd wait 'til you're hanged. Can't chance actin' hasty with you still alive and with what you know."

Neville nodded in appreciation of what the sheriff was saying. He'd brought up a valid and comforting point.

He turned to Marshal Schaeffer.

"Just so's yuh know, I purty much plan to ride straight through," he said. "Ride at a good pace with no stoppin' longer than necessary. That way I should get back to the farm in two days—maybe less."

Schaeffer was agreeable. "Got that fresh horse out back. Let's get movin'."

J ust down the road from the Municipal Building was a quaint if brightly painted two-story house with large front windows and a wraparound porch where an elderly widow named Mrs. Ella Slate took in boarders by the week or month. A second-floor room was occupied by a man who had paid for a week's lodging, a stranger who, for the past several days, had not been seen by Mrs. Slate or the other boarders, though he had been noticed sitting by the window in his room for lengthy periods, just gazing out onto the street, watching.

. . . A man whose patience was finally rewarded when he saw a tall, official-looking man ride his horse up the street at a slow pace, bringing his mount to a halt outside the Municipal Building.

Lance Denning smoked what was left of his cigarette and wore a contented expression. It looked as if Neville had played his part well, and he was pleased. The man's concern for his wife and children was touching and admirable. Lance almost could feel regret at what was to come.

But that was a thought he could dismiss quickly.

As Lance spent those days sitting alone inside his room he began to develop a resentment that his *Sarah-gal* had turned so coldly against him. It was an abrupt and unforeseen change in attitude for which he firmly blamed Neville. But what Sarah didn't know was that he wasn't through with her yet. Despite what he'd promised her husband and his obligingly riding away from Sarah the day he visited her at their dirt farm, Lance had not forgotten her betrayal. Nor was he ready to release her from his life. The way he saw it, with Neville providing no defense at his trial, it shouldn't take longer than a few weeks for him to be hanged at the state prison. And then Lance would come back to visit Sarah. Not to provide her with a packet of cash, as he'd told her trusting husband, but to persuade her back into the life she chose to walk away from—enticing her the same way he did with Neville, with the offer of providing her children with a more prosperous life.

Regardless of her feelings toward him, Sarah couldn't deny her daughters a better future. And Lance was now the only one who could provide that for them. The white knight riding to the rescue.

Lance left his room, walked out onto the street, and took a moment to savor the freshness of the cool air that drifted in from the valley and also absorb the warming rays of the sun, both of which he'd denied himself sitting inside his room keeping watch through the window, waiting for the U.S. marshal to show up. Patience was a requirement of his job, and it was a quality he had learned to master.

He looked down the street at the Municipal Building, and his lips creased in an intimate smirk. Everything was working according to plan. All he needed was to watch Neville be led away from town by the marshal.

But to his dismay, that wasn't what he saw. Not exactly. The man Lance assumed was the federal lawman exited the Municipal Building alone, mounting his horse and holding the animal steady, as if waiting. Moments later a horse came galloping around from the rear of the building. Lance narrowed his eyes and held his squint. The rider looked to be Neville. Looking closer, he saw that it *was* Neville. He joined up with the marshal and the two men rode off together, heading in the opposite direction of the courthouse at Fort Sampson, where Neville should have been taken to stand trial.

In fact, they looked to be riding back toward Neville's farm.

Lance tossed aside his cigarette with an angry flourish. It looked as if Neville had crawfished on their bargain . . . and if that was so, he'd likely told both the sheriff and the marshal everything . . . including that he, Lance, had admitted to the killing of the mayor.

Lance glanced toward the Municipal Building. The sheriff would have to be silenced, but Lance didn't have time to deal with that. First he had to catch up to Neville and the marshal along the trail. This was no longer personal as much as a practical decision. If word got back to San Francisco that a government-appointed lawman knew of their involvement in the Commercial City killing, that would jeopardize their whole gambling parlor venture . . . and Lance would be blamed for fouling up by not just sticking to the job at hand, and would be made to pay.

Lance hurried to collect his horse. Neville and the marshal had a good head start, especially since they had picked up an even swifter pace as they neared the edge of town, but Lance's horse was a pistol. He would ride fast and keep them within his sight while maintaining a far enough distance behind to not be noticed. Lance reckoned that at some point they would have to stop, either to sleep or to water and rest their horses, and that was when he would come upon them and make his move.

EIGHTEEN

Neville and Marshal Schaeffer rode hard, following the exact trail Neville had used when he had traveled the many miles from his farm into Commercial City—a ride he'd made just days before but that seemed to Neville a lifetime ago. Their horses kept almost a rhythmic pace with each other as they galloped side by side. Neither man spoke to the other, nor did they so much as exchange a glance. Their focus was solely on the road ahead. Neville's only thought was getting to his family.

His heart was racing, seeming to keep pace with the rapid gait of his horse. He reproached himself for the terrible mistake he'd nearly made, angry that his discouragement and crippling despair had so clouded his reason that he'd actually accepted the word of a man like Lance Denning. How could he have forgotten all that Sarah had told him about Denning those many years ago, when his fear of her ending up with such a cruel and sinister man had prompted Neville's proposal of marriage? Neville now had to consider that Denning might even have engineered this scheme to get him out of the way so that he could try to win Sarah back. Neville wasn't concerned about Sarah being tempted by such an offer; he trusted her enough to know she would never accept Denning back into her life.

But that refusal was also what troubled him.

If she rejected him, Neville couldn't know how Denning might react. Lance Denning was a confessed murderer who, even though he denied it (perhaps as part of his clever strategy), likely still held resentment toward Sarah for choosing another man over him. Neville recalled how he spoke of his pride and how it had been injured. For her to turn him away now could have terrible consequences . . . and maybe not only for Sarah, but for the children as well.

They had a far way to go. Even keeping up a brisk pace, stopping just long enough to rest and water their horses, they were looking at a two-day ride. It had taken Neville nearly a week to reach Commercial City, but he had stopped to rest at night, fortified himself with saloon visits along the way, and ridden slow when on the trail. Of course that was when he was riding toward a hanging. Now there was no time for leisure with his concerns over his family driving him forward.

After a long stretch when both horses were kicked into a dead run, maintaining a breakneck pace sure to wear down their endurance, Marshal Schaeffer signaled to Neville to bring his mount to a halt. He sidled up alongside and told Neville they'd best rest the animals for a spell. Neville was reluctant to interrupt the progress they'd made, but the marshal gave him a hard, no-nonsense look that prompted Neville to slow his pony.

"Understand you're in a hurry," Schaeffer said firmly. "But you won't be gettin' anywhere fast with a dead horse 'neath yuh."

Neville complied. They pulled off the trail and led the horses through an overgrowth of trees and dense shrubbery to a clearing where both animals could cool themselves in the shade after their extended run. Neville dismounted and stepped away while his animal cropped the grass, and Schaeffer did the same. He stretched out his arms and legs to lessen their stiffness and then leaned back against a tree and watched as Neville paced restlessly, taking quick, nervous sips from his canteen.

"Sometimes feel I'm gettin' too old for this line of work," Schaeffer remarked lightly.

"Been at it long?" Neville asked with no real interest, his thoughts elsewhere.

"Long 'nuff," Schaeffer answered. He then looked critically at Neville and said, "You gotta relax. Y'heard what the sheriff said. Ain't much chance of anything happenin' to your kin."

"No way of knowin' for sure 'til I get there," Neville returned.

"You're thinkin' the worst, boy," Schaeffer told him.

Neville gave Schaeffer a hard look.

"Name's Neville, Tom Neville," he corrected. "Ain't been a boy in a long while."

Schaeffer was taken aback by the peculiar response. He didn't expect to provoke a defensive reaction. He regarded Neville with a contemplative look but didn't comment.

Neville brooded for a few moments before he flickered his eyes toward Schaeffer. He simply couldn't curb his restlessness. For him, the ten-minute break was sufficient. Schaeffer thought it prudent to allow their horses a longer rest, but he saw that Neville was not of that mind and so he sighed, slapped his hands against his thighs, then rose, walked over to his animal, and mounted it. Neville quickly followed suit. He just wanted to get back on the road.

The brief stop they made proved beneficial for Lance Denning. He sat atop the rise that sloped into the woodland trail and watched as both men emerged from the thicket, resuming their journey. Denning considered how if he'd carried a long-range he easily could have picked them both off right from where he was, but all he wore was his Colt .44 sidearm. He'd have to bide his time. But he knew he'd get his opportunity, and so he was patient.

He'd caught up to them as his horse was a good pacer and would now follow their trail at an easy gait, keeping enough of a distance off to the side of the road where if necessary he could veer into the camouflage of the brush and not be spotted.

It was nearing sundown and Marshal Schaeffer suggested another stop. The horses were holding up well as the men alternated their pacing between a gallop and a canter, but with nightfall soon to be upon them it was time for the animals to be fed and the men to eat supper. Neville was resistant and urged his companion that they go on just a little farther, but Schaeffer reminded him that he wouldn't do any good for himself if he didn't eat and keep up his strength.

Neville grudgingly agreed.

"We ain't too far from a crick I passed on my ride into Commercial City," he said to the marshal. "Good place to water the horses. Just gotta go us a couple more miles."

"All right. But smart if we camp out for the night, get an early start in the morning," Schaeffer suggested. "Need some rest as well as nourishment."

Neville nodded at Schaeffer, and each slowed his horse's gait to a trot.

They reached the creek before it got dark and set up camp not too far inland from the rippling of the water's edge. By the time night descended they had built a small fire. It was late in the season and the night was chilly, and the men sat wrapped in their saddle blankets near the warmth of the fire. A pot of coffee and a pan of beans were cooking over the flames.

"If'n we keep up a good run, figger we might be able to reach my place come the day after next," Neville said optimistically as he settled down to partake of the canned beans and strips of jerky that Schaeffer withdrew from his saddlebag.

"Just keep sensible," Schaeffer advised him, biting off a piece of the beef. He talked while his mouth worked aggressively around the thin, hard meat. "Apologize that beans and jerky are the best I got to offer. Didn't figger on makin' this run. Generally eat light on the trail anyhow."

"This'll do just fine," Neville said. He spooned up some

beans and looked thoughtful. "Can't offer much myself, but I'm sure my missus can rustle us up somethin' once we get there." He managed a smile. "Even if it's just watery vegetable stew."

Schaeffer smiled under his mustache. "I et worse."

The night air was quiet and still with the occasional whisper of wind interrupting the calm as it rustled through the leaves and stirred the scrub. There was the sporadic quick scurry of a small night critter as it foraged for food, attracted by the smell of the beans but keeping a safe distance from the campsite. The distant call of a bird. Other than that the most pronounced sound was the crackle of the campfire. The two men finished their supper, sipped at their coffee, and didn't speak much, enjoying the silence.

After a bit Schaeffer looked hard at Neville and said, "Aw, the hell with it," raising Neville's curiosity. Schaeffer rose and walked over to his horse, standing by the creek, and reached for something in the saddlebag. He walked back, his tall, lanky form illuminated by the campfire flames.

He held up a flask of whiskey in an inviting gesture.

"Reckon we could both use a belt," he said.

The flask passed between them until its contents were gone.

Schaeffer looked content, and Neville felt warmed and much less restive.

Neville laid his head back on the saddle he used as his pillow and stared up into the night, dotted with stars and the slow passing of silver-edged, deep purple clouds, which blended against the sky like paint sweeping against a canvas.

His thoughts were on his family. And for the first time in a long while he felt a certain peace, a calm and a tranquillity. Even with the knowledge that he was going back to a situation that was no better than when he had left, he was grateful to be doing so. Maybe, he philosophized, he needed what he had gone through to give him the proper perspective. Maybe his efforts had not succeeded because he'd considered himself a failure. He thought it ironic. Here he was half-drunk and yet he was sure he'd never before thought so clear in his life.

All was quiet except for the faint sound of water babbling in the creek. It was a peaceful sound and Neville drifted off to slumber and slept soundly—so soundly that it seemed it was only in the next moment that he was being nudged awake by Marshal Schaeffer, who hunkered down before him, looking ready to get back on the trail.

Neville stared up at the skies, which were no longer holding the night but not quite ready to announce daybreak. Schaeffer evidently was an early riser, which was all the better for Neville. He yawned, nodded at the marshal, then wiped the sleep from his eyes and permitted himself a few moments to collect his thoughts. He crawled out of his bedroll, stretched his arms and shoulders, and walked stiffly down to the creek to revitalize himself with a face dip into the cold water.

"Coffee'll be waitin'," Schaeffer called after him.

Neville heartily anticipated the taste of a good morning brew. He knelt to a crouch beside the creek and splashed several handfuls of water against his face. It was cold all right and instantly snapped him to wakefulness. He wiped his eyes with his shirtsleeve, then swept back his hair with his fingertips. He stood upright and started back to the campsite for that welcome cup of coffee.

To his puzzlement he couldn't see Marshal Schaeffer. Neville glanced about and noticed that Schaeffer's horse was where he'd tethered it, but as his eyes searched the area he could see no sign of the lawman. Neville halted his step. He was curious and felt a little unsettled. It appeared that Schaeffer hadn't even started to make the coffee he'd promised.

Neville heard a quick sound that he couldn't identify. Maybe a rustling from somewhere in the brush. He spun around to the source . . . saw nothing. He suppressed a shiver from the cool of the morning and his own uncertainty.

Then—a voice, seeming to emanate from no specific location, traveling in the still, morning air:

"Not a smart move yuh made, Neville."

Neville froze at the accusing tone. He could not mistake the voice:

Belonging to Lance Denning.

Neville felt the nerves in his body seize. He slowly looked around . . . and it was then that he found himself staring into the barrel of a Colt .44 revolver.

"Stand easy, pardner," Lance instructed him.

Denning, Neville mouthed.

"Shoulda stuck to your end of the bargain," Lance said.

Neville glanced about and asked, "Where's the marshal?"

"Next to where I'm standin'. Only he *ain't*," Lance said humorlessly.

Lance reversed his hold on the gun so that he was gripping the barrel and wielding the butt like a club, thrusting it downward, a pantomime to indicate that he'd coldcocked the lawman. Then he tilted his head downward and as Neville's eyes followed he could just make out Schaeffer's boots, his legs stretching out from behind the leafy overgrowth of a shrub.

"Coulda come up on yuh both when you was sleepin'," Lance declared. He drew a slow finger across his throat to illustrate his point. "But that wouldn't have been fair."

Neville hitched a breath. He instantly knew that he was a dead man but tried to hold himself steady. He wasn't about to give Lance Denning the satisfaction of watching him die shaking in his boots.

"Unbuckle your gun belt, slow, and toss it deep into the brush," Lance said. "And don't try nothin' funny with those hands."

Neville did as he was told, then said, "Sarah . . . and the girls?"

"Yeah, well, what yuh done sorta complicates things," Lance said in reply.

Neville's blood quickened. "I don't care 'bout the money. All I'm askin' is that they be left alone."

Lance yipped a short laugh. "I ain't forgettin' 'bout the money, Neville. Keepin' my word . . . just a slight change in our arrangement. Yeah, yuh might as well know that after you was hanged I planned on goin' back to Sarah-gal. Not to cause her no harm. Couldn't do that no matter how she cheated on me. Couldn't hurt your kiddies, neither, so rest easy. No, was gonna offer her the chance to reconsider. To accept the life we was gonna have a long time ago . . . 'fore you came along. Figger once we spend time together, I can get her to think different . . . and if'n I can't, well, can't see no mother not wantin' to provide her young'uns with a better life."

"She'll never go back to you," Neville said with conviction.

Lance shrugged. "Mebbe. Thing is, *you'll* never know."

"Sheriff Rawlins knows 'bout you," Neville stated deliberately.

"Figgered that after I saw you and the marshal ride away from the jail."

"Don't see your plans goin' very far with you bein' a wanted man."

"You let me worry 'bout that," Lance replied as he cocked the hammer on his revolver. His eyes looked off beyond Neville. "You just walk yourself over to the crick."

Neville slowly craned his neck toward the water's edge.

"Won't find yuh so quick with you and the lawman sunk to the bottom," Lance explained with a chilling smile. "And by that time won't be much left to recognize either of yuh."

Neville stayed put. With a bullet facing him either way, he stood in defiance, determined not to give Lance the satisfaction of accommodating him.

Lance regarded him admiringly. "You got guts."

Neville swallowed, and in what he saw as his final moments he decided to justify Lance's comment. But his heart was racing and he could feel a nervous tremor in his hands, which he didn't want his killer to detect. So he focused his thoughts on Sarah and his daughters. He wanted to leave this life with the memory of his family, and he prayed a silent prayer that they would be looked after. He kept his eyes riveted on Lance and maintained a rigid expression as he waited for the tug on the trigger.

And then Lance hesitated.

"One thing I gotta know," he said. "Was you really gonna go through with our bargain . . . or maybe was you countin' on a way out?"

Neville cleverly thought out his answer. "Reckon you'll never know anymore'n I coulda known if you'd have kept your end."

A smile crept across Lance's lips, and he looked strangely impressed. "Reckon I can live with that."

In the very next instant Neville heard the explosion. It was loud, produced an echo that disturbed the morning silence, scattering the birds nesting in the trees. But it didn't register with Neville—not until he felt the impact of the bullet as it slammed directly into his breast. He fell backward to the ground and let out a groan. He felt as though he'd been kicked in the chest by a mule, and at once his breaths were coming fast and heavy. Yet he was still conscious and could hear Lance's footfalls soft against the dew-moistened grass as he came toward him, walking at an even pace. No rush now. Neville struggled to lift his head. Lance had stopped just a few feet away from him and wore a curious expression as he inspected where the bullet had struck. The hole in Neville's shirt indicated that the bullet should have pierced not far from his heart, which if it didn't kill Neville outright certainly would have proved a mortal wound.

Only . . . no blood seeped through the shirt. Neville turned his eyes to Lance, who now stood before him with his features screwed into an incredulous look.

Lance straightened his arm, cocked the hammer and aimed his Colt at Neville's skull.

The expression on Lance Denning's face would be the last sight Neville would ever see . . . as if welcoming a passage to hell.

Of a sudden he heard a rapid round of gunshots and Lance's body seemed to swing in a crazy dance as slugs ripped holes straight through his midsection, spattering blood onto the grass and some spurting onto Neville. The surprise of sudden death twisted Lance's features before all expression left his face, leaving a vacant mask, and he collapsed on the ground next to his intended victim, his body twitching in a final spasm before he died.

Neville managed to maneuver away from the corpse,

surprised that he still had the strength to do so. He'd been
shot in the chest at a close distance.

He was sure that he had to be dying . . . until he reflexively dropped his hand to touch the wound. His brow creased
as he felt no sticky wetness indicating blood. He drew his
hand up toward his face to make sure. His fingers were dry
and clean. It wasn't possible! Neville was stunned, unbe-
lieving. But as he once more touched his breast, fingering
the unmistakable bullet hole, he felt something hard and
solid inside his shirt pocket. His mind cleared enough for
him to understand what had happened. He reached inside
the pocket and slowly withdrew the ten-dollar gold eagle.
Miraculously, the coin had absorbed the impact of the bullet.
Neville inspected the coin and noticed how its surface had
been deeply indented almost dead center.

Neville laid his head back on the grass to give himself a
needed moment to recover. It had to be a million-to-one
fluke. Lance Denning had aimed right for Neville's heart.
He'd missed his target by just inches, but enough for the
gold eagle to deflect the bullet.

Still, his chest was aching from the bullet's impact. He
struggled to pull himself upright but couldn't quite lift himself from the ground, though he managed to raise his head.
And that was when he noticed Marshal Schaeffer standing
not far from where he'd lain after being knocked unconscious by Lance Denning, gripping his still-smoking Henry
rifle in both hands. There was a trickle of blood on his
forehead where he'd been slugged.

Neville managed a weak smile of gratitude.

He held out the ten-dollar gold eagle for the marshal to see.

Schaeffer didn't acknowledge. The expression on his face
was peculiar. Neville assumed he might be a bit dazed from
the blow to his head.

But then Schaeffer did something equally peculiar. Neville watched the marshal swing the barrel of his rifle slowly
in his direction.

"Hoped to end this on the trail takin' you to Fort Sampson,"

Schaeffer said in an unemotional tone, his face devoid of expression. "Woulda been a whole lot less trouble."

Neville just stared at him with an uncomprehending expression.

"Still, Denning makin' his fool's play will make my story more credible," Schaeffer added. He dramatized the scenario. "Came upon us sudden like. Gunned yuh down 'fore I could get to him. But I managed to finish him. And with me bein' a lawman, no questions asked."

"You—ain't no lawman," Neville said as he slowly recovered from his shock.

"Am for the time bein'," Schaeffer said tonelessly.

Neville pulled himself up on an elbow.

Schaeffer went on. "Will be 'til I report back to Sheriff Rawlins, then ride on outta Commercial City. After that, makes no matter. I'll be long gone."

"So what are yuh then?" Neville wanted to know. "*Who* are yuh?"

Schaeffer lowered to his haunches. He laid the Henry aside but withdrew the 1873 Colt Peacemaker from his holster and kept it trained on Neville.

"Someone hired to finish what our dead friend there started," he answered, gesturing bluntly at Lance's bullet-riddled body.

Neville slowly turned his head toward the dead man, then looked back at Schaeffer, unable to make sense of any of this.

Schaeffer felt he could afford him an explanation. "He worked out a clever scheme, talkin' you into turnin' yourself in for the killing *he* done. Your misfortune 'cause yuh went and married his gal. Too bad things didn't work out like they were s'posed to back at the jail. People I work for had a feelin' that might happen. Yeah, that Sheriff Rawlins proved himself a pretty smart fella. Seems he saw right through yuh, your confession and all. In any case, you weren't goin' to make it to Fort Sampson for trial. You was gonna die on the trail and I was gonna just disappear."

"Rawlins sent for a U.S. marshal," Neville said.

"Did indeed," Schaeffer beamed. "Was on his way, too. Only . . . he didn't make it."

"You—killed him?"

"Bushwhacked," Schaeffer clarified with pride. "Skill learned in the war that's proved mighty profitable since."

Neville summoned his courage. "You got no objection shootin' an unarmed man?"

Schaeffer cocked an eye. "Make your point."

"Just did."

"You suggestin' I give yuh a chance?"

Neville nodded carefully. "You can kill me with a clean conscience, if'n that matters to yuh."

Schaeffer furrowed his brow and said cynically, "Think that's a concern?"

"Reckon no more than it was to Denning."

"Downright astounding how that coin of yours saved your life," Schaeffer remarked. "Only a man can't get lucky twice."

"Maybe not," Neville returned flatly.

"I'd wager you lose either way," Schaeffer reminded him.

"Ain't your worry," Neville stated boldly.

Schaeffer rubbed his long, nimble fingers along both sides of his drooping mustache, considering. "No, reckon not." He indulged a moment to contemplate. "Can't rightly recall ever killin' a man fair before." Another pause and then: "All right, pick up that buzzard meat's gun and I'll give yuh your chance."

Schaeffer watched Neville grimace as he painfully clambered to his feet. His fingers were stiff as he stretched out his arm to retrieve the Colt .44 still clutched in Lance Denning's dead hand. Neville was a left-handed draw; that was how he'd learned when his old boss Carter Wilde taught him how to use a gun. He knew he wouldn't stand a chance against Schaeffer with his aching from where Denning's bullet had struck.

Schaeffer kept his six-shooter leveled on Neville and watched his movements attentively. Schaeffer couldn't know if Neville possessed any prowess with a handgun, and being a cautious man he wasn't going to take any chance to find out.

Daylight had arrived, the lemon glow of the morning sun

spreading over the countryside. Schaeffer took an instant to gaze up admiringly at the sky. Then he turned to Neville with a look that seemed to express it was too bad Neville wouldn't be around to enjoy the day ahead. Neville fixated his opponent with his stare. He held the Colt .44 loosely at his side.

Schaeffer's eyes glinted coldly as he started to step backward to widen the distance between them.

"I'll holster my side iron," he said to Neville, fancy-twirling the Colt, then sliding it into the leather at his side—just a little display to show Neville what he was up against. He added with a sneer, "Might give yuh a bit of an advantage."

Neville wasn't immune to the realization that for the second time that morning he was staring into the face of death. Challenging Schaeffer to a duel was a ticket to the grave . . . but at least he would die knowing he'd tried to defend himself. He would have been denied that opportunity with Lance Denning.

"You make the call," Schaeffer said.

Neville could not acknowledge through his words; his mouth felt bone dry. He merely rocked his head.

Schaeffer held himself calm and steady, confident of the outcome.

Neville tried to swallow but couldn't get anything past the lump in his throat. He stood with arms akimbo in an awkward attempt to replicate a gunfighter's pose.

Schaeffer could tell instantly that Neville possessed all the shooting skill of a tenderfoot. He would have preferred just to shoot him dead as he had planned and save Neville this final humiliation.

But he dismissed any notion of regret. This was how Neville chose to die, and he would oblige him as would a prison warden granting a condemned man his last request.

Neville didn't want Schaeffer to notice the fear that twisted his stomach into a knot. He watched how Schaeffer positioned himself even more steadily, the fingers of his gun hand flexing in eager anticipation of his draw.

He could detect the smile widening under Schaeffer's mustache, accentuating his narrow cheekbones. The man was as much a killer as Lance Denning . . . and he enjoyed it just the same.

Neville's fingers were trembling. His grip was uncertain.

"Make your move, Neville!" Schaeffer barked.

"Try it and you're dead, Schaeffer!" a voice commanded.

Schaeffer swung around. Neville suddenly had the advantage and could have shot him dead right then had his hand been steady. Instead his gaze veered off to behind where Schaeffer was standing . . . and he watched as Sheriff Rawlins stepped clear of the trees, standing on a slight rise holding an eight-gauge, aimed dead center at Schaeffer.

Rawlins edged forward down the grassy slope. He glanced expressionlessly over at the body lying near where Neville stood. "Take it that was Lance Denning . . ."

Neville nodded.

"Sheriff Rawlins," Schaeffer greeted superficially. He dropped his gun hand limply to his side, though his fingers still gripped the weapon. "Yeah, Denning all right." He gestured with a nudge of his head toward Neville. "Once I took him down, our boy here made a grab for Denning's gun. Seems he wanted a showdown. Maybe not so innocent like yuh thought."

Neville opened his mouth to protest, but Rawlins signaled for him not to bother.

He spoke directly to Schaeffer.

"Strange thing. Not a half hour after yuh left town, a fella rode in packin' a body on the back of his horse," Rawlins told him. "Said he found him dead on the trail leadin' into Commercial City. I'm wagerin' that was the real U.S. marshal. A man you murdered, Schaeffer . . . if'n that's your name."

"Pretty slim assumption, Sheriff," Schaeffer said, unscathed by the accusation.

"Don't think so," Rawlins said confidently. "Go by my gut, and my gut ain't usually wrong. And it started to upset me ag'in when I got to thinkin' 'bout you offerin' to ride out with Neville here. Fine gesture, but with him bein' a free man and there likely bein' no immediate threat to his family, a busy territorial marshal willin' to accompany him on a long, unnecessary ride got me a little suspicious."

Schaeffer tried to explain. "Was ridin' with him in case there was trouble along the way . . . and as you can tell, there was." He placed a hand against his head wound, pulling it away and checking his fingers for blood. "Denning come up on us and gave me this here head butt."

"Well, you killed him real dead, just like the U.S. marshal," Rawlins said outright.

"Y'find any identification on this supposed lawman?" Schaeffer asked slyly. "Anything to confirm who yuh *think* he was?"

"You mean like a badge, credentials? 'Course not. You took 'em."

"Then you can't really prove who he was, can yuh?" Schaeffer said with a sneer. "All yuh got is a dead man. Could be anyone unlucky 'nuff to get ambushed along the trail."

"That's how yuh made it look," Rawlins said. "But I can wait to have my suspicions verified. Question is, can you?"

"You arrestin' me?"

"Holdin' yuh. 'Til we get this straightened out."

Schaeffer smirked. "Seems to your way of thinkin' that you already have."

Rawlins kept a careful eye on the bogus marshal. Schaeffer held firm with his icy-eyed bravado, and Rawlins intended to remain on his guard. He prepared himself by thumbing back both barrels on the shotgun. He wasn't leaving himself open for a clever move from this man who he suspected was a wily killer.

"I'll back up your gut feelin', Sheriff," Neville said, eyeing Schaeffer defiantly. "He already fessed up to killing the real marshal."

Schaeffer half turned toward Neville, who by now had also raised his gun at him. The trembling had ceased and his hand was poised and steady. Schaeffer noticed the renewed confidence and tossed Neville a derisive wink. He then breathed in and out through his nostrils and seemed impressed by his predicament.

"Suggest you drop your hardware, Schaeffer," Rawlins said. "'Less'n yuh wanta ride back to town draped over your saddle."

"Reckon I'm the one in the middle now," Schaeffer remarked casually, almost with a dash of humor.

Neville was playing it cautious. He didn't trust Schaeffer's easygoing attitude. He seemed just a trifle too sure given that he had two guns drawn on him.

Schaeffer spoke a little arrogantly to Neville. "Reckon you never suspected that the fella ridin' alongside yuh was plannin' to kill yuh."

"I'm advisin' you to let loose that gun," Rawlins said again, his voice harsher.

Schaeffer slowly started to turn his head back toward Rawlins.

"The way I see it, man caught in the middle's got but one of two choices," he said.

And Schaeffer made his choice.

He shifted his body, maneuvering with amazing speed and precision. He dropped to a crouch and swung completely around to Rawlins, fanning the palm of his hand against the hammer of his .44 and getting off three quick shots. Rawlins half expected such a move and twisted his torso reflexively so that only one of the bullets connected, winging Rawlins just above the left bicep, close to the shoulder. Still, Rawlins's body staggered at the impact; the eight-gauge went loose in his grip, leaving him vulnerable.

But then Neville—either intentionally or by reflex—fired off two well-aimed shots, both bullets puncturing Schaeffer's back. Schaeffer was propelled forward by the blasts, dropping face-first and spread-eagled onto the ground. He didn't move.

Neville looked stricken, stunned that he had actually shot a man—and in the back. To his way of thinking, that equated dirty play. He dropped his gun hand to his side. Then his fingers went slack and the weapon fell onto the grass.

Rawlins appeared as surprised as Neville by his action . . . even as a trace smile of thanks crept across his lips.

Neville spoke numbly, pensively. "When I first rode out

to Commercial City, stoppin' in saloons for a shot of whiskey
and a glass of beer, think damn near everyone figgered me
for a gunman. Not understandin' I wasn't no threat, just
someone who'd given up what he'd had and was readyin' to
give it all up." He gazed over at Rawlins, looking distressed.
"Now I s'pose I mighta earned that reputation. By shootin'
a man in the back."

"No, I figger they'll see you done what yuh had to," Rawlins said reassuringly. He pressed his hand against the
wound near his shoulder and grimaced. Although it was
painful, it didn't appear to be an injury he needed to be too
concerned about. Once cleaned and bandaged, it would hold
until they rode back to Commercial City and he had the
doctor tend to it.

Neville walked over to help dress the sheriff's wound.
He tried to appear comforted by Rawlins's words, but it was
evident he still had his doubts.

But he could ruminate on that later. What was most
important now was that he get back to Sarah and the girls.
Rawlins recognized that he was itching to continue his journey for home.

"Still gotta get back to my family," Neville said. He
sighed and said with a faint smile, "Gotta come clean with
Sarah."

Rawlins examined his upper arm. It hurt, bleeding a little
through the cloth ripped from the shirt of the dead Schaeffer
with which Neville had prepared a bandage, but he knew
he could manage on his own.

"S'pose you might at that," Rawlins agreed. He offered
an encouraging smile. "Go on, git . . . and then wanta see
yuh back in Commercial City. We got us some talkin' to do."

Neville regarded him with a questioning look.

But Rawlins was not yet ready to oblige.

"It'll hold," he told him.

NINETEEN

———

Neville looked at the bank draft in astonishment. He'd blinked his eyes several times to be sure he wasn't misreading the figure.

Seventy-five hundred dollars!

He and his wife were back in Commercial City and, as Sheriff Rawlins had requested, Neville had come by his office. His two girls were instructed to stay put in the buckboard, which was parked outside the Municipal Building. Neville didn't know why the sheriff wanted to see him, and frankly he was a mite worried. Whatever other possibilities he might have considered, he certainly did not expect to be handed the reward offered for the apprehension of Mayor Ford's killer—plus what appeared to be a bonus of some sort.

Sarah looked almost faint, and Rawlins helped to ease her into the chair next to his desk. Curls popped out from under her pale blue bonnet and her eyes were wide. But she recovered swiftly and her face beamed as she rose from her seat and took her husband's arm.

Sheriff Rawlins looked pleased. "Well, 'sides the federal reward, the townspeople put up twenty-five hundred dollars on their own. That's how much the mayor meant to them. Looks like you got yourselves a nice stake."

Neville nodded, speechless.

Rawlins said, "You know, Tom, you could have a good future in Commercial City. The town's still growin', plenty of opportunities. Plus, you're kinda a hero 'round here. Think you'd have no trouble fittin' in." He joked, "Probably never have to pay for another meal." Then he turned serious. "Reckon what I'm sayin' is we'd be mighty pleased if'n you'd stay."

Neville didn't have to consider his answer.

"Flatterin' offer, Sheriff," he said. "But decided me and my family are gonna head north. See what prospects might be there. Can afford to do so now."

Rawlins smiled as he scratched behind his neck. "Well, reckon after what you been through, can't rightly say I blame yuh."

Neville again regarded the bank note. He shook his head in wonderment.

The tone of his voice light, Rawlins remarked, "Still think you might be the biggest horse's ass I ever met, but I'm glad things worked out."

Neville smiled . . . and then a concerned look crossed his face.

"Have they?" he asked with seriousness.

Rawlins gave a sober nod. "Still work to be done, but we're aimin' for a federal investigation into the corruption comin' out of Frisco with these gamblin' halls and the methods they been usin'. Don't think that with the government backin' 'em, people are gonna be much 'fraid to come forward. So I reckon we both came out ahead."

"With you doin' your part, Sheriff, I know it'll all get fixed," Neville said, his words sincere.

"Thank yuh, Tom," Rawlins returned modestly.

"What 'bout that other matter I asked yuh to look into?" Neville then inquired.

"Duke Marbury?" Rawlins said, referencing the name in a sneer. "Yeah, coulda told yuh 'bout him a while back.

Punk outlaw. Him and some other gun-crazy cowboy were killed in a holdup in Santa Fe."

Neville squinted his eyes. "Fella named Rafe, by chance?"

Rawlins grunted. "Yeah, Rafe Cutler. Bad sort. Loco as they come. Shot down two people inside the bank 'fore him and Marbury were gunned down." He gave Neville a curious stare. "Still can't figger why the interest."

"Just a coupla names from long ago," was all Neville offered.

Rawlins let it go at that.

Neville felt relief and a sense of justice that Sheriff Dan's killer and his partner had met fitting ends. Two other dark blotches from his past that he was grateful would no longer pose a threat either to him or his family. True, it had been a long time, many years in fact, but he'd still lived in the shadow of their return.

For just a moment Neville considered asking Sheriff Rawlins if he knew anything about Duke Marbury's sister, Jessica. Then he decided it, too, was long ago and he really didn't need to know. He did hope, however, that she'd gone on to a good life. Neville gave a loving glance to Sarah and could feel satisfied that *he* had.

Neville smiled and extended his hand. The sheriff accepted the handshake with a strong grip.

"Good luck to yuh," Rawlins said.

Neville's daughters excitedly climbed down from the buckboard and rushed toward him and Sarah when they walked from the Municipal Building.

Neville happened to peer down the street and noticed a boy of about ten years old and his father loading burlap sacks onto the back of a wagon. The lad looked thin and hungry, and his pa appeared strained and overworked. Neville watched them for a moment, then smiled at Sarah before stepping away from her and his girls and walking over to the boy, reaching into his shirt pocket and withdrawing the ten-dollar gold eagle. He looked at the coin affectionately. He massaged it between his thumb and forefinger, then tried to trip it between his fingers as he'd often done but couldn't manage the trick because of its damaged and dented surface. He smiled to himself and gave his head a little shake. The coin had served a special purpose in a way he could never have expected.

Now it was time to fulfill the vow he'd once made to himself. A vow that despite the odds he would now be able to keep.

Neville stopped before the boy, and the freckle-faced, redheaded lad looked up at him with eyes squinting against the midday sun. Neville gently took the boy's hand and pressed the coin into his palm.

"Wish it were in better condition, son," he said. "But don't think that really matters. Was special to the man who gave it to me, was special to me . . . and I reckon it'll be just as special to you."

The boy stood statue-still and regarded the unique coin with eyes wide and his jaw hinged open.

"That is, if'n you hold on to it," Neville added seriously but with a wink meant to impart his message.

The boy's father stepped over and looked at Neville questioningly.

Neville spoke to relieve his doubt. "Had a few years on the boy when that gold piece was handed to me. Took me some years to realize its value. Maybe givin' it to him now will give him a head start to 'preciate its worth."

The father didn't know what to make of either Neville or his gesture. He stood there in awe as much as his son as Neville then tipped his hat and turned to go back to his family.

Sarah and the girls, though not understanding what had just transpired, watched with happy expressions as Neville walked back over to them. He wrapped one arm around his wife and embraced his two bonnet-wearing daughters with his other arm, drawing them close. Sheriff Rawlins had stepped outdoors and had watched Neville with the boy. While he also didn't know what had gone on between the two, he looked on approvingly. Because he knew that Tom Neville was a good man. He couldn't be otherwise with a family as loving as the one he had been blessed with.

The family for whom he had been willing to sacrifice his life.

As Neville piloted the buckboard along Archer Street, past the stone-structured Municipal Building, Rawlins gave a brisk wave. Keeping both hands steady on the reins, Neville responded to Rawlins's gesture with a broad smile and a firm nod.

But as the wagon rolled down the street, the two little girls sitting in back waved their tiny gloved hands enthusiastically at the sheriff.

"Bye!" they both shouted.

Rawlins chuckled to himself, feeling pretty good that afternoon. He looked up at the clear skies, shading his eyes against the bright sun. He drew in a deep, contented breath, then turned and sauntered back toward his office.